THE GREAT MEADOWS

THE GREAT MEADOWS

❖

CHRISTOPHER WALSH

For my wife, Sallie, and for our parents, Richard and Judy Walsh, and Haydon and Ann Spalding.

CHAPTER
ONE

THIS IS WHAT *a hangover tastes like,* I thought. *Cigarette ashes soaked in bourbon and bacon grease.*

The cab of the pickup suddenly felt like a sweat lodge as beads sprouted like liquid polyps on the surface of my throbbing forehead. I stuck my head out the window to cool down, but the wind felt more like a furnace blast than a fan. So, I pulled my head inside and white-knuckled the wheel as the acrid taste of bile rose in my throat. I desperately drained the remaining few ounces from a water bottle and tossed it on the dusty floorboard where it landed next to a crumpled foil sandwich wrapper. The thought of the greasy bacon and egg sandwich I had eaten an hour earlier made my stomach heave in revulsion and I gagged, trying to fight back the involuntary urge to vomit. Sensing the inevitable, I eased the truck onto the gravel shoulder and prepared to make a run for the weeds by the side of the road.

But after a minute or so of drawing in and exhaling deep draughts of air, my heart rate slowed and the tingling sensation in my face and hands began to subside. I pulled the hem of my T-shirt up and wiped the sweat from my face. Then I sat for a long moment with my eyes closed, focusing on breathing in and out in a steady rhythm. Eventually, my temperature dropped to a tolerable level, and it appeared the "spirits" had granted me a reprieve. Blowing out a relieved sigh, I maneuvered the truck back onto the roadway, slumped in my seat, and stared through the grimy windshield at the blue-sky horizon in the distance.

"It's a great life if you don't weaken," I said to no one.

My father used to say that. He didn't say it to me. He didn't say it to anyone. He just said it. I don't know where he picked it up. And I don't know what it meant to him. But I know it means something to me. Mainly because there's not much else I remember about him, not much else I remember him saying. I say it, too, sometimes. Usually at times like this. Times when I'm driving and at loose ends. Which is to say I drive a lot, and I think a lot. And all that driving and thinking makes me wonder if I'm really at loose ends, or if what I think of as loose ends is just a convenient reason to move on, and if moving on is the same thing as starting over, and if starting over is just a way to avoid tying up loose ends.

Minutes and miles ticked by as the truck wheels hummed against the faded gray of what used to be interstate blacktop. Just beyond the garish marquee of an adult theater, I saw a white billboard with large black letters that read "Do you know where you will spend eternity?". As I passed the sign, my hand went instinctively to the naked left wrist where my father's watch should have been, and I felt a flush of hot shame. Again, I stuck my head out the window, not for succor, but to scream into the oncoming wind. My shame unassuaged, I pushed the silver knob of a lighter into the pleather dashboard and fished a cigarette out of the crumpled pack that lay on the torn vinyl of the bucket seat. I positioned the cigarette in the corner of my corrugated lips, draped my forearm over the steering wheel, and waited.

The soft bur of the truck wheels lulled my restive mind, providing a welcome moment of clarity during which I reflected upon the truth. Not about the destination of my eternal soul, but about moving on and starting over. Upon that subject, the truth was quite clear despite my aversion to admitting to it. But if I had the mettle to admit to it, then I'd say the truth is if you move on and start over enough times for the same reason then you aren't really moving on or starting over at all. You're just moving on for the sake of being in motion and starting over for the sake of believing in hope. That's the truth. And now that I think about it, I don't know why I shy away from admitting to it. I mean, who doesn't want the feeling of motion fueled by the aphrodisiac of hope? It's a combination elemental to the perpetual love affair between a wanderer and the town that doesn't know his name.

The lighter popped free, its metallic click sounding like a hammer dropping on an empty chamber. Splitting my concentration between the highway and the lighter, I raised the black speck at the center of the simmering red circle to the waiting cigarette. It flared as my lips puckered and pulled, and the tar ignited causing the paper to crisp and crackle in response. I felt the dry lining inside my throat inflame from the irritants as my nostrils expanded and blasted forth a misshapen funnel of effluvia that floated above the steering wheel. The tendons of my jaw tightened, and my tongue glued to the stippled roof of my mouth as I drew in the misty air.

"I am Levi Motley, master of loose ends," I said before letting loose a sweet breath of toxic humidity. "As for tying them up?" I made a sound like a miniature bomb exploding, and the question hung in the air like an invisible mushroom cloud.

For the next few miles, I dragged on my cigarette and gazed out the window as my mind wandered to the previous night and the old college buddy who had bellied up to the bar next to me at a place where we used to hang out. Truth be told, he was more of an acquaintance than a buddy. A friend of a friend from back in the day, that sort of thing. I wasn't a bit surprised to hear he was still slinging weed to the ever-replenishing customer base that is the staple of a college-town pharmaceutical venture. He was with a guy I didn't know, but who immediately struck me as a caricature. Fairly or not, I tagged the guy as a hanger-on who spent the tips he earned waiting tables on booze and drugs while student loan bills piled up next to the always-blinking answering machine in his one-bedroom efficiency apartment.

There I had been, sitting alone and nursing a beer in silent reminiscence, when I heard a familiar voice exclaim a coupling of expletives that are for some reason socially acceptable when uttered in a certain locale, with a certain level of excitement, and, ironically, preceded by the qualifier "holy". Soon, shots of bourbon appeared, and the three of us eagerly descended into the void of college bar nostalgia and the kind of raging drunkenness that erases any distinction between acquaintance and friend, between friend and buddy. Hell, I even told the hanger-on I'd look him up next time I was in town.

Thinking about it now, I realize the fact that a couple of guys pushing thirty and yet still hanging out at the old college pub were so casually down for the descent into darkness didn't say much about their prospects for the immediate future.

Yeah, well don't kid yourself, Motley, I thought, my face contorting in ironic disgust. *You were down for the ride as much as they were.*

With that ignominious reality check, I took a final drag on my cigarette, flicked the butt out the window, and scanned the radio for inspiration. Forgoing the saccharine sounds of a boy band, I landed on a grunge rocker that normally would have had me enthusiastically butchering the high notes. But for whatever reason the song didn't kindle my inspirational fire, so I turned the radio off and settled for the sound of the wind whipping outside my window.

Staring ahead in distracted absence, I rubbed the rough stubble on my chin and thought maybe it was something his father said that time he came home with a black eye and a split lip, having run up against it with the wrong guy, on the wrong block, in the old neighborhood. Of course, I'm talking about what my old man used to say. Maybe he got his ass kicked and that's what his father had to say about it. After all, what can a father offer in a moment like that? Words of understanding? Of disappointment? Of solace or disgust? What can a father say? Something. I'm sure his old man gave him at least that much because what father can remain silent at the sight of his broken son? He must offer him something so that someday when the son becomes the father, he'll know what to say to his own son when he comes home with a black eye and a split lip, having run up against it with the wrong guy, on the wrong block, in the old neighborhood.

It's as good a story as any, I thought.

But was it?

My eyes narrowed in curiosity as I wondered what other potential sources might exist for that cryptic phrase. As my imagination wandered, a faint image flitted before me like a snippet of a barely remembered dream, and I found myself reflecting on the sepia-drenched photograph of some matriarchal ancestor that used to hang on the wall of the house where I grew up. Calling the image to mind, I imagined the woman – my old man's great-something-or-other – wringing her hands over the pitiful state of the food staples in her garden during some pre-postmodern era when such concerns were not only necessary, but honorable. And then I imagined my father eavesdropping from some secret burrow only a child could know about as the woman muttered that phrase in tense anticipation of the familiar look of disappointment her husband would unsuccessfully try to hide from her when he arrived home dirt-streaked and bone-weary from whatever job he was able to hold down that week. I was surprised by the twinge of grief I felt at imagining that long-dead ancestor whose name I didn't even know, distraught and afraid as she mouthed those words as a mantra of self-reliance to help her get through another day in the life she didn't ask for but ended up living all the same.

Again, it was as good a story as any. But what if, I supposed, it wasn't a person at all? What if the phrase was an original thought, the real McCoy, sui generis? Maybe it was something the old man plucked out of thin air like a contemplative epiphany or a private revelation. Or maybe it was part of a prayer card that he carried around in his wallet, a pious adjuration he would recite while kneeling at the foot of The Cross. Or it could have been an advertisement, or a throwaway line from a movie, commercial, bumper sticker, billboard, or political slogan; something vacuous, repeatable, and sure to elicit Pavlovian commitment to a rally-around-the-rooster cause whose effects were predictable, and yet predictably unavoidable.

"Hell, who knows," I said, blowing out a deep sigh. "Maybe it came to him in a dream."

Maybe. But like I said, I don't know where he picked it up or what it meant to him. I only know that he said it. And so, I say it, too, pretending it was something he meant to say to me. I'd like to think he gave me at least that much. Something simple to help me become a good man. Something like, put the tools away when you're finished with them; run out every ground ball; keep your own counsel; stay loyal to your friends; be your brother's keeper through adversity; wash your hands before supper; eat everything you put on your plate; and say your prayers at bedtime.

But he never said those things to me. He said, "It's a great life if you don't weaken." And he didn't say it to me. He just said it. And so, I say it, just as he did. To no one. I say it as I'm driving, thinking, moving on, starting over, in motion, and without much hope. And I find the words to be less a north star than a transcendental warning. I find the words to be a telepathic entreaty to open my eyes to see the hour is later than it seems.

I say those words and the words form a thought, and the thought forms the shape of who my father was: a worm that long ago burrowed into my brain, died, decayed, decomposed, and became a fossil buried in the sediment of my childhood consciousness. I exhume the fossil in moments like this. Moments when I am suffering from having fucked up, underachieved, disappointed, quit, and fled the field in my attempt to outrun the guilt of unfulfilled promise. I exhume the fossil in moments when I have surrendered to being the worst kind of liar there is, a hypocrite. In such moments, I turn the fossil over in my hands. It is rough-edged and radiating all the colors in the kaleidoscope of time. But I know someday it will become smooth and nondescript. I know someday it will become a stone.

And then what will I do?

CHAPTER
TWO

THE HOUSE WAS empty except for a wooden table and two chairs in the main room. I sat at the table and poured a neat slug of Old Fitzgerald. Raising the glass in a silent salute, I sipped the drink and wondered what kind of questions the woman would have for me when she arrived. The woman was an investigative reporter with the Louisville newspaper. I had spoken to her the previous day, agreeing against my better judgment to meet with her. I say against my better judgment because during our conversation, the woman seemed to know things about me that she shouldn't have known. I didn't like that. So, as I sat waiting for a knock at the door, I sipped my drink and weighed what I thought I knew about what happened against the counterweight of my suspicion that there might be more to it.

After several minutes of waiting, I blew out my cheeks and looked around the room, bored with idle speculation. My gaze came to rest on a satchel that lay on the knotty planks of the hardwood floor. I opened the satchel and began shuffling through the various notebooks stuffed haphazardly inside, pulling out a black spiral edition whose cover was faded by years of wear and idle scribbling. Turning it over, I smiled wistfully at the words "The Search for Answers" written on the subject line.

To kill time until my inquisitor arrived, I sat at the table and meandered through the well-worn volume, stopping to peruse a page dated "December 5, 1990". It was a journal entry that spoke of a night out with two college buddies that ended with me caring for an old flame who had passed out drunk at The Peach House, an apartment building near campus notorious for parties among the eclectic crowd that eschewed the buttoned-down priggery of Greek Row. The entry described how I had asked if she knew who I was, and that she had taken my hand without opening her eyes and whispered my name. I flipped to the next page hoping to find that maybe we had gone to lunch or done laundry together the next day, but the pages that followed were filled with pseudo-philosophical musings and bad poetry. The next entry I found was dated "January 2, 1991", and there was no mention of the girl.

A knock at the door shook me from my reverie.

"Yeah, just a minute."

I downed the remainder of my drink and asked who was knocking.

"Regina Sandoval," came a faint voice from the other side of the door.

I opened the door to a woman bundled up and hugging herself against the cold.

"Mr. Motley?"

"Yeah, I'm Levi Motley. Here, come in." I ushered her inside. "You must be Regina Sandoval." She offered a polite smile as she pulled off her gloves and extended a hand. "Of course, you are," I said, taking her hand. "You just told me that."

"Thank you for agreeing to see me," she said, unraveling her scarf. "I'm glad I finally got a hold of you. You're a hard man to reach."

"Ah, well, you know," I said with an apologetic shrug. "I haven't gotten around to hooking up the phone."

"Well, that's inconvenient."

I cocked my head and stared as she unbuttoned her coat. "Inconvenient for who?"

She stopped with the buttons and gave me a chastened look. "My apologies, Mr. Motley. Sometimes I speak before thinking. I shouldn't presume."

"Call me Levi."

She resumed with the buttons and said, "It's the nature of my work, you see."

I waited to see if that was the extent of the apology. Realizing it was, I shook my head and said, "No worries. Let me get your coat."

I took the coat and searched the room for a respectable place to lay it. "Oh, really, it's fine anywhere," she said. "And no offense, but I prefer to keep things on a strictly professional level."

"Professional level it is," I said, draping her coat over a backpack and camera case that sat on the floor. "And you're probably right about the phone. But in my experience, it's not such a bad thing for bill collectors and pissed-off boyfriends to be inconvenienced."

Again, she offered a polite smile as she scanned the room, taking in what little there was to see. "At the risk of sounding rude yet again, I must ask...moving in or moving out?"

I surveyed the room, turning in a full circle until I arrived back face-to-face with my guest. "I'm usually doing both at the same time, Miss Sandoval."

Her smile tightened into a thin line as her eyes continued to roam about the room, taking it in from corner to corner and from floor to ceiling. After a moment, I gestured for her to sit, and she placed her leather bag on the floor and took a chair.

"Want a cup of coffee?" I tapped the bottle of Old Fitzgerald that sat on the table between us like a mischievous chaperone. "I can make it Irish."

"Thanks, but I'm more of a Vodka Tonic kind of girl. Besides, it's a bit early in the day for me."

Undeterred, I gave her a waggish grin and displayed the bottle like a model on a game show. "You're in the bourbon capital of the world, lady. Meaning it's never too early. Or too late, for that matter."

"Yes, well that may be, but I don't know the first thing about bourbon," she said, removing a legal pad and file folder from her bag. "Coffee would be great."

I walked to the kitchen and returned with a cup of coffee that I sat on the table in front of my guest. She offered a curt nod of thanks as she pulled an article from the file folder and placed it on the table next to the legal pad. I took a seat and folded my hands across my stomach, waiting for her to complete her preparations. For my part, I was as ready or unready for this conversation as I needed to be. After all, she had called me. Sure, I had called her back, but not until the secretary at *The Bardstown Observer* chewed me out after giving me the message for the fourth, and as she was quite clear in telling me, final time. It wasn't that I was avoiding the woman. I just didn't see the point of talking about it, and I told her so.

"Like I told you on the phone, I really don't see the point in all this. I mean, I don't know what I can tell you that you don't already know."

"I think there's plenty you can tell me."

I gave dubious shake of my head. "I can't imagine what."

"How about telling me your story, Mr. Motley?"

"My story?" I said with a snort. "What's that got to do with it?"

"It has everything to do with it." She headed and dated a page on the legal pad. "After all, you spent time with him."

"Twenty minutes, Miss Sandoval. I spent twenty minutes with the guy. Maybe half an hour. I hardly see how that can help your investigation."

"You picked this young man up and took him to his destination. You conversed with him along the way. You shared time, even if it was brief. And you were at the scene where his body was found. That's quite an interesting circle of events, don't you think?"

I narrowed my eyes and said, "And how is it you know I was at the scene where his body was found?"

"I'm damn good at my job, that's how."

She regarded me with an inquisitive gaze as I mentally ran through the list of people who knew I had been at the crime scene. It was a short list. Perhaps sensing my wariness, she relaxed her inquisitive posture and sat with her hands folded neatly on the table. But if she had intended this action to ease my suspicion, it didn't. Instead, it gave the impression that she had all the time in the world to crack me open and explore what was inside.

"Why are you here, Miss Sandoval?"

A gold medallion visible between the open collar of her ivory blouse moved in rhythm with her breathing as she continued to regard me with relaxed ease.

"I'm here because I want to know what happened. And I don't think you would have agreed to see me if you didn't want to know the same."

"Is that from *The Observer*?" I said, pointing to the article.

"It is."

"I assume you've read it?"

"I have."

"Well, there you go," I said, displaying my hands like a blackjack dealer. "You know what happened."

"Hardly. Especially since the article has no mention of how you came to meet him. Nor does it say what you said to him, nor what he said to you. I'd like to know those things. Just as I'd like to know how your path intersected with his, and how all of this has impacted you."

She leaned forward and fixed translucent green eyes on me.

"I'm here, Mr. Motley, because I want to know what really happened to Moussa Diab. And I want to know what has happened to you because of it."

Despite her previous demure, I tipped the bottle in her direction. She lifted her coffee cup and took a sip, and I poured a shot and drank it down. It was at that point of conversational stasis that she made a rather innocuous move. Or so it seemed at the time.

"When we spoke before, did I mention I'm headed to a conference tomorrow?"

She had mentioned it, and of course, she knew she had mentioned it.

"You mentioned it. Nashville. Good town."

"Yes, well, I'll get a room here tonight and drive down in the morning. The conference doesn't start until late afternoon and even then, it will be mostly drinks and socializing before we get down to business. You know how it is."

Actually, I didn't know "how it is," though I did wonder how much horse manure a gaggle of reporters could shovel during an extended happy hour with the phrase "charge it to the room" floating ubiquitously around the bar.

"What is it?"

"Oh, nothing," I said, realizing I had been smiling. "Just wondering if there will be any sessions on blogging."

"Blogging? Oh, I'm sure it's part of the program. After all, it's the current boogeyman scaring the bejesus out of the industry."

"It sure takes a lot less paper and ink. But the idea that it could replace print journalism..." I gave a dismissive wave, indicating the absurdity of the notion.

"You think so?"

"Well, I hope so. I remember Professor Goben used to quote Arthur Miller, saying a good newspaper is a nation talking to itself. If you ask me, this online crap is more like a sanctimonious circle jerk than a nation in conversation."

She gave a slightly embarrassed look, and I made a clumsy apology for my crudity.

"Goodness knows I've heard worse in my newsroom. And from Artie Goben," she said with a soft laugh. "I think I mentioned that I called our mutual friend and checked you out a bit. Do you mind?"

She had mentioned it, and again, she knew she had. I shrugged and said, "No skin off my back."

"I plan to stop and see him on the way to the conference. I told him I'd take him to lunch."

"Good luck with that. If somebody sees Arthur Goben stop working long enough to take an actual lunch, they should engrave the date and time in stone."

She smiled and regarded me with that keen, inquisitive light in her eyes. "Professor Goben tells me you're quite a handful. 'A pain in the ass', I believe were the words he used."

"Yeah, well it takes one to know one."

"True enough. But he also said you have good instincts and an interesting take on a subject. He said you even surprised him a time or two."

"Coming from him, that's high praise. Especially since Artie Goben don't trade in bullshit as he likes to say."

"Oh, that's Artie to a T. A real straight shooter," she said. "You know, we worked together in Chicago before he got into academia."

"Oh yeah? Well, he had no shortage of stories about Chi-town. Head-bustin' unions, ball-bustin' politicians, and the dad-blamed Cubs that can't get their ass above five hundred."

Again, she smiled as she studied me with her eyes.

"Yeah, no doubt he loved to talk about Chicago. He made those days sound so heady. Made you wish you had been around for it. Like it was the best time to be alive even though he'd complain about it to no end."

"That's an interesting take. Tell me something, Mr. Motley. Are you a man out of time?"

The question surprised me, and I had to resist the sudden urge to squirm in my seat. To cover, I decided to counterpunch. "You know I checked you out, too."

"Is that right?" she said with what I thought was a nervous laugh. "And?"

"You know Danny Brewer?"

She cocked her head and appeared to be searching her mental Rolodex for the name. That seemed strange to me, but given what Danny had told me, I figured Regina Sandoval was in The Show while Danny Brewer was still ham and egging it in the minor leagues.

"Danny Brewer. He's with your paper in Louisville. Covers local and state politics."

"Oh, right. Danny," she said. "He's good people."

"Yeah, he is good people. He was a year ahead of me. Good dude, Danny. And a damn good wingman." She looked amused and I frowned inwardly at my second sophomoric remark. "Anyway, Danny Brewer. Good guy and a good writer. He said you're one of the best in your field."

"Wow. That's high praise from a gifted journalist."

I searched her face for a sign of condescension, but she looked almost embarrassed by the compliment.

"You know, I read the Louisville paper every day now that I'm back," I said, tapping an index finger against my chin. "But I don't recall seeing any of your work."

"Oh. Well, that's no surprise, really. You see, I've been on sabbatical for the past few months, pursuing some stories that are outside the realm of my normal journalistic duties."

"Is that what this is? A story outside the realm of your normal journalistic duties?"

"That remains to be seen," she said, giving me a coy look.

We sat in silence for a moment. Our verbal fencing hadn't taken us far, but I was okay with that. She seemed like a real professional, but I wasn't sure I was ready to talk about this.

"I understand you're from Louisville."

I gave a slight nod as I absently traced a line along the edge of the table. "What part?"

"Portland."

"Ah."

I stopped running my finger along the table and looked at her. "And you're from Chicago?"

"Umm-hmm." A half-minute or so of awkward silence passed. "So, now we know where each of us is from."

"Yeah. Guess so."

She gave me an earnest look and spread her hands apart as if offering me a truce. "I'd like to hear your story, Mr. Motley. But I get the feeling it's going to be opening day at Santa Anita by the time we get into this."

I gave a frustrated sigh and said, "I thought you wanted to know about Moussa."

"I do. And as we've established, I already know what was in the paper. So, what I'd like to learn is how his path came to intersect with yours. I think that's where the story lies, somewhere in the reason why the two of you connected." She picked up her pen and positioned it above the legal pad. "Why don't you start with how the two of you met?"

"How I met Moussa. That's what you wanna know?"

She gave a single nod and waited, knowing I had to come to it on my own. For a long moment, I stared at the label on the bourbon bottle, trying to decide how much I wanted to reveal to this stranger. Finally, I decided there was at least one thing I did want her to know.

"I'm celebrating a birthday today."

"Oh? I wish I'd known," she said, scribbling a note on the pad. "I could have brought you a gift."

"Oh yeah? What kind of gift would you have brought me?"

She stopped writing and looked at me. "Well, umm...I'm not sure. I don't really know what I would have brought."

"That's right," I said, eyeing her narrowly. "You don't know. You just blurted out something people say when you tell them you're celebrating a birthday. You were being...polite." She stared at me, and I thought I detected a slight fissure inside those sparkling green eyes. "But, hey, don't worry about it. It's not my birthday. It's Declan's."

"And who is Declan?"

"Declan's my brother."

She set the pen down. "And where is your brother?"

"My brother is in Manchester." I let a silent interval pass. "You know what Manchester is?"

The fissure in her eyes widened to a crack, but she remained resolute. "Yes, I know what Manchester is. I'm sorry to hear that."

"Don't be," I said with a soft laugh. "To Declan, doing time is something to be proud of. Thinks he's upholding the old man's legacy."

"The old man?"

"Ray Motley. People called him Rock. He died a long time ago."

Her tongue slid back and forth along her lower lip, and she looked like wanted to inquire further. But for a long moment, the only sound between us was a repetitive *ting* as I flicked a fingernail against the glass bottle. Finally, she cleared her throat to signify it was time to move things along.

"I don't mean to press you, Mr. Motley, but I do have a conference to get to."

"I don't," I said, pouring another drink.

At that her eyes narrowed as she regarded me with a cold stare. Then she stood and began gathering her things, stuffing them unceremoniously into her leather bag. "You know, I made quite an effort to locate and contact you. And I made the effort to come down here to meet with you. So, I really don't appreciate you wasting my..."

"He was hitchhiking."

She stopped and blinked as if I'd suddenly flipped on the light switch in a dark room.

"Moussa. He was hitchhiking. That's how I met him."

Again, she blinked and said, "Hitchhiking from where?"

"Down south. Louisiana."

"And where were you coming from?"

"Bowling Green. I'd stayed there the night before, after driving in from Colorado."

"Colorado?" she said, a curious look on her face. "What for?"

"What do you mean what for?"

"I mean, what brought you to Kentucky from Colorado? What did you come back for?"

"Well, shit, Miss Sandoval," I said, resting my chin between my thumb and forefinger. "What for is the whole story."

She placed her palms on the table and leaned toward me with an intense look. "And I'd like to hear that story, Mr. Motley. Will you tell it to me?"

I let out another frustrated sigh. "For Christ's sake, woman. A man died. Do you understand that?"

She nodded and said, "Yes, I understand that."

"Well, then you should know it's not an easy thing to get to."

"I understand that as well. Just as I understand we're not getting to it today." She looked at me with a scrutinizing gaze and appeared to be weighing her options. "Tell you what. Why don't you get to it on your own, Mr. Motley, and then if you feel like telling me about it, I'm all ears."

Her eyebrows arched into her forehead as she gave me a look that seemed to inquire whether we had a deal. I nodded and said, "Fair enough."

She slung her bag over her shoulder and said, "Given that I can't reach you by phone, how will I..."

"Nine o'clock tomorrow morning at Café Mozart." She gave me a blank stare. "It's a café about a block and a half from the courthouse."

"Okay," she said in a cautious tone. "And if after having gotten to it, you still don't feel like talking?"

"Then I guess we'll have a pleasant conversation about the weather."

She gave me a mirthless smile as she walked to the door. "I wouldn't count on it, Mr. Motley."

A burst of cold air lingered in the room as the door shut behind her. For a long time, I sat at the table and thought about what she had said, about her reason for wanting my story. "What do you mean what's happened to me?" I said with a dismissive snort. "Nothing's happened to me."

But I knew that wasn't true. Something had happened to me. It had been happening for years and I didn't want to face it. I looked over at the camera case and at my backpack and satchel. Except for the crumpled sleeping bag in the bedroom, everything I owned was sitting on the floor in front of me. And that was fine. After all, I never wanted a life burdened by possessions. But why did I remain in a perpetual state of being packed and ready to go? Hell, I didn't have anywhere to go to.

I sighed and looked at the drink sitting on the table before me. Pushing it away, I stood and reached inside the canvas satchel, fishing around until I located a leather journal faded by years of wear and use. Turning to a fresh page, I wrote "What really happened to Moussa?" at the top. For a long moment, I stared at the words and thought about the question. Then I thought about Regina Sandoval's hypothesis that there was something meaningful in the way my path had crossed with his. I wasn't sure I agreed with that, but what was the harm in exploring the idea?

Oh, there's harm in it, I thought. *I just won't see it until it's bit me in the ass.*

Even so, I picked up my pen and added something to the phrase I had already written on the page and stared at the two questions.

"What really happened to Moussa? And what has happened to me?"

I thought about the juxtaposition of the questions and whether there really was some meaning to be found in the space between or around or within them. Then I thought about the tacit agreement I had made with Regina Sandoval to at least give it some thought.

I sighed and said, "I guess a deal's a deal."

Then I started writing.

CHAPTER
THREE

THE EXIT FOR the Bluegrass Parkway was a mile ahead, but I was in desperate need of a fill-up and twenty minutes of shut eye lest I end up on the side of the road or in a ditch.

I dropped my pen on the open journal and frowned as Professor Artie Goben's phantasmic presence perched on my shoulder like a bird of editorial prey. "Typical Motley," I could hear him saying. "Always the gardener planting pretty flowers instead of the carpenter building a sturdy box."

"Fine," I said, revising the sentence to suit the editorial predilections of my fastidious mentor.

I passed the parkway exit because I was tired and needed gas.

I looked at the sentence and shook my head. Scratching it out, I rewrote and continued with my original thought.

The exit for the Bluegrass Parkway was a mile ahead, but I was in desperate need of a fill-up and twenty minutes of shut eye lest I end up on the side of the road or in a ditch. So, I ramped onto state Highway 62 where a mega-station promised half-decent coffee and a restroom that didn't require a key. I turned instead into the empty parking lot of a rundown shanty of a station that promised nothing.

"Take that, Goben. After all, even a sturdy box deserves a colorful inlay."

I looked over my shoulder and smiled, imagining Artie's shaggy-haired head moving in slow disdain. "Typical English major," he would have said. "Too young to understand it'll take half a lifetime to become even a serviceable novelist, and too naïve to know that in the meantime, a man's got to eat."

I gave a wistful laugh and continued writing.

Having pulled into the parking lot of the rundown shanty, I parked on a patch of gravel at the far end of the lot next to a cinderblock building baking in the midday sun. A crusty mophead leaned against the building's gray wall and a few feet away a hose lay coiled like a snake beside an old-fashioned water pump. Looking around, I saw what might have once been a going mom-and-pop outfit situated on the edge of town, the last chance to fill your tank or chew the fat with a farmer for the next thirty miles. But that day had passed. Now, it lay in the shadow cast by the neon light of its corporate neighbor, a dingy remnant of an era when "urban sprawl" was not part of the community lexicon.

I killed the engine, slid across the seat, and leaned against the passenger side door. The window crank bore into my back, so I gave it a half-turn and the glass squeaked up a few inches from the metal doorframe. Again, I nestled my back against the door, closed my eyes, and slipped into a peaceful repose. I had no idea how long I had been asleep when the belligerent sound of knuckles rapping on the hood of my truck jerked me into bleary consciousness.

"Hey, boy," I heard a bellicose voice say. "This look like a goddamn rest stop to you?"

I sat up and groaned in painful awareness of the unabated throbbing in my forehead. Attempting to focus, I squinted and rubbed my eyes as a man with a dark brow and meaty jowls gripped the doorframe as he glared at me and said, "You hear me boy? This look like a rest stop to you?"

I raised a quieting palm. "Hold up," I said as I swung my feet down, kicking the crumpled foil wrapper that lay on the dusty floorboard. It ricocheted off the door and rolled up against an empty water bottle.

"I ain't holdin' nothin'," he said. "I done asked twice. But you seem a little slow on the uptake, so I'll ask again. Does this look like a damn rest stop to you?"

My jaw opened in a gaping yawn as I looked out the window at my surroundings. The old-fashioned water pump stood in a grassy area enclosed by a wooden fence in need of fresh paint. Beyond the fence, there was a little pond with a stand of magnolia trees shading the far bank. It might have been my imagination, but I thought I heard a bullfrog belch as I turned to look at the man. "A rest stop, you say?" I surveyed the bucolic scene once more before turning back to the man. "Looks pretty restful to me."

The man leaned in through the window and said, "You don't wanna be a smartass with me, boy."

I shrugged. "Too late."

The man pushed back from the truck, his jowls quivering as he glared at me. I decided it was best to try and lower the temperature a few degrees. Unfortunately, my effort came off less diplomatically than I had intended. "Look, man, I'm going to fill up, so why are you givin' me shit?"

"Givin' you shit? I'm the man around here," he said, poking himself in the chest. "And this ain't no rest stop for no loiterin' drunks who ain't got no business but stinkin' up my lot."

A surge of adrenaline rushed to my temples, and I felt my face go flush. Still, I took a deep breath and raised both palms in a gesture of truce. "Look. I've got a killer hangover, and I'm on practically no sleep. I just wanted to..."

"And I'm supposed to give a shit?" he said, cutting me off. "Asshole."

At that I ripped the door open. It took only three long strides to reach the tailgate, but the belligerent clerk was already beating a path back to the store. As he retreated, the cowardly prick had the balls to call out over his shoulder, "Buy somethin' or hit the road, drunkard."

I watched the man strut toward the storefront, swinging his arms in exaggerated arcs as he flung open the door and disappeared inside. I stood beside the truck, my chest heaving in rhythm with the air rushing in and out of my nostrils. After a few minutes of staring at the rundown storefront, I exhaled a slow breath and made my way over to the water pump. I gripped the handle and flailed, but the arm clanked loosely against the metal tank. Cursing, I looked around and saw a spigot protruding from the wall of the cinderblock building. Turning the wheel, I leaned down and cupped my hands, grateful as the water flowed warm, lukewarm, and then cold from the metal spout. I drank and soaked my face and the back of my neck. When I was finished, I turned the wheel and the waterflow stopped, leaving a muddy pool on the ground.

Back in the truck, I lit a cigarette and gazed in the rearview mirror at the oasis of cheap gas, clean toilets, and fresh coffee across the highway. A Greyhound bus sat on the far side of the parking lot, the sun glinting off its silver chassis. I watched as a man emerged from the bus and walked across the parking lot onto a grassy berm bordering the highway. I turned to look out the back window of my truck and saw the man wore a backpack and carried what looked like a piece of cardboard under his arm. I continued to watch the man in absent wonderment until my curiosity was distracted by a red dually rumbling up to one of the gas pumps. A stout, gray-bearded man wearing overalls got out of the truck and walked into the store.

Tossing the spent cigarette, I pulled up to the pump opposite the dually and climbed out, immediately taking note of the sorry condition of the parking lot. The gas pump was adorned with a colony of weeds that grew out of busted concrete littered with brown shards of broken glass, the source of which had rolled up against the base of an adjacent pump. It was a busted beer bottle with jagged edges and a long thin neck. As I shook my head at the sad state of the former mom-and-pop outfit, the gray-bearded man emerged from the store. He nodded a greeting, yanked the handle from the diesel pump, and started filling his tank. I returned the nod and then stood over the broken bottle, nudging it with the toe of my hiking boot. The bottle rolled, revealing a familiar but crusty label.

"That ain't gonna do nobody no good," the man said in a deep baritone.

I looked at him and said, "Looks like Mr. Personality in there isn't too concerned with keeping up appearances."

The man snorted and said, "Vernon ain't got the sense God give a tadpole."

"Gave him a hell of a chip on his shoulder, though."

"Yeah, ol' Vernon ain't no hail fella well met, that's for damn sure," he said with a chuckle. "Truth is he ain't nothin' more than a doorknob. Gets pushed and pulled on all the time, so he thinks he's got to do the same to others."

I glared at the storefront and said, "Guess he thought he'd pull my number today."

"He told me." The man looked me up and down. "I reckon he thought wrong."

I gave the man a nod and then retrieved a Styrofoam cup from my truck. Emptying the dregs onto the concrete, I crouched down, stuck my index finger in the bottleneck, and maneuvered the bottle squeaking and biting into the foam. Then I walked toward the storefront, holding the cup before me as the bottleneck jutted forth from the rim. Behind me, I heard the pop of a truck hood followed by the sound of the gray-beard's deep voice.

"Ain't gonna do nobody no good."

Stepping inside the store, I wrinkled my nose at the rank smell permeating the air. The place was a dump with half-stocked shelves, grimy windows, and a sticky floor that caused my boots to make a sucking sound as I walked. The clerk was hunched over a magazine with his back to the counter. He wasn't wearing a belt, and I could see curly black hair on the pasty skin that poured out of the gap between his T-shirt and jeans. I stood, cup in hand, and knocked on the counter. He glared at me over his shoulder as I set the cup down and said, "You mind throwing this away for me?"

He turned back to the magazine and extended his arm, pointing toward a coffee stand beside the entrance. "You offering me coffee?"

"Offerin' you trash," he said.

I bit my lip as I picked up the cup and walked to the coffee stand. "Hey, I appreciate you letting me grab a few winks. Had a rough one last night. You know how it is."

He flipped a page, ignoring my attempt at magnanimity.

I set the cup on the coffee stand and pushed the door of the trash receptacle, but it wouldn't give. "Of course," I said with a sigh. Lifting the coffee pot, I placed my palm a few inches above the burner and swirled the contents of the pot. The burner was cold, and the contents of the pot were sludge. "Of course."

I walked back to the counter, threw down a twenty, and said, "Fill up on two."

As I exited the store, I held the door for the gray-bearded man as he walked inside and said, "Gimme my change, Vernon, and hurry up about it. I got places to be."

Back at the pump, I slipped the handle from its niche, flipped up the lever, and stared at the white tiles as they flipped by with an occasional *ding*. As the tank filled up, I glanced at the opposite station, wondering how far down the highway the man and his sign had gotten.

"Be good now," the graybeard said as he slipped inside his truck.

"Too late for that."

"Ain't never too late this side of the dirt. But if ya can't be good, then be good at it."

I flashed him a knowing grin and said, "That I can do."

The man started up and pulled away as the tiled numbers slowly crawled to a stop at $12.72. I slipped the handle into its niche and walked back into the store where the clerk was still hunched over his magazine.

"Hey, man. You got a restroom?"

He extended his arm and said, "You see that sign on the door?"

"Yeah, I see it. It says, 'Notice to customers'."

"It says 'Notice to customers, restroom out of order'. Looks like you read about as good as you hear, drunkard."

I felt the familiar surge of adrenaline causing my face to go flush. "The top half of the sign says, 'Notice to customers'. The bottom half's torn off." I placed my fists knuckles down on the counter and leaned toward the clerk. "But judging by the way my boots stick to the floor, it should say, 'Notice to customers, the whole place is a shitter, so just piss wherever you want'."

The clerk turned on me with an angry flash in his eyes.

"It sure smells that way. Or maybe that's just you, Vernon." His jowls quivered, and his mouth hung open as he searched for a retort, but I didn't wait for his pea brain to register a suitably noxious comeback. "How about you tear yourself away from that porn rag and give me my change?"

"How about you kiss my fuckin' ass?"

"Woah, now," I said, backing away with my hands raised. "Where'd you learn those big words? Redneck Sesame Street?"

"Fuck you, asshole."

"Oh, come on now, Vernon. Haven't you heard that foul language is a symptom of a weak mind?"

His fists were balled up and his breathing was heavy as he glared at me. I halfway hoped he would come across the counter, but I knew he wouldn't do anything more than posture to try and save face.

"Got an idea, Vernon. You get yourself a jar and every time you insult a customer with an F-bomb or call somebody an A-hole, you drop a five in the jar. I bet in a week you'll have enough money to fix that restroom right up."

"Go fuck yourself."

"Now you see, that'll be five bucks for the jar," I said, extending a hand. "At the rate you're going, you'll be able to fix that restroom tomorrow."

We stood glaring at each other, violent tension radiating in the space between us. I rapped my knuckles on the counter three times and said, "Give me my change. Asshole."

The sound of car wheels whirring out on the highway was the only accent to the thick silence that pervaded the dingy little store. Our standoff had lasted for a full minute when I saw the clerk's lips curl into a sardonic smile. Appearing satisfied with himself, his rigid posture loosened as he un-balled his fists and stepped to the cash register. With deliberate calm, he took out two one-dollar bills and then dug out a quarter and three pennies. He flung the money down and the change skidded across the counter and onto the floor. Then he took a five out of the register and displayed it for me to see.

"That'll be five bucks," he said, snapping the bill. "Rest stop fee."

Little yellow teeth showed beneath a snarled upper lip as he folded the five and slipped it into the breast pocket of his T-shirt. Then he crossed his arms and leaned back, a victorious look on his piggish face.

I kept my eyes on him as I bent over to pluck the change off the sticky tile. Standing, I placed the coins next to the two bills that lay on the counter. He watched me as I did this, his lips contorted in a contemptuous knot. I regarded him carefully for a moment as I rubbed my stubbled chin. Then I turned to look at the coffee stand, my eyes fixed on the neck of the broken bottle that jutted forth from the cup like the hilt of a sheathed dagger. Looking back at the clerk, I held his eyes as I walked over and retrieved the cup. Returning, I placed the cup on the counter next to the bills and the coins. The clerk looked at me, his contemptuous satisfaction evaporating as he watched me grip the handle of the bottle.

"You can keep the five, Vernon." The bottle squeaked as I gripped the cup and pulled. "But you damn well better be ready to earn it."

CHAPTER
FOUR

A ND WAS HE ready to earn it? Not hardly. He threw the five on the counter and told me through a string of expletives to beat it. And I did. Right after I told him to throw the bottle away, which was all I had asked for in the first place. I mean, really, I was just trying to be helpful.

"Yeah right," I said, dropping my pen.

I leaned back and linked my hands behind my head, thinking back to that day. I could see in retrospect that the guy was a bitter man who probably had no control over his life except for what happened at that gas station. I knew people like that guy. Hell, I grew up with them. People vying for just a scrap of control over their lives. People who had choked down a lot of bullshit in life and because of it, they just wanted a little bit of control. Vernon was like that. And then a guy like me comes along, acting the way I did. I shook my head, knowing that my behavior wouldn't have done much to change the man's outlook on life. Not that I thought it was my job to improve the worldview of Vernon the gas station clerk.

"But it's not my job to make it worse, either."

Perhaps as a subconscious reaction to that notion, my eyes settled on the drink I had poured earlier. Mr. Fitzgerald sat like a friend whose feelings were hurt at having been ignored. Unwilling to appease my forlorn friend, I left the drink on the table, walked to the window, and reflected further on my behavior that day at the gas station. Was that me? Was I really the guy who menaced a down-on-his-luck gas station clerk with a broken beer bottle? And all over a five-dollar bill?

Outside, the waning rays of sunlight signaled that dusk would soon fall on the peaceful houses lining the quiet street in the charming town that I was admittedly beginning to like. I frowned, feeling a sudden resistance to the notion I had a growing affinity for this place. I looked over at my packed bags and felt the familiar urge to pick them up, walk out, and drive away. Instead, I let out a slow breath, turned back to look at the tranquil scene outside and thought about Regina Sandoval. What was it she had asked me to do? Get to it? I looked over at the journal laying open on the table.

Well, I'm getting to it, all right, I thought. *And if I wanna keep getting to it, then I better put a cap on that bottle.*

"Besides, I think I've toasted big brother just about more than he deserves."

With that thought in mind, I walked to the kitchen to put on a pot of coffee. A few minutes later, I returned to the table freshly fortified and ready to continue with the account of how I met Moussa Diab.

CHAPTER
FIVE

A FTER MY CONFRONTATION with the gas station clerk, I went to the station across the highway for a restroom and a cup of coffee. The encounter had left me with a pang of regret previously unknown in the aftermath of similar experiences. So, I pulled onto Highway 62 and searched the radio dial to distract myself from the rueful notion that I might be maturing. But the radio offered little reprieve as one talking head after another spouted caustic assessments of society's ills, and worse yet, their banal solutions to the problems. I was about to tune out the political palabra in favor of classic rock when I drove past a man holding a piece of cardboard displaying the single word "Gethsemani" in large black letters. My interest was immediately piqued, so I watched the man in the rearview mirror until he disappeared behind a bend in the road.

"Gethsemani." As I spoke the word, I felt the strangest sensation of déjà vu that I had ever experienced. Another mile or two passed and I spotted the gravel lot of a garden nursery just ahead. I slowed the truck and pulled into the lot, trying to get a grasp on the pervasive feeling that this moment had happened before. As I did so, the talking head returned from a commercial break to continue his vacuous rant. With a twist of the radio knob, I silenced his insipid nonsense and sat for a moment, contemplating the hitchhiker and his cryptic sign. "Gethsemani." The word echoed in a familiar chamber of my mind and without another thought, I put the truck in drive and hit the gas pedal. My truck wheels crunched and sprayed bits of gravel as I exited the lot and headed back up the highway.

A few minutes later, I came around the bend and saw the man, luckless in his attempt to lure a passerby to his aid. I eased the truck onto a grassy spot on the shoulder, leaned out the window, and said, "Where you headed?" The man put a hand to his ear as cars whisked by. Once I saw the highway was clear, I proffered my question again.

"Where you headed?"

He pointed to the sign.

"Gethsemani, huh?" I said with a nervous chuckle. "Aren't we all?"

He looked at me without expression as more cars whooshed by. I studied the sign and the man holding it. He had black hair that unlike my own, was closely cropped, and his young face was brown, and again unlike my own, cleanly shaven.

"You could be here a while."

"I'm not in a hurry."

"Good thing," I said under my breath. "Look, you wanna tell me where you're going? I might be able to help you out." Again, he pointed to the sign. I frowned and said, "You know, it's too damn hot to stand on the side of the road."

He didn't move or speak. In fact, he seemed oddly indifferent to my presence. Despite that, I found myself wanting to help him. More than that, I found myself wanting him to want me to help him.

"Hey, I'm headed to a town about twenty miles from here. If you want, I can at least get you that far."

As if I'd uttered some magic phrase, he picked up his backpack, slung it over his shoulder, and ran across the highway, sign in hand. He threw his backpack in the truck bed, unzipped it, pulled out a book, and opened the door and climbed in. I stared in curious fascination at this stranger who, as if conjured from thin air, was suddenly sitting beside me in the cab of my truck.

"Thank you for stopping."

"My good deed for the day," I said, still staring at the man. "Helps to balance the scales."

"And how are the scales balancing today?"

The question surprised me. Buying a second to think, I looked out my window to check for traffic. Seeing things were clear, I pulled onto the highway and made a U-turn back into the eastbound lane as I said, "Tilting in the wrong direction."

"Well, the day isn't over yet."

I glanced over at the young stranger, thinking I had detected a glib undertone in his remark. But he sat looking straight ahead, his face smooth and impassive.

We drove for a few miles in silence, and I felt a curious irritation growing inside me. I tried to rationalize it as a byproduct of my pounding headache, but I knew that wasn't the source. I fished a pack of cigarettes out of my jeans and motioned toward him, but he gave a slight shake of his head. The cigarette lighter was activated, and a moment later the silver knob clicked. I lit up and took a drag.

"Sorry about the heat," I said, blowing smoke out the window. "My air went out a couple of weeks ago. I didn't know at the time that I'd be in..."

A squeaking sound interrupted my thought, and I looked over to see my new passenger rolling down the window. His action made sense given my remark, but I thought without reason that maybe he was reacting to the cigarette smoke and that thought caused my irritation to tick up a notch. But after another couple of miles had passed, I realized the actual reason for my irritation was that my passenger hadn't introduced himself. Of course, the thought occurred to me that I could simply introduce myself, which would in turn prompt him to follow suit. Instead, I took a deep drag on my cigarette and exhaled the fumes inside the truck. Naturally, that didn't help matters as my passenger waved a hand to fan away the smoke causing my irritation to ratchet up another notch. I tried to shake it off with idle chatter.

"Back at the gas station. You were on the bus?"

"Yes, the Greyhound."

I guess that was the icebreaker we both needed, because he suddenly shook his head and extended a hand in my direction. "I'm sorry for my rudeness. My name is Moussa Diab."

"Levi Motley," I said, shaking his hand. And just like that, my irritation dissipated like air being let out of a balloon.

"How did you come to pass by me?"

"Same as you," I said with a shrug. "I'd just left the gas station."

"And you saw me get off the bus?"

His question left me feeling exposed. Of course, I had watched him get off the bus, but that wasn't something I wanted to admit to a stranger. "Well, I figured, umm...you know, based on you hitching and all, that you must have been on the bus."

"But you arrived from the opposite direction."

"Huh? Oh. Yeah, I passed you and then came back around."

"Why did you turn around?"

The young stranger had an interrogative self-assuredness that left me feeling a step behind in the conversation. Still, I figured there was no harm in telling the truth. "Your sign," I said, motioning to the cardboard. "I was intrigued by your sign."

He seemed to consider that but didn't follow up on the point. Instead, he resumed his line of questioning. "Were you at the gas station when the bus arrived?"

"No, I was at the station across the highway."

"So, you stopped at the opposite gas station at the same time my bus pulled in?"

"Yeah," I said, as if this fact had just dawned on me. "I guess I did."

I flicked the cigarette out the window and glanced over at my passenger. He looked pensive, like he was trying to work out a riddle. Whatever the case, I was thankful for the break in the interrogation as this young stranger had rubbed me the wrong way. It wasn't that he was impolite or sarcastic. In fact, he was rather uptight and stiff. But in addition to being slow with his introduction, he had yet to look directly at me and that bothered me. I glanced down at the sign sitting upright between his leg and the truck door, but the blank back of the cardboard told me nothing.

"Thank you for the ride, Levi. Speaking of which..." He reached down and retrieved the book he had pulled from his backpack. Opening it, he took out a map and set the book on the seat between us.

"The Boy's King Arthur," I said, reading the title.

He nodded and said, "A gift from someone very special to my family. Someone who is no longer with us."

"Sorry to hear it. But it's good you have something to remember him by." Instinctively, I rubbed my left wrist.

"The town you are going to," he said, tracing a line on the map with his index finger. "Is it Bardstown?"

"Yeah, that's right. Why?"

"Well, if that is most convenient for you, then I'm happy for you to take me to Bardstown, and I'll find a way from there to my destination. But Gethsemani is a relatively short distance from where we are. In fact, if you were to take a right on..."

"Hold up," I said, shaking my head in confusion. "When you said you were going to Gethsemani, I assumed you were speaking in some kind of spiritual metaphor."

"Why did you think that?"

"I don't know," I said defensively. "I thought your sign was some kind of...wandering gypsy voodoo message or something."

"Gypsy voodoo?"

"Oh, wait," I said, shooting him a concerned look. "I didn't mean to imply that..."

"Well, I am, in fact, going to Gethsemani," he said in a direct tone. "More specifically, the Abbey of Our Lady of Gethsemani."

A long moment of silence passed. The truck meandered over a concrete bridge spanning a river whose banks were shrouded by a tunnel of trees that stretched back into dense woods. I took a drink of my coffee and turned to him with what I hoped was an apologetic look and said, "Hey, about what I said earlier. I wasn't making a comparison or anything because of your..."

"It's a monastery."

I glanced over at him, bemused. "A monastery?"

"Yes, a monastery. The road to get there is just ahead." For the first time, he turned to look at me, and I thought I detected something of a plea in his gaze. "That turn just ahead," he said, pointing.

A monastery, I thought. *That's a unique adventure.*

"Okay, sure. Let's go to Gethsemani." I slowed and turned onto a highway heading south. My passenger let out a sigh that I took to be an expression of relief. "Anxious to get there, huh?"

"Excited more than anxious," he said. "I've been traveling for two weeks and it's good to be on the last leg of the journey."

"Yeah, I get that. I'm something of a traveler myself. It's always a good feeling to know you're close to your destination."

"Which leg of the journey are you on?"

I barked a dry laugh and said, "Man, I've lost track. But tell me more.

You've been on the road for two weeks and now you're on the last leg of your journey. What's it all about?"

He considered the question and said, "I suppose I should not refer to it as a journey. It's really a quest."

"Okay. So, what's the difference?"

Again, he considered the question. "I recently graduated from university, and I'm trying to decide what to do with my life."

"Well, there's something we've got in common. The 'what to do with my life part', that is. I'm still figuring that out, and I graduated seven years ago."

"What did you study?"

"English lit. But I wrote for the college paper, so I took a bunch of journalism classes, too."

"And that's why you are here?"

"What do you mean?"

"I mean, are you here for work?"

"Eh," I said, unsure how to answer. "Not exactly."

His brow wrinkled in puzzlement. "What then?"

"I'm here to see a friend. Beyond that, I don't really know. But look, I'm curious about your quest. So, you're trying figure things out, huh?"

"Yes, I am."

"And how do you plan do that?"

"Through discernment. By searching for answers."

"Another thing we have in common. What kind of questions are you asking?"

He paused for a moment, and I glanced over to see he was looking out his window. "You might laugh."

"No, I won't."

He turned to me and said, "I want to know if God is calling me to be a priest."

A bark of laughter shot through the truck cab. My passenger shook his head in disgust and turned away.

"Hey, I'm sorry. Look, I wasn't laughing at you. It's just that we were kind of on a roll there with things we have in common, and well...that one through me for a loop." I could see he was hurt. "Look, man, I'm sorry. Truly, I wasn't laughing at you. I was just...surprised, that's all."

He stared straight ahead as I fumbled for words to convey my sincere contrition. As usual, my effort came up short of the mark. "Thing is, I can be kind of an asshole." I gave a nervous laugh and shrugged, hoping he would warm to the idea of me as a hopeless buffoon.

He shot me a pointed look, but then softened in apparent acceptance of my second ham-handed attempt at an apology. "Anyway. My quest is part of my discernment, and this monastery has a special role to play."

"That sounds interesting," I said in a cautious tone. "What kind of role?"

"The abbey is consecrated to Our Lady. Do you know Our Lady?"

"Well, umm...yeah, I guess I think I know what you're talking about."

"You guess you think you know?" he said, taking advantage of the fact that I did, in fact, sound like a buffoon.

I squirmed in my seat and gave him a wary look as I offered my answer. "Mary?"

"Yes, Mary," he said, looking pleased. "Are you Catholic?"

Again, I squirmed, feeling like a kid the teacher won't stop calling on because she knows he didn't complete the reading assignment. "Let's just say I haven't thought about what I am in those terms for a long time. But how does all this figure into your quest?"

"I have a devotion to Our Lady. And as I stated, it is to Our Lady that this monastery is dedicated. So, to answer your question, I would say my quest is a kind of journey, but one prompted by a specific purpose. One driven by faith that God will guide me to where He wants me to be."

The truck rambled over a railroad crossing, causing us to bounce on the seat. I thought about his answer, and it resonated with my own experience coming out of college. Back then, I had been all about the journey, although according to Moussa's definition, my journey had lacked the ingredient of faith that might have turned it into a quest. I certainly couldn't argue that I had been trying to figure out what God was calling me to, but I had possessed a sense of purpose, a sense that I wanted to live a meaningful life. I had always despised the idea of a domesticated existence, longing instead for adventure. But the truth is I never gave much thought to where the journey was taking me, or what I was meant to learn from it all. And adventure? Yeah, sometimes. But lately most of my travels felt more like random series of events than adventures. And what I had learned from it all?

"So that, I think, is the difference."

"The difference?" I said, coming back from my reflection.

"Yes. The difference between a journey and a quest."

"Oh. Right. That makes sense." I glanced over at my passenger and said, "You know, two weeks is a pretty good stretch to be on the road. Where'd you come from?"

"New Orleans."

"You went to school there?" He nodded. "You're a better man than me."

"What do you mean?" he said, cocking his head in curiosity.

"I mean I barely graduated as it is. If I'd gone to school in New Orleans, I would've ended up in a gutter."

"Why do you say that?"

"Well, let's just say I tend to be easily distracted, and New Orleans is a place with lots of distractions."

As he thought about that, I thought I detected a slight smile on his face as he said, "It is a fun place."

"Oh yeah? You had some good times, huh?"

His smile widened in an innocent childlike way. "I have friends. We had fun."

"That's good to hear. So, why not keep riding that train?"

"What do you mean?"

"Well, this is a pretty serious endeavor you're undertaking. I mean, don't get me wrong, I like where your head is on this quest for truth and all that. But look it, man, you're young and, well..." He looked at me with an air of expectation, as if I was about to impart some wisdom upon him. "It's just that...I don't know." I hesitated. "Have you tried drugs?"

His face drooped in a disappointed frown.

"Okay, okay. I get it. Just say no. Solid policy. How about an internship? Have you done that yet?" He rolled his eyes as he looked away. "Right. You've done an internship. What about six months backpacking abroad? Hookah bars and youth hostels and all that stuff."

I looked over to see if I was getting through, but he was hunched over, studying his map.

"A mentor. Do you have a mentor?"

"Why?" he said in a dry tone. "Are you volunteering for the job?"

Yeah, right, I thought. *Like I'm qualified to give advice on how to live your life.*

"Turn left," he said as we approached a T in the road.

"Look, I'm really not trying to be flip," I said, taking the turn. "It's just that you're a young guy and you just graduated. Don't you think you should live a little?"

"Do you always provide life coaching to the hitchhikers you pick up?"

I shot him an ironical look and said, "Yeah, well the last hitchhiker I picked up was on one hell of a lot different quest than the one you're on."

"So, you have picked up a hitchhiker before?"

"Sure. In fact, the last time I did was kind of like this time."

"How so?"

I scratched my stubbled chin and thought back to a summer afternoon a few years earlier when I had given two hitchhiking hippies a ride to Memphis, Tennessee. "I was pulling onto the highway when I saw this hippie standing on the side of road holding a sign. I pulled over, and when I did, I saw in the rearview mirror that there was not one, but two shaggy-ass hippies running toward my car. I don't know where that second guy had been. Probably off taking a piss in the weeds."

"Where were you?"

"Oklahoma."

"What was in Oklahoma?"

"A fresh start."

"Why did you leave?"

"For another fresh start," I said in a frustrated tone. "Look, man, you sure ask a lot of questions. Have you ever thought maybe..."

"Why did you leave Oklahoma?" he said, cutting me off.

"So back to my story," I said, ignoring his question. "I stopped and now there's not one, but two guys standing beside my car expecting a lift. I mean, of course they did. Hell, I stopped after all. But I drove a two-seater back then, a hatchback, and everything I owned was stuffed in the back. Like, I could barely see out the back window, it was so packed. So, I told them I didn't have much room, but they were good with it and piled in on top of each other. Of course they smelled like they hadn't showered for a week, so that made for a pleasant drive."

"And how was their quest different from mine?"

I let out a sharp clap of laughter and said, "How wasn't it?"

"I don't know. That's why I asked."

"Well, to start with, they told me there'd been a dozen of them that had driven out west in a converted school bus. When the bus broke down, they split up and these two decided to hitchhike to Mississippi to pick mushrooms. So yeah, it's pretty safe to say they had a different kind of quest in mind."

"Or maybe not."

I gave an incredulous grunt and said, "How do you figure?"

"Didn't you just ask if I had tried drugs as a means of finding the answers I am looking for? Maybe they were looking for their own answers in their own way." He turned and gave me a satisfied look. "Just as I'm seeking my own answers in my own way."

He had a point. I lit a cigarette and fell into a sullen silence as we drove through a small community nestled at the foot of dense green hills that dominated the landscape. The streets were lined with modest homes fronted by small patches of grassy lawns, many of which were adorned with statues of Mary recessed in concrete basins. All around there were people mowing their lawns, fetching their garbage cans from the roadside, or rocking in chairs that rested on small porches covered by aluminum awnings of green, or white, or rusty gray.

"What did the sign say?"

"What sign?" I said, my brow wrinkling with fresh irritation.

"The guy, the hippie. You said he was holding a sign. What did it say?"

I took a long drag on my cigarette before answering. "Be kind," I said, exhaling a cloud of smoke out the window. "It said 'be kind'."

"Then I guess the last time was like this time."

I glanced over to see a gratified smile across his face. Sensing the scales had tipped further in the wrong direction, I gave a quick nod and looked away.

"Did you take them to Mississippi?"

"No," I said in a small voice. "I was on my way back to Kentucky, so I dropped them in Memphis."

My mind wandered back to that day. We had been on the road for more than five hours, my two passengers sleeping through most of the drive. How they managed to sleep was beyond me, as they were pressed up against the door and all tangled up in arms and elbows. Just as we came into Memphis, one of the guys woke up and told me to take the next exit. I remembered thinking that didn't seem like such a good idea given the blight in the neighborhood we were driving past, but I obliged his directive.

"It was raining." My passenger looked over at me with a quizzical gaze. "That day in Memphis," I said, more to myself than to my passenger. "It was raining. But they didn't care. One of them told me to pull underneath an overpass. So, I did and just like that, they grabbed their stuff and ran off. Didn't even say anything. They just took off. And there wasn't anything for me to do but...I don't know...just keep trying to..."

"Turn right," he said, jolting me out of my reverie.

Refocusing my attention on the road ahead, I saw we were approaching a T in the road. I took the turn, and we passed a sign indicating we were in New Haven. We drove through the community, taking in the vibe of the small town as we passed St. Catherine Catholic Church; the Grab-and-Go liquor store advertising half-pints of V.O.B.; and the Mattingly Funeral Home where a black hearse sat parked beside a two-story white-brick house bordered by a turf walkway that reminded me of a putting green. We drove past an aluminum-sided V.F.W. lodge; a burned-out clapboard house; and Rhonda's Hair Salon where a wicked black Mustang was parked on the front lawn. Finally, we passed the Mainstreet Methodist Church and the community park baseball field before a sign on the edge of town thanked us for visiting and encouraged us to come again.

"It's been like this for me the whole way," he said.

"Like what?"

"I left New Orleans two weeks ago with no money and no clear path to my destination. I had my backpack, my sign, and a map. Since then, God has continually placed people in my life to help me on my way. It has been a providential road I have traveled."

Moussa's eyes gleamed as he shared this description of his travels. I thought of my own travels and the not-so-providential debauchery that had led me into a nasty exchange with a gas station clerk not an hour earlier. It struck me as ironic that such a debased confrontation could be followed by an encounter with this young stranger and his mysterious sign. As I considered the irony, it dawned on me that if I hadn't stopped,

I'd probably be in Bardstown by now, crashed out in some low-rate motel room. Instead, I was on my way to Gethsemani. The thought rather
amazed me.

"God's providence," he said.

"Come again?"

"You are an angel of God's providence."

I shot him a sharp look, expecting to see some trace of sarcasm on
his face. But he was looking straight ahead with the calm demeanor
that seemed to be his natural disposition. I nodded awkwardly and said,
"Yeah, well, umm...thanks for saying that."

For a moment, the only sound was that of truck wheels humming
against the blacktop.

"What will you do when you get to Bardstown?"

"Not sure. I'm supposed to meet up with my friend later today. We'll
see where things go from there."

"You're going to take a left up ahead."

A half mile up the road, I turned at the sign for Monk's Road and
asked my companion what he planned to do while he was at the
monastery.

"Walk, pray, read, reflect. Seek God's guidance."

"For how long?"

He shrugged and said, "Until I know what to do next."

"Do you know anyone here?"

He hesitated and I sensed some emotion pulling at him. "I did know
someone. The man I told you about earlier. The one who gave me this
book." He lifted the book from the seat. "His name was Brother Llewellyn.
He was a monk here, but...well, as I said before, he recently died."

I kept quiet rather than offer any banal words of condolence.

"Brother Lew is the one who prepared my quest."

That statement struck me as interesting, but before I could ask what
he meant, a large cross appeared atop a hill beside the highway and just
seconds later, the white walls of the Abbey of Our Lady of Gethsemani
rose up ahead of us, shimmering in the bright afternoon sun. I hadn't
thought about what I expected to feel upon seeing the place for the first
time. But looking at my passenger, I could see he was awed by the sight,
and I found that to be moving. After all, he had endured a considerable
challenge and made real sacrifices to arrive at this place. And what

part had I played? Was I an angel of God's providence? I wasn't so sure about that, but I did feel pleasure at having played some small part in the young pilgrim's quest.

I turned into the monastery entrance, circled the parking lot, and pulled into a spot facing a walled enclosure. "Here we are," I said with little understanding of what that statement truly meant.

Moussa, who appeared well aware of what it meant, extended his hand and said, "Thank you. You have been a blessing to me."

Whatever words I might have offered were lost to me in that moment, so I took his hand and offered a single nod. With a quick nod of his own, the young man gathered his things, climbed out, and retrieved his backpack from the truck bed. Then he stood outside the truck, looking at me as he held up the cardboard sign and said, "Gethsemani." Then he stepped onto the sidewalk and began to walk away.

"Hey, Moussa." He stopped and turned to look at me. "I just want to say good luck with everything and...I'm glad I turned around."

His face broke into a wide smile as he said, "I think the scales might be tilting in your favor, Levi Motley."

I offered my own embarrassed smile and watched as Moussa Diab made his way down the sidewalk toward a portico underneath which stood a pine-colored door. He opened the door, stepped inside, and was gone.

CHAPTER
SIX

I LAID THE PEN on the journal and got up to stretch as I was feeling the mental and physical impact of pouring my thoughts onto the open page. For years it had been my practice to keep a journal, and though that practice had never been what I would call a daily routine, it had recently become somewhat more inconsistent than usual. Still, I had to admit that Regina Sandoval's request for me to "get to it" had led to a productive session that I felt like continuing. Given that she knew and yet wanted to know more about how I ended up at the crime scene, I thought it would be good to record the events that led up to that point in "my story," as she had referred to it. With that objective in mind, I resumed my account of what happened after my encounter with Moussa.

For some time after Moussa's departure, I stared at the walled enclosure, mystified by the day's events. "Gethsemani," I said in a small voice. "How the hell did I end up here?" I exhaled a slow breath. "I bet Jesus said the same thing."

The throbbing in my forehead had been somewhat assuaged by my conversation with Moussa and the anticipation of arriving at our intriguing destination. But that rush was fading, and fatigue was rushing in to take its place. So, I pulled the truck into a spot comfortably shaded by the limbs of an oak tree as fatigue turned into outright exhaustion. Collapsing on the seat, I slept.

Sometime later, a breeze flowing through the truck cab brought me out of my slumber. I sat up, yawned, and looked out at the hazy afternoon glow permeating the landscape. My head felt groggy, but the pulsing sensation that had plagued me throughout the day had receded to a tolerable dullness. I calculated it must be around four-thirty, and though I wanted to explore the place, I was supposed to meet Dominick at six o'clock. So, I figured I better get moving.

Twenty minutes later, I saw a sign for "My Old Kentucky Home Motel" and another across the street that read "Stephen Foster Restaurant". My stomach rumbled at the sight of the restaurant, reminding me that it had been hours since I had scarfed down that sandwich. I turned into the motel lot, got a room key, took my gear inside, and returned to the lobby to ask the clerk for directions to The Prep Room, the bar where I was set to meet Dominick.

"Oh, that's easy, hun," she had said as she chomped on a piece of bubblegum. "It's down the street in the basement of Spalding Hall. That's the brick building behind St. Joe's. You can't miss it."

The motel clerk had been accurate as my destination did turn out to be just down the street. Thus, it wasn't more than ten minutes after settling up at the restaurant that I found myself standing in front of a sign that read "St. Joseph Proto-Cathedral". The red brick structure was fronted by a colonnade of white pillars that stood like sentinels guarding the stone images of saints who stood in oval niches above the church doors. As I admired the façade of the old cathedral, a question Moussa had posed drifted into my mind. He had asked if I was Catholic, and my answer had been rife with ambivalence. And rightly so. For many years, I hadn't thought of faith as anything more than a remnant of my childhood, a piece of my family history.

Family history, I thought, my mind floating back to memories of my grandmother.

Her name was Lenora, but to Declan and me she was Grandma Lenny. She had raised us, and part of that upbringing included Grandma Lenny scolding and cajoling and guilt tripping us as only an Irish Catholic grandmother can do, insisting we make the walk from our house to Notre Dame du Port for Mass every Sunday morning. As he got older, Declan refused more often than not to go, though I dutifully made the trek every Sunday, so Grandma Lenny wouldn't have to go alone. When she died, I think Declan was genuinely grieved to be unable to attend her funeral. But I also think he knew the old lady would have rolled over in her coffin at the sight of his unrepentant ass warming one of those old pews. After all, if there was one thing Grandma Lenny despised, it was a hypocrite. And whatever judgement the old lady, God, the court system, or the streets dared to pass on Declan Motley, they could never find him guilty of hypocrisy.

Shaking away thoughts of family history, I walked up the steps onto the cathedral portico. To the right of the entryway, a brown plaque read "THE BASILICA OF ST. JOSEPH PROTO-CATHEDRAL. The Mother church of the first diocese west of the Alleghenies, St. Joseph's was constructed between 1816 and 1819 under the Sulpician Bishop Benedict Joseph Flaget (1763-1850), first Bishop of the Diocese of Bardstown".

The plaque went on to explain that because of its historical significance, rich paintings, and liturgical celebrations, the church had been recognized as a national treasure by the United States Congress, the Kentucky Heritage Commission...

"And the Vatican," I said, stepping back to examine the statues above the doors. "Impressive."

"Isn't it though?"

I started and turned to see a priest standing at the edge of the porch. "What's that?"

"You remarked that our dear cathedral is impressive," he said with a gentle smile. "I was agreeing with you."

"Oh, right. Yes, it is impressive. I mean, the history and all...it's really something."

"It isn't locked," he said, motioning to the main entrance. "Would you like to go inside?"

"Oh, no thanks, Father. I mean, I would but, umm...well, you see, I'm on my way to meet somebody."

"Another time then," he said with that soft smile.

He walked through the white, double-doored entryway, and I retreated down the steps, craning my neck to see the time on the clock tower. It was six-oh-five.

"Brick building behind St. Joe's," I said, making my way behind the cathedral rectory.

Again, the motel clerk had been spot on. Spalding Hall, a stately, three-story brick building, stood directly behind the old church. If the clerk's accuracy held, then it was a safe bet The Prep Room was in its basement. Arriving in front of the building, I stood before two antique lampposts on either side of stone steps that led to a set of black doors constituting the main entrance to the building. At the top of the steps was a sign that read "Oscar Getz Museum of Whiskey History". Another set of steps led down from this main entry point to a sign that read "Xavier's". Looking at the sign, I thought for a moment that the motel clerk must have been mistaken. But I walked down the steps anyway and entered through a door that led into a vestibule.

Nice place, I thought as my eyes met those of an attractive young woman standing behind a kiosk.

"Welcome to Xavier's," she said. "Getcha a table?"

I grinned sheepishly as I ran a hand through my hair and wished I had bothered to shave. "Hey, sorry. I'm kind of a mess," I said with an apologetic laugh. "Just got into town."

I whisked my fingers over my T-shirt, attempting to flatten the wrinkled cloth while figuring my blue jeans and hiking boots wouldn't do much either to improve her first impression. But the dark-haired woman's smile, coupled with a glint of mischief in her eyes, indicated that I might be doing better than my vain attempt at a debonair appearance would suggest.

"How 'bout a table?"

"A table? No, I don't want a table. I mean, don't get me wrong, a table sounds good and all, but...I think I might be in the wrong place."

"Well, that'd be a shame," she said with a twangy lilt in her voice that I found fabulous.

"Yes, it would. But I'm supposed to meet a friend at a place called The Prep Room, so..."

"Then you're right where you need to be, darlin'. Follow me."

Lead the way, I thought.

We walked through a brick archway into a low-lit area containing an old-style bar replete with spirits bottles of all shapes, colors, and sizes. The stools were occupied with patrons bellied up and imbibing the happy hour specials.

"This is The Prep Room. See your friend?" I nodded toward the back of a bald black head sitting atop a broad-shouldered man at the far end of the bar. "You're friends with Dominick?" she said, touching me lightly on my forearm.

I nodded and said, "Join us for a drink?"

She let out an exasperated sigh and said, "Don't I wish. I still have almost an hour left on my shift."

"Well, with any luck we'll still be here when you get off."

"Then I guess we'll just have to see if lady luck is on our side, now won't we?" she said, flashing a radiant smile. I let out a low whistle as I watched her turn and sashay out of the bar.

Once she was gone, I looked over at my friend, surprised to feel a lump in my throat at the sight of him. But the last thing I wanted was to give him fodder to grieve me with, so I cleared my throat and swung around beside him, leaning casually against the bar as I said, "You know, Dom, a real friend would've told me there'd be pretty girls here."

He wrinkled his beefy brow and gave me an incredulous look. "Like you wouldn't still be wearing those raggedy-ass jeans and that ratty T-shirt even if I had." I laughed as he slipped off the stool and gripped me in a warm embrace. "My man, Lee-mo."

"Hey, don't start with that," I said, pointing a warning finger at him. "You've been calling me that since freshman year."

"I swear, when I got that rooming assignment in the mail, I thought, Levi Motley? That ain't no brother they got me rooming with." We laughed and embraced again. "Good to see you, my brother. You're lookin' good, like you ready to go." I took a step back and extended my arms, a look of mock arrogance on my face. "Not the distance, but maybe a round or two. Not in my class, of course. Welterweight is more your speed."

"C'mon, now, Dom. You know I'm good in any class. And when have you known me to not go the distance?"

He put a hand on my shoulder, and said, "Well, my friend, right now the only round you got to worry about is the next one." He drained his pint and slid the glass toward me.

"And here I am, a guest in your fair town," I said, shaking my head as I pulled out my wallet.

"Oh, I'm gonna take care of you, 'cause you need taking care of, Levi Motley. Damn skippy, you do."

I hailed the bartender and ordered two pints. Then I turned to my friend and said, "Since when do I need taking care of?"

"Since day one, that's when." I gave him a dubious frown. "Well, go on, then. Enlighten me on the great job you been doin' taking care of yourself."

"I'll tell you what. You wanna take care of me? You can start by introducing me to her." I pointed toward the archway and the dark-haired beauty standing in the vestibule beyond.

"Uh-uh," he said, shaking his head.

I wrinkled my brow and said, "Umm, why?"

"Because I know her, that's why."

"That's exactly my point."

"Yeah, well I know you, too, Motley. That's exactly my point."

I feigned offense and said, "What's that supposed to mean?"

"It means, I got to live here once your dumb ass is long gone."

The bartender placed two pints in front of us, and I pulled out a five and slapped it down on the bar. "This one's on you, Vernon," I said with a sly grin. Dominick raised an eyebrow, but I waved him off saying, "Come on, let's grab this table."

We sat, clinked our pints together, and took deep draughts of beer.

"So, you have to live here once my dumb ass is gone. That's how it is?"

"Damn skippy. And you know this to be true."

"Well, maybe it was once true. But who knows, Cotter? Maybe my dumb ass wants to stick around for a while."

"Please," he said with a dismissive wave. "When have you ever stuck around for anything?"

"Maybe I've changed. People can do that, you know. Change."

"Yeah, well change is what you should've done before your raggedy ass came up in here wanting to be seen with me."

"If it ain't broke," I said, to which he waved another dismissive hand. "But back to the question at hand."

"I didn't know there was one."

"Well, there is."

"Well, if it's will I introduce you to that fine young thing, let me make it abundantly clear...N-O."

"Oh, don't worry, we'll get back to that," I said, shooting a coy look in the direction of the kiosk. "I'm talking about the question of me sticking around."

"That ain't no question."

"Give me one good reason I can't."

"It's not that you can't, Levi. It's that you never do, and therefore you won't. Man, come on. How many places have you lived since we graduated?"

"Well, if I never stick around, then how is it that you know me so well as to conclude that I won't stick around?"

He pressed his hands together, a long-suffering look on his face. "The good Lord knows I have not had enough to drink to venture into the Godforsaken world of Mot-logic, where you will argue whether grass is green."

"Well, we are in the Bluegrass State," I said with a facetious smile.

"You know something, Motley, I wish you could've met my Great-Grandma Beatrice. Five minutes of you and she would have said thank the heavens that after God made that fool, he broke the damn mold." We laughed. "But I have missed you brother. I truly have."

"Good to see you, my friend," I said, and we clinked our pints again.

The bar was filling up with locals who were letting off the day's steam as they swapped war stories and made bold predictions about the next day's college football lineup.

"Tell the truth, Levi. You're not really thinking about staying, are you?"

Dominick regarded me with a penetrating gaze and my eyes fell to the tabletop.

"Gimme one of those," he said with a sigh, and I handed him my pack of cigarettes. "We've been friends a long time, Levi," he said, lighting up. "But you shouldn't expect me to tell you why you're here or what you should do next."

I snorted and said, "That's funny, I don't remember asking you to tell me any such thing. And besides, I already know why I'm here. I'm hanging out with you."

"You're here because you got tired of whatever it was you were doing out there. I just happened to call as you had one foot out the door."

"Now you see, that's also funny 'cause I thought you said you weren't going to tell me why I'm here."

"No, I told you that you shouldn't expect me to tell you why you're here."

"Same damn thing."

"Actually, it isn't," he said with an annoyed frown. "Why do you always do this?"

I polished off my pint and slid the glass toward him. "Your round."

He stared at me for several seconds, and then walked to the bar while I sat sulking. He was right, of course. He knew the game I was playing, baiting him to get a reaction so I could then deflect, obfuscate, and avoid accountability for whatever decision I would ultimately make. Dominick had seen my act a thousand times, and that made me an asshole for playing him. He knew it, and I knew it. But there it was. I had done it anyway.

The conversation level in the bar was rising as Dominick returned to the table with only one pint. "Okay, I see how it is," I said.

"Just pacing myself. After all, some of us have to work in the morning. And if you spent last night in B.G., I know damn well you ain't long for this world."

"I might surprise you. And why are you working on a Saturday? What, are you late on a deadline?"

"As if," he said, rolling his eyes. "I'm covering for somebody. An event over at..."

Just then a woman walked up to the table and shot my companion a sly look as she said, "Well, if it isn't my eighth-grade crush, sitting here in all his sexy glory."

"What's up, girl?" Dominick stood and the two hugged.

"Haven't seen you in forever," she said. "Who's this?"

"This is my boy from college," he said, motioning toward me.

The woman was blonde, late twenties, and brimming with exuberant personality. She looked at me with a wide smile and said, "Hey there, boy from college."

"Hey yourself."

"I don't recollect I've seen you before. Where you from?"

"Just got in town from Colorado."

"Oh, wow. Is that where you live?"

"Not anymore," I said. "Sorry, I didn't catch your name."

"Oh, for heaven's sake, my manners are terrible. I'm Tonya. I went to school with this big hunk." She nudged Dominick in the gut with her elbow. "We've known each other more than twenty years. Went to school together since kindergarten."

"Damn, girl, you're making me feel old."

"Old enough to know better, too young to care," she said, a mischievous glint in her eyes.

Dominick shot me an apologetic glance and I excused myself saying, "I'll leave you two to, umm...well, whatever. I'll be right back."

"Okay, then," she said in a bubbly voice. "Don't get lost, college boy."

The kiosk was absent the lovely young hostess as I made my way to the restroom where I stood at the mirror inspecting the three-day-old growth on my face and a mess of hair that resembled a misshapen mop head. I ran water over my hands and tried to smooth the mess into a somewhat respectable coif. Staring at the mirror, I gave a wry smile at the road-worn image staring back at me.

Raggedy ass is right, I thought.

As I returned to the bar, I was happy to see the hostess standing at the kiosk with the relaxed grace of woman who knows the power of her charms. As I walked past, I tapped an imaginary watch on my wrist. "Tick-tock, tick-tock," she said with a smile.

Back in The Prep Room, I frowned at the flippant reference to my missing watch, though I really hadn't meant anything by the gesture.

Just trying to be charming, I thought, shaking it off.

I found Dominick still talking with Tonya, so I sat people watching as a thin man with long hair parted sharply in the middle carried a guitar case through the crowd. He wore khaki cargo pants bunched up around his sandals and was bespectacled in round frames. He disappeared though a door at the back of the bar, reemerging a moment later with a speaker cabinet that he placed on a stand. Dominick spotted me, and I heard him say, "Okay, girl, good to see you," as he hugged Tonya and returned to the table.

"Ten bucks says he opens with Van Morrison," I said, motioning to the guy setting up for his gig.

Dominick quickly examined the guy and said, "Beatles, for sure."

I lifted my pint, noticing that my friend was properly fortified with a pint of his own. "Look, man, I'm sorry. You know how I get."

"It's all good. A man develops thick skin being friends with Levi Motley." He gave me a quick once over. "You look like you've recovered well enough from whatever havoc you wreaked last night."

"I'm 'bout half-way there. I might get all the way there if I keep working at it." I took a deep draft of my pint as Dominick furrowed his brow.

"What'd you get into?"

"Ahh, you know," I said with a shrug. "Some of the boys from back in the day showed up."

"Showed up where?"

"Baker Street."

"For real? What was your old ass doin' at the pub?"

"Just trying to catch a glimpse of my former glory." Dominick shook his head, but he had a slight smile on his lips. "What? You never think about those days?"

"Of course I do," he said. "Those were good days. But maybe you've heard the rumor that life goes on?"

"Yeah, I've heard. But on to what?"

"Levi, your problem is you're a dreamer, always searching. And I admire that. I really do. But don't you ever think about putting down roots, building a career, starting a family? You know, normal life kind of stuff?"

I let the question get lost in the noise around the bar.

"So, who were the boys?"

I hesitated. "Well, actually there was just one," I said, absently tapping my fingers on the table. "You remember Dave?"

His face wrinkled as he searched his memory for the "Daves" we used to know. Then he sat up in his chair and said, "Dave, as in 'Doctor Feelgood Dave'?" I took a meek sip of my beer, and he slumped back in his chair. "Damn, Motley. You're lucky your ass ain't in jail." He shook his big bald head in disbelief. "Or a body bag."

"Yeah, whatever. You would've been right there with me, and you know it."

"Ten years ago, maybe."

"Oh, come on. It hasn't been that long."

"Gettin' close. But I guess that explains why you look like you spent the night in a box car."

"Yeah, that's right," I said, relaxing back in my chair. "Get your shots in while you can."

We sat in silence for a few minutes as the house entertainment went through the guitar-tuning and mic-check ritual ubiquitous among the singer-songwriter set.

"So, I know you were just shit-talking earlier," Dominick said, breaking the silence. "But just for the sake of discussion, is sticking around something you might actually consider?"

I took a moment, giving the question its proper due. He was right, I had been talking out of my ass when I said something about sticking around. But hearing the question posed as an honest inquiry from a friend gave me pause. I shrugged and said, "I guess it's worth talking about."

"I want you to think about it," he said, seizing upon the opening. "I think it'd be good for you, Levi."

The bar was full of people now, and the energy in the room was buzzing. I scanned the crowd, thinking that I liked the place.

"I talked to my editor about bringing you on staff."

I shot him an incredulous look and said, "You got me a job before I even got here?"

"Not exactly. But I think I can get you a gig that could lead to a job. You interested?"

I gave an ironic laugh and shook my head, but Dominick held me with a questioning gaze. After a moment, I gave a helpless shrug and said, "What's the gig?"

"A freelance job. You know the drill."

"Covering what?"

"You know anything about bourbon?"

"Well, I know how to order it," I said. "And I know what do to do with it once it arrives."

"Yeah, well, you been knowin' that for a long time."

Again, I shook my head, genuinely not following his train of thought. He picked up on my confusion and expounded on his thinking.

"There's a bourbon festival coming up. Been going on for years. It's grown into a big-time event with a bunch of high society types that..."

"Hold up," I said, cutting him off. "You know I'm not the guy to cover some black-tie ball."

"I know, I know," he said, putting his hands up. "Look, there's all kinds of stories here, Levi. About bourbon, about people, about the town. There's all kinds of stuff to write about here."

"Okay, but you said the gig is covering a festival."

"Well, yeah, but that's just the start of it. There are a lot of characters that live here, a lot of interesting personalities. The festival is just a jumping-off point."

"Well, if it's so interesting, then why don't you..."

Just then, an ear-splitting shriek ripped through the bar as the Lennon-esque musician plugged in his guitar. "Sorry about that," he said into the microphone.

I took a drink and said, "Like I was saying, why don't you write it?"

"You know I'm not a storyteller, Levi. I'm technical, succinct, precise, efficient."

"You're damn good, Dom."

"Yeah, I'm good. But you're..." He searched for the word. "Literary." I rolled my eyes and frowned. "Oh, come on, Motley. You were the best longform writer at *The Heights*, and you've got killer instincts. You know when to lay back, and you know when to stir shit up, to provoke a reaction. I write articles, but you tell stories. There's a difference." He paused, gauging my reaction. "There's a lot of good stories here, my friend, and you'd be great telling them."

"Plus, it would keep me around, so you can keep an eye on me."

"Brother, I know why you move around so much. I know it's about your old man, about Declan."

I shot him a sharp glance and said, "What the fuck does that have to do with anything?"

"I'm just saying I understand," he said, putting his hands up in a calming gesture. "I get you."

My jaw clenched as I struggled to tamp down the rush of adrenaline heating up my face. I took a deep breath as Dominick gave me a knowing smile and said, "I told you I'm gonna take care of you. Besides, what do you have to lose? You'll get a good story and some cool photographs for your portfolio. And you'll get paid."

I'd known Dominick a long time and we were similar in that neither of us was prone to dole out unwarranted praise. He knew I'd walk in a heartbeat if I thought he was trying to blow smoke up my ass, so I had no doubt he was coming from a place of friendship.

"I'll think about it," I said irritably. "But you gotta tell me something first."

"What's up?"

"Don't you get thirsty talking so much shit?"

He gave a wide grin and said, "I got nuttin' but love for ya, Lee-mo."

We stood, clasped hands, and did that shoulder-to-shoulder bump that passes for a hug when male conversation cuts a little too close to the heart. That settled, I scanned the room and noticed the young hostess sitting at a table next to a guy in dark jeans pulled down over crocodile-skin cowboy boots. Ignoring the guy, I smiled at her and though she demurred, I could see the slight curl playing on the edge of her lips.

"Hey, lover boy. It's your round."

I turned to look at Dominick and said, "You mean I gotta sit here and listen to you pump sunshine up my ass and I gotta buy the next round?"

"Hey, I'm just trying to get what I can before that wallet dries up."

A moment later, I returned from the bar and presented two shots of bourbon. Per usual, Dominick shook his head in a mixture of humor and disapproval. Still, he took the shot, and we raised our glasses and drank. I slammed the empty shot glass on the table and motioned toward the woman. "Think I got a chance?"

He looked over at the couple and said, "Best leave it alone, Motley."

"Oh, I forgot. You gotta live here once I'm gone."

"No, it's not that," he said, his eyes lingering warily on the couple. "You're just better off staying away."

"And why is that?"

He turned to me and said, "If your dumb ass would just listen for once, then you might hear what I'm saying to you. Stay away."

I gave him a curious look and was about to question his cautious advisement when the singer-songwriter began picking a delicate opening on his acoustic guitar. A familiar melody wafted through the bar as the singer crooned in a pleasing voice. Dominick and I looked at each other and called out the song in unison.

"Sweet Baby James."

CHAPTER
SEVEN

I HAD BEEN SURPRISED to learn that the editor of *The Bardstown Observer* was willing to meet with me on a Saturday morning, though it had not surprised me to learn that Dominick set the meeting up before I had even gotten to town. Upon hearing of my prearranged appointment, I reminded my friend that it was presumptuous to make demands of a person's time without his knowledge. In truth, I appreciated his considerate foresight even if I did resent coming off as a foregone conclusion. Dominick had filled me in on some of the professional peccadillos of his boss, George Hawley, as we lingered over our final pints the evening before. Most notably, he described Mr. Hawley's irascible disposition and penchant for peppering his conversation with curse words.

"He's kind of an odd duck, but he's a good boss," Dominick had said. "He's done some fantastic stuff, and really knows how to get inside a story. I think you'll dig him, but just know that he can be a bit temperamental until he gets to know you."

The Observer office building was located on the court square. I approached a metal door off an alley at the back of the building and as instructed, pushed the buzzer. A moment later, a middle-aged man in blue jeans, tennis shoes, and a well-worn University of Kentucky sweatshirt appeared in the doorway.

"Hellfire and damnation, who's this buzzing at my door?" Before I could answer, he said, "I reckon you'd be Motley?" I extended my hand, and he pumped it enthusiastically. "Yes, yes, damn good to know ya.

George Hawley's the name." He then turned abruptly and gestured for me to follow. "A rollin' stone gathers no moss, no sir, indeed."

I followed him down a hallway and into an office lined with faux wood paneling and redolent of a strong cigar.

"I brought my portfolio for you to..."

He cut me off, gesticulating as he said, "Yes, yes, damn good of you. Just lay it on the table there. Yes, over there. That's right, very good."

I searched the table for an open spot to lay the portfolio, finally setting it upright between two sets of thick file folders. The office was a mess. There were stacks of old newspapers on the floor and practically every inch of the walls was filled with pictures of George Hawley posed with all manner of people in all manner of settings. I surveyed the photos, stopping to peer at one depicting my host with his arm over the shoulder of a wildcat mascot. The two stood in the end zone of a football field amidst the faces of college coeds whose celebratory expressions were frozen in time.

"That was a hell of a good night right there. Yessir, indeed it was," he said, standing next to me as he gazed at the picture. "That was in seventy-seven. The Cats over the Nittany Lions. Hell of a good night, yessiree."

"Were you a student?"

"No, I was class of sixty-eight. Although I acted like a damn fool student that night, throwin' 'em down like I was back at the old fraternity house. Yessir, indeed I did."

I looked at the man, amused by his frenetic energy and peculiar speech pattern. But as we sat and began what was presumably a job interview, I was taken by his sudden transformation as he adopted a stoic poise accompanied by a steady tone that belied what up to that point had been a scattershot style of conversing. He gave me a direct look as I sat uninvited in the only other chair in the office.

"So do you want to hear about my experience?" He stared at me without reply. "Would you like to see samples of my work?" I said, motioning toward the portfolio on the table. He frowned and gave a slight shake of his head. "Well, has Dom told you anything about me? About our time working together at *The Heights*?" He gave a little shrug. "Okay, then."

I folded my hands in my lap, and we sat in silence. At least five minutes passed before he spoke. "You know, Mr. Motley, I have found the most effective means of getting someone to talk is to simply shut my big yapper."

I nodded agreement but was unsure of what to say.

"You see, it has been my observation that people are damned uncomfortable with silence. So, when a man shuts his piehole and confronts the person in front of him with the discomfort of silence, well, that person typically just turns into a regular ol' chatterbox."

Again, I nodded, not knowing what else to do.

"But here we are, having sat in silence far beyond the limits of what most people are comfortable with, and you have not turned into a damn chatterbox."

"Well, I guess that's just my..."

"Which would seem to indicate that you are not discomforted by silence," he said, cutting me off. "Or at least not intimidated by it."

I kept my mouth shut, wondering if his pause was my opening to speak. "Well, I'm happy to talk your ear off if...."

"And from that I gather that you are not overly eager to offer your thoughts unsolicited. Would that be an accurate assessment of your personality, Mr. Motley? At least on this topic?"

I cleared my throat, buying time to see if he really wanted me to answer. "I guess I haven't really thought about it before, Mr. Hawley," I said, pausing to see if he would interject. "But I suppose that's true, although it probably depends on the circumstances."

"Fair enough. But damnit don't stand on formality, Motley. Call me George. And to answer your question, Cotter has told me a thing or two. Hell, he thinks you're the regular cat's pajamas. Won't stop talking about ya."

"Well, Dom's a good..."

"He tells me you just got to town. From whence have you arrived?"

I decided brevity was the best strategy in answering the man's questions. "Out west."

"Well shit fire, son, 'out west' ain't a place. It's a helluva wide open space is what it is. A space I'm damn fond of occupying. But it ain't no place. Where ya coming from, son?"

"Colorado."

"That's more like it. Were you working for a paper out there?"

"Freelance stuff." Seeing the way was clear, I added, "A good bit of photography. Building my portfolio."

"What kind of photography? Landscapes?"

I shook my head and said, "Only as far as the landscape involved a person."

"Explain."

"I mean, I'm not as interested in the mountain as I am the woman who's climbing the mountain just a year after having her left leg amputated below the knee."

"That in there?" he said, his eyes flashing toward the table. I nodded, and his eyes narrowed as he regarded me in a close inspection. "What's your first impression of our little town?"

"Well, it's actually not the first time I've been here. Dom brought me to the Turkey Crawl back when we were in college."

"Crawl? Hell fire, son, it ain't no crawl. It's a Turkey *Kick*."

"Sorry. Turkey Kick. Hell of a good time, as I recall."

"Well, you got that part right. So then, what's your accumulated impression of our fine town?"

"I like it. It seems like a place with a unique story to tell."

"I reckon I'd say you're right about that," he said, nodding with approval. "And how long do you plan to stay in our historic little hamlet?"

"Well, to be honest with you, George," I said, clearing my throat to see if it was in fact, okay to refer to him by his first name, "I didn't plan to stay at all. But here I am, so I guess we'll see how things play out."

"That's rather noncommittal," he said, eyeing me with his narrow gaze. "You got a better offer someplace else?"

"I don't have any offers. And I don't mean to be noncommittal, but I also don't intend to bullshit you, if you'll pardon my French."

"Oh, go on now. Don't apologize on my behalf. I ain't no delicate daisy. But if ya ain't fixin' to stay around here, what in the hell would you do otherwise?"

"Well, George, I tend to drift about and go from place to place without much of an alternative plan."

"Boy oh boy, you said a mouthful there. When I was young, I surely did the same." His face softened in a wistful gaze. "But tell me, what have you been doing since you got to Kentucky?"

"Since I got to Kentucky? Well, let's see. So far, I got drunk at the college pub where I used to hang out, nearly got into a fight with a gas station clerk over five bucks, picked up a hitchhiker and took him to a monastery, and had a few pints with Dom down at The Prep Room." He gave me a knowing smile. "And, oh yeah, I caught the eye of a pretty girl, too. But that story's yet to be written."

He arched his eyebrows in genuine appreciation. "A damn fine couple of days, right there. And how do you plan to follow up on all that?"

"I don't know. I suppose I'd like to walk around the town, get a feel for the place."

"I see you brought your camera," he said, motioning to the case beside my chair.

"Gotta be prepared. Never know when the moment will arrive until you find yourself in it."

He took in a long breath and regarded me with a dreamy, nostalgic air. "Hell of thing, ain't it Motley? A moment?"

I found I couldn't contain a soft laugh. Dominick had been right. I liked George Hawley.

"Well, let's get down to the brass tacks of the matter. You looking to do some work?"

"Yes sir, I'd appreciate an assignment. Dom mentioned something about a bourbon festival?"

He shuffled the papers on his desk. "Yes, yes, of course, the bourbon festival. You understand I need words and pictures? No room for any specialization at a small-town outfit."

"Yeah, of course. I'll give you something good, George. Although, I have to admit I don't know much about the ins and outs of the bourbon industry."

He dropped the papers and waved at me with a disgusted look on his face. "Hell, I don't give a damn about the industry. It's the people that tell a story, Motley. Focus on the people, son, and you can't go wrong."

He looked at me with that narrow gaze, seemingly deciding which way to go with me.

"I tell ya what, young Motley, I got a proposition for you. You get yourself out there and walk the town like you said and then meet me back here at three o'clock with five hundred words on what you found. By God, I want to see what kinda chops you got."

"You're not giving me a lot of space to stretch my legs in there, George."

"Well, shit fire, if you're any good then the five hundred ought to get me to pining for a thousand more."

I thought about his proposition and liked the sound of it, especially the challenge of making him want more. "Yeah, okay. I'll give you what you asked for and make you wish you gave me five thousand words to work with."

"Yessiree Bob, that's what I like to hear. That's damn good stuff right there. Damn good, indeed."

That seemed to settle the matter. But before we wrapped things up, he motioned for me to lean in toward him, which I did.

"This here town has got loads of good stories, young man. Bring me the one that all the others missed. Bring me the story it still wants told, and this old town will forever remember your name."

"I hope I can surprise you," I said, leaning awkwardly over the edge of the desk. "But Dom tells me you've been editor here for going on twenty years. What can I tell you that you don't already know?"

His face broke into a wide grin, and he said, "Well, that's trick, now ain't it?" Without another word, he got up and walked out the door. I heard his voice from down the hallway as I picked up my gear to follow. "Yes sir, that was some good stuff right there. This way, Motley. Come on, son, get your ass out there and talk to the people."

"You want me to leave my portfolio?" I said, hurrying after him.

"Sure thing," he said, not breaking stride. "Leave it."

He opened the door to the alley and extended his hand as I stepped out. "Thank you for the opportunity, George," I said, shaking his hand. "I'll do my best to...."

"Aww, hell, Motley, the day's a wastin'. Get out there and talk to the people, son."

With that, the metal door slammed shut. And that was how I made the acquaintance of George Hawley, editor of *The Bardstown Observer*.

CHAPTER
EIGHT

A MAN WALKING HIS dog eyed me with suspicion as I stood in the alley. "Job interview," I said, pointing to the closed metal door. He frowned and shook his head as he and his snippy companion hurried by.

"Well, you heard the man," I said with a sigh. "Let's go talk to the people."

I walked toward the town's main drag, plucking a tourist pamphlet from a rack on the sidewalk as I went. According to the pamphlet, I was standing at the intersection of Third Street and Stephen Foster Avenue, the commercial center of the town presided over by a four-story red brick courthouse that the pamphlet explained had been completed in 1892 in the Richardson-Romanesque style. Not that I had a clue what the Richardson-Romanesque style was, but it sounded impressive.

I took several photographs around the perimeter of the courthouse and then wandered down the main thoroughfare, capturing the small town coming to life as local shop owners prepared for what they surely hoped would be a bustling Saturday trade. Along the street I saw an old-fashioned fountain inside a drug store, its red-cushioned stools occupied with people drinking coffee and swapping local gossip. There was a five-and-dime advertising "toys, souvenirs, housewares, and gifts" next to a shoe store with a glass display stocked with boots, wingtips, high-heels, and shoeshine kits. Halfway down the block, I paid a visit to a bookstore whose counter was stocked with caramelized popcorn, chocolate-covered peanuts, and multicolored candies that customers grazed on as they sauntered around the shelves filled with local history, best sellers, and classic children's books.

Making my way across the street, I stopped in "Spalding and Sons" and spoke to the fourth-generation owner who proudly told me that the retail clothing store had been in continuous operation in the same family since 1856. I listened as he regaled me with the story of how the store's founder, W.T. Spalding, had once been forced by a Union general to hide horses in the store's cellar to prevent the equine animals from falling into the hands of Confederate rebels. I thanked the man for the story and moved down the street, stopping in a café where I drank a cup from a French press prepared by the immigrant owner who sat with me and described in broken English how he and his family had fled their war-torn country, settling in this small town through the help of the good people at the local Episcopalian Church. His wife joined us, dabbing her eyes as she shared what it was like to lose her home and country and wondered aloud if they could ever return.

I photographed each stop along the way, including a horse stable across the street from the café. I had stopped to capture the image of a horse tethered to a rail next to a carriage advertising "Tours Around Historic Bardstown" when a woman walked out from behind the stable and said, "Ol' Moots is at lunch right now, but you can catch the next tour when he gets back."

"Wish I could, but I'm on a deadline. I'll have to catch it another time."

"You work for the paper?"

"I will if I can prove I've got the chops for the job."

She gave me a wary look and walked over to the horse. "This here's Roscoe," she said, gripping the bridle and stroking the horse's snout. "I never much cared for that name myself. But it's not my horse, so I don't have much say in the matter, now do I?"

"I guess that depends."

I hadn't meant any disrespect, but the woman immediately straightened, her brow creasing in disapproval. "I wouldn't imagine you'd speak to Judge Harry McGill that way, so you should know you are in the company of his only daughter." I stammered, taken aback by her reaction and unsure how to reply. "Well, don't stand there with your mouth open. You'll catch flies." I clamped my mouth shut. "Now you tell me," she said, eyeing me with suspicion. "What depends?"

She was a diminutive woman who barely came up to my chest even in cowboy boots. Her short auburn hair framed a lightly freckled round face bearing a look that warned me to tread with caution.

"Well, what I mean is...I mean, what I meant to imply is that...well, I just assumed that you were the proprietor of this stable, and therefore, could have a say in the name of the horse."

"You think I own this place?"

"Well, it seemed a reasonable premise. I mean, you are Judge Harry McGill's daughter."

Her eyes flashed as she searched my face for a sign of sarcasm. But I stood tall with what I hoped was a look of earnest respect. After a moment, her features softened as she apparently concluded that I had shown her the proper level of deference. After all, she was the daughter of Judge Harry McGill.

Whoever that is, I thought.

"I suppose I can see how you arrived at that conclusion. After all, I did solicit your participation in the next tour, which would be the act of a concerned party." She smoothed the front of a leather vest that covered a long-sleeved, white collared shirt. "I suppose you were just exercising your powers of reason, and Judge Harry McGill always did say that reason is the compass of the soul."

"Wise words."

She flashed another look of suspicion, but my face was a mask of stoic reason.

"Well, he was a wise man," she said, walking over to, again, stroke the gentle horse's snout. "Anyhow, his name is Roscoe, and I did not have a say in the assignment of that moniker. But if I had been invited to offer my opinion, I would have recommended he be called Biscuit after the stouthearted little warrior who took on that monstrosity, War Admiral, and showed him what for." She made a punching motion as she said this, and I had to stifle an amused smile at her intensity. Relaxing, the woman sighed, and said, "But he's Moots's horse and ol' Moots liked the name Roscoe, so there you have it."

Hearing his name, the horse nudged her, and she stroked his snout with a loving hand.

"You know, I think I have decided Roscoe is a fine name after all."

She shot me a look that solicited my agreement.

"Absolutely," I said, not daring to challenge her. "Roscoe. A fine name."

Again, the horse nudged her, and she kissed him. Then she straightened her vest, and turned to face me with a look that indicated the matter was now closed.

"Well, I hope you will be able to join us for a tour in the not-so-distant future. I'm sure you'd be pleased to learn about this beautiful flower growing here in the heart of The Great Meadows."

"The Great Meadows?"

She frowned at my lack of understanding. "When Daniel Boone looked down upon the Cumberland Gap, he said Kentucky was the most beautiful land he'd ever seen, calling it 'The Great Meadows'. Although that was hardly an original description, since the Shawnee and Mohawk had already named the land 'Kenta', which as everybody knows, means meadow."

She looked at me with the penetrating gaze of a teacher who had offered a point in her lecture that required a response from her student, so I said, "That's interesting. I didn't know that." She glared at me with a peeved curl of her lip as if my comment had been completely inane, which of course, was true.

"Anyhow, Daniel Boone called it the most beautiful land he'd ever seen. And rightly so. It's the best kept secret in the union, and I for one hope it stays that way."

"You'll get no argument from me. In fact, just yesterday I drove through the country just south of here admiring the hills and the lush..."

"Hills? Those are knobs," she said, correcting me. "And those knobs are part of an ecologic subregion that stretches from across the river in southern Indiana, through Kentucky, and all the way down into Alabama. This whole area is filled with limestone and shale, which is one of the primary reasons the water in Kentucky is perfect for the distillation of that magical brown elixir for which we are so well known."

"Well, I for one like both the hills and..."

"Knobs," she said.

"Right. Knobs. I like both the knobs and that brown elixir. Sometimes more than I should."

She snorted and said, "Judge Harry McGill always did say that moderation is the key to happiness. Although everybody knows he was merely drawing on Aristotle in making that derivative observation. Still, imitation is the best form of flattery."

My stroll through the town had introduced me to some unique personalities, but this professorial woman with her didactic manner of conversing was someone I found truly mesmerizing.

"You seem to know a great deal about the history of this area."

"I thought you couldn't stay for the tour," she said, her suspicion returning.

"Well, that's true, I can't. But I'd like to ask you a few questions. Can I do that?"

"May," she said, to which I offered a puzzled look. "Of course you *can*, but what you want to know is whether you *may* ask me a few questions."

"Oh, right. And wouldn't you know, I was an English major." I gave a nervous laugh, attempting to build rapport, but she stood with her hands on her hips and her face set in a frown. I decided to take another tact and fished a ten-dollar bill from my wallet. "Look, I'm happy to pay the fee for the tour. Or at least the highlights of the tour."

"Moots gives the tour, and Moots is at lunch."

"Right. You said that. But look, I really do plan to come back for the tour, but I've got someplace I have to be this afternoon and..."

"Young people today," she said with a disapproving shake of her head. "Always rushing about like a chicken with its head cut off."

"Yeah, I suppose that's true," I said, trying for an apologetic look. "Do you work for Moots?"

I immediately regretted the question as she folded her arms with an indignant huff and said, "Certainly not."

"Oh, I'm sorry. I didn't mean any..."

"If you must know, I am a local historian conducting research for my upcoming book on the history of Nelson County. Therefore, I do not work for Moots nor for any other man."

"I see."

"You see what?"

"Well, you know, umm...again, I thought it was a reasonable assumption."

"You make a lot of those, now don't you?" she said, raising an eyebrow. "And do you know what they say about assumptions? Hmmm. Do you?"

"Yes, I've heard the..."

"Although I refuse to lower myself to say such things. That saying is profane and Judge Harry McGill always did say that profanity is a sign of a bankrupt mind."

Seeing an opening, I went for it. "You know, I said that very thing to a man just yesterday."

Hearing this, her features softened, and she looked almost pleased. "Is that so? That very thing, you say?"

"Well, I think what I said was that profanity is the symptom of a weak mind, but close enough. I even suggested he start using a swear jar."

"A what?"

"A swear jar. It's when you put money in a jar every time you swear. Then you spend the money on something you need, or something you wouldn't otherwise spend it on."

She considered this with great interest. "I've never heard of such a thing. But I think I'll recommend the idea to Moots." She leaned toward me and in a low, conspiratorial voice said, "His speech can be a bit rough around the edges at times." I nodded sympathetically. "Perhaps this jar could help with that. He could spend the money on Roscoe's feed."

"I think that's a great idea. In fact, maybe my token of appreciation could also go toward Roscoe's feed?"

A thoughtful look came over her face as she looked at the sawbuck drooping from my fingers. "Well, it is true that feed costs are on the rise." I nodded my understanding. "I suppose that would be an acceptable use of a gratuity."

The matter settled, she reached out and took the bill, folding it before she tucked it into the breast pocket of her shirt. I had to smile.

"So, what is it you would like to know about our beautiful town?"

"Well, I know you don't work for Moots, but you help him out from time to time?"

"I assist Moots on the weekends. As you might imagine, those are his busiest days. I have been doing so for a few years now, and we have become quite the team. He provides the color, what with his anecdotes and local slang, and I provide the accurate history of Bardstown, Kentucky, the seat of Nelson County." I opened my mouth to ask another question, but she was already off and running in full lecture mode. "Which of course, was the fourth county founded in Kentucky in seventeen-eighty-four. It was named after Thomas Nelson, who was a signer of the Declaration of Independence."

"Good to know," I said. "But I wonder if you could tell me..."

"The Shawnee lived in Kentucky during the seventeenth century," she said, operating on autopilot. "But a prehistoric race of people lived on this great land far earlier than the Shawnee. Mound builders, they were, and the Shawnee shared the legend of this mysterious race of people with the white settlers when they arrived in..."

"Yes, that's fascinating. Truly," I said, taking my own turn at interjection.

"I was coming to a point of transition," she said, glaring at me. "The point at which I begin my soliloquy about the spirits of the ancestors of the mysterious race who built the mounds and how this influenced..."

I held up a hand and said, "I'm sorry, umm, Miss McGill, I assume?"

"I believe we already covered assumptions, young man. And the word you are looking for is not assume, but rather..."

"Right. I should have said Miss McGill, I presume."

She straightened up and lifted her chin. "Well, that would be a reasonable presumption. After all, I am the daughter of Judge Harry McGill, who always did say that..."

"Just to be clear, is it Miss or Mrs. McGill?"

"I most certainly am not a Missus," she said in a defiant tone. "I speak for myself, thank you very much."

I sighed. Conversing with this woman was like gardening in a minefield.

"Well, Miss McGill, my name is Levi Motley."

I extended my hand, which she examined cautiously before extending her own hand.

"Olive McGill."

"It's nice to meet you, Olive McGill. May I call you Olive?"

"You most certainly may not," she said, withdrawing her hand. "And I will refer to you only as Mr. Motley."

"Of course," I said with another sigh. "Miss McGill, I'm interested in the history of Bardstown. Truly, I am. But what I'd really like to know more about is the people of this area. Can you tell me about the people?" She started to launch back into a lecture, but I beat her to the punch. "You see, as I said earlier, I'm a journalist, and I'd like to write some stories about this area. But to do that I really need to know more about the people, about what makes them who they are. Does that make sense?"

I looked at her expectantly as she considered my point. After a long minute during which I almost decided to thank her for her time and walk away, she relaxed her rigid posture and said, "Yes, Mr. Motley. That is a most reasonable request."

She then took a deep breath and appeared to be searching for the transition point in her lecture where she would normally begin her elocution on the people of her beloved town and state. Having landed on that transition point, she began in a tone filled more with endearment than erudition.

"What you need to know is that the people of Kentucky are among the kindest, friendliest, most generous, and most hospitable people you are likely to meet anywhere in the world." I nodded, encouraging her to continue. "However, it is well known that they are also something of an enigma, which is not uncommon among people who live in a border state."

"A border state?"

"Yes, a border state," she said, cocking her head to one side. "If you don't mind me asking, Mr. Motley, where are you from?"

"I'm from Louisville."

"Umm-hmm," she said, her lips pressed together like those of a disappointed teacher. "And don't you know the basic history of your own state?"

"Well, I know some things. But where I grew up the history of the neighborhood was more important than state history, I guess."

"Which neighborhood?"

"Portland."

"An old neighborhood with a rich history to be sure," she said with an appreciative nod. "But I will remind you that Portland is in Louisville, which is in Kentucky. And Kentucky is a border state by virtue of the fact that its sons fought on both sides of the late unpleasantness, though it is well known that most people at the time sided with the Confederacy. Still, I am of the opinion that there is a kind of psychological struggle that has plagued the collective consciousness of the Kentuckian ever since its divided allegiance during the Civil War. That struggle, I think, is a historical antecedent that contributes to what makes the people of this state who they are." She shot me an icy glare and said, "And I would be remiss if I did not remind you, Mr. Motley, that you are one of those people. Thus, it would behoove you to brush up on your own history."

I gave a chastened nod.

"But returning to the point. The question of whether the character and identity of the people of Kentucky is derived from its being a border state is often driven by the question of whether Kentucky is the northernmost southern state, or the southernmost northern state. My unequivocal position on that question is that it is neither. I believe the character and identity of the people of this great commonwealth is derived from its roots as a western frontier, a wild land that captured the imagination of adventurers possessed of a frontier spirit and pioneer mentality."

I listened with genuine interest as people started to gather on the sidewalk, inspired by the eloquence and passion of this diminutive orator. For her part, Olive McGill seemed oblivious to the audience. It was as if she were strolling alone and without a care through The Great Meadows she called home.

"It is from that historical genesis that Kentuckians derive their unbridled spirit, for they are adventurers, a people who thrive on exploration and discovery. They are the sons and daughters of the surveyors and huntsmen, the traders and scouts who defied the injunction of the tyrant King George the Third to leave that area west of the Appalachian Mountains unsettled, so he could corral the people and check their instinct to wonder at what lay beyond the horizon. They are the inheritors of the adventurous disposition that brought veterans of the Revolutionary War west from Virginia and the Carolinas to stake their claim in the wilderness, hoping to harvest the deer, elk, bear, and wild turkey in the same way that the Indians who were native to this land had done for centuries. They are the descendants of the English, Irish, Scotch, and German settlers, who found in Kentucky the glory of God's handiwork with its knobs, and valleys, and rivers, and streams dotting and crisscrossing the unspoiled landscape with the promise of milk and honey. And they are the sons and daughters of the enslaved peoples of Africa, for whom the land was a prison, but through whom the land thrived and produced a bounty from which they could not partake despite their tireless toil."

I looked around at the people who had gathered to listen, and I could see that like me, they longed to see the unspoiled terrain that those settlers cultivated into the frontier society that formed the hard bark covering the people of this border state.

"They are the cultural beneficiaries of the Presbyterians, Catholics, Baptists, Methodists, and Lutherans, who traversed the Ohio River and the wilderness trail, who forded swollen rivers, who cut paths through the dense forests that would provide the wood used to build the churches, the modest but sturdy places of worship where priests and ministers would preach the Good Word. And those priests and ministers in time oversaw the building of much fairer churches, and indeed, the first cathedral erected west of the Alleghenies. And those priests and ministers preached to the congregations, to the people whose names are still among those who live here in our community today. And some of those in the congregation were lawyers and legislators, while others were farmers and blacksmiths, cartwrights, millers, tailors, shopkeepers, and teachers. And still others were slaves and freemen, and others stone masons and carpenters. Some were the proprietors of taverns and inns, which were then and remain today a most important aspect of Kentucky culture. For as the father of American literature, Mark Twain, once said, there was never a Kentuckian who didn't have a fifth of whiskey and a deck of cards at the ready."

As she neared the climax of her exegetical sermon, Olive McGill took on an exalted appearance as if she were channeling the spirit of one of those frontier priests or ministers preaching to the assembled congregation.

"And as one of our native Bardstownian authors once wrote, 'When God almighty created the heavens and earth, He made the little birds to sing, the flowers to bloom, and the sun to shine and nature all grand and beautiful. He made Kentucky the garden spot of the universe and Nelson County the heart thereof'."

With that conclusion, a delighted smile spread across Olive McGill's face as she approached me and looked up into my eyes. "That is who the great people of Kentucky are, and you sir, are one of them."

The crowd erupted in applause as people reached into their wallets and purses to fish out bills, stuffing them into a tip jar beside the carriage. After a few minutes, the murmuring crowd dissipated, and I stood alone with Olive McGill as she brushed Roscoe's light brown mane.

"Did that answer your question, Mr. Motley?"

"It more than answered my question. But there is one more thing."

She cocked her head in curiosity.

"What about the bourbon?"

Just then, a man walked around the corner of the stable. He had a long black beard speckled with gray and wore a brown Stetson atop his head.

"Well, if it isn't ol' Moots," she said, smiling. "Now there's the man to answer that particular question. So, join us for the next tour, young man, and you're sure to hear all you ever wanted to know about that magic brown elixir."

"Next time, Miss McGill."

"Next time indeed," she said with a nod. "Although one wonders when that may be. After all, Judge Harry McGill always did say that one path leads onto another and next thing you know, you are far from home." She stopped brushing, her brow furrowed as she said, "But of course, everybody knows he borrowed that from Robert Frost."

After listening to Olive McGill and speaking with the other good people of the town, I knew exactly what kind of story I wanted to write. Realizing I needed a place to make that happen, I headed back to *The Observer* office building anxious to capture what I had experienced that morning, though I was more doubtful than before that I could do the experience justice in five hundred words. Before I left, I bid Olive McGill farewell as she stood lovingly brushing Roscoe's mane.

"Young people, today," I heard her say as I scooted down the sidewalk. "Always on the move, always someplace to be."

CHAPTER
NINE

Aᴛᴇʀ ʀᴇᴀᴅɪɴɢ ᴍʏ five-hundred words, George Hawley delivered an enthusiastic "attaboy" to me for capturing the essence of a story he admitted to having overlooked. "Damn hell, Motley, but I tell ya, sometimes a man can't see the forest for the trees," he had said, laying the story on his desk. "This here's a fine profile of the people of our lovely community and the soil they grew out of. I tell ya I enjoyed the hell out of it, and you got me wantin' more."

It was good news to hear that George enjoyed my essay, but I would venture to say he didn't enjoy it nearly as much as I enjoyed seeing Dominick's reaction when I told him that George had given me space in an upcoming edition to expand my article. The look on my old friend's face when I dropped that tidbit of information on him made the whole trip to Kentucky worthwhile.

I dropped the pen onto the journal and rose to again stretch my legs after having been glued to a chair for most of the past few hours. Walking around the room, I gnawed a piece of crust left over from a pizza I had popped in the oven earlier in the evening. Then I fetched one more cup of coffee from the kitchen, thinking the caffeine boost would help me power through another half hour of writing.

Returning to the journal, I leafed through the pages with a familiar sense of affinity for this "beautiful flower growing in the heart of The Great Meadows" as Olive McGill had referred to her beloved Bardstown. But I was also keenly aware that my affinity was undercut with a pang of...

what? Regret? Sadness? Uncertainty? What did I feel about what had happened to Moussa Diab?

"All of the above and then some," I said with a heavy sigh.

And then there was the matter of my visitor from earlier that day, Regina Sandoval, the curious inquisitor who had planted the idea in my mind that not only was there something more to what happened to Moussa, but there was also something meaningful in the way that I came to briefly know the hitchhiking pilgrim. I mean, of course I had reflected on the circumstances that brought me to meet the young man on his quest. And sure, I felt the weight of his tragic demise. But what exactly was it this mysterious investigative reporter wanted to know?

Do I take her at face value? I thought. *Is it really a matter of, as she'd said, wanting to know what happened to Moussa, and what had happened to me because of it?*

"Well, either way, it's time to figure out what comes next."

What comes next? That's what Moussa wanted to know.

It occurred to me that the lingering weight of my encounter with Moussa Diab was a product of the sad reality that a young man who only wanted to find his way in life never got the chance to do so. And what did that say about me? I mean, I had wasted years moving from place to place indifferent to the question of where that movement was taking me, yet I still had a chance to figure out "what comes next" while Moussa did not.

I sat for a long time, thinking about chance. Regina Sandoval had a point when she said I had completed quite a circle of events with Moussa. After all, what were the chances that I would cross paths with the young man, deliver him to his destination, and then get called to the scene of his death? I didn't bother trying to calculate the odds, opting instead to continue writing my account of what led Dominick and me to that grievous site.

Dominick had recommended a local favorite called Tom Pig's for a Monday afternoon lunch, during which I was sure he intended to grill me about the interview he had engineered between me and George Hawley. To my surprise, I found myself anxious to fill him in on both my conversation with George, and my walk about his fair town, a walk that yielded what I thought was a pretty good story.

I arrived and sat in a booth amidst the farmers, construction workers, businessmen, and civil servants whose voices buzzed about the restaurant in casual banter. I was perusing the menu when my brow furrowed in confusion at one of the items. I hailed the waitress, who had a few minutes earlier explained to me that "Bless my heart, The Pig only serves sweet tea," and asked for clarification.

"Umm, what exactly are lamb fries?"

"That's the daily special," she said in a matter-of-fact tone.

"Yeah, I get that. But what are they?"

Her tongue worked back and forth between her lower lip and gums as she regarded me with amusement. "Sweetheart, if you got to ask, then you don't wanna know." My brow furrowed as my confusion deepened. "You might ought to go with the chicken fried steak," she said, tapping her pen against my menu before moving on to the next booth.

I shook my head, still confused, as Dominick arrived and offered his apologies for being late. "What the hell kind of place did you bring me to, Dom?" I said in a sharp whisper as he slipped into the booth opposite me. "The special is lamb fries and according to the waitress, I don't even want to know what they are."

"Is that so?" he said with a grin. "Then just wait 'til I get you to Colonel Hawk's for some rocky mountain oysters. We'll make a country boy out of you yet, Motley."

I gave him a wary look as the waitress reappeared. "Hey there, D.C.," she said with a sly grin. "What's poppin'?"

"Girl, I was just gonna ask you the same thing. What's good today, Deanne?"

"Aww, c'mon now. You know you can't go wrong at The Pig. Need a couple minutes?"

"Nope," he said, not even glancing at the menu. "Catfish sandwich on rye with fries and coleslaw."

"Drink?"

"Girl, you know I want your sweet tea."

She winked and wrote down the order. Then she turned to me and her grin morphed from sly to sardonic. "How 'bout that special, nature boy?"

I handed her my menu and said, "I'll take the vegetable soup."

She shook her head in mock disgust as she gathered up our menus. "Where's your sense of adventure, stranger?"

Dominick chimed in and said, "Yeah, what about it, stranger? Cat got your balls?"

"We got some in the fryer if you need extras," she said, and the two of them high-fived and howled with laughter before the waitress turned and walked away.

I looked without humor across the booth and said, "D.C.? Really?"

"My friend, I'm a reporter on the prowl for the skinny. I make it my business to be on a first-name basis with waitresses, bartenders, cops, hair stylists, and anybody else in this town who can give me the scoop."

I leaned in and regarded him with a pleased look. "You know, now that you mention it, being on a first-name basis is a good way to get the scoop. And now that I'm on a first-name basis with that lovely hostess from the other night...well, let's just say I'm looking forward to prowling for her skinny."

"And how, pray tell, did that happen?"

"Well, if you must know, I went up to that tavern on the courthouse square Saturday night. And wouldn't you know it, she was there with that shitkicker we saw her with in The Prep Room."

"Is that a fact?"

"Indeed, it is."

"Well, I imagine she would be there with that shitkicker, genius, since that's her boyfriend."

"I got that under control," I said, waving him off. "The bartender at the tavern filled me in already. Guy's name is Lance Coletrain."

"Coleridge, dumbass."

"That's it," I said, snapping my fingers. "Lance Coleridge Dumbass. Bet he's got a big ol' belt buckle with the initials L.C.D. on it."

"Keep your voice down, fool," he said, glancing around the restaurant. "Everybody's related to somebody around here. It's not the best idea to throw names around too loosely."

I grinned as Dominick cautiously said, "You take her home?"

"Nah, nothing like that. But we did slip upstairs for a minute. Did you know Jesse James once stayed at that tavern and shot up the place?"

Dominick rolled his eyes and said, "Please don't say dumb shit like that to a local."

"What's that mean?"

"That means everybody from around here knows Jesse James stayed at that tavern and shot up the place." He buried his face in his hands. "Jesus, Motley, I'm trying to help you out here."

"With my love life?"

"No, with your reputation. And with keeping your hide intact."

"I just got to town, Dom. I don't have a reputation yet."

"Yet being the operative word."

Now, it was my turn to roll my eyes as I said, "And what do you mean keeping my hide intact? What, you think I can't handle that goon? Come on, man."

"Yeah, yeah, you got mad skills. That's not the point."

"Then what is the point?"

"The point is that it's not just that guy you got to handle. That dude's into some shit, Motley. I'm telling you, brother, it's best to steer clear of this one."

I casually threw an arm over the back of the booth and said, "By the way, her name's Daphne Rose."

"Yeah. I know her name. First-name basis, remember? It's my policy."

"Daphne Rose," I said dreamily. "What a great name."

The waitress returned with our order. "Catfish sandwich for D.C.," she said, placing the plate on the table. "And vegetable soup for the nature boy. Get you boys anything else?"

"All good, Dena," I said, smiling up at her.

"It's Deanne, smartass," she said, shooting me a nasty glance before she walked away.

"Moving on," he said, picking up the ketchup bottle. "How'd it go with George?"

"George, is it? Wow, you really take that first-name basis thing seriously."

"Don't even try it, Levi. I'd bet good money that you called him Mr. Hawley, and he said something like, 'Well hell fire, son, don't be so formal, call me George'."

I laughed and said, "Pretty close to it. But you were right. I like the guy."

"That's because he's old school," he said through a mouthful of catfish. "Like you."

"He's one of kind, that's for sure. So, what's his story?"

"Grew up down near the Tennessee line. Went off to Lexington and then worked in Cincinnati after college. He was up there until around nineteen-eighty, I believe. Then he had the opportunity to come back closer to home as an editor and took it. He lives out in the county. Likes to refer to himself as a gentleman farmer, but that's just his sense of humor. Bottom line, he's a hell of a good journalist."

"Yeah, you said that before. What's he done?"

A knowing smile spread across Dominick's face. "Cornbread Mafia."

I gave him a vague look as I slurped my soup.

"It was a huge story several years back. You'd love it."

"Okay. Give."

"It was a bunch of good ol' boys that got busted with tons upon tons of pot up in Minnesota. Turns out they were running the largest marijuana-growing syndicate in United States history."

"They were from Minnesota?"

"Nah, from just south of here. Marion County. But they had farms set up in multiple states from the Southeast through the Midwest. Did some international trade, too, if I recall correctly. It all got busted up around eighty-nine or ninety. Can't remember exactly."

"And our boy George did what? Broke the story?"

"No, not that," he said, dipping a fry in a pool of ketchup. "He got to know the guys that were part of it and hung out with them, gained their trust. The way I understand it, he actually got to be friends with some of them. He's a country boy at heart, like them, so they trusted him. They knew he wouldn't screw 'em over, wouldn't exaggerate for effect. He and another guy, a reporter from Louisville, they wrote some great pieces on the whole deal."

"Is it still going on?"

"The marijuana business? Of course. I mean, you gotta figure pot's the largest cash crop in Kentucky next to tobacco. But it's not like before."

"What do you mean? It's not the Cornbread Mafia anymore?"

"Nah, when the feds busted 'em, they went up on RICO charges. Took down most of the crew. But not one of those boys took a deal. Not one."

"How many we talkin' about?"

"I think like, sixty or so. And every damn one 'em kept their mouth shut. Feds said they'd never seen anything like it."

I seasoned my soup with the saltshaker and said, "Where are they housed?"

"I don't know," he said with a shrug. "LaGrange, Manchester, Eddyville. Which one's federal?"

"Manchester."

Dominick sighed and said, "Right. Manchester."

We ate in silence for a few minutes.

"So, what's George got you doing?"

"Well, he asked me to give him five hundred words on my experience wandering around town talking to people."

"And?"

"And I like the place. I talked to all kinds of interesting people and got a damn good story out of it."

He regarded me with a curious expression. "What'd George say about it?"

I grinned and said, "He told me to expand it to twelve hundred words."

He dropped his fork on his plate. "He's giving you column space? Are you serious?" I shrugged in mock humility. "You're a bastard, Motley," he said, pointing a thick finger at me.

"Hey, you're the one who set up the meeting. It's not my fault I'm that damn good."

Dominick gave a wry smile as he wiped his hands on a napkin. He looked like he was ready to say more, but the pager on his belt buzzed. He checked the number and said, "Speak of the devil."

Dominick walked over to a payphone near the entrance as the waitress stopped and asked if everything was okay. I told her everything was fine and that my sense of adventure would be in full effect if I were lucky enough to see her the next time I dropped in.

"You should be so lucky," she said. But then she shot me that sly smile and wrote something on the check before slapping it down on the table and walking away.

Dominick returned to the table and looked at the check. Then he looked at me, shaking his head in amused disbelief as he said, "You got her number?"

"What can I say, my friend? Evidently, raggedy-ass chic is all the rage."

"Yeah, well we gotta move," he said, throwing some bills on the table to cover the tab. "Sheriffs found a body down near New Haven."

"We?"

"You're coming with. Boss's orders." He took one last bite of his sandwich and said, "Actually, he asked me to ask you to go. So, Mr. Legend-in-His-Own-Mind, would you be so kind as to grace me with your presence?"

"Damn skippy."

Dominick frowned as I dropped a tip on the table, picked up the check, and smiled at the sight of Deanne's number scrawled across the top. As we headed out the door, I heard an old man say...

I jumped at what sounded like someone tapping on the window and looked around, disoriented. Evidently, I had fallen asleep. The room was dark, but I didn't remember having gotten up to turn out the light. Still, I must have done so at some point. But then why I had sat back down at the table in the dark? The tapping sound came again, and I turned toward the window to see pellets of rain peppering the glass. I got up and turned on the light. Rubbing my eyes into focus, I scanned the room. Everything appeared the same as before. I yawned and wondered at the time with a vague notion of some responsibility I had to attend to nipping at the edge of my mind. What was it I was supposed to do?

Regina Sandoval, I thought. *Café Mozart.*

"Shit," I said, suddenly wishing I hadn't set the meeting.

I turned out the light and walked over to the window where the tapping had become a steady cacophony of rainwater pounding against the glass. I stood listening to the rain as I tried to remember what that old man had said. But the moment had passed, and I couldn't fit the old man's message into my memory of walking out of that restaurant with Dominick's words echoing in my mind.

"Sheriffs found a body down near New Haven."

CHAPTER
TEN

THE COZY CONFINES of Café Mozart were redolent of fresh pastries, assorted muffins, and various beans and brews, the comingling of which made for a pleasant aroma. I blew lightly on my mug of black coffee as Regina Sandoval sipped a steamed latte from a delicate cup etched with a vivid floral pattern of swirling green and pink hues. She set the cup gently on its saucer, and just as she had done the day before, opened with a simple query to get our conversation moving.

"So, Mr. Motley, did you get to it?"

I sipped my coffee and thought about her question, deciding it was not so simple after all.

"Well, if you mean did I reflect on how I've come to find myself as a temporary citizen of the bourbon capital of the world, then yes. I got to it."

"What else could I mean?"

"I think you know what else you could mean." She gave me a quizzical look. "Okay, Miss Sandoval, I'll play along. You could also mean, did I reflect upon the cosmic import of how my path crossed that of Moussa Diab?"

"And did you?" she said with a nonchalant glance at her fingernails.

"Yes and no."

She shot me an ironic look. "Now who's playing games, Mr. Motley?"

"No games here. Just answering your question."

"Then I gather from your answer that you did, in fact, reflect upon your travels but not so much on your interaction with Moussa."

"No, my reflection included my interaction with Moussa. I just don't know yet what it all means in the broader scheme of what I'm doing here." Her look softened and she nodded in appreciation of my point. "Which is to say I'm not sure how I can help if you're still wanting to know how all of this has impacted me."

"And if I were to focus my attention squarely on what happened to Moussa?"

I considered her question for a moment and nodded my assent to her investigative parameters.

"Good. Then we won't have to talk about the weather, after all. Let's go back to where we left off yesterday. Namely, the question of how the two of you met."

The bell above the entrance rang and a burst of cold air shot through the door as a customer exited the café. Regina Sandoval hugged herself and then sipped her latte.

"We can do that," I said, and she motioned for me to begin. "I was on Highway Sixty-Two headed for Bardstown, and, umm…well, I guess I'd say it had been a pretty shitty day up to that point."

"Would you like to tell me about it?"

My face wrinkled in angst at the thought of relating my confrontation with the gas station clerk. "Let's just say I was hungover and in a foul mood and leave it at that."

She gave me a look that said she would like to have heard more but nodded in acceptance of my succinct explanation.

"Anyway, I was headed toward Bardstown when I saw this guy holding a sign."

"A sign?"

"Yeah. He had a sign. And looking back on it, that makes sense."

"How so?"

"How so, Miss Sandoval, is that in my experience, they always have a sign. And it's the sign that gets you."

She cocked her head in curiosity and for the next ninety minutes, I gave her the unabridged version of the Bardstown chapter of my life story. She listened intently, taking notes and asking questions along the way. I found her claim from the previous day that she was damn good at her job to be true, as she adeptly clarified points of confusion and elicited details that I had glossed over. I wrapped up the story of my walk around town right about the time the server brought my third cup of coffee.

"So, the Bosnian couple that spoke to us earlier was the same couple you met the morning after you arrived in town?"

I nodded and blew lightly on my fresh cup of java. "And you probably already realized it, but over there," I said, pointing across the street, "is Moots's tour-around-town operation."

"Olive McGill," she said. "She sounds like a lady I'd like to meet."

"Yeah, I stop by every week to chat. She's actually a bit of a card, but the lady knows her stuff. And not just local and state history. Olive knows World War Two historians like I know the beat poets."

She nibbled on her biscotti and said, "Sounds like you're on a first-name basis."

"Well, not exactly," I said with a soft laugh. "I call her Miss Olive, and she calls me Mr. Levi, so close enough. I guess that makes you the only holdout on that front."

"Well, now that I know a fair chunk of your life story...but no. Unlike George Hawley, I prefer to stick to formality."

She sat with her fingertips steepled beneath her chin, considering how to proceed.

"I think I have a pretty firm grasp on your story, Mr. Motley, and I appreciate you telling it to me. But what I'd really like to know is how you ended up at the murder scene of man you had coincidentally picked up while hitchhiking just three days before."

"He wasn't charged with murder." She shot me a cool, questioning look. "You called it a murder scene, but the guy wasn't charged with murder." Her look went from cool to icy, and I felt the temperature in the room drop a few degrees. "Reporting one-oh-one," I said, raising my hands in a meek gesture. "Just saying."

She glared at me as I rubbed my hands together, attempting to thaw the chilling effect of having taught my superior journalistic colleague a lesson in the basics of reporting. "Thank you for the correction," she said in a dry tone. "Now, if you could please continue?"

I shrugged and said, "I was at lunch with Dom when George called and said sheriff's deputies were responding to reports of a dead body found near New Haven. He wanted us to go down there and check it out." She leaned in, her sharp, green eyes keen on my description of how things unfolded. "The body was found by a couple of guys who were floating the Rolling Fork River. They had just pulled their canoe out and were walking down to the riverbank to smoke a joint when they saw a shovel."

"They told the cops that?"

"No, they told me that when I spoke with them the next day."

"So, you did look into it," she said with a knowing look.

I took a drink of my coffee. "Yeah, well anyway, what they told the cops was that they were walking down by the river to take a leak when one of them saw the shovel. He picked it up and saw it had blood on it, so they started looking around the area. They found the body in some high grass near the bank of the river. At that point, they drove up the road to a store and called the police. Somebody in the sheriff's department tipped off Hawley and he called Dom."

"What did you see when you arrived at the scene?"

"We were a good half-hour getting there, so the area was already taped off. Dom got to work chatting up a deputy he knew, and I walked the riverbank until I found a spot to cross. Then I came back up the other side and climbed a tree to get a better look at things."

"That was resourceful of you. Could you see the body?"

I shook my head and said, "All I could get were shots of the deputies surrounding the body."

"Surrounding it?"

"That's what it looked like to me. After a while, the coroner got there, and they hauled him away in a body bag."

"How long until they removed the body?"

"Maybe twenty minutes after we got there."

Her face wrinkled in puzzlement. "So, it couldn't have been more than what, an hour between the deputies arriving and removal of the body?"

I nodded and said, "Yeah, I'd put it somewhere around an hour."

"Not much time for forensics to conduct an investigation." I didn't reply but thought she raised an interesting point. "How did you find out it was Moussa?"

"One of the deputies told Dom that the dead guy was..." I frowned. "He said he was an Arab-looking dude."

"An enlightened one," she said, scowling.

"Yeah, well that wasn't enough to know for sure, but it damn well made my stomach tighten up. I mean, what are the odds, right?" She nodded, conceding my point. "Anyway, Dom kept working his source and got the name."

"Had you already told him about your encounter with Moussa?"

"Nah, I wasn't in the head space to get into all that when we first met up. You know, we hadn't seen each other in a long time, and I really just wanted to catch up."

"But you told him after the body was found?"

"Sure. No reason not to at that point."

"Did you go to the police?"

"Nah, I thought I might eventually, but..."

"But?"

"But I don't usually make it a point to put my name up on the po-po's radar."

"So, they never questioned you?"

"No, they questioned me. But what could I tell them? Like I keep saying, I was with the guy for all of thirty minutes max. I told them what happened and what I knew about him, which if you think about it, really wasn't that much."

"Did they question you just the one time?"

"Yeah," I said, rubbing my chin. "A cop called me, I don't know, maybe two or three days after."

"Called you where?"

"*The Observer*. The secretary gave me the message and I called him back. He said he had a couple of questions and asked if we could meet."

"A deputy?"

"No. City."

"Why a city cop?"

I shrugged and said, "It's a small town. Maybe they were working together."

"Maybe," she said, a pensive look on her face. "Did you meet at the station?"

"No. He said he was on his way to the courthouse and asked me to meet him in the parking lot behind *The Observer* building."

"Did that seem odd to you?"

"At the time?" I said, thinking back. "Not really. It's an open lot, so all kinds of people who work or have businesses downtown park back there. The courthouse is right there across the street."

"So, he knew you were working for *The Observer,* knew to call you there. How? Did you give your credentials at the scene?"

"I didn't have any credentials. I'd just met with George Hawley two days before."

We looked at each other and I caught her drift.

"How could he have known to talk to you? Why would he have any inkling that you'd have something to say on this? I mean, you didn't tell Mr. Cotter about your encounter until after the body was found, correct?"

My brow furrowed and I heard myself answer in a small voice. "Yeah, that's right."

"Do you think he told the cops?"

"Hell no."

Her eyebrows arched into her forehead, and I blew out a slow breath as the import of her implied question settled upon me. It was a good question. Namely, if Dominick didn't tell the cops about my encounter with Moussa, then who did?

"Daphne?" She cocked her head, waiting for me to expound. "That Saturday night when I saw her, I told her about meeting Moussa. You know, in the context of telling her about my trip from Colorado."

"Perhaps playing up the rambler who's unafraid to pick up a random hitchhiker angle?"

"Whatever," I said, waving a dismissive hand. "Point is, I told her about it."

"And you think she told the police?"

I considered that possibility, but it didn't make sense. "No. I don't think that."

She raised an eyebrow in speculation and my face contorted as I tried to imagine Daphne telling the cops about my interaction with Moussa. I couldn't see her doing that. Especially since, as Regina Sandoval had correctly surmised, I was playing up my role as the free-spirited wanderer who had just blown into town when I told her about it.

"Lance Coleridge, on the other hand..."

"The boyfriend?"

"Ex-boyfriend," I said, pointedly. "Dom told me the dude was into some shit, and that's why I should steer clear of Daphne. I didn't know what that meant at the time, but now..." She waited. "Let's just say Daph told me a little and I've pieced the rest together myself. He's mid-level on the pecking order of some crew trying to pick up where the cornbread boys left off."

"A marijuana-growing operation?"

"That's the word. But Coleridge is a punk. And Daphne's not with him anymore, which is a good thing."

"So, is she with you?"

I hemmed and hawed, trying to explain our relationship, but Regina Sandoval managed to sum it up best. "Moving in and out at the same time, huh Mr. Motley?" I gave her a dumb shrug. "Kind of makes a relationship difficult to maintain. But she was Coleridge's girlfriend back when the police reached out to you, and you were sniffing around his girlfriend at that time. Correct?"

"In a manner of speaking," I said flatly.

"And you say Coleridge is wrapped up in the dope trade. Is it coincidence that Dale Goodlett claims Moussa was snooping around in a marijuana field? Could that field have been connected to Coleridge's outfit?"

"Eh, that might be a stretch. I mean, from what I hear, Coleridge's crew is hardly the only one that's stepped up to fill the void left by the downfall of the Cornbread Mafia."

She tapped her pen on the legal pad as we silently considered the possible ways that the police could have known to contact me. It was clear that the list of potential sources included Dominick, Daphne, and Lance Coleridge, but lacking any clear evidence of who the leak might have been, we moved on.

"Getting back to the interview. A parking lot still seems to me an unusual place to question someone about a crime." I shrugged it off, but in truth, her suspicion was contagious. "For the moment let's assume good faith, that it was simply a matter of making things convenient for you. What did he ask you?"

"He wanted to know where I was coming from, why I stopped to give Moussa a ride. He wanted to know about our conversation. What did he say, did he know anyone around here, was he visiting someone, did he give me anything or contact me while he was here? Stuff like that."

"So, he knew enough to ask informed questions?"

"Well, he knew I picked the guy up. That's really all you need to get to the other questions."

She nodded slowly and said, "I suppose that's true. What did you give him?"

"I'm not exactly a fan of the cops, Miss Sandoval," I said with a wry smile. "Not saying I've got something against them, but I'm not one to open up and bare my soul when conversing with the boys in blue, if you know what I mean." I could see she understood where I was coming from, but she waited for me to expound. "I didn't give him anything because I didn't have anything to give."

She sighed as she rubbed her eyes, and despite my caffeine overload, I found the fatigue of thinking through it all getting to me as well.

"Okay, well let's put a pin in it and go back to the crime scene for a moment. Does the Rolling Fork River pass near the monastery? I mean, could Moussa have been walking back to the monastery by way of the river?"

"I don't know the area well enough to say for sure but based on what I saw driving to the monastery, I don't think so."

"Okay," she said, her pen pressed against her lips. "What did they say about where he was found?"

"What was there to say? Within twenty-four hours, they had a guy in custody, and he confessed. The cops took his story at face value. That was it. Case closed."

"Case closed," she said in a whisper.

She thought in silence for a moment, and then dug in her bag to fish out a file folder that contained a newspaper article. "The guy that confessed, Dale Goodlett," she said, perusing the article. "He said he came upon the victim, Moussa Diab, walking along the bank of the Rolling Fork River carrying a shovel. Goodlett said Diab became agitated when he was questioned about his intentions and that after a heated conversation, Goodlett concluded that Diab was either a narcotics officer or a thief attempting to seize or steal marijuana plants from a nearby field. Goodlett claimed that Diab became aggressive when confronted about his intentions, and that he, Goodlett, seized the shovel after Diab punched and attempted to tackle him. Goodlett said he was only defending himself when he struck Diab in the head with the shovel." She looked up from the article and said, "How big of a guy was Moussa?"

"Probably five-nine, one-fifty soaking wet."

She took a breath and continued. "The county coroner's office concluded that the victim sustained an open head wound in the conflict. Speculation is that the victim was found near the riverbank because he was attempting to reach the water to gain relief for his wound. The coroner concluded that the victim lost consciousness and bled out." She stopped reading and looked at me with a bemused expression. "Do you have any idea why he would have been walking along that river?"

"None."

We sat in silence for a long moment, the constraint of time creating a palpable tension that permeated the air around us. Again, I could see that she was good at her job. She had asked good questions and had probed the issue of why I had been contacted by a police officer in a way I hadn't even considered. She even pointed out that the officer contacted me after Dale Goodlett, the man ostensibly responsible for Moussa's death, had already confessed. That was another good point to which I hadn't really given much weight. But we'd been at it for going on two hours and there were more questions now than when we began.

The one question that remained a constant for me was how I fit into her investigation and what kind of story she intended to write. I mean, on the one hand, there was the factual matter of what happened, but on the other was the notion that there was a deeper meaning to all of this. So, was I the source or the actual subject of the story? I didn't know, but one thing I was sure of was that the clock was ticking, and that meant Regina Sandoval would soon be hitting the road on her way to Nashville.

CHAPTER
ELEVEN

WELL, ARE YOU gonna fold or push all your chips in?"
Regina Sandoval pursed her lips and considered the question before posing one of her own. "Do you believe Goodlett's account of what happened?"

"Occam's razor, Miss Sandoval."

"The simplest explanation is usually the correct one? Say more."

I folded my hands on the table, thinking how best to illustrate my point. "Remember what I said to Moussa when he was standing on the side of the road? That he might be there for a while?"

Her lip curled in a sardonic half-smile as she said, "You think I'd have a hard time hitching a ride around here. Is that what you're saying?"

"That's the way things are," I said with a shrug. "We don't have to like it, but there it is."

"You're awfully young to be this cynical, Mr. Motley."

"Yeah, well, naïveté was never a luxury I could indulge in. So, I wouldn't call it youth as much as necessity."

She tapped her pen against the yellow pad as she considered my point and countered with one of her own. "But he had hitchhiked all the way from Louisiana. He'd made his way through the Deep South."

"True. But if you recall, he said he'd been on the road for a couple of weeks. That's longer than I would have expected the trip to take. And don't forget he ended up on a Greyhound."

She kept tapping her pen, and I saw that now she was the one catching my drift.

"And let's not forget he was carrying a shovel in the vicinity of a field full of pot plants."

"That's only true if you believe Goodlett's story," she said. "And is there any evidence that there was, in fact, a marijuana operation in proximity to where Moussa's body was found?"

"I didn't hear anything about a drug bust if that's what you're asking. But whether you believe Goodlett's story or not, I've heard enough about pot operations around here to know it's entirely possible that Moussa stumbled near enough one to put himself in danger whether he knew it or not. And what was it that deputy said to Dom?"

She blew out a disgusted sigh and said, "That it was some Arab-looking dude."

"All I'm saying is that going with a plausible explanation doesn't make it any less tragic."

"Occam's razor, huh?"

"That's all we have to go on." I took a drink of my coffee, set the cup down, and shot her a sly gaze. "That and whatever card you've got in the hole."

Her eyes narrowed, and I could see she was about to respond when a man walking by our table stopped and asked if I was the reporter who had written the article on the bourbon festival several weeks back. "Well, that depends on whether you liked it or not," I said to the man. He replied that he did like it and for the next couple of minutes he gushed about the piece.

When the man moved on, I saw a look of genuine admiration on Regina Sandoval's face. "Looks like you've got a fan club."

I feigned humility, but in truth, I felt pride at having praise heaped upon me in her presence. "Chalk it up to me being the new kid in town, but I did get some nice notes. I even got a couple from some industry bigwigs who read my piece."

"Nicely done. Next thing you know, you'll be drinking fine bourbon from Waterford tumblers and rubbing elbows with the bourbon glitterati, the Connie Westcotts of the world."

I gave her a skeptical look, thinking she might be laying it on a bit thick to distract from my point. "So back to that hole card," I said, leveling her with my own inquisitive gaze.

"You certainly like your poker metaphors, Mr. Motley."

"Yeah, well call it what you want, but I don't see a seasoned professional like you chasing this story without having at least one good card to play." Her eyes became green slits of light, and a smile played at the edges of her mouth. "What about it, Miss Sandoval? Is that the ace of spades you're about to turn over?"

She regarded me carefully, considering how much she wanted to tell me. Finally, she said, "I wouldn't exactly call it an ace. More like a wild card."

"Meaning you have to match it with another card for it to have any value. Is that why you're willing to spend all this time listening to me drone on about myself? You trying to match that wild card up with a card I don't even realize I'm holding?"

She continued to regard me with a narrow gaze. After a full minute of silence, she reached inside the file folder and pulled out a map. Clearing the dishes to one side, she spread the map on the table before us and traced a line with her finger as I leaned in to see what she was searching for. "That's funny," I said with a grunt. "You say you don't know where the Rolling Fork runs, but here you are with a map of Nelson County."

She glanced up at me, but there was no apology in her eyes. "In my line of work, you ask the question not to verify what you already know, but to read the person who is answering."

"Talk about poker metaphors," I said, glaring at her.

"I have it on good authority that Moussa was seen walking along this highway toward Monk's Road," she said, ignoring my comment. "That's the same route you took. But we know the body was found off Howardstown Road." She pointed to a spot on the map south of Highway 52. "Right here. Near this bend in the road."

"Good authority?" She flashed me a look that did not invite inquiry into her sources. "Okay, I get it," I said, turning my attention to the map. "Yeah, you can see the highway dips in near the riverbank. That's a natural spot for the two guys that found the body to pull their canoe out of the river. But how is that your hole card?"

"It isn't." She retrieved another document from the folder. "This is."

My brow furrowed in confusion as I examined the document. "Looks like a copy of a receipt from Brothers Hardware Store in New Haven. But how is that a wild card? It just has a time stamp and an amount on it. There's no..." I looked at her, realization dawning across my face. "The shovel. He bought the shovel."

She nodded and said, "Where did you think it came from?"

I shrugged and said, "Goodlett, of course."

"So, you didn't believe his story after all?"

"Well, not that part. I mean, come on. To think that Moussa was out there carrying a shovel? I didn't believe it, but now..."

She arched her eyebrows and folded her hands in her lap.

She's right, I thought. *It is a wild card.*

"But why? He told me he was going to the monastery for reflection and prayer, not manual labor. Why would he need a shovel? And wouldn't the monks have one he could borrow?"

"I would think so. My guess is he didn't want to ask them, from which we can surmise he didn't want the monastery to know why he needed a shovel." I considered the plausibility of her reasoning. "Occam's razor. Right, Mr. Motley?"

I picked up the copy of the receipt and said, "How do you know about this?"

"The sheriffs found it in Moussa's pocket." I scratched my head, wondering why we never got wind of the receipt. "Think about it. Goodlett took a deal within twenty-four hours. That means this piece of information wasn't entered into any public court record. You would have had to petition for the evidence, but why would you? Goodlett had already confessed."

"And this piece of information probably played into Goodlett getting the deal that he did," I said, continuing the thread of her logic. "The receipt confirms what he said about the shovel belonging to Moussa. I still call bullshit on Moussa as the aggressor, but Goodlett was telling the truth about Moussa carrying the shovel. He bought it. It was his."

"But how did he get a deal in the first place?" she said, craning her neck as she stretched her back. "I saw Mr. Goodlett's mug shot, and at the risk of sounding judgmental, he didn't look like he was from the social set that keeps an attorney on retainer."

"And not just any attorney. He had Sidney Marksbury."

The bell above the door rang as a couple entered the café. More people came in immediately after and I realized it was getting close to lunchtime.

Regina looked at me and shook her head, bewildered. "How did Goodlett manage to get a high-powered attorney to defend him?"

"From what Dom heard, Marksbury served in Nam with Goodlett's grandfather, so he took the case pro bono to help out his old comrade in arms."

"It's quite a favor for a prominent attorney to put his name on the line for a racist killer," she said, incredulous. "Old war buddy or not."

"But that's not the story they sold. And there's no witness to dispute their story."

She nodded in agreement, though I could see her eyes had become clouded by the mental fatigue that was taking a toll on me, as well.

"Can I ask you something, Miss Sandoval?" She gestured for me to go ahead. "Why are you pursuing this? I mean, I get that you don't buy the official account of what happened, but there had to be something that initially piqued your interest in this story. What was it?"

Her eyes dropped to the porcelain cup she was cradling in her hands. She seemed on the edge of a strong emotion, and it took a moment for her to answer.

"My brother was murdered. He was out with friends in a bougie area of the city where a brown face draws unwanted attention. He defended himself against some asshole who didn't want any filthy 'Spic in the bar where he liked to hang out. My brother defended himself and it cost him his life. And like Moussa, my brother's killer had a big-time attorney who got him a lesser charge. The bastard was out on shock probation in six months."

"Damn. I'm so sorry." She nodded in appreciation and put on her coat as cold air chilled the space around us with the coming and going of café patrons. "Do you think Goodlett could get out that quickly?"

"I don't know Sidney Marksbury," she said, pulling her coat tightly around her. "But if he's got any kind of reputation in this town, then he's not going to allow it to be sullied by having a man he represented rotting away in the county lockup."

I considered her point, imagining the small-town politics that could pave the way for Dale Goodlett's early release. I couldn't see who might benefit from that, but I conceded that she could be correct. After all, why would Marksbury take the case if there weren't a built-in safeguard for his credibility?

"My mother never recovered from what happened," she said, toying with a paper napkin. "I told Hamia Diab I'd do my best to make sure that didn't happen to her."

"You've talked to Moussa's mother?"

"I have. A lovely woman. I told her who I am, what I do, and that I want to look deeper into her son's death. I was surprised that she wasn't all that eager for me to do so, but she didn't outright object." She tossed the napkin on the table and looked at me. "Just so you know, Mrs. Diab's version of her son's journey, his quest...it's all consistent with your account of what Moussa told you."

I glazed her with a fierce look, but she didn't back down.

"You can be angry if you want, but I know my craft."

"Yeah, so you've said. But why not level with me from the beginning? Not about your brother, I get that. But about Hamia. Why didn't you tell me you spoke to her?"

"I'm telling you now," she said, poking her index finger on the table. "Look, this is how things work in an investigation. You don't reveal what you know before you've asked the right questions. If I had told you what I already know, then your own account of what happened would have been colored by that information. And I didn't come here for corroboration, Mr. Motley. I wanted your version of what happened, unfiltered."

I continued to glare, but I could see her point.

"By the way, Hamia gushed about you. She said it gives her comfort to know of your kindness to her son."

The compliment didn't exactly fall on deaf ears, but it did compete with the feeling that I had been played.

"How long did you speak with her when the two of you met? When you gave her your account of meeting her son?"

Of course, I thought. *She knows about that, too.*

"I don't know," I said in a curt tone. "Less than an hour. We were in the county attorney's office."

She leaned in with that inquisitive spark alight in her eyes. "Have you heard from Hamia since?"

"Why would she contact me?"

"You never know what someone needs to process this kind of loss. I thought maybe she had reached out to you. Has she done that?"

"No. She hasn't."

She continued to regard me with an intense gaze. "Would it surprise you to know that Hamia thinks her son's journey was tied to your own, and that like Moussa, she believes you were an angel of God's providence?"

She seemed to be searching my face for a reaction, but I only shrugged, finished off the dregs of my coffee, and said, "So, what now?"

She simultaneously considered my question and mentally evaluated her options, as I had noticed she was prone to do. "I'd like to ask a favor. I know you think the matter is probably closed, and maybe you're correct. But I need to know two things to be resolved in my own mind." I gestured for her to continue. "First, I'd like to know if the owner of the hardware store knows why Moussa bought that shovel."

"Why would you think he'd know that?"

"Because small-town hardware store owners like to chat up customers about the projects they're working on. And customers like to oblige them with details."

I conceded her point and said, "What's the second thing?"

"The monastery. I want to know if anyone at the monastery spoke to Moussa, if he shared anything that might shed light on what he was doing. Maybe someone knows why he was down near the Rolling Fork."

"Maybe he was just out exploring," I said. "You gotta remember, the guy hitchhiked from Louisiana. He was an adventurer."

"Well, I'm sure that's true. But I keep coming back to that shovel. Why the shovel?" The same question was plaguing my own mind. "Somebody might have spoken to him. He might have opened up to someone in casual conversation about what he planned to do with that shovel."

"On the other hand, Miss Sandoval, there's probably not a lot of casual conversation happening in a monastery."

"Hey, I thought we already broke the ice on the whole first name basis thing," she said, giving me a playful wave. "I've called you Levi, so call me Regina from now on."

My brow furrowed as I thought back through our conversation. "You called me Levi?"

"Sure, I did. And look, we're not in twelfth-century Europe. People talk in monasteries."

My face must have conveyed my confusion as I tried to remember her calling me by my first name. "When did you call me Levi?"

"You know, the more I think about it, it's not really a favor I'm asking for, Levi," she said, ignoring my question. "I think what I'm asking is for you to partner with me. Are you interested?"

Her question supplanted my confusion with a sudden flush of pride. Throughout our conversation, I had thought of her as the expert, a seasoned investigator who was adept and instinctive in applying her craft. And as much as I had chafed at the bits of information she had concealed, I had to admire her technique. Now, here she was, the investigative pro asking me to partner up with her.

"Partners," I said, eyeing her narrowly. "What would that entail?"

"That would entail you following up on the matters of the hardware store and the monastery. If you uncover a lead that takes us further down the road, then we follow it and see where it takes us."

"And if we don't?"

She sighed and melted back into her chair. "Then we tell Hamia that we did our best. She's clearly a woman of great faith, but I think knowing somebody cared enough to try to find out what really happened to her son will help her heal."

Right, I thought. *And help you heal, too.*

"Partners, huh? Look, I'd have to run it by George, but I think he'd be good with me following up on a couple of leads. After all, it is a local story and..."

"Oh, before I forget," she said, cutting me off. "Do you have the name of the police officer that questioned you in the parking lot?"

"Actually, I do." I pulled a business card out of my wallet. "Nathan Hadley," I said, handing her the business card. "That name mean anything to you?"

She considered the question for several seconds. "No, I don't think so." She slipped the card inside her leather bag and said, "I'll be in Nashville until Monday. I'm staying with a friend through the weekend following the conference. Do you think that will give you enough time to move on those two questions?"

"Yeah, sure. I've got a couple of assignments this afternoon and tomorrow, but I should have time Friday. I'll get to it." I shot her an ironic smile and said, "Regina."

"Good. I'll follow up with you on Monday."

Since there was nothing more to discuss, we stood and shook hands in a manner that despite her sudden urge to be on a first name basis, I found rather formal.

"You're a tough man to get a hold of, Levi Motley. But I'm glad I finally did."

I was about to offer some words of gratitude for the chance to work with her, but before I could, she turned on her heel and walked out the door, the little bell ringing brightly as she left.

CHAPTER
TWELVE

JERRY EDELEN LEANED against the counter with a dip tucked behind his lower lip as he took great care in explaining the genealogical connection between himself and the business he ran, Brothers Hardware Store. According to Jerry, Vincent Brothers founded the store as the community of New Haven experienced the growth that swept across the country following the Second World War. His mother was Vanessa Brothers who married Bill Edelen at St. Catherine's on a day so hot, Jerry said, "Daddy told me you could've fried an egg on the hood of a car." Since Vanessa was the only child of Vincent and Margaret Mary Brothers, Bill Edelen came into the business, inheriting ownership through his wife when old man Brothers died in 1974.

"That's how come it's Edelens now that operates the store," he said, spitting into an empty soda can. "Just in case you was wonderin' why it ain't a Brothers that owns it. 'Course I run it with my brother Pat, but he ain't here right now, seein' as he's took an order to a customer up in New Hope. But I run it with him, my brother Pat that is, so I guess it makes sense that it's called Brothers Hardware seein' as how we're brothers and all. Know what I mean?"

I told him the name was still a good fit and asked if he remembered Moussa Diab coming into the store.

"Nah, Pat was here that mornin'. I was makin' a run that day. Think it was to, umm, let's see...umm...I believe it was to a fella' down in Hodgenville, but the name escapes me. You see, we make special deliveries when the need arises. It's good for business and all."

"Did you and your brother talk about it later, about Moussa coming into the store?"

"Oh, sure, we discussed the matter thoroughly. Especially since the boy was found on a Monday morning."

"Why was that significant?"

"Well, you know there's some hell-raisin' gets done around here. And plenty of people get, you know, stabbed and beat up and whatnot. But not on no Monday morning."

"More like on a Saturday night," I said.

"Oh yeah, that'd be the time, all right. Lotsa hell-raisin' and drinkin' on the weekend. Some pot-smokin' and probably some other chicanery, too. Most people don't mean no harm, just gotta know where ya are and who you're with. I used to run and gun, so I ain't pointin' no fingers. But I got a wife and kids and a store to run, so I ain't out too much no more."

"So, you're saying people do get hurt. But this guy wasn't hurt, he was killed."

"Yessir, he was," he said, spitting into the can. "Kilt deader 'n a doornail."

"So, it's not unusual for there to be violence around here, fighting and all, but not killing."

"I mean, it's happened before 'cause like I said, we've always had our share of hell-raisers 'round here. And sure, there's lots a people got crops in the ground, but most that sells or smokes it don't mean no harm. We got us a fair number of people with wild hairs up their butt, that's all." His face contorted in incredulity. "But me and Pat talked about it and can't neither one of us reconcile no killin' happenin' on a Monday morning. Not along the river nor elsewhere."

"Did somebody from the sheriff's office question you?"

"Yeah, ol' Donnie Ball stopped in. You know, to verify that the boy had been here and all. And then there was that city cop that come by a couple days after."

"A Bardstown cop?"

"Yessir."

My face wrinkled in puzzlement. "What would a Bardstown cop be doing down here?"

"Same as you. Askin' questions."

"What kind of questions?"

"Had ya seen him before, did he say what he was doin' 'round here, did he mention any names, anybody he was gonna meet up with, anything about where he was goin'? Stuff like that. I told him I wasn't even here at the time, but Pat told him he asked the boy what he was doin'. You know, just being friendly and all. Pat said the boy was brown as a biscuit. Didn't make no matter though, 'cause Pat treated him like he would any other, meaning he always asks what a person's up to with their tool buyin'. See, if ya know that, then you might be able to sell 'em on another product or two."

"And did he say what he was doing?"

"Yessir, he did." Jerry Edelen fiddled with the bill of his John Deere cap, seemingly befuddled by the answer Moussa gave to his brother's question. "He told Pat he was on a grail quest."

I blinked. "A grail quest?"

"That's what he said. Well, Pat didn't rightly know what in hell the boy was talkin' about, so he just sold him the shovel and didn't ask no more questions."

A quest is a kind of journey, but one driven by faith, I thought, remembering Moussa's description. *But a grail quest?*

"He didn't say anything about that," I said, thinking out loud.

"What's that now?"

"Oh," I said, shaking my head. "Nothing."

"Well, is there anything else I can do for you? Damn shame what happened to that boy."

"Actually, there is. If we could go back to the officer for a minute. Did he ask why Moussa bought the shovel?"

"Oh, yeah. He wanted to know all about that shovel. Surprised the hell out of him when he seen it."

"Why is that? I mean, a shovel's a shovel. Right?"

He set the soda can on the counter and walked down an aisle, motioning for me to follow. Halfway down the aisle, he picked up a three-foot-long shovel with a wooden handle and a bright, silver spade. He handed it to me.

"This can't weigh more than three or four pounds," I said, balancing the shovel in one hand. "What would you use this for?"

"Small projects, mostly. Things like gardening where you ain't got to dig too deep."

"Gardening? You mean like planting? Or digging up plants?"

"Well, that's gardenin' all right. Of course, sometimes ya see offi-cial-type folks using something like this for groundbreaking ceremonies and stuff like that."

"But the story is that he was killed with a shovel." I held the tool in both hands like a bat. "How could somebody kill a man with this? He'd have to pummel him with it over and over."

"Or put the spade through him. But even that'd be tough. I suppose you could open him up with the edge. Come to think of it, ain't that what the paper said happened?"

I looked down at the shovel, shaking my head in bewilderment. "That's what the paper said."

Just then the front door opened, and a man walked into the store. He slapped his hands on the counter and in a loud voice said, "What the hell ya gotta do to get some service in this joint?"

Jerry Edelen winked at me as he said, "By God, that sounds like Tommy Johnson. And I guaran-damn-tee he ain't here for nothin' more than scuttlebutt."

"Now, see, ya just lost a sale," the man said. "I was in the market for a key ring, but reckon I'll just have to take my dern business elsewhere."

We emerged from the aisle to see the man leaning against the counter, smoking a cigarette. "Hell far, Tommy, don't be stinkin' up the place. And what in the hell ya need a key ring for anyway? You never lock your door."

"Well, see now, your old lady gimme a key to your front door, so's I don't have to be sneakin' in through the window. Thought I'd put it on a shiny key ring bought right here in your own place of business."

"Well, I guess ya ain't got no choice but to buy it here since you're banned at Walmart."

"It'll be a cold day in hell, Jerry Edelen, when I can't go inside a damn Walmart."

The two men continued as I stood aside, enjoying their good-natured ribbing.

"Gimme just a minute, Tommy." The man waved a hand and walked away, perusing the shelves as he puffed away on his cigarette. "Anything else I can do for ya, mister? I'm sure sorry about that boy, Pat and me both. Terrible thing."

"Let me ask you this. Do you think the man who confessed was telling the truth? That the man you sold this shovel to was out there trying to steal from a marijuana field?"

He adopted a serious look, like a scholar about to deliver a simple answer to a complex question. "Like I done said, there's lots of people 'round here with plants in the ground and most of 'em don't mean no harm to nobody. But that don't mean a man got a right to go wanderin' where he ain't welcome, neither."

He gave me a challenging look, as if he was assessing my level of agreement with his statement.

"You make a good point, Mr. Edelen. And I appreciate your time, but I've taken enough of it. I'll let you get back to your business."

"Business? What, you mean Tommy?" He removed the dip from his mouth and stuffed it in the soda can. "Shoot, he ain't hear for nothin' but gossip. Tell the truth, he's about to jump outta' his damn skin wantin' to know what business a stranger like you got here. Probably the only reason he come in."

"Okay, well just one more question, then. Do you remember the name of the officer that came in asking questions?"

"Hell yes, I do. Same one that got me for expired tags last year when I was drivin' through town up there. He knew damn well I was paid up, but he wrote me a ticket anyway. Had to waste half a day goin' to court to show what everybody and their brother already knew...that I was paid up full." I looked at him, waiting for the name. "Hadley. Nathan Hadley. And you didn't ask but I'll tell ya, anyway. Steer clear of that one, 'cause he's a sonofabitch. Know what I mean?"

Ten minutes later, I glanced over at the small shovel sitting on the seat next to me in the truck as I approached the turn onto Monk's Road. I figured Jerry Edelen deserved a little business for the time and information he gave me, so I bought the little gardening tool. But when he asked if I wanted the receipt, I said, "No," and walked out the door.

CHAPTER
THIRTEEN

A S I PULLED into the monastery parking lot, I turned toward the passenger seat attempting to recall the awed expression I had seen on Moussa's face when we arrived at that same spot several weeks before. But time had attenuated the memory, and I struggled to recapture the young pilgrim's visage. The walled enclosure, on the other hand, was as blank as it had been when I had first stared at it in mystified wonder at the circumstances that led me to the Abbey of Our Lady of Gethsemani.

The truck door creaked as I got out and walked down the sidewalk, stopping to observe the words "GOD ALONE" engraved in stone above a gated archway. Across from the gate, the door Moussa had walked through was tucked into a recess in the wall. The word "PAX" was engraved above the door with the years "1098" to the left and "1848" to the right. For a moment, I hesitated. Then, with a deep sigh, I opened the door and walked inside.

The far wall of the room was comprised of a bank of windows with a glass door leading onto a patio where several chairs were scattered about. The patio overlooked a wall enclosing a park-like scene with a gravel path that looped around in the shape of an ellipsis. I watched through the glass wall as a man traversed the path, stopping along the way to kneel at monuments I recognized as Stations of the Cross.

Turning from the scene, I walked down a corridor toward a light emanating from an open door. Peeking around the edge of the door, I saw a man sitting in the corner of an office. He wore a white tunic and brown scapular and appeared to be reading. I knocked lightly on the doorframe, and he raised his head. "The peace of the Lord be with you," he said, standing and offering a slight bow.

"Hello, Father."

He laughed and said, "I'm afraid that title is a bit above my paygrade." I must have looked confused because he said, "What I mean is, I am not a priest. My name is Brother Simon. I'm the abbey's retreat director."

"Ah, got it. Well, I'm Levi Motley, and you see, I was hoping I could, umm...you know, speak with somebody."

"Upon what subject?"

"What's that?"

He gave a patient smile. "What is it that you'd like to speak about?"

"Oh. Right," I said with a nervous chuckle. "Well, it's about a guest. I mean, he was a guest. He's not now. It's about, umm...somebody who was here visiting a few weeks back."

"I see," he said, his brow furrowing. "Well, in that case, you must understand that I am not at liberty to discuss any particulars regarding our guests."

"Sure. Right. No, I understand. Umm, this matter, you see, pertains to Moussa Diab. He's the guy that was killed not far from here back in September. Do you recall Diab being here?"

"Well, yes, of course. His death was a great tragedy, and we continue to pray for the repose of the young man's soul, just as we pray for the souls of all the faithful departed." He cocked his head and scrutinized me, his dubious eyes conveying that I did not cut the figure of a man on official business. Still, he extended his hand toward a chair, inviting me to sit. "May I take your coat?"

"Oh, no thanks," I said, removing my toboggan. "I'm good." I shifted under his gaze as he regarded me carefully. "I guess a lot of people come here for retreats, huh?"

I groaned inwardly at my insipid attempt to break the ice. But he was a man of grace and good manners, so I didn't suffer long.

"Indeed, they do. We have visitors from all over the country. Sometimes beyond. But winter fast approaches, so we won't receive as many guests over the next few months."

He took a seat behind a desk and folded his hands in his lap, waiting for me to explain the purpose of my visit. I cleared my throat and tried to adopt an air of professionalism.

"I'm here, Brother Simon, because I am an investigative reporter and... well, actually I'm not an investigative reporter, per se, but I'm working with an investigative reporter. She's one of the best in the field, you see, and I've shared my experience with Moussa Diab with her, and...well, I wonder if you could share, umm, you know, any details that stand out about his visit here."

I sat back, thinking I had summed up the reason for my visit with aplomb. To my dismay, a grave look came over the monk's face as he leaned forward, placed his palms on the desk, and said, "Young man, why don't you start over."

"Start over?"

"Yes, start over. Perhaps you could begin by telling me the capacity in which you are here to ask the questions that you would like to put to me. I think that would be a good place for you to begin."

"Okay. Well, like I said, I'm working with an investigative reporter. I'm partnering with her, you understand?"

"No, I'm afraid I do not understand. Perhaps you could tell me what news organization you and this reporter with whom you are partnering represent."

"Well, I'm with the Bardstown paper, *The Observer*. You know, mainly freelance stories and filling in where George needs me. High school sports, civic events, stuff like that."

I knew I sounded ridiculous, but my nerves were on edge, and I couldn't put together a cogent thought. Brother Simon looked at me with a practiced patience that did not belie the doubt written on his face.

"Sorry, I know I'm rambling. But you see, this is where I...this is where I dropped him off, and well, I haven't been back here since."

The monk stood and walked around the desk. "Why don't you let me take your coat?

"My coat? Yeah, okay. It is getting a little warm in here."

He took my coat and hung it on a rack in a corner of the room. He then slid the chair he had been reading in next to my chair and sat down. "Here's what I understand so far. Your name is Levi Motley, and I gather you knew the young man who was killed near the river. You work for the newspaper in Bardstown, and you're partnering with an investigative reporter presumably to investigate the death of the young man in question.

Is this information accurate?" I nodded, grateful for his charity. "Good. Now why don't you briefly tell me how you knew the young man?"

I gave him the abridged version of my encounter with Moussa, and he listened with rapt attention.

"Given what you have told me, I can understand why you are a bit out of sorts," he said after I had finished my account. "For heaven's sake, anyone would be." The monk stood and retook his seat behind the desk. "Now that I understand the basics, perhaps you can explain why you are here and how you think I can help."

At that I went on to briefly describe how I came to be contacted by Regina Sandoval, how I told her my story, and how she asked me to assist her in looking further into what happened to Moussa Diab.

"And you say this reporter, Regina Sandoval, has spoken to the young man's mother?"

"That's correct. Hamia Diab. I spoke to her too, when she was here in town. You know, after he was killed, and the plea deal was being worked out."

He considered this information with a pensive expression. "And the young man's mother has endorsed the work in which you and Miss Sandoval are engaged?"

"Well, to be honest, Regina told me that Moussa's mom wasn't overly enthused about us digging into this. But she didn't say no, so..."

"Not exactly a ringing endorsement."

"No, I guess not. Look, we just want to know if there's anything more to this. Seems to me that Moussa deserves that much. And his mom does, too. If we don't find anything, then so be it. No harm done."

We sat in silence for a long moment, and he seemed to be considering my argument. The fact that he was considering it at all made me think that the monk must have something to offer. I thought about that, and the notion made the hairs on the back of my neck stand up.

"Let me ask you this," he said, leaning forward and folding his hands together on the desk. "Is this matter under investigation by the police, and if so, will any information I provide interfere with that investigation?"

Interfere? I thought. *How about help with the investigation?*

I shook my head and said, "It's my understanding that this case was closed when Dale Goodlett confessed and took a plea deal."

"Yes, I remember hearing about that."

"We're not working with the authorities. So, we're not impeding any-thing. As far as I know, this case is closed."

"Then what is it you hope to find?"

"To be honest, Brother Simon, I'm not sure there's anything to find. It's Regina who's on fire for this. She's convinced there's more to the story."

He cocked his head and eyed me with a narrow gaze. "And you?"

The hair on the back of my neck began to tingle, but I tried to answer in a dispassionate tone. "I guess I wouldn't be here if I didn't think it was worth checking out. Fact is, I've already managed to uncover some infor-mation that raises an interesting question or two."

Brother Simon's shrewd gaze gave me the same feeling I'd had with Regina, that he was deciding whether to shove his chips in or fold. It was clear to me that he knew something, so I decided it couldn't hurt to try and push him off the dime. "Did the police question anyone here at the monastery?"

He was silent, still considering whether and how much he wished to participate in my, our, pursuit. He continued to eye me narrowly but ap-peared to have made the choice to talk. "To my knowledge, no, they did not."

"Don't you find that strange?"

"No, I don't," he said, leaning back in his chair. "This monastery is a place of God, open to all people. And yet to many, it holds an air of fore-boding. There are people who drive by our monastery every day who I suspect haven't a thought in the world about what goes on here."

"Why do you think that is?" I said, slipping a small notepad out of my shirt pocket.

"It is my observation that our world is in short supply not only of faith but of wonder, which I consider to be a doorway to faith. This is not surprising to me, mind you, as so many see our way of life as out of step with the modern world. And of course, they are correct. Yes, we are in the world like everyone else, but we live our lives according to promises we have made. Promises to live lives of stability, of fidelity, and of obedience to something greater than ourselves. Tell me something, young man, do you find those promises and the way of life they prescribe in keeping with this world as it sits on the brink of a new millennium?"

I studied the monk as he sat in his chair. Maybe his reflection on my query was an honest one, but to me it sounded like he was sidestepping the question.

"Respectfully, Brother Simon, a man was killed, and at the time of his death he was a guest here. I don't know anything about why people don't understand your promises and all, but it seems normal to me that the cops would've had some questions for you and your, umm..."

"My brothers in Christ?" he said, raising an eyebrow. "To my knowledge, they did not."

"What about Moussa's family? Surely his mother wanted to know more about what happened while he was here."

"Naturally. In fact, I've heard from others that she was friends with Brother Llewellyn, God rest his soul. It is my understanding that this friendship is what led her son to visit our monastery in the first place."

"So, you met her? You met Hamia Diab?"

"Briefly. She met with the abbot, of course, but I am not privy to the contents of that conversation. I only know that the abbot directed me to gather the young man's belongings so his mother could retrieve them. This, I did."

"Did you speak with her?"

"Very little. As you would expect, she was profoundly grief stricken, so I assured her of my prayers. Beyond that, I delivered the young man's belongings to her as instructed. He didn't have much, but then young men usually don't, now do they? And Moussa seemed to me a free-spirited sort who wished to be unencumbered by personal possessions."

"Yeah, I know the type." He cocked his head in curiosity, but I waved the comment away. "Can you tell me what he had? What possessions you handed over?"

"No great secret there." He opened the desk drawer and pulled out a leather-bound ledger. Putting on a pair of spectacles, he flipped through the pages, using his index finger to locate the information he sought. "I am fastidious in my note-keeping. I find that to be most helpful as I welcome many repeat visitors who appreciate that I know their preferences before they arrive. Ah, yes, here it is." Brother Simon read a list of items recorded on the page. "A pair of blue jeans, a pair of khakis, two pairs of shorts, one collared shirt, three T-shirts, socks and undergarments, a journal, a copy of *The Devout Life* by St. Francis DeSales." He looked up and nodded in appreciation and then continued with his inventory.

"Let's see, there was a bottle of red wine." He chuckled. "He had writing utensils, a prayer card seeking the intercession of St. Charbel...and, oh yes, a copy of *The Boy's King Arthur*."

He concluded his account of Moussa's belongings and looked at me.

"And you gathered these things together for Moussa's mother?"

He shrugged and said, "It was a relatively short task."

"Did you interact with Moussa while he was here?"

"I greeted him and helped him settle into his room. He struck me as a gracious young man, somewhat serious, yet earnest in a way that I found endearing."

"Were there any details that stood out about his visit?"

"Such as?"

"You know, anyone that he met or spent time with? Anything he might have talked about with another guest or with a monk?"

He cleared his throat in the way people do when they're about to school you on a subject. "Young man, the people who come here for retreat are seeking solitude for prayer and reflection. Moreover, my brothers and I do still attempt to follow the rule."

"The rule?"

"The Rule of St. Benedict. It calls for the observance of silence. Thus, we do not engage in idle chatter." He frowned sheepishly. "Well, at least not much idle chatter."

"So, even the Rule of St. Benedict can be bent a little, eh brother?" The monk leaned forward and leveled me with a gray stare. "Anyway. Back to my question."

"And what question would that be?"

"Are there any details that stood out about the young man's visit?"

He looked at me with a cautious gaze, and again I had the sense that this monk knew something. But he was clearly hesitant to share whatever it was with me. Not that I could blame him. I mean, I'd walked in unannounced, looking every bit the ragamuffin Dominick so gleefully made me out to be. I could see how that might not engender confidence in my interview subject. Still, my spider sense was picking up that this man had something I needed to know, and that instinct came with a kind of investigative rush I had never experienced before.

"Brother Simon, I know I just busted in on you uninvited," I said, regarding him with what I hoped was a look of earnest appeal. "And while you were cozied up with a good book at that. But I'm being straight with you when I say that I'm trying find out if there is something more to Moussa Diab's death. I believe he deserves that much."

His cautious demeanor softened a bit, but he didn't speak.

"Please, Brother, if there's anything you can tell me?" The man still didn't speak. He just looked at me, his lips pursed tightly in a thin line. I began to lose my patience. "You know, I find it interesting that he was staying here, and yet the cops didn't want to talk to any of you after he was killed."

"How dare you insinuate that anyone here had..."

"Had what? Information that might have helped uncover the truth? Information that could still help uncover the truth?" His face hardened in defiance of my impudent remark. I didn't let up, but I did soften my tone. "That's all I'm asking, Brother Simon. For you to help me uncover the truth. What's your rule have to say about that?"

For a moment, his face reddened in anger. But then he sighed, and I felt his defiance giving way to what I imagined was his natural inclination toward assisting those who ask for help. Even so, he remained silent, and I decided that was answer enough for me.

"I appreciate the time." I stood and walked toward the coat rack.

"I received a call prior to the young man's arrival." I stopped and watched as he scanned the leather journal on the desktop. "As I stated before, I keep careful records of my interactions with guests."

He again slipped his spectacles on, pulling them down onto the bridge of his hooked nose. Then he peered up at me with an irritated expression and motioned for me to sit, which I did.

"Here it is," he said, peering down at the ledger. "August twenty-ninth, nineteen ninety-seven. I received a call from a woman who stated that a young man named Moussa Diab was scheduled to visit the monastery sometime in September. I asked for the exact date of his arrival, but she did not have that information. She then asked if I would convey to Mr. Diab that the Westcotts would like to have him over for dinner at some point during his stay."

I scribbled on my notepad as Brother Simon spoke but stopped after writing the name he had cited. It sounded familiar, but I couldn't remember where I had heard it. "The Westcotts," I said, trying to pull up the name from my memory bank. "Who are the Westcotts?"

"Precisely my question to the woman on the phone. She told me they were friends of the young man's family and that she learned of Moussa's impending visit from his mother, Hamia." He reviewed his notes. "She asked me to tell Moussa that he was invited to the home of Conrad and Isabelle Westcott, who would be most pleased to welcome him in the interest of learning more about his quest. She then gave me an address in Bardstown, as well as a phone number for Moussa to call."

"Quest? She said she wanted to know about his quest?" Brother Simon gave a curt nod. "Do you know if the woman who called was Mrs. Westcott?"

"I did not ask for her name, but my presumption is that the woman on the phone was Isabelle Westcott." He removed his spectacles and regarded me with a stern gaze. "Perhaps now you understand my reticence on this matter." My face wrinkled in confusion as his took on an expression of irritation. "Someone calls to give me information about the impending arrival of a guest Brother Lew is aware of but that I know nothing about. What if I failed to have a room ready?" He gave a disgusted huff, and I realized it was wounded pride that had kept him from talking.

"Yes, of course, Brother Simon, I understand. And I'm grateful to you for helping me. I wonder, could you tell me the address and phone number the woman gave you?"

He closed the ledger with pointed deliberation. "I would think that an investigative reporter should have no problem locating that information on his own."

"Yeah, fair enough. Is there anything else? Any other details you remember about Moussa's stay at the monastery?" He gave me a questioning look. "I don't know...maybe a project he was working on?"

"A project? I know nothing about any project." The monk removed his glasses and rubbed the bridge of his nose. "Mr. Motley, I think you'd agree that I have been most cooperative with your request for information." He folded his hands and placed them on the closed ledger.

"Yes, I do agree, Brother Simon. You've been a tremendous help." I stood and extended my hand, and he stood and gave me a curt bow. "Right. Well, truly, I can't thank you enough."

"I'm pleased to have been of assistance. I shall hold you and Miss Sandoval in prayer. As you seek, so may you find that which God wishes to reveal to you."

As he walked to the rack to retrieve my coat I said, "May I ask one more question, brother?" His icy glare told me I was pushing my luck, but I asked anyway. "Did you relay the invitation to Moussa?"

"Of course I did," he said, as if the alternative was unthinkable. "After I assisted him in getting settled, I told him the Westcott family wished to welcome him to their home for dinner and conversation regarding his quest."

"And did he take them up on the offer?"

"In truth, I don't know. I recall that he looked puzzled, or perhaps even...I don't know. Maybe it was a look of concern. But beyond that I don't know what he did with the information."

Knowing my time was more than up, I thanked Brother Simon once more and made my way outside. Gray clouds pressed low with the threat of rain, but I had a strong impulse to explore the grounds. Leaving the sidewalk, I made my way to the outer corner of the walled enclosure I had seen earlier. I walked the perimeter of the wall, which ran parallel to the highway, hoping to get a different perspective on the high monastery walls. After fifty or so paces, a trailhead on the opposite side of the highway caught my attention. Intrigued, I crossed the road and stepped onto the trail where I saw a white sign that read "To the Statues". I had taken only a couple of steps down the trail when a thought occurred to me that stopped me in my tracks.

Conrad and Isabelle Westcott, I thought. *Regina Sandoval called him Connie.*

"That's kind of familiar for a woman intent on formality. And why did she send me here asking questions if she already knew the name of the people who invited Moussa to their home?"

A few minutes later, I was in my truck, hightailing it back to *The Observer* in the hope that Danny Brewer hadn't yet left his office for the day.

FOURTEEN

Dominick was walking out the front door as I pulled to the curb in front of *The Observer* office building. I exited the truck, and we stood on the sidewalk talking until the heavy clouds decided to make good on their threat of rain. It didn't take long for the rain pellets to turn into a steady downpour, so we jumped into the cab of my truck to continue our conversation.

"So, I hear a city reporter's been doggin' you," he said. "You headed to the big time, Motley?"

"And not take you with me? Never."

"Well, since you're sticking with us small-timers, you might wanna know that Rebecca at the front desk told me to tell that deadbeat friend of mine that she's not Sarah from that show."

"What show?"

"That show," he said, trying to call up the name. "The one with the little red-headed kid and the sheriff."

"*The Andy Griffith Show?*"

"That's the one," he said, and then turned to me with an incredulous look on his face. "You realize there's not one brother or sister in the whole town of Mayberry? That's got to be one boring-ass town. Anyway, you best be making up to Rebecca, 'cause she's ticked."

"I'll buy her a bottle of wine. Women always like wine."

"Rebecca don't drink."

"Huh? I thought everybody in this town drank."

"Best stick with flowers," he said, peering despondently out the window at the monsoon. "I had to run into you, didn't I?"

"Just your good luck, I guess. Grab a drink later?"

"Yeah, that'll work. I want to hear more about this city girl chasing you."

We jumped out of the truck and Dominick sprinted down the sidewalk as I leapt across a puddle and entered the building. "Rebecca," I said as if she was my long-lost best friend. "Young lady, you're looking especially lovely today."

She flipped me the bird and said, "Get a phone, loser."

"Ooh, obscene gestures from such a pristine girl."

"I'm not that obscene," she said, with a sardonic curl of her lip.

"Actually, I think the line is I'm not that pristine. But in your case, well..."

"What the hell ever, Motley. What is it you're here for other than to harass me?"

"The man himself, of course. Is he around?"

"He's in his office."

I leaned toward her and said, "You have a lovely day you obscenely pristine girl, you."

She rolled her eyes, and I made my way down the hall to George Hawley's office. I rapped on the doorframe to get his attention.

"Damnation, Motley, where you been at?"

I ignored the question and plopped down in a chair. "You need a haircut, boss. And a shave."

With one hand he pulled at the bristly tip of his widow's peak, while the other rubbed his stubbled cheek. "Yessir, I'm probably due for a visit to George's Clip Joint. But damnit, who has time for such things? And what's the difference? At my age, if you've got a patch, you might as well grow the sonofabitch." He shot me an annoyed look. "And why am I justifying myself to a pissant like you, anyway?"

"Just trying to help you stay on top of your game."

"I'll have you know I'm the most eligible divorcee in the tri-county area, and don't you forget it," he said with a cocky air. "But enough of all this nonsense. What can I do you for, Motley?"

"Well, you told me this morning to check in with you later on about an assignment. It's later on, so I'm checking in."

"Yes, yes, of course, I surely did say that. Look here, there's a Christmas event every year called Christmas 'round the town or somethin' like that. Hell, I can't be expected to remember such things. Anyhow, it's a fundraiser for some such civic club or another, organized so that people can wander around historic homes and gawk their covetous little eyes out."

"And this has what to do with me?"

His face widened in a malicious grin. "You're covering it." I slid down in my chair and groaned. "Now, don't give me no guff, Motley. This here's a good deal for you. Probably get you another story that'll be popular with the masses. On top of that, you'll get to meet some of the right people in the community."

"The 'right people'? And who would they be?"

"Just, just, just," he said, struggling to find his point. "Just, just listen to me for once, Levi. You know I wouldn't give a wooden nickel for the approval of some uppity sumbitch. But it does a man good to hold his own with that sort of folk. Sure, they'll try to put their thumb on you, but if you don't let 'em, then they'll hold you in good stead and won't try any monkey business with you. You see, you got to stand up and show 'em who you are, or they'll leave footprints as they walk right over ya. That's the damn truth, indeed."

I sighed in acceptance of his reasoning, bullshit though it was. "Okay, I hear you. And I do serve at the pleasure of one, George Hawley." I sat up in my chair and adopted a serious tone. "Since we're talking about the quote, unquote, right people, I wonder if you can tell me anything about the Westcotts?"

"As in Westcott Bourbon Company?"

"If you say so," I said with a shrug. "Conrad and Isabelle Westcott?"

"That'd be them. Connie and Belle Westcott. Big time society types. They got a single barrel called Old Royal. Damn fine stuff, indeed. You ought to try it and find out for yourself."

"Connie, huh. Does everyone call him that?"

"I guess people around here do. That's how I've hailed him whenever I've been in his company. What do ya got cookin' there, son?"

"Not sure. But you did tell me to find you a good story, so..."

"So, what?" he said, but my mind had drifted as I wondered in vain at how Moussa Diab could have possibly been connected to a family in the bourbon industry. George Hawley pointedly cleared his throat and repeated his question.

"Not sure," I said, slapping my thighs and standing. "But I'm on the hunt for a good one."

He stood and walked around the desk, a serious look on his face. "Now you listen good, Motley. Don't go poking a bear unless you're carrying an awful big stick. Or better yet a Winchester."

"I hear you, George."

He gave me a single poke in the chest and walked back behind his desk. "Well, how's the house working out for ya?"

"Good. I really want to thank you for hooking me up on that."

"Just don't go throwin' any wild parties, at least not without invitin' me." He shot me a perturbed look. "And get a damn phone hooked up already. Rebecca's going crazy. Said she feels like that woman on that show, whatever it's called. Hell, I can't be expected to remember such things."

"Yeah, yeah, I've already heard. Hey, speaking of phones, I've gotta make a call. Mind if I use the spare office?"

He gave me a wave indicating I should make myself at home. As I shuffled down the hall, I heard George yelling after me from his office. "Now, don't forget to invite me if ya have a party. Especially if you want any ladies there. I'm a hell of a draw, Motley. Like flies to honey. Yessir, indeed."

CHAPTER
FIFTEEN

AN HOUR LATER, I walked out of *The Observer* building, thankful the rain had stopped. After running a few errands around town, I headed home to shower before my planned meet up with Dom. As I climbed out of my truck, a car pulled up and parked at the curb. To my surprise, Regina Sandoval exited the vehicle and began walking up the sidewalk toward the house.

"New car?"

"It's a rental," she said.

"With temporary tags?"

"Well, aren't you the observant one? That instinct will serve you well as an investigator."

"Yeah, well my current observation is that you're standing in front of my house on Friday afternoon when you said you'd be in Nashville until Monday."

"My plans for the weekend fell through, so I thought I'd stop by on my way home to get a status report."

My brow creased as I looked quizzically at my unanticipated guest. Something seemed different about her. "What is it?" she said, picking up on my vibe.

"Nothing. Come on in."

Inside the house, we went through the same routine we had gone through during her first visit. "I see not much has changed here," she said, scanning the room with interest. "Still moving in and moving out, huh?" I didn't reply but continued to regard her with a scrutinizing gaze. "You know, if I've got a piece of food stuck in my teeth, then I really wish you'd just be out with it already."

"Oh, right. Sorry. It's been a busy day and...well, I didn't expect to see you today. That's all."

"I hope my presence isn't a disappointment to you," she said with what I thought was a slight flirtation in her tone.

"Oh, no. Not at all. Hey, how was the conference?"

I went to the kitchen to put on a pot of coffee while she draped her coat over my backpack.

"Oh, it was fine. Nothing groundbreaking. But a good opportunity to stay up to date on professional best practices, as they say."

"Hmm. Sounds interesting."

I let the coffee brew and returned to the main room where we sat at the table.

"So, you've had a busy day. Have you gone and cracked the case without me?"

She gave me a sly smile, and again, I had the feeling she was flirting with me.

"Yeah, right." I gave a nervous laugh.

"Anything to report?"

"Not much," I said, picking at the edge of the table.

Her eyes narrowed and she cocked her head to one side. "Have you had a chance to follow up on those leads?"

"Actually, that's what I've been doing today," I said. "I had some time on my hands, so I went down to New Haven, and umm..." Her eyebrows arched in anticipation of my report. I shifted in my seat and said, "Well, you know, I went to the hardware store and, you know, talked to the owner. His name's Jerry Edelen. But he wasn't there the morning Moussa came in."

"Was he able to confirm that Moussa bought the shovel?"

"Yeah, he confirmed that."

"And was the person who sold Moussa the shovel there when you spoke with Mr. Edelen?"

"No, he was out making a delivery."

"Did Mr. Edelen tell you who sold Moussa the shovel?"

She was posing her questions like a teacher trying to pry information out of a third grader who'd rather be at recess.

"Oh, sure. It was his brother," I said, again picking at the edge of the table. "But he wasn't there. I mean, he wasn't there when I was there. At the hardware store, that is. But there's not much to say. He sold Moussa the shovel and that was that."

"So, no chummy conversation then?"

"Nah, nothing like that."

I shifted again as she regarded me carefully and said, "Do you think the coffee might be ready, Levi?"

"The coffee?" She pointed toward the kitchen. "Oh, right. The coffee. Let me check on that."

I walked to the kitchen and brought one cup back, setting it on the table in front her.

"Why don't you have a seat?"

"Oh, that's okay. I've been sitting all day," I said, leaning against the doorjamb. "Need to stretch my legs."

"And no coffee for you?"

"Nah, I'm about coffee'd out for the day."

She took a sip of her coffee and regarded me with a narrow gaze. "So, they didn't have much to offer at the hardware store?"

"Sounds like it was just a typical morning. At least that's what they told me."

"Typical morning?" She set her coffee cup down. "Is it typical for a dark-skinned, twenty-two-year-old who had hitchhiked from Louisiana to stay at a nearby monastery to come in their store and buy a shovel? Or typical that this very man would be dead within an hour of leaving their store? Is that what you mean by 'typical'?"

"They didn't know any of that at the time."

"Of course they didn't. But it stands to reason that our young friend might have stood out among their regular customers. After all, it sure didn't take long for that enlightened deputy to point out what was different about our friend, now did it?"

I shrugged and said, "Jerry Edelen acted like that wasn't any big deal."

"I thought Jerry Edelen wasn't there that morning."

"Yeah, that's right. But he and his brother heard what happened and put two and two together, realizing it was the same guy that had come into their store."

"Sure, they did." Her lips were pulled tight, and her jaw muscles clenched and unclenched as she studied me. "Were they questioned by the police?"

"Yeah, a sheriff's deputy stopped by. You know, because of the receipt and all."

"Is that in your notes?" she said, pointing to the notepad in my shirt pocket.

"Nah, I didn't take any notes. At least not at the hardware store. Mr. Edelen was more of a good ol' boy, so I just wanted to be conversational. I didn't want him to think he was being quoted or anything."

She lifted her coffee cup but stopped midair and set it down. Letting out a frustrated sigh, she pushed the cup away. "So, what about the monastery? You come up empty there, too?"

"Sorry to say it, but yes. I talked to the retreat director, a monk, but he couldn't say much. You know, because of guest confidentiality and all."

She gave me a condescending half-smile. "I'm afraid your career as an investigator is off to a bit of a slow start, Mr. Motley." I gave her an apologetic, dunce-like nod of agreement. "But on the other hand, you must be rather satisfied. After all, it appears there really is nothing more to this. At least nothing you can find."

"Guess not."

We locked eyes for a moment and neither of us looked away as we both knew this was the most honest moment we had shared.

"Well, then," she said, laying her palms on the table. "I didn't anticipate such a brief working relationship, but it appears our work here is done. Guess I'll be going."

"To the Westcotts?"

She was about to stand, but stopped, her eyes glowing with suspicion as they locked onto mine. "Well now. Maybe little mister man learned something after all."

"Are you working for the Westcotts?"

"A piece of advice, Mr. Motley," she said, eyeing me with a patronizing gaze. "Don't fall into the void of conspiracy theory. You'll lose what little credibility you have."

"How do you know the Westcotts?"

"Who says I know the Westcotts?"

"Maybe I'll get the chance to rub elbows with the bourbon glitterati, the Connie Westcotts of the world. Isn't that what you said?" She didn't speak, but I detected a slight wariness in her keen eyes. "And it's Connie, huh? That's pretty familiar for someone so intent on formality."

She gave a mirthless laugh. "You're showing yourself to be quite the amateur, sir. I have a perfectly good explanation for why I know the name Conrad Westcott." I held up my hands, welcoming her explanation. "Hamia Diab, of course. She spoke to Moussa the day he arrived at the monastery, and he mentioned to her that he had been invited to dinner at the Westcott home. If you do a quick check of the phone book, you will find there are precious few listings for Westcott in this town. It wasn't difficult to deduce that he was referring to Conrad and Isabelle."

"And was it difficult to deduce why a society couple like that would invite a college kid over for dinner?"

"According to Conrad Westcott, that never happened. He claims it was a misunderstanding, that someone at the monastery misheard the message and wrote down the wrong name."

"So, you talked to Westcott?" I shook my head in disbelief. "This shit just gets better and better."

"I'm an investigative reporter, Mr. Motley, and I am damn good..."

"Yeah, yeah, I've already heard. You're great at your job. No need to remind me."

She took a deep breath and let out a slow, steady breath. "I contacted Conrad Westcott to see if I could ask him some questions. He agreed, and during the interview he insisted that I call him Connie. I could see it was part of his good ol' boy schtick, so I went along. That's why I made the offhanded remark to you about Connie Westcott."

I sat down at the table and said, "So why not tell me that?"

She leaned toward me with a pleading look. "Because I'm trying to help you, that's why. You're a talented reporter, Levi. I thought if you got involved in the story it would be a way for you to grow and that it might lead to..."

"I called Danny Brewer."

She froze mid-sentence and blinked. "Who?"

"Danny Brewer. You know, my wingman in college. The guy you said was good people. Danny Brewer?"

"Oh, yes, of course. Danny. So, what did he..."

"Turns out he goes by Dan now, for professional reasons. He said

Dan sounds more grown up. That may be true, but to me, he'll always be Danny."

I could see the gold medallion she wore rising and falling with the quickened pace of her breathing.

"Anyway, I called my old buddy Danny, or Dan, as his colleagues like you should know him. He was surprised to hear I'm in Bardstown. Said he thought I was out west. In fact, he thought I'd ended up in Seattle." She began to chew on her lower lip. "I said, 'Damn Danny, why'd you think that?' And he said, 'Well, because last time we talked, you were asking about Regina Sandoval.' So, I said, 'What do you mean, Danny? I thought you worked with Sandoval there in Louisville. The best investigative reporter you've ever worked with. Isn't that what you told me?' So, he says, 'Yeah, she is. But she's not in Louisville anymore. She took a job out in Seattle maybe five or six months ago.'"

Regina picked up her leather bag and slung the strap over her shoulder.

"That's a funny thing, don't you think? My buddy Danny Brewer hasn't spoken to you in six months. You see, he figured I was trying to get a job in Seattle and that's why I called asking about Regina Sandoval. You know, networking. Is that the right term, Sandoval? Networking? Is that what you were doing down in Nashville?"

Her right hand slipped inside the bag as she slid the chair back from the table.

"Good ol' Danny. Now that I'm just down the road, he wants to get together to have a couple of beers. I mean, he's married now, but I bet he can still set me up just like the old days."

Her eyes moved from me to the door and then back to me.

"Say, why don't you come with us, Sandoval? You, me, Danny, let's all go have us a drink and chew the fat about news and politics and the impending demise of the newspaper, what with all these websites and blogs taking over. It'll be like a mini conference." I leaned in across the table, glowering at her. "Just say the word, Sandoval. Hell, we can even invite Artie Goben. That's your old buddy from Chi-town, right? How about it, Sandoval?"

She stood, her right hand still inside the leather bag.

"Now check this shit out. What, you got something in that bag for me?" She slid around the table and moved toward the door. "Do you even know how to use it?"

"I know how to use it."

"Yeah, right," I said, placing two fingers against my temple as I stood, menacing her. "But do you *really* know how to use it?"

"I'm leaving now."

"So, who the hell's stopping you?"

She scooped up her coat, opened the door, and slipped out of the house. I followed her outside as she hurried to her car. As she pulled away, the temporary tag flapped in the wind, revealing a license plate underneath. I pulled out my pad and scribbled the number down. Then I stood in the yard and looked around at the neighboring houses, half expecting to see eyes peering out of windows and cracked doors. But the neighborhood was peacefully disinterested in the drama playing out in the front yard of George Hawley's rental house.

I walked back inside and scanned the room, the disquiet in my mind growing into the firm and certain knowledge that I had been played for a fool. But why? Who was Regina Sandoval, and what was the motivation for her charade?

On top of all that, I thought, *how is it her green eyes have turned blue?*

CHAPTER
SIXTEEN

I AWOKE TO THE sound of a fist pounding like a battering ram against the front door as a muffled voice called out, "Open the door, Motley." The light cascading through the windows stung my eyes like needles, and my head felt like it had been split open with an ax. I wriggled out of my sleeping bag, pulled my knees up to my chest, and buried my face between them as I sucked in and slowly blew out huge draughts of air. As life seeped into my bones and muscles, I became aware of a sharp pain in my right hand. I looked down and saw dried blood crusting at the edges of a wicked gash snaking across my knuckles. I balled my hand into a fist and threw my head back in pain as the wound opened, causing a fresh flow of blood to trickle down my fingers. Outside, the fist continued to batter the door as the muffled voice called out for me to open up.

"Stop banging the damn door," I said.

"I'll stop banging when you start opening."

Though dulled to the point of being nearly inoperable, the synapses in my brain had enough spark to register that the voice was Dominick's. But that realization and his offer of truce did nothing to make me move faster as all I really wanted was to crawl back into the cool darkness of my sleeping bag. Still, I was cognizant enough to know that the wound on my hand needed attention. Knowing that, I attempted to stand, but the house teetered as if balanced on the tip of a knife blade. The best I could do was to slide along the wall, eventually slipping into the bathroom where I gripped the porcelain sink to steady myself.

Again, I sucked in a long breath and as I exhaled, I looked up to see blood smeared across the spiderwebbed mirror. Ignoring two menacing shards of glass in the sink, I turned on the cold water, grimacing as it ran over my outstretched hand. I dried and wrapped my hand in a white towel and gingerly made my way toward the sound of the fist, ardent in its attempt to break down the door. I unlocked and opened the door, releasing the fist from its toil. Then I collapsed in a chair and laid my head atop the wooden table.

"Holy shit, Motley. You look like hell."

"You woke me up to tell me that?"

I heard a chair slide against the floor and glanced up to see Dominick sitting opposite me. He took a foil-wrapped sandwich out of a bag and placed it along with a Styrofoam coffee cup on the table in front of me.

"You were in rare form last night, brother." I didn't speak or move. "Come on, now. Soldier up. You down, but you ain't out."

"I was out. And if not for you, I'd still be out."

"Well, then it's a good thing I came along to nurse you back to life. Speaking of which..." He walked over and unwound the bloodstained towel from my hand. "Jesus, Levi. What the hell did you do?"

"Bathroom."

Dominick walked to the bathroom where I heard him let out a low curse. "This is probably a stupid question, but you got any first aid stuff around here?"

I groaned what I intended to be a negative reply.

Dominick returned to the table and pushed me up by my shoulders, leaning down to look me in the eyes. "What's the deal, tough guy? You look in the mirror and see Lance Coleridge?"

"No. I looked in the mirror and saw Levi Motley."

His look of concern was accompanied by the all too familiar despondent shake of his head. "I'm gonna run up to the drug store," he said, rewrapping the towel around my hand. "Be back in a few."

He returned to find me sitting upright and drinking the coffee he had brought. The breakfast sandwich, however, sat untouched on the table. "You need to eat that," he said. "Make ya feel better to get something on your stomach."

"I need more than that to feel better."

"Come in here." He walked into the kitchen and laid the first aid materials out on the kitchen counter next to the sink. "Put your hand in here."

"Damnit Dom, that's hot."

"Mama always ran hot water over a cut. Said you got to get the blood flowing to flush out the wound." I gripped the edge of the counter as bloody water flowed into the sink. "Okay, here comes the cold." The hot water turned icy, and my hand went numb. By the time he was finished, the ragged wound was clean, and my hand was wrapped tight in a brown cloth bandage. "I won't bother saying you might want to see if that needs stitches, 'cause I know good and well you won't."

"Thanks," I said as he handed me two aspirin and a glass of water. "I appreciate it."

"I told you I'm here to take care of you, brother." I gave him a pitiful half-smile. "Somebody sure has to. Now, where you wanna eat?"

I sat down and asked what time it was.

"Where's your watch at?"

"What time is it?"

"Almost twelve-thirty."

I took a drink of my coffee and said, "Gimme about a half hour to get myself together."

"Cool. Where you wanna go? Tom Pig's?" I leveled him with an icy glare. "Yeah, buddy," he said, grinning. "A big ol' plate of fried cow balls will cure that hangover right up. What do you say, Motley?"

I dropped my forehead onto the table. "How about we keep things simple and find a place that serves a good burger? Preferably quiet and away from other people."

"So let me get this straight. You want me to take you someplace good, but empty."

"You got it."

"I'll pick you up at one," he said, and headed for the front door.

"Hey, Dom." He turned. "Thanks."

"You know I got you, Lee-mo. See you in thirty."

I sat for a while drinking coffee and for whatever reason, my thoughts drifted to memories of Grandma Lenny. Though she didn't receive much formal education, Grandma loved to read, and she was proud to be able to cite passages that she learned from classic literature, capturing the essence of a great line in her own rough-hewn patois. I could still see her leaning hard on that old-fashioned black cane as we walked home from church, imparting wisdom to her young wards in a voice made raspy by years of smoking.

"Boys, I despise death and the gates of hell," she would say with a wag of her finger. "But I despise even more a man that has truth in his heart and yet spits forth a lie." Then she would look at us with a serious expression on her face. "That's Homer. And what that means boys, is that it's a disgrace to be a liar, but it's a goddamn tragedy to be a hypocrite." She would then cross herself at having taken the Lord's name in vain and continue the walk home, chatting amiably about what she had prepared for Sunday brunch.

Declan respected Grandma every bit as much as he loved her. In a way, he took her message to heart more than I did, in that he eventually chose not to make the Sunday Walk to Our Lady's so as not to appear a dreaded hypocrite to Grandma Lenny. After all, everybody knew the road he was on, and it wasn't one that led to absolution. In the end, my brother may not have wanted to be a hypocrite, but he sure was hellbent on becoming a tragedy.

I let out a deep sigh as I thought about the tragedy of Declan Motley. Then I looked down at my bandaged hand as it lay on the table, and I felt a sudden pang of envy toward Dominick and the mother who had taught him what I thought to be a task of fundamental importance.

Namely, how to mend an open wound.

CHAPTER
SEVENTEEN

Y OU'VE GOT TO be kidding me," I said, staring at a sign that read "Bardstown Bowling Center".

Dominick didn't even try to suppress the gleeful grin on his face.

"Let me give you an image, Dom. You know those wall clocks where there's a little guy dressed up in a mountaineer outfit? You know how that little guy comes out of the clock and bangs his sledgehammer against that little bell? You know what I'm talkin' about?" His grin widened as he nodded enthusiastically. "Well, let me tell ya, Dom, that little bastard is in my head right now swinging his little hammer against my brain about every three seconds. Can you picture that?"

"Umm-hmm," he said, his jughead nodding atop his thick neck.

"And knowing that, you brought me to a bowling alley where according to that sign, kids under twelve bowl free from noon to three. Am I summarizing the situation accurately?"

"Yeah, that's pretty much it," he said. "But you left out the part about you saying you wanted a good burger, and this place cooks the mac-daddy of all burgers."

"But you're leaving out the part where I said I wanna be away from people. Take a look around, man. This parking lot is packed."

"It's all good. There's a lounge inside. Probably be empty this time of day."

As we walked inside, my senses were immediately assaulted by the sound of bowling balls crashing into pins as preteen kids begged their moms to give them quarters for the arcade while their toddler siblings squealed in decibels somewhere in the range of a dog whistle.

Thankfully, Dominick was partially right about the crowd in the lounge area, which contained only a handful of patrons. We sat and the bartender sallied up to take our order. He was a willow-thin, greasy-haired specter of a man with a towel draped over his sloped shoulder and a look of indifference plastered on his narrow face. Naturally, Dominick greeted him by his first name. I ordered a beer and a shot, ignoring the sideward glance of my disapproving companion. The bartender set the drinks in front of me, and I downed the shot, gripping the bar as I tried not to puke. Dominick gave that familiar shake of his head and said, "How you gonna try to cure an illness by dosing yourself with the same poison that made you sick in the first damn place?"

Still gripping the bar, my chest heaved with the rhythm of my breathing until I was sure the alcohol would stay down. Once my breathing became normal, I took a long draught of my beer and told the bartender to bring me the fattest cheeseburger on the menu. Dominick said he'd have the same, and the bartender nodded and walked away.

I took another swig of beer and squinted as I looked over at my frowning friend. "That you up there on that high horse, Mr. Cotter, sir?" He waved a disgusted hand. "I do recall that you yourself have partaken of that time-honored cure known as hair of the dog on more than a few occasions. But by all means, rain your judgement down upon thee."

"Yeah, well, it's called maturity. You oughta give it a try sometime."

"Sounds like good advice," I said.

"Okay, well I also advise that you spill the goods on what happened last night."

"What do you mean spill the goods? You were there."

"Yeah, but by the time I showed up, you were already half-lit. Do you even remember the rest of the night?"

"I remember it, umm...what's that saying? As through a glass darkly?"

"You remember almost pummeling Lance Coleridge?"

"I have a vague recollection," I said, lighting a cigarette. "But I'd appreciate it if you'd fill me in on the details."

"First half of the night was a pretty good time," he said, bumming and then lighting a cigarette of his own. "I mean, watchin' your white ass trying to cut a rug with Daphne was entertaining as hell."

"Let me guess, things took a turn when puss n' shit-heel boots showed up."

"Yeah, the two of you were eyeballing each other hard. You almost went after him when he pulled Daphne aside, boo-hoo'n that he wanted her back."

I grunted and said, "I wish I could remember that part."

"You had the bouncers on high alert. Lucky for you they're my boys and I told 'em you'd be cool, or I'd whoop your ass myself."

"What happened then?"

"Coleridge split, and you ordered shots for everybody sitting at the bar." I put my head in my hands and groaned. "So, what set you off? I mean, it's one thing to blow off steam, but you had that monkey on your back. And you wouldn't tell me nothin' about it."

I shook my head is disgust and said, "Lying bitch."

"Who, Daphne? What, she not give it up? As if your drunk ass could've done anything with it if she had."

"Not her," I said, shaking my head. "Regina Sandoval."

"Sanda who?"

"The reporter from Louisville that you asked about."

"Oh, right. I tried to get you to speak on it, but you wouldn't say squat. So, what's she want with you?"

"That's what I have to figure out."

The bartender brought our food and for a minute I ignored his questions as I devoured half the burger in three massive bites.

"What do you mean you have to figure it out? I heard she was at your place Tuesday and that you met the next morning, too."

"You heard?"

He gave me a sly look and said, "You in my hood, Levi. I got eyes and ears everywhere."

"Yeah, well, you see that's the thing. I spent all that time with her only to find out she was playing me."

The plates rattled as I slammed my good hand down on the bar, causing the normally impassive bartender to look annoyed.

"It's all good, Rick," Dominick said. "Women, ya know? No worries, my man." He turned and scolded me in a harsh whisper. "You want to sink so low as to get your dumb ass thrown out of a bowling alley?" I shot him a rueful expression and took a drink of my beer. "So, this Sandoval. What's her game?"

"I'm not exactly sure," I said, rubbing my bleary eyes. "What she said is that she wants to know what really happened to Moussa."

"And that's not true?"

"No, I think that part is true. But that's not her end game."

"So, what is her end game?"

"I don't know, Dom. But I know I got played."

"You did that to yourself because you got played?" He pointed to my bandaged hand. "Uh-uh. I don't think so."

I shot him a wary look that was meant to convey that I didn't want to go into it. But of course, he went into it anyway. "I'll repeat the question. What set you off?"

"It's nothing," I said, pushing my plate away. Dominick turned in his chair and gave me a stern look that was evidently meant to convey I wasn't getting out of this without an explanation. I shook my head and tried to change the subject, but he stared at me as he waited for my response. "This is all I'll say and then I want you to leave it alone," I said, leveling him with a stern glare of my own. He nodded his agreement. "You remember a few months after we started rooming together, we were the only two people on our floor who didn't go home for Thanksgiving break?"

"Of course I remember," he said, smiling mischievously. "We smuggled a twenty-four pack of Beast Lite into the dorm, got smashed, and ran around the tower like the hopped-up freshmen idiots that we were."

"That's right. And that was also the first time we had a drunken woe is me, tell me your life story session. You remember that, too?" His eyes dropped to the floor as he realized where I was headed. "I told you how my mother walked out on us, right?"

His gaze rose to meet mine and he said, "You don't need to say anything else, Levi. I understand. But let me help you figure this out, brother. Tell me what happened with this Sandoval woman."

I hesitated for a moment, but it was obvious he truly did want to help. So, I shared, as he'd said, what happened with this Sandoval woman. Dominick already knew the story of my encounter with Moussa, so I was able to relate my conversations with Regina Sandoval in relatively short order. He listened attentively as I then described my meetings with Jerry

Edelen and Brother Simon, bringing him all the way up to the point of our conversation the day before in the cab of my truck.

"Okay, so where'd you go after you saw me?"

"I went inside, teased Rebecca, talked to George for a little while, and called Danny."

Dominick knew Danny Brewer from our days in Bowling Green. I told him about my conversation with Danny and how he said the Regina Sandoval he knew had split for the Pacific Northwest months earlier. Upon hearing that tidbit, Dominick hailed the bartender and said, "Rick, I'm going to need a tall boy right here."

"Make it two."

The bartender brought our beers and cleared away the plates.

"So, what happened next?"

"I took care of some random stuff and then headed home. But as I pulled into the driveway, I noticed a car parked in front of the house. Turns out it was Regina Sandoval. Or at least that's who I thought she was."

For the next ten minutes, I related the details of my third encounter with the duplicitous mystery woman. Dominick leaned toward me as I spoke, engrossed in the details of the interaction. I finished the story by addressing the question he had posed as to why my most recent encounter with the so-called Regina Sandoval had set me off. "Look, I don't want to get all Oedipal about it, so let's just say I've got female trust issues and leave it at that."

"All good, brother," he said, raising his hands in a gesture of acceptance. "But what the hell are you into here? I mean, you got some dragon lady from who knows where trying to uncover what you know about... about what exactly? This kid from Louisiana? That shit don't make sense."

I stared straight ahead, trying to work out what I had missed in my encounters with the woman while Dominick provided his own cautious insight into the matter. "Maybe you should back away from this. I mean, you've got a big-time name in Conrad Westcott getting thrown around in connection with this kid's death, however it happened. And you've got this Sandoval woman who's trying to play you to get information about it all. And apparently packing heat, I might add. I don't know, man, maybe the best thing is to leave it alone."

I looked down at the bandage on my hand, stroking the cloth with my good hand as Dominick took a drink of his beer and stared at me in anticipation. But my mind was too clouded to sort and organize the facts of what had transpired in a way that made sense, much less give honest consideration to Dominick's counsel. I lifted my beer to buy another moment to think but stopped midair when I suddenly heard the sorrowful twang of a country music song emanating from a jukebox in a corner of the lounge. I set the mug down, dropped my throbbing forehead onto the bar, and said, "Thanks, Dom."

"For what?"

"For bringing me to the seventh circle of hell. Much appreciated."

"Whatever, Motley. I'm the best thing you got going."

Lifting my head, I leaned back in my chair and let out a heavy sigh. "And what's that say about the current status of my existence?" He grunted and took another drink of his beer. "Hey, Rick. Can I get some change?"

I threw a dollar bill down on the bar and he changed it with four quarters. I walked over to the jukebox, dropped in three quarters, and made my selections. Returning to the bar, I looked at Dominick, who was eyeing me with a wary expression as he said, "Knowing your taste in music, I know not one of those songs came out in the last decade."

"Guess you'll just have to wait and see, now won't you? Now, are you gonna help me think this through or not?" He continued to eyeball me warily, but I knew he was dying to quarterback the situation with me. "I hear you telling me to leave it be, but you know I can't."

Dominick regarded me with a knowing look. "You mean you don't want to."

"Whatever, man," I said with an exasperated sigh. "Look, my brain feels like one big cotton ball, so I could use the help. How about it, Cotter? What do we know and what do we need to know?"

He blew out his cheeks, knowing that given the level of betrayal I felt, there was no way I was dropping the matter of Regina Sandoval. So, after another moment of working through whatever internal debate he had to settle, he slowly nodded as he rubbed his hands together. He was about to speak but stopped as he listened to the opening notes of the song floating from the jukebox.

"'Lyin' Eyes'?"

"Seems apropos."

He gave a soft laugh and focused on the task at hand. "Okay, now this fake Regina Sandoval. You said she called *The Observer* looking for you, correct?" I nodded. "So, she knew you worked there."

"She knew that and a few other things, like that I had been at the crime scene. Hell, she already knew the deal about me and Moussa before I told it to her."

"How do you mean?"

"She'd already talked to Moussa's mother. That morning we had coffee, she told me she had already spoken to Hamia Diab and that my account of things squared with what Moussa's mother had told her."

"And she told you Hamia Diab was the one that tipped her off about the Westcotts?"

"I don't follow," I said.

"Her explanation of how she knew about the Westcotts. You said Hamia told her that Moussa had called when he got to the monastery, and that he told her he had been invited to dinner at the Westcott house."

"Yeah, that's right."

"And you said that she reached out to Conrad Westcott to get an interview." Again, I nodded. "And he gave her the interview."

"Yeah. So?"

"Well, that means Westcott knows something's up."

I put my head in my hands and groaned. "I'm in a fog, man. Spell it out for me."

"Follow along with me. If she did in fact interview Conrad, or Connie, or whatever he likes to be called, then we have to assume that the questions she asked him speak to her true motivation, her real purpose in all this." I nodded for a third time, indicating a tenuous grasp on the first point of his argument. "That means we also have to assume that Westcott knows something about her purpose, and knowing that, he's probably on to her."

"Eh, I don't know, Dom. Why do we have to assume that? I mean, we don't even know what they talked about."

"True, true. But check this out. A wealthy cat like that gets contacted out of the blue by a reporter, you know he's got his antenna up. The only way she gets in the door is if she's selling something that makes him look good."

"But she probably lied to him to get him to see her," I said.

"No doubt. But whatever she sold him on as the reason for the interview, we know at some point in the conversation she asked about the connection between him and Moussa, and Westcott denied that connection. He denied ever having contacted the monastery to put that invitation out there."

"Yeah, all right. I see what you're saying. So, Westcott may have realized that she was there under false pretenses because she segued into questions about the supposed invitation to Moussa. But if he's lying about not having delivered that invitation, then he probably knows that Sandoval knows that he's lying. That could mean that he's on high alert when it comes to Regina Sandoval. Same as me."

"That's right. And then there's the matter of your boy Brother Simon, who's a meticulous notetaker, right? So, if he didn't get that invitation wrong, and it sounds like he's not one to get that kinda thing wrong, then why would Westcott deny it unless he has something to hide? I mean, the monk told you whoever he talked to on the phone said the Westcotts were friends of Moussa's family. If that's true, then what's the big deal about saying so unless you don't want Sandoval to know that?"

"I see your point," I said. "Especially after Moussa turned up dead. If you're a friend of the family, you'd be offering condolences to the family, not denying any connection to it."

"Exactly. I'm surprised Westcott took the meeting with Sandoval in the first place. But like you said, we don't know what kind of angle she sold him on. If I'm Westcott, I'm wondering where she got her information,"

"Well, he'd have to figure she got it from Hamia or from Brother Simon. But Westcott wouldn't have known that Moussa or Sandoval ever spoke to Hamia unless Sandoval told him, which I highly doubt. So, he'd have to conclude she got it from Brother Simon. He's the only source for the information that Westcott would have known about. At least the only one we're aware of."

"And that's all the more reason for Westcott to be sweatin' it," he said. "After all, why is she talking to the monk unless she's investigating Moussa's death? And through that investigation, she discovered a connection that Westcott for whatever reason, denies."

"So then, we can extrapolate what from this? That the connection between Moussa and the Westcotts was Sandoval's motivation for contacting me? Is that it?"

"I'm not sure. But I do think her saying that she learned about the dinner invitation from Hamia and that's what led her to contact Conrad Westcott tells us something. And his denial of that invitation tells us something."

"Which is?"

"That somebody's lying," he said.

The next song came on the jukebox. "Evil Woman."

"You raise some good points, Dom. Problem is, the only reason we know any of this is because she told me she had spoken to Westcott, and she only did that to save her ass when I confronted her about how she knew to call him Connie."

"Yeah, but think of the timing," he said. "She'd already talked to Westcott before she talked to you."

"Okay."

"So, it's conceivable that what she was looking for from you was rooted in something she learned from him."

I frowned and said, "Sorry, Dom, but I'm not sure about that part."

"Yeah, me neither. I got on a roll and stretched it too thin, didn't I?" He took a swig of his beer, and we both sat pondering for a minute.

"Do you know anything about this guy?"

"Who, Westcott? I know he's a rich bigwig and that his son's in politics. But the whole bourbon industry connection? That ain't my scene. That's why I wasn't interested in writing that story about the festival."

I feigned a hurt expression and said, "And here I thought that was part of your master plan to get me to stay in town."

"Yeah, well you know...that, too."

"All right, well let's look at this from Westcott's perspective. He's a somebody, an influential guy, big in the industry and all that. And you've got this reporter..."

"Maybe she didn't sell herself as a reporter," he said, interjecting.

"Maybe not. But whatever the case, she's asking questions about his connection to this kid that got killed. I mean, yeah, you'd probably wanna distance yourself from that. Look for the simplest explanation, right? Westcott wanted to stay out of it. He didn't want his name associated with Moussa's death. That's understandable, isn't it?"

Dominick sighed as he slumped back in his chair. "Yeah, I guess so."

"So, what do you think, Dom? Where's that leave us?"

He considered the matter for a moment. "Here's what I think we know. One, I think that Brother Simon's notes are reliable. He got that call. Two, I think Hamia did talk to Moussa, who said he received that invitation. I mean, how else would Sandoval have known about it? Three, I think Conrad Westcott is denying the connection to Moussa for some reason, and that reason could be the one you named. On the other hand, it could be something nefarious. Or it could be somewhere in between." He stopped and looked at me. "What do you think?"

"I think given the way she played me, Regina Sandoval played or at least tried to play Conrad Westcott, too."

"Which brings us back to the original question," he said. "What's her motivation?"

"What's her end game?"

Dominick gave me an enthusiastic slap on the back. "Good to see those brain cells aren't completely dead."

I looked at the half-full beer mug sitting on the bar in front of me and pushed it away.

"So how do we get at this? I mean, if we can figure out Sandoval's part, then we can figure out how to move forward."

"I like the *we*, brother," I said, offering him a warm smile.

"Always takin' care of your dumb ass, Motley," he said, shaking his head in mock exasperation. "Always working double-time to keep you straight."

I clapped him on the shoulder as "The Bitch is Back" came on the jukebox.

"Let's think about what she asked you to do. She wanted you to go to the hardware store and to the monastery."

"Yes," I said. "She did."

"And if you hadn't gotten suspicious and called our boy Danny, then she would've heard everything you learned on your field trip."

"Yes, she would have."

"Well, that speaks to at least part of her motivation then, right?"

I thought about that and said, "I suppose it does."

"Okay. Then what'd you find that she never got to hear?"

"Well, at Brothers I guess the main things were the size of that shovel and that this cop Hadley was asking questions. And at the monastery it's that the Westcotts invited Moussa to dinner, but she already knew that part." He ruminated on this information for a long moment. "You think she was after something else? Something different I was supposed to have learned?"

"It's hard to say," he said with a pensive look on his face. "So, what now? What are you gonna do next?"

"First I need to talk to Hamia Diab to find out what Sandoval said to Hamia and what Hamia said to her."

"Agreed. You have her number?"

"I don't even know where she lives."

"Let me handle that," he said. "I've got a friend at a major outlet who can help."

"What does that mean?"

"It means don't ask questions that you don't want the answers to."

"All right," I said in a cautious tone. "What about the sheriff's department? Is there anybody you can talk to?"

"Yeah, you know, I got somebody inside."

"I think it'd be helpful to know more about that shovel. They've gotta have it in evidence. Think you can find something out?"

"The dude I need to talk to is on duty right now," he said. "I saw him going through town after I left your place. I can hunt him down, no doubt."

"Okay, get me back to my truck and then you can hunt your guy down and get that phone number while I try to find out more about Conrad and Isabelle Westcott."

"How you plan to do that?"

"Well, who do we know that has the four-one-one on all things local?"

"That McGill lady?" he said, chuckling as he shook his head. "I'll leave that one to you."

"Oh, come on now. Miss Olive is just a tad eccentric, that's all. Anyway, we'll run our errands and meet back at *The Observer* later in the afternoon."

Dominick looked at me and said, "And you're sure you wanna keep going down this road?"

Given the persistent pounding in my head, I wasn't sure I could say definitively that I wanted to do anything other than go to sleep and wake up whole again. But I knew there was enough gas in the tank to at least get through the afternoon.

"I don't know what in the hell we're going to find, Dom, but I know I'm chasing Regina Sandoval until the road dead ends. Plus, I told George I'd bring him a good story. Maybe this is it."

"Or maybe it's more than that," he said with a sideward glance.

It seemed we had taken our speculative inquiry as far as possible, so we stood and made for the front door. As we did, my attention was drawn to the lights and sounds coming from the arcade across from the lounge. "Hey, Dom," I said, nodding toward the game room.

He caught my drift and said, "Damn skippy."

Making my way back into the lounge, I threw a five on the bar and said, "Hey, Rick. I need some change. That old-school arcade is calling my name."

CHAPTER
EIGHTEEN

I STOOD ON THE sidewalk and watched as Roscoe meandered down Third Street, no doubt anticipating the bounty of oats awaiting him at the end of a long day's toil. As the tour group turned into the stable lot, I heard Olive henpecking Moots, whose shoulders drooped in mock discouragement. "Folks, I tell ya there has never been a man more in need of a woman to tell him what to do than this one right here," she said, jerking a thumb toward the carriage's pilot.

Moots waved her off and said, "Ah, what do you know?"

"What I know is that Judge Harry McGill always did say that behind every good man is a good woman ready to bring a rolling pin down on his fool head."

The smiling tourists climbed down from the carriage, offered their gratuities, and shuffled down the sidewalk in search of a Saturday afternoon sale or an open table at one of the local restaurants.

With a nimble athleticism that belied her age, Olive slipped off her seat, leapt to the ground, and said, "Well, I do declare. If it's not my new old best buddy, Levi Motley."

She pulled the collar of her coat up as she walked toward me, her wry smile forecasting disapproval of my timing. "Since Moots and I just finished the last tour of the day, you're typically out of luck to join a tour yourself. However, I suspect per usual you are not here for a tour but rather to be edified on some topic related to the history of my beloved hometown."

"You see, that's what I like about you, Miss Olive. Not only are you a living, breathing font of historical knowledge, but you're a mind reader, too."

"A one-track mind is not so hard to read, young man," she said, studying me with a shrewd gaze. "I don't suppose those dark rings under your eyes are the result of you staying up all night reading the Good Book."

"No, but they are the result of me staying up all night, so do I get partial credit?"

She stood with her hands on her hips and regarded me with a stern glare. "Judge Harry McGill always did say that you can't expect to soar with the eagles in the morning if you're out hootin' with the owls at night."

"Now, there's a lesson I should probably take to heart."

"Well, while you ruminate on today's lesson, I'm going to help Moots get things settled. When I'm finished, we can talk about the day's topic. That is, once you've informed me what it is."

I wandered across the street for a coffee. By the time I returned, Moots and Olive had wrapped up the day's business, and Roscoe was happily munching on his well-earned reward. I leaned against a rail and sipped my coffee as Olive made her way toward me, her boots clip-clopping on the concrete as she walked.

"Well now, Mr. Levi. Have you taken today's lesson fully to heart, or do you first need to take it to the Lord in prayer?"

"You know, that's probably a good idea, but I'm a little rusty on that front. Maybe you could offer one up on my behalf."

Her rigid posture relaxed, and she said, "Why, I already have. More than once." She reached out and gently lifted my bandaged hand. "But I get the feeling I need to put St. Jude on your case, young man. So, you can expect him to be tapping on your shoulder any day now."

I felt my face go flush as I said, "Well, I umm...I'll keep an eye out for him." I cleared my throat. "In the meantime, I wonder if you could enlighten me about one of the kingpins of your favored local industry."

Her eyes brightened with curiosity. "I do my best to stay current on the biographical sketches of the leaders in our signature industry. You see, I think our guests appreciate the personal touch that comes from offering an anecdote or two about the local gentry. Who is it you wish to inquire about?"

"Conrad Westcott."

She let out a high-pitched peal of laughter. "Well, that one is quite the character indeed."

"How do you mean?"

"Well, for starters, Mr. Westcott is known to be quite the gregarious sort who very much enjoys imbibing the product he sells. And his home is regularly buzzing with activity."

"Meaning he knows how to throw a party?"

She gave me an amused look and said, "Saying Connie Westcott knows how to throw a party is like saying Secretariat knew how to run a horserace."

"Sounds like a regular Jay Gatsby."

"A more apt description than you perhaps realize. You see, like Mr. Gatsby, Conrad Westcott is a first-generation baron of our fine capital export. Which is to say that his is not old money."

"A self-made man, huh?"

Her nose wrinkled as she considered this. "I don't know if I buy into that social myth. After all, it surely takes not only luck but the help of others for one to ascend to great professional heights, don't you think?"

"I can agree with that. But it does seem to me that some people are, I don't know, fated for greatness."

She cocked her head and said, "And are you such a man?" I put up my hands and feigned retreat. "And may I ask why not?"

I gave a dubious laugh and then hesitated, hemmed, hawed, and fell all over myself explaining why that was not the case.

"I think you sell yourself short. Like the great Frederick Douglass once said, the next best thing to success is a valid apology for non-success. It possesses the means of covering the small with the glory of the great." She took a step forward and poked me in the chest. "You are too young, Levi Motley, to be making apologies for not succeeding."

Staring down at this diminutive force of nature, I felt the sense of pride that springs from the seed of another's belief. The last time I had felt that was with Artie Goben, who after gracing me with one of his rare words of praise, told me I damn well better have enough sense to not diminish the moment with my stupid words. So, instead of offering my stupid words, I looked Olive McGill squarely in the eyes and gave a single nod of appreciation.

"But here I am going on and on. Tell me how I can help."

I cleared my throat again, and said, "Well, do you have a Westcott anecdote?" She gave me a confused look. "You said you like to have an anecdote ready to tell tourists. Do you have one for Conrad Westcott?"

She frowned and said, "I leave that one to Moots."

I gave her a curious look. Olive rolled her eyes and called out for Moots, who sauntered across the parking lot puffing on a pipe.

"How's it going, Moots?"

"I'd complain, but who'd listen?" He shot a sour look at Olive. "What about you, Levi? How's the world treatin' ya?"

"About as good as I deserve."

At that Olive piped up and said, "Mr. Levi is in the process of taking certain lessons to heart. Lessons that will surely improve both his outlook and his prospects."

"Sounds good."

Moots could make two syllables sound like molasses being poured over a warm biscuit. On top of that, his voice was the perfect converse of Olive's birdlike chirp, providing another reason, I was sure, why tourists found the pair so endearing.

"And I might add, they are lessons that you, Mr. Moots, should give some serious consideration to as well," Olive said.

"That what you brought me over here to say?"

"Well, it bears saying, and you should listen."

"Maybe so, but I reckon next time you wanna preach, ya ought to take the trip over to me to do it."

I fought back a smile and said, "Actually, Moots, Miss Olive called for you because I have a question."

"Rather answer a question than stand here listenin' to a sermon. Hell far, Sunday ain't 'til tomorrow, unless I forgot the order of days in the week."

Olive withered him with a fierce glare as I continued to suppress my smile. The two of them always went at each other like an old married couple, which was another reason why I enjoyed seeing them.

"Well, Moots, Olive and I were discussing Conrad Westcott. You see, I'm doing some research on local figures in the bourbon industry for a story I'm writing, and his name came up."

"Sounds good. What's the question?"

"Now you see, that's another lesson you need to learn," Olive said. "Namely, how to exercise a little patience in your discourse with others."

"Hell far, the man said he had a question. I'm just wonderin' when it's coming forth, that's all."

She folded her arms and glared at him.

"Fair enough. I'll get to the point. Miss Olive said you have a story you like to tell about Westcott."

"Sure do. But what's the question?"

Olive sighed loudly.

"Well, I'm wondering what it is you say."

"That ain't no question."

Olive buried her face in her hands.

"The question, Moots, is what do you say when you go past the Westcott house?"

"Oh, that. Well, I tell 'em ol' Connie was bein' interviewed by some writer one time when the woman doing the interviewin' looks at him and asks if he likes to take a drink of anything other than bourbon. He says to her, 'I didn't know there was anything but bourbon worth likin'.' So, she says, 'Well, vodka's the most popular spirit in the world, so it seems like lotsa people think it's worth liking.' So, ol' Connie, he looks at her like she got three heads and says, 'Lady, that don't make a bit a sense.' And the lady says, 'Why's that?' So, Connie says, ''Cause vodka ain't go no taste to it.' So, she says, 'Well, whaddaya mean it ain't got no taste?' So, ol' Connie, he says, 'Well, if ya put it with orange juice, it tastes just like oranges. And if ya put it with lemonade, it tastes just like lemons. And if ya put it with grape juice, it tastes just like grapes. Hell, I reckon if ya put it with piss, it'll taste just like piss. And who in the hell wants to drink piss?'"

I laughed out loud as Olive shook her head in disgust.

"And dang if she didn't print it just the way ol' Connie said it."

"That story is crass and uncouth," Olive said. "I prefer my part in this stage of the tour."

"Which is?"

Olive drew herself upright, preparing to recite her part. "I tell them Conrad Westcott, a product of our very own Nelson County, is the founder of Westcott Bourbon Company. Mr. Westcott purchased the Old Stump distillery, which had shuttered its doors in the late nineteen-sixties. Despite the ups and downs of the industry during the seventies and eighties, Mr. Westcott persevered to produce a single barrel bourbon of the highest quality called Old Royal, of which the advertising tag line is 'Old Royal, a bourbon fit for kings and queens.'"

I looked at her deadpan as Moots blew a billow of smoke from his pipe.

"What?" she said indignantly.

"Well, you know that sounds very factual and all. And I'm sure people appreciate having that umm...information. But to tell you the truth, Miss Olive, it doesn't have quite the same pizzazz as Moots's part. Meaning no offense."

She raised her chin in defiance. "How did I know you would say that?"

Moots grinned and said, "Then again, I suppose it's a fer sight better than sayin' 'Old Royal, at least it don't taste like piss.'"

I coughed to hide my laughter as Olive spun on her heel and took several steps away before turning and walking back in a huff. "The two of you are a couple of...a couple of..." She pointed a menacing finger in our direction, the tornado of frustration bottled up inside her ready to explode. "Well, I just don't have words for what you are."

Moots shook his head and said, "Y'all need me for anything else?"

Olive's mouth was shut tight, so I said, "Thanks for the story, Moots."

He tipped his Stetson and ambled over to the stable like a man with all the time in the world.

"Well, sir," Olive said, glaring at me. "Did you get the information you were looking for? Which is to say, did you acquire the sufficient crudity needed to titillate your audience in the effort to sell more newspapers?"

"Come on, Miss Olive. You're the one who said Moots had a story to tell, remember?"

She snorted but the stiffness in her spine yielded a smidge. "I suppose that's true. Still, you could at least acknowledge that for my part, I provide a succinct and accurate account of the history of Westcott Bourbon Company. And accuracy is the bellwether of truth, is it not?"

"Is that something Judge McGill used to say?"

"No. It's something that I'm saying right at this moment."

"Well, of course. Your part is quite important. It counterbalances Moots's story with actual history, which is good and necessary."

Her face softened just a hair. "Do you really think so?"

"Absolutely, I really think so. It's important to provide both color and historical accuracy. Isn't that what you told me that the first time I stopped by?"

"Well, it does sound like something I would say," she said, softening a bit more. "Especially since it's a true statement."

I nodded and gave her an affirming look. "Is there anything else you can tell me about the Westcotts? I get that he throws a great party, but is there anything else noteworthy about Conrad and Isabelle Westcott?"

"Well, there is the son," she said. "Rogers Westcott."

"And why is that noteworthy?"

"Well, he's only the most gifted young politician in the state of Kentucky. In my estimation, he is still a bit too green to put up a challenge for the governor's mansion in the next cycle, but I do believe he has a chance to be a viable candidate six years from now."

"What's he do?"

"He's an attorney and a state representative in Lexington. That's where his mother Isabelle is from. A most powerful platform from which to further his political ambitions, I must say."

"What party does he represent?"

She gave me a look of profound disappointment. "You really need to do your homework on our state history, sir. If you had even a basic understanding of our politics, then you would know that a Republican hasn't won the governor's seat in Kentucky since Louie Nunn in sixty-seven. And before that, it was Simeon Willis in forty-three. Which is to say that Republicans do not frequently occupy the office of governor in our state."

"So, I take it you're a Democrat?" She closed her eyes in dismay. "Okay, I get it. It's bad form to talk religion and politics."

"Oh, please," she said, waving a dismissive hand. "That silly rule shouldn't govern informed discussion, no pun intended. Besides, Judge Harry McGill always did say that a Democrat is just a person who thinks they were born thirty years too early."

"And a Republican?"

"What do you mean?"

"Well, I guess it would stand to reason that Judge McGill would have said a Republican is somebody who thinks they were born thirty years too late. Correct?"

"Judge Harry McGill never spoke about Republicans. Southern Democrats, yes. But never Republicans."

"Okay, so what's a Southern Democrat?"

"Why, that's no great mystery," she said in an obvious tone. "It's a Republican who wants to get elected."

Having thus been schooled in Kentucky politics, I thanked Olive for her time, her prayers, and for the lessons on life and history she had shared with me. As usual, she asked when I planned to join a tour, and as usual, I promised her I would make a point of it. In fact, I told her it might be nice to take a tour during the upcoming holidays, to which she replied that tours during the Christmas around Bardstown festivities were particularly enjoyable. That serendipitous pronouncement prompted me to share with her that my editor had asked me to cover the Christmas around Bardstown event and that seemed to please her a great deal.

"And since you have an interest in that particular kingpin, as you called him, it might interest you to know that the Westcott home is part of the Christmas tour. Perhaps the two of you can share a glass of eggnog, Mr. Levi. Spiked with Old Royal, of course."

CHAPTER
NINETEEN

THE RUSH OF energy that came with the hunt was pushing me onward, but I knew that rush would fade as the afternoon wore thin. Inertia was the primary factor that would hasten my inevitable crash, so I tried to stay active until Dominick arrived back at the office. Unfortunately, I soon found myself with idle hands and I was just about to give in to the tightening grip of fatigue when the thought of driving out to the monastery to see if Brother Simon could share any additional details about Moussa's visit popped into my mind. And while the prospect of the monk coming forth with more information seemed unlikely, the urge to go home and crawl into my sleeping bag was fast emerging as the only alternative to immediate action. Thus, I decided a field trip would at least provide an activity to fill the time until I could track down Dominick.

Arriving at Gethsemani, I parked in my usual spot and made my way inside where my hopes were buoyed by the light I saw emanating from the good brother's office. But my greeting to the monk was stymied by the sight of an unknown man in blue jeans sitting in the corner reading a newspaper. The man looked up with a jovial smile and said, "Hey fella. How can I help ya?"

"Well, I'm, uhh...looking for Brother Simon. Do you know when he'll be back?"

"He's gone over for Vespers. I usually fill in for him for an hour or so before my shift is up just in case a guest needs help with somethin'."

"So, you're a monk?"

The man let out a boisterous laugh and said, "Not even close. Name's Denny. I work in the mailroom."

He rose, and we shook hands as I introduced myself.

"So, did you want to be a monk?"

"You mean was I cut from the team like at a grade school basketball tryout?" He let out a good-natured chuckle. "Nah, I work here but I live down the road in Culvertown. Got me a wife and two kids, which is kindly a problem when it comes to bein' a monk."

"Right. Yeah, sorry. I'm still learning about all this."

"You and me both, friend."

I looked at him blankly as he looked back at me with an amused expression.

"So, you work in the mailroom?"

"Yeah, I'm kinda like the postmaster general for the monastery. But beyond that, I do all kinds of odd jobs. Try to make myself useful so they won't get ridda me."

"I see." I tried not to sound disappointed. "Well, look, Denny, I won't keep you. I just stopped by to see Brother Simon, so I guess I'll just..."

"You a guest?"

"No, I'm not staying here. I came by to ask a few questions."

"How do you know Brother Simon?"

"Well, I wouldn't say I know him. In fact, I just met him yesterday. He's helping me out with a story I'm working on. I'm a reporter."

"For the Bardstown paper?"

"Yeah, that's right."

"What a coincidence. I was just readin' that paper. The sports section, anyway." He displayed the front page of the latest edition of *The Observer* as evidence, and I gave him an awkward thumbs-up. "So, what's the story about?"

"Well, it's umm..." I hesitated to get into it, but didn't want to be rude, either. "I'm looking into the death of a retreat guest who was staying here a couple of months back. You know about that?"

His jovial face turned grim. "Hell, everybody knows about that. You know we're good people 'round here. Hate for something like that to give outsiders the wrong impression."

"I don't think people jump to that conclusion. But I have been told that there are...well, let's just say some hijinks going on down here."

He frowned at that and said, "Where you from?"

"I'm from Louisville."

"So, tell me, friend. Y'all got any hijinks goin' on up that way?"

"You got me there," I said, chastened. "Anyway, it was nice meeting you, Denny. I'll just show myself..."

"How's Brother Simon helping you?"

Again, I hesitated, unsure if I wanted to share details about our conversation, particularly since confidentiality had been foremost in Brother Simon's mind when I showed up asking questions.

On the other hand, why go home empty handed? I thought. *Plus, this guy's a local. Maybe he's got an interesting perspective on things.*

"He told me a few details about the man's stay here that were helpful," I said.

"Such as?"

"For one, he told me the Westcott family in Bardstown invited the young man to dinner before he even arrived here. I find that puzzling."

"Why's that puzzle you?" he said, ironically sporting a puzzled look of his own.

"Well, here you've got this young guy, Moussa Diab, a hitchhiker from Louisiana, and there you've got the Westcotts, who are from the highfalutin' world of bourbon." The man looked at me with a patient expression, awaiting my conclusion. "I don't know, Denny. It's just kind of hard for me to see the connection is all."

His face turned pensive as he thought about that. "From what I hear, this Moussa fella was some kinda friend of Brother Lew. Is that right?"

"I don't know about friends. But yeah, my understanding is that Brother Lew was a big part of the reason Moussa came to the monastery."

A smile formed at the tips of Denny's mouth. "Well, friend, I can make that connection for ya real easy." I cocked my head in interest. "She was his sister-in-law."

The muscles in my stomach tightened a bit and my mouth felt suddenly dry. "You have any water?"

"Fountain's right around the corner," he said, pointing.

I found the water fountain and drank as if just realizing how thirsty I had been.

"You mind if I sit down?" I said, returning to the office. He motioned for me to take a seat as he dropped down into his own chair. "Go back a minute. You said she was his sister-in-law. Who's sister-in-law? Moussa's?"

"Nah, not him. Brother Llewellyn."

I pulled out my notepad and pen and said, "You mind if I take some notes?"

He shrugged and said, "Fine by me. It ain't no big secret."

"What's not?"

"What you're askin' about. The connection between Brother Lew and the Westcotts."

I did the math on the simple equation he had put before me. "Are you saying that Brother Llewellyn was a brother to Conrad Westcott? Like, an actual blood brother?"

"Sure was. Don't really see what the big deal is. Everybody knows they was brothers."

"Brother Simon didn't seem to know that."

He gave a dry laugh. "You got to understand that Brother Simon's old school. I mean, as retreat director, he likes to chat up the people who come to visit. Chats 'em up good. I think it's his way of connecting with the outside world. You know, gettin' to know people from various parts who come to visit. That's why he takes all them notes on people. Don't get me wrong, Simon's good at his job, but when he's not workin', he ain't exactly the talkative type, if you know what I mean."

"Not one to engage in idle chatter," I said reflectively.

"Nah, not Brother Simon. He takes his vows serious. Obeys all them old rules. I'd wager he never had a conversation with Brother Lew long enough to learn nothin' much about him. I mean when he was alive and all." He crossed himself.

"What about you? Did you have any conversations with Brother Lew?"

"Oh, sure. Brother Lew was an outgoin' sort. I mean, he was a good monk and all, but he loved talkin' to people. He'd talk a blue streak if you'd let him. Of course, when he did, he'd walk off with ya down a trail or someplace out of the way, so he didn't ruffle no feathers."

"A gregarious sort of guy, huh?"

"Oh, yeah. A good fella. And talented. He was real good with drawin' and woodwork, stuff like that. Reckon a guy like that, a talented outgoin' sort and all, must've really heard the call to come in here and not have no interactions with people on the outside."

"Wow," I said, thunderstruck by the information. "So, Brother Lew, before he came here, was Llewellyn Westcott."

Denny smiled like a man who's about to give you the inside scoop. "Like you said, you're still figuring this stuff out. So, here's a little bit of learnin' for ya. When a man comes into the monastic life, he leaves the name people knows him by and takes on a new name. You know, like he's got himself a new identity now that he's given his life to God."

I nodded, my pen deployed over the notepad. "So, what was Brother Llewellyn's name before he became a monk?"

"James Westcott. He was Connie Westcott's older brother. That's how come I said Isabelle Westcott was his sister-in-law. Now ya see?"

"Now I see," I said in a small voice. "A friend of the family."

"Come again?"

I waved the comment away and blew out a long, low whistle. I didn't yet know how this information was pertinent, but my gut told me it was something good to know.

"Denny, you have been one hell of a big help to me."

He gave me a wide grin. "Happy to do it, friend."

My brow furrowed and I chewed on my lip as I considered a new question. Denny's grin vanished as he leaned forward in anticipation as I said, "But there's still one thing I can't quite figure out."

"Shoot."

"It's just that Brother Simon said he got a call from someone he assumed to be Isabelle Westcott. You know, the call where she invited Moussa to dinner. I can't figure how she knew to make that call. How did she know Moussa was going to be at the monastery in the first place?" His lips drew together in a tight line as he considered my conundrum. "You know anything about that?"

"I reckon I might," he said in a cautious tone. "I mean, it's possible I do. You see..."

"What is it, Denny?"

He hesitated, rubbing his chin in an anxious gesture. "Well, back when Brother Lew died, Mr. and Mrs. Westcott was here for the funeral and all." He hesitated again, seemingly conflicted as to whether he should share what he knew.

"Okay, they were here for the funeral," I said, urging him onward. "And what?"

"Well, the thing is...ya see, it goes against policy. And I don't wanna get in no trouble. Hell, I got enough problem payin' high school tuition at Bethlehem for my oldest on top of my youngest being at St. Catherine's."

"I'm not here to get you in trouble, Denny. I'm trying to figure out what happened to a kid who got killed."

"But they arrested the man that done it. At least that's what the paper said."

"You're right, they arrested a man. But I think there might be something more to it. And if you can tell me something that might help me figure it out...well, it seems to me that'd be the right thing to do."

"Shit," he said. "Leave it to me to open my big mouth. My wife's gonna kill me."

I let him work through his moral dilemma in his own time. To my eventual relief, some variable in the ethical equation must have fallen into place, prompting him to act in my favor.

"Like I said before, when Brother Lew died the Westcotts was here for the funeral. And well, there was a letter that had just arrived. I think it come the day before and it was addressed to Brother Llewellyn. I thought, why not give it to his family? That goes against policy, ya see, but I figured they'd be the ones to eventually get it anyway, so what the hay."

"Who was the letter from?"

"Well, I didn't make the connection at the time. But now...well, I guess it was from the boy's mama."

"Hamia Diab?" I said, my heart picking up a pace. "Was the letter from Hamia Diab?" He dropped his head and groaned. I felt bad for the guy, but I needed to know. "Look, it's important that you tell me who sent that letter to Brother Llewellyn. Was it Hamia Diab?"

His head bobbed up and down. Then he looked up at me with a deflated expression and said, "Yeah. That was the name. Kinda' hard to forget bein' that it's not one you see every day."

"You did the right thing, Denny. I'm grateful."

He gave me a wry half-smile and said, "Me and my big mouth."

"You got nothing to worry about, my friend. Mum's the word."

As I drove back to *The Observer*, my initial excitement at learning about the connection between Brother Llewellyn and Conrad Westcott was tempered a bit by the realization that such information might already be common knowledge. After all, Denny had said it was no big secret, so it occurred to me that it might be nothing more than an explanation for why Moussa was invited to dinner. But the more I thought about it, the more difficult it was to square that explanation with the fact that Westcott denied an invitation was ever proffered in the first place.

There must be something more to this, I thought. *And whatever it is, that's what Sandoval is after. And it could be that Conrad Westcott is after it, too.*

With that thought in mind, my initial excitement, having gone from heightened to tempered, was piqued yet again by the notion that the nexus of the entire investigation might be something Conrad Westcott and Regina Sandoval thought Moussa Diab knew or had. If that was so, then something about my brief encounter with Moussa was the real impetus for Regina Sandoval's inquiry into my story, and her stated purpose of finding out what really happened to the young pilgrim was nothing more than a ruse.

"What is it I'm supposed to know that I don't know that I know?"

The answer to that question, I surmised, would lead me to whatever it was that Sandoval and Westcott wanted from Moussa Diab. But at the moment, whatever it might be remained a total mystery.

Arriving at *The Observer*, I rushed inside the building and called out for Dominick, but he either hadn't arrived, or had arrived and left. I thought about paging him, but I felt too restless to sit and wait for him to call back. Instead, I drove around town for the better part of an hour trying to spot him, but without luck. That didn't sit right with me. After all, he said the sheriff's deputy he needed to talk to was on duty, and I couldn't imagine it would have taken this long to get Hamia Diab's phone number. I mean, since we left the bowling alley, I had quizzed Olive McGill about Conrad Westcott and driven to the monastery where I had engaged in a substantive conversation with Denny the postmaster.

"You're telling me he couldn't find that deputy and call his friend to get Hamia Diab's number in the time it took me to do all of that?"

What the hell is he up to? I thought. *It's not like him to say he's going to be somewhere and to not only not show up, but to be scarce around town.*

Still, I didn't see that there was anything left for me to do. By the time I gave up the search for Dominick, it was too late to call Hamia Diab even if I did have her phone number. My tank was about empty, but I wasn't ready for the day to end. So, I pulled up to the curb in front of the tavern on the courthouse square with the queasy sensation that I was returning to the scene of the crime. I went inside, sat at the bar, and ordered a beer and a shot of my usual.

"You know what, scratch that," I said to the bartender. "Make it a shot of Old Royal."

The bartender brought the beer and the shot of bourbon, but just as I was about to sample the goods, Daphne Rose sidled up beside me.

"What is light if Daphne be not seen?"

"Hmm. That sounds nice. But it'll take more than pretty words to impress me."

"Sounds nice is good enough for me," I said, lighting a cigarette.

"Can I ask you something, Levi?"

"No, I'm not married."

She shot me an ironic smile and said, "What a relief."

"Okay then, yes. I am the handsome galoot who tried unsuccessfully to sweep you off your feet last night. And wouldn't you know it, I'm back to try again."

"If at first you don't succeed...but that's not my question."

I let out a deep sigh and said, "Then it looks like the well of my conjecture has run dry. So, what's the question?"

She gave me a sad look and said, "You know how we all have a devil that sits on one shoulder, and an angel that sits on the other?" I looked at her, waiting. "My question is, do you ever listen to the angel?"

I gave her a wan smile and said, "Well, you see, Miss Rose, the thing is...that angel? She talks to me. But my problem is I think too much, and it's the devil who hears my thoughts." I downed the shot of Old Royal. "And that bastard's a damn good listener."

Her sad eyes dropped to the floor.

"I suppose I owe you an apology."

"You don't owe me anything."

"Well, I'm told I almost tore up the place with my old buddy Coleridge."

"Oh please," she said, looking up with a spark in her eyes. "Lance Coleridge has got sugar in his britches. He'd never stand up to you. He might try if he's got a posse of his loser friends around. But even then, my money's on you."

"It's probably a bad idea to drop a bet on my nose, Daph."

She looked at me with a sense of pained longing, like I was sitting on the other side of the world instead of right in front of her, and she just wanted to reach out and touch me.

"You know something, Levi Motley? I'd probably fall in love with you if I thought you'd be around long enough to learn how to love me back."

My throat tightened and I cast my eyes downward, not knowing what to say. Daphne leaned in and kissed me. Then she turned and walked away. And I wanted to stand up and go after her.

But I didn't.

CHAPTER
TWENTY

AFTER MY ENCOUNTER with Daphne, I headed home to crash for the night. That was a prudent move, as I was set to cover an event at the Oscar Getz Whiskey Museum the next day. An evening with bourbon historian Randall J. Minkins was to feature a presentation on the early roots of the industry going all the way back to Elijah Craig, the Baptist minister who first distilled bourbon in 1789. But the doors didn't open until six o'clock with the program scheduled to begin at six-thirty, so I had plenty of time to track down Dominick and grieve him for not updating me on his part of the investigation.

"What happened to you yesterday? You never showed up at the office, and I couldn't track you down anywhere around town."

Dominick cleared his throat and said, "I have a private life, you know."

"Meaning what?"

"Meaning someone of a feminine persuasion who is a damn sight more appealing than you got to me first."

"Okay, well that is a pretty good explanation. But you could have at least let me know what you found out."

"How the hell am I supposed to do that, Motley? With smoke signals?"

His caustic remark might have landed for points had not the grief I'd taken over not having a phone led me to call the phone company and put in a work order to get a line hooked up. "So, there," I said in a petulant tone. "Now what'd you learn from that deputy?"

"Dude wouldn't hardly say anything. I asked about the shovel, and he said, 'What the hell are you asking me Cotter, whether a shovel's a freaking shovel?' I told him I wanted to know what kind of shovel it was, and he said, 'Get a picture of a shovel in your head. Got it?' I said, 'Yeah.' So, he says, 'Good, now leave me alone.'"

"What the hell does that mean?"

"I took him to mean it was a regular shovel."

"A regular shovel," I said, confused. "But that's not what Jerry Edelen showed me."

"It is what it is," he said with a shrug. "So did you head home?"

"No," I said, still trying to puzzle through the deputy's description of the shovel.

Dominick's eyebrows rose into his forehead as he waited for more. I proceeded to fill him in about my most recent visit to the monastery, including the new information that there was a familial link between Brother Llewellyn and Conrad Westcott. I also shared the interesting tid-bit that Denny the postmaster had given Isabelle Westcott a letter from Hamia to Brother Lew while she was attending Brother Lew's funeral.

"Hence, the Westcotts knew of Moussa's impending arrival."

"Nice work," he said, looking impressed.

"Yeah well, I was lucky, and Denny was talkative. A fortunate combi-nation. But what about Hamia Diab? Were you able to get her number?"

Dominick produced the phone number. I praised him for the gen-tleman and scholar that he was and headed home to break in my new phone. During my conversation with Mrs. Diab, it evolved that she and her husband, Nassar, emigrated to the United States from Lebanon in 1974. They remained in Louisville until 1981, when a friend of Nassar presented a business opportunity in the automotive industry that took them to Detroit. By that time, Moussa was four years old, so most of his formative years were spent in Motor City, U.S.A.

Hamia was gracious throughout our discussion, answering my ques-tions despite the grief of having lost her son. Of course she remembered me, saying that she would be forever grateful for the kindness I had shown Moussa. And then she a did curious thing. She gushed with profound appreciation for my attempt to learn the truth about what happened to her son.

"I'm a bit surprised to hear you say that Mrs. Diab."

"Why would this surprise you?"

"Well, I recently met with a reporter who said she had spoken to you about her intent to dig deeper into Moussa's case. This reporter said that you were lukewarm to the idea of her investigating Moussa's death to see if there was more to what happened." The line hummed for several seconds. "Mrs. Diab?"

"Yes, I am here. Mr. Motley, no reporter has contacted me. At least not prior to your phone call. But if I had been contacted, I most certainly would have been grateful that someone was advocating for my son."

"I see. Then may I ask if someone other than a reporter contacted you? Someone asking questions about the case, or about Moussa's time at the monastery?"

"Yes, I was contacted by someone inquiring about Moussa's case."

"Was it a woman?"

"Yes. She was from the United States Attorney's office in Louisville. She said she was looking into whether federal charges should be filed in the case of Moussa's death."

"Do you have the woman's name?"

"I wrote it down. Just a minute." Again, the line hummed as I waited in eager anticipation. "Her name was Cynthia Wilcox."

I wrote the name in my notepad. "And what did Miss Wilcox want to know?"

"She wanted to know about Moussa, about why he was making the pilgrimage to Gethsemani. She wanted to know of his plans, if he was going to meet anyone specific when he arrived. Those kinds of things."

"Did you tell her about Brother Lew?"

"I told her that Brother Lew had been a friend to me for many years, and that he had arranged a quest for Moussa. A quest that would lead to a great treasure."

"A great treasure?"

"Well, that's what his letter said. But you would have to know Brother Lew to understand his meaning. You see, he loved to create quests that would lead a person to some kind of spiritual enlightenment. Kind of like a spiritual treasure hunt."

"Did you explain that to Miss Wilcox?"

"I did, but she pressed me on this point, speculating that this treasure might have been real and that it could have been motivation for the man who killed Moussa. I told her she did not understand Brother Lew and his ways, but she didn't seem to hear me. So, I decided to say no more on that point."

Hamia went on to explain that she and Brother Lew had become friends during her time in Louisville. They met in 1987 when Hamia and Nassar were on a guided retreat at the monastery. Brother Lew had spoken on the topic of the spirituality of St. Francis de Sales, and Hamia had several questions for him following his talk.

"His personality was such that he couldn't help but make friends with people," she said. "I liked him right away."

"Did you have any contact with him before he died?"

She took a moment before answering. When she did respond, I could hear the emotion in her voice. "I had not seen him for three years. I was sad that I could not go to his funeral, but my husband has been having health problems, and we could not travel. But to answer your question, yes. I received a letter from him this past August. That was the last time I heard from Brother Lew. I replied to his letter just before he died."

"I'm sorry, Mrs. Diab. From what I've heard Brother Lew was a great guy."

"Indeed, he was. Warm, funny, talented. And above all, a true follower of Our Lord."

I asked her about the contents of the letter she had sent to Brother Lew. She explained that it was mostly pleasantries. She said she had thanked Brother Lew for his prayers for her husband, and for all that he was doing for Moussa. She said she spoke of Moussa's discernment regarding the priesthood and his effort to understand God's call in his life.

"And I thanked him for sending the book."

"The book?"

"The King Arthur book," she said. "It was one of Brother Lew's prized possessions given to him by his father when he was a boy. He mailed it to Moussa before he left Louisiana. It was part of Moussa's quest."

"Did you tell all of this to Miss Wilcox?"

"Yes, of course. I wanted her to have all the available information."

I asked Hamia if she thought there really was more to what happened to her son. She answered by speaking about her faith and how she believed she would see Moussa again in Heaven. But she also said that justice in this world is important, and that she was skeptical Moussa's death was as random as the supposed facts made it appear.

"I am not naïve, Mr. Motley. I know how the color of a person's skin can fan enflame a man's hatred. I do not understand why this is so, but I know it is true all the same. But Moussa was a gentle young man. So, the idea that he incited this man's rage is preposterous. That's why I think it is just that you are seeking the complete truth on behalf of my son."

Hearing this gave me a sense of encouragement. But I also had to admit to a twinge of guilt in that I didn't know whether I was pursuing this so-called "complete truth" in the interest of justice, or because I was pissed off at being played by the mystery woman who now had two known aliases.

"Have you heard anything more from Cynthia Wilcox?"

"Not yet. But it has only been two weeks, so I am hopeful."

I felt a flash of shame and wondered if I should tell her the truth. But I decided to stay silent on the matter, reasoning that I needed to better understand Miss Duplicity's purpose before dropping that information on Moussa's grieving mother. We talked further about the dinner invitation, and Hamia confirmed that Moussa had shared that information with her by phone. She said when she pressed her son on the matter, he blew it off. He was more interested in telling her about his journey from Louisiana to Kentucky than he was talking about a random dinner invite.

"He was a typical young man. He was excited about his adventure, about being at the monastery. I don't think he gave much thought to the invitation."

"Do you know the Westcott family?"

"I do not," she said, to which I let out a frustrated sigh. "What is it?"

"Well, it's just that I was told the reason the Westcotts invited Moussa to dinner was because they're friends of your family. Sounds like that's not true."

"I do not know these people," she said in a definitive tone.

"Well, it turns out that Brother Lew was the brother, the sibling, of Conrad Westcott. Did you know that?"

"I knew that he had a brother. But he never spoke about him. The one time I asked him about his family, he became uncharacteristically somber, so I didn't push him on the subject."

"Did you tell Miss Wilcox about the invitation?"

"Yes. As I told you, I wanted her to have any information that could possibly help my son."

As we wrapped up our conversation, she again thanked me for my kindness both to her son and to Mrs. Diab herself, when we had spoken during her time in Bardstown.

"I believe that you were meant to meet my son, Mr. Motley. I believe that your path and his path were meant to cross."

I was silent for a moment, knowing I had heard this before, though not from Hamia Diab. Finally, I said, "Mrs. Diab, did you share what you just said with Cynthia Wilcox? Did you share how you feel about me helping your son?"

"Oh, yes. I told her that I believe in God's providence, and that there is meaning in the intersection of our lives and the lives of those we meet. Especially when that meeting occurs through charity."

After we hung up, I sat for some time trying to reconcile my strange sense of ironic confusion. If what Hamia said to me was true, that there was meaning or providence in how we cross paths with others, then what a special thing it had been for my life to have intersected with the life of her son. But then I also had to consider what to make of my life's intersection with a hypocrite like Sandoval. And how could I resolve the fact that it was her duplicity that got me into this pursuit?

And what is this pursuit about? I thought. *Truth or retribution?*

As I considered the question, a rumbling in my stomach brought me back to more practical matters. Deciding the question of motivation would eventually work itself out, I picked up my satchel and headed down to The Prep Room to grab a quick bite before the event in the whiskey museum.

CHAPTER
TWENTY-ONE

Sam Everett moonlighted at The Prep Room to supplement his teacher's salary, and in his words, to keep on the right side of the bar. I told him if that's what bartending was all about, then maybe I should give it a shot, pun intended. I hadn't caught his name when Dominick and I had shut the place down during my first night in town, but during subsequent visits I had come to know him as a solid guy who shared my sense of wanderlust.

"I love teaching," he said as I sat at the bar with my dinner. "And I know it's a cliché to say the summers off are great, but they are pretty killer for a guy who wants to see at least some of the world before his ass gets chained to the stake of domesticity."

"Damn, brother. You make it sound like death and taxes."

"Nah, I know I got a choice. And I'm probably overdramatizing the stable life as some kind of soul-sucking existence."

"No, I suspect you probably have that part about right," I said with a dry laugh.

He smiled as he wiped down the bar. "Actually, I really do want the house and the picket fence and the wife and two-point-five kids. But before that day comes, I want to be able to inspire my students to go out and at least get a taste of what the world has to offer. Seems to me I'd be a hypocrite if I told them to do something I never had the balls to do. Does that make any sense?"

"Perfect sense."

Sam excused himself to take care of a couple that had taken a seat at a high top. I ate in silence for a few minutes contemplating, to my chagrin, the topic of hypocrisy. Thankfully, I hadn't delved too deep into the topic before Sam returned to engage in more casual banter.

"Hey, you should come down here Wednesday night," he said.

"Why Wednesday?"

"It's Turkey Kick. The night before Thanksgiving. The whole town will be out on a bar crawl."

My mind wandered back to our college days when Dominick invited me to Bardstown for this annual tradition. I remembered having a hell of a good time as a twenty-year-old, hellbent on my own destruction and not giving a damn when it came. I also recalled, with a rueful cringe, that not a single person asked to see our I.D.'s, nor those of revelers who were obviously not of a legal drinking age.

"Yeah, good ol' Turkey Kick," he said. "The place will be wall to wall with college kids getting hammered. Looking for a security gig?"

"Hell no. Sounds like a nightmare."

"Fair enough," he said with a laugh. "So, what do you have going on tonight?"

"Covering an event in the museum upstairs. An author giving a talk on a book he just put out."

"Topic?"

"Well, the talk is in a whiskey museum, so..."

"Right. You gonna be out later?"

"Eh, doubtful," I said. "I might come back down and bug you for a while, but beyond that...let's just say I'm due for a chill evening at home."

"Yeah, I get that. Well, either way, I'll be here."

"On the right side of the bar," I said.

"You got it, my man."

The Oscar Getz Museum of Whiskey History boasted an astounding array of posters, advertisements, bottles, and rare artifacts such as Abraham Lincoln's liquor license, and a still that reputedly belonged to George Washington. I gazed at the items with interest, stopping to study a poster that featured a tuxedoed courtier sitting wide-eyed and despondent beneath a heading that read "Every Day Will be Sunday when the Town Goes Dry". I chuckled at that facetious proposition and continued along, stopping at a piece of prohibition propaganda titled "The Drunkard's Progress from the First Glass to the Grave".

"And upon which step in the drunkard's journey do you find yourself, Mr. Levi?"

I was unsurprised to look over and find that Olive McGill was on hand for the evening's program.

"Well, today I'm on step two, 'a glass to keep the cold out,'" I said, examining the poster. "But I have admittedly been, on a recent occasion, somewhere between 'drunk and riotous' and 'the summit achieved with jolly companions.'"

"On a recent occasion?" she said with a slight frown. "Even so, you have recovered well enough to look lively this evening."

I gave her an ironic smile as I pointed at the poster and said, "Well, that's because I've not yet reached the stage of being 'forsaken by friends', which appears to be a precursor to 'desperation, crime, and death by suicide.'"

She gave a dubious grunt and said, "I shall try to take heart that you are not only well shy of those deleterious effects, but also aware that such possibilities exist. Perhaps Prohibition-era slogans can have a positive effect, after all."

"I guess so. Especially since I just turned down an invitation to hoot with the owls at the upcoming Turkey Kick festivities. Although you can probably chalk that up to common sense more than anti-booze propaganda."

"A vulgar display of intemperate indulgence," she said, frowning. "The city leaders really should put an end to that nonsense. But I'm sure they fear a revolt of the local barkeeps if they were to so much as lift a finger to try."

The next poster in the display featured an armored woman sitting on a horse and wielding an ax in defense of the temperance league. Behind her a banner read "In the Name of God and Humanity".

"Sounds like you would have been on her side back in the day," I said, pointing to the poster.

Her face took on that imperious look I had come to recognize as her default reaction to being challenged in a way she didn't care for. "I most certainly would not. Prohibition shuttered the doors of more than half the working distilleries in this state. For a Kentuckian it was the political and economic equivalent of cutting off your nose to spite your own face."

"So, then you're not opposed to people taking a drink?"

"Of course not. I am a daughter of the bourbon capital of the world. And besides that, I am a believer in the free exercise of personal will."

I adopted a scholar's pose and said, "And let us not forget the wise words of Judge Harry McGill, by way of Aristotle, who said that moderation is the key to happiness."

She straightened her back and looked at me with a mixture of pride and pleasure. "I do believe your time in our fair town has had a positive impact on you, Mr. Motley."

"Yeah, well like another wise man once told me, it's never too late this side of the dirt."

She considered this for a moment and said, "Well, that is putting it a bit simplistically. But then Judge Harry McGill always did say that simplicity is the seal of truth." I arched my eyebrows and gave her a sidelong glance. "Young man, there is no shame in repeating the great pearls of wisdom that have been passed down through time. After all, does not the Book of Ecclesiastes tell us there is nothing new under the sun?"

With that, we continued down the hall, stopping at a display of plates hanging above a case filled with artistically rendered bottles, some of which were no longer extant. There was Cream of Kentucky, an eighty proof with a heart-shaped label pierced by an arrow; Old Woodpecker, which featured what else but a red-headed woodpecker sitting in a tree; Old Rosebud with its narrow neck and fat body displaying a jockey atop a thoroughbred; and Kentucky Owl, which had the intriguing image of a tugboat pulling a load of bourbon barrels away from a burning building.

"That's an interesting one."

"Ah, yes," she said. "The story goes that Al Capone stole a warehouse full of Kentucky Owl before it burned down at the hands of temperance zealots. Of course, it didn't burn down at all, and Mr. Capone was not a hero but a thief who spirited away, pun intended, a healthy number of barrels for sale on the black market. Thus, the label depicts that story."

I shook my head in appreciation and said, "Damn, I hope that tale is true."

"Indeed. Sometimes the mythology surrounding a bourbon is a more powerful marketing tool than its taste. It provides an air of mystery that consumers find alluring."

"What about that one," I said, pointing to a bottle sitting next to the Short Horn Club bottle.

"Old Relic," a man standing next to us said. "That was the Westcott distillery's original brand."

"A Westcott brand, huh?" I said. "How about that."

I studied the label, which was in the shape of a triangular shield of light green hue. Beneath the bourbon's name, written in gold script, was the neck and head of a snake. The image was white, outlined in black, and the snake had one red eye and a red tongue that lashed out toward a golden apple.

"Is that some kind of allusion to the Garden of Eden?"

"Could be," the man said with a shrug.

I looked over at Olive and saw that she was transfixed in her study of the image. "What do you think Miss Olive?" For a long moment she was silent, which was odd since Olive always had an answer to my questions no matter how esoteric. "Miss Olive? What do you think? The Garden of Eden?"

"Hmm. I suppose it could be." She appeared deep in thought. "But it reminds me of something else. Something on the edge of my memory that I can't quite recall."

She continued to study the image, as if burning it into her mind's eye as the man piped up and said, "I rolled barrels for Westcott for two summers back in college. It's not the biggest operation going, but they put out a damn good product."

"I just recently had my first taste of Old Royal," I said, nodding. "I'd have to say I agree with you."

"For a hundred proof whiskey, it's damn smooth. You can put that down to the way they..."

"Can you get a picture of this for me, Mr. Levi," Olive said, interrupting the man's point.

"For you, Miss Olive? Anything."

I thought at the very least that comment would elicit a roll of the eyes, but she remained lost in her study of the image. I took the photo and was assuring my curious companion that I would send it right over when a woman at the podium called out for people to begin moving toward their seats for the start of the presentation.

I moved around the room throughout most of the talk, capturing images of the speaker, the crowd, and the museum. Once the presentation ended, I looked around the room, trying to spot Olive as I wanted to get her take on the evening's topic, but she was nowhere to be found. So, after spending a few minutes with the historian to clarify some points from his talk, I made the prudent decision to forego the author-guided bourbon tasting and headed for the door.

The next day, I polished up and filed my article and developed the picture of the Old Relic label that Olive had asked for. I stopped by the stable to drop it off, but Olive wasn't around. So, I left the picture with Moots who promised to pass it along.

Later that week, John and Esther Cotter, who remembered me from previous visits with their son, graciously welcomed me to their home for Thanksgiving dinner. At some point after our second helping, I pulled Dominick aside and filled him in on my conversation with Hamia.

"Am I hearing correctly that you think there really is more to what happened to the kid?" he said. "Or are you still pursuing this because of Sandoval's trifling ways?"

"I've been asking myself that same question. I guess from a pragmatic standpoint, it doesn't really matter. Hamia Diab is appreciative of the effort, no matter what the motivation."

"She say anything interesting?"

"She said she was contacted by someone representing the U.S. Attorney's office. Someone named Cynthia Wilcox. You find that interesting?"

His eyes widened as he said, "You check it out?"

"Yep. No Cynthia Wilcox."

"Reppin' a U.S. Attorney's office," he said, shaking his head. "Damn, that's bold. You tell her?"

"Nah, not yet. I figure I need to know more. And who knows, maybe fake-Wilcox will contact her again, and we can find out what Sandoval is up to."

He nodded and said, "What else?"

"Mostly information about how she came to know Brother Lew, what kind of guy he was, stuff like that. She mentioned the letter he sent her."

"Anything interesting there?"

"She said Brother Lew commented on the great treasure Moussa was set to find on his quest."

"Great treasure? What's that mean?"

"She said it was all about a spiritual treasure. She said that Brother

Lew liked to create, I don't know...like, little adventures that would lead a person to discover something meaningful about themselves."

"Okay. That it?"

I thought about whether I should share Hamia's comments on my kindness toward Moussa and how our paths were meant to cross but decided to keep that part to myself. "Yeah, that's it."

"Cool," he said, rubbing his hands together. "Let's go back for round three."

The rest of Thanksgiving weekend passed quietly. On Sunday, I called Daphne, but she didn't answer. I let her machine know that I now had an honest-to-God phone number and told her to give me a call if she wanted. It wasn't until Monday that my phone finally rang, but it wasn't Daphne on the other end of the line. It was a secretary for the county attorney letting me know there was a package at their office with my name on it. I called her back and said, "What kind of package?"

"The kind that's wrapped up so that only the person it's meant for can unwrap it and find out what's inside," she said testily.

"Well, can you at least tell me who it's from?"

"The return address is Detroit. The sender's name is Ham-ya Dub."

"Hamia Diab," I said, correcting her flawed pronunciation.

"If you say so. Listen, if you wanna know more, then you can march your little feet over here and look at it your own self."

I did want to know more, so I marched my little feet over to the county attorney's office to pick up the package. Later, when I opened the package, I found a book, and inside the book I found a clue. Upon following that clue, I would come to find that Hamia Diab was right.

There is meaning in the way our paths cross the paths of others.

CHAPTER
TWENTY-TWO

THE FIRST TIME I met County Attorney Jack Merrick was a few days after Moussa's death. Hamia Diab had come to Bardstown to confront the tragedy of her son's death and since I was one of the last people to have spoken with Moussa, she asked to meet with me. Jack Merrick was present for that conversation, as he wanted to glean any information he could from the description of my encounter with Moussa. I found that to be reasonable, given he was still negotiating the plea deal with Dale Goodlett's attorney, Sidney Marksbury.

During that initial meeting, I found Mr. Merrick to be an equitable man who displayed open compassion in assisting Hamia with the enormous challenge of processing her son's death. Based on that experience, I thought Mr. Merrick's request to speak with me about the package Hamia had sent to his office would result in a meeting similar to our previous encounter. I was incorrect, as Jack Merrick wasted no time getting to the point.

"You know anything about this?" he said, tapping a package that sat on his desk.

I leaned forward to look at the package. It was wrapped in brown paper and bore a label with the county attorney office's address beneath the words "In the care of Levi Motley".

"I don't. And no offense, Mr. Merrick, but even if I did, I'm under no obligation to tell you about it."

"And here I thought you were a reporter, Mr. Motley. Hell, I didn't know you passed the Bar Exam."

"Look, I'm not trying to be confrontational. The simple answer is no. I don't know anything about this package."

"Well, then let's open her up and find out together. How'd that be?"

"I don't think so. That package is intended for me. I assume Mrs. Diab sent it here because I'm not in the phonebook."

"Maybe, maybe not," he said, leaning back in his chair. "After all, she knows you're a reporter. So why not send it to *The Observer*?"

"I don't know. I guess you'll have to ask the grieving mother of the man that was slain in your jurisdiction why she didn't mail this package to my place of employment instead of yours."

"It's a bad idea to stick your finger in my eye, young man," he said, leveling me with an icy glare. "My point is that a logical argument can be made that she mailed it to my office because she intended for me to know the nature of its contents."

"Or she didn't know my address."

County Attorney Merrick was an intimidating presence, broad-shouldered and sharp-witted. I understood that he was not a man to trifle with, especially given the weight of his office.

"What's your objection to opening the package here?"

"It's not an objection, it's a choice. My choice. But like you said, I'm no attorney. So, you tell me, Mr. Merrick. Do I, in fact, have a choice as to where I open a package intended for me?"

He studied me for a moment. "I hear you've been asking questions about Moussa Diab's death. That true?"

"Yes."

"Why?"

"Just exercising my rights as a member of the free press."

"But the case is closed. Dale Goodlett copped to it and took a deal. He's locked up, and you're out there stirring the pot, trying create a story where one doesn't exist."

"And you're free to exercise your right to express that view. But then again, I guess you know that since presumably, you did pass the Bar Exam." The tension between us was palpable. "Can I have the package now, Mr. Merrick?"

He tapped his index finger on the desk. "It's addressed to this office."

"And it clearly says, 'In the care of Levi Motley.'" He looked at me for a full minute without speaking. "You know, I should probably contact my editor." I stood as if to leave. "I'm sure it's not the first time George Hawley has had to defend the rights of one of his reporters against government overreach."

Jack Merrick chewed on his lower lip as he weighed his options. After another long moment of silence, he begrudgingly relented. "Take the package, Mr. Motley. And do let Mrs. Diab know your address for the purpose of any future deliveries."

I picked up the package and walked out without further comment. Back at my truck, I made a beeline for *The Observer* offices. But as I parked in front of the building, a police cruiser pulled in behind me. The cruiser's lights were not on, so I exited my truck and walked toward the building. Officer Nathan Hadley exited the cruiser, approached me on the sidewalk, and said, "Motley. You got a minute?"

"Officer Hadley. You seem to be in the habit of wanting to talk to me in public places."

"Maybe you should be grateful for that."

"Meaning what? That you're a guy that I don't want to meet in a dark alley?"

"Meaning I'll talk to you where I damn well please."

I spat on the sidewalk.

"You best be careful, boy."

"Careful of what?" I said, taking his measure.

He bristled as he squared up to me, but then he seemed to remember what he was about, and his posture relaxed. "I saw you leave Jack Merrick's office. I got some questions."

"You saw me leave?" I said with a grunt. "Guess you just happened to be driving by."

"Don't get all dramatic about it. I've got some questions you need to answer, that's all."

"I tell you what, officer, you wanna ask me some questions, then you give me your card, and I'll schedule a time to come to the station. We'll sit down and have us a nice conversation on the record. How'd that be?"

"We can go that way," he said, taking a step toward me. "But I'm trying to keep this, umm...what's the word a writerly sort like you might use? Conversational. That sound about right, paper boy?"

"You know what, I've got work to do. And that work doesn't include conversing with you, Hadley."

"Well, you sure seem to wanna converse with all sorts of other people. Especially that blackboy Cotter you're always with."

I felt a surge of adrenaline rush into my temples and my right fist, sore though it was, balled up involuntarily. He pointed to the package in my other hand and said, "Who's that from?"

I glared at him, silent.

"I said, who's that from?"

I tucked the package under my coat and folded my arms across my chest.

"I told you, you best be careful," he said, raising a finger to my face. "This ain't your town, and you ain't got no business asking questions about matters that don't concern you."

"And you've got no business trying to intimidate me, so you best be stepping the f..."

"Well now, lookie here." I turned to see George Hawley skipping down the steps. "Looks like we got us a regular old meeting of the minds. Yessir, it does, indeed. And what a mind to meet with," he said, smiling. "Say now, what can we do ya for, Nathan?"

"It's Officer Hadley."

"Aww, come on now. Let's not get all uppity about it. Hell, you can call me George if ya want."

"And you can call me Officer Hadley."

"Well, now, Nathan, we don't normally stand on formality around here. But if that's the way you wanna play it, then this here's reporter Levi Motley and you can call me George goddamn Hawley, editor of *The Bardstown Observer* newspaper. How's that sound to ya, Officer Nathan? Did you get it straight the first time, or do you want me to say it again?"

Hadley's glare shifted from me to George.

"Ya see, by God, if we gotta get all formalized in our titles, well I reckon we oughta get straight and formalized about the law, too. Now, how's that proposition sound to you, Mr. Crimefighter?"

He didn't speak, but the look of contempt on his face conveyed volumes.

"I mean, after all, you are an officer of the law, ain't that right, Officer Nathan? And the law, you know historically speaking and all, does derive I believe, from a little piece of paper known as the United States

Constitution. You've heard about that development, haven't you Mr. Law Officer?"

"I'm not violating the law by having a conversation," he said, his lip curling in disgust.

"Oh, oh, oh, is that what this is? Oh, well then, by all means let's converse. I'll start." George put his hand to his chin, feigning deep thought. "Well, shit fire, officer, I can't rightly think of one damn thing I got to say to you. What about you, reporter Motley? You got anything you wanna converse about with Officer Nathan the crimefighter?"

"Nope."

"Well then, I reckon what we got us here is a regular ol' one-sided conversation, officer. And bein' that's the case, I suppose you ought to get right on in that cruiser there and talk amongst you and yourself. What do you say there, Officer Nathan?"

He glared at me and then looked down at the arms folded across my chest. Then he spat on the sidewalk, turned, and walked back to his police cruiser.

"Well, gosh darn it, Motley, I'm freezin' my ever-lovin' tail off out here. Let's get inside."

As we entered the building, Rebecca gave me a look as if to say I saved your dumb ass, which was one, something that Dominick would've said, and two, accurate. I gave her an appreciative nod and walked down the hall with George.

"You know, Hawley, you might be a bigger smartass than I am."

"Ah, you got to learn to play the man not the hand, that's all."

"Meaning what?"

He stopped outside his office and turned to me with a serious look on his face. "Meaning what we do is important, and don't you forget it. Never willingly concede power over your own future to another man, Levi."

"I wasn't giving him power. I was standing up to a jackass on a power trip."

"And if you'd taken that swing? Who'd have the power then?" I dropped my eyes, conceding his point. "A man like Hadley wants you to get sideways, son. That's his game, and you better learn it."

"Okay."

"Don't okay me, Motley. It's not about defending your pride, it's about defending something greater than yourself, namely the democracy we stand for against people that will drag it through the mud for their own agenda. 'Bout time you figured that out."

I nodded and said, "Okay, but why the attitude toward Hadley?"

He looked at me with a sly smile and said, "'Cause he's an asshole, that's why."

George walked into his office and closed the door, and I walked down the hall to the spare office that day by day was becoming my own. Sitting at the desk, I placed the package before me and stared at the words "In the care of Levi Motley". I felt somewhat daunted, as if those words had meaning beyond merely listing me as the recipient of whatever contents the package held. But I also felt a rush of excitement, so I grabbed a pair of scissors, cut open the package, and laid its contents out on the desk. There was a book and a sealed envelope. I spoke the title of the book the same way I had when it sat between Moussa and me on the seat of my pickup.

"*The Boy's King Arthur.*"

I studied the cover, which displayed the image of two knights sitting astride warhorses, their swords drawn and at the ready, as a woman in a pale blue dress stood with her face buried in her hands. The scene unfolded in the shadow of a castle high atop a hill. I ran a hand over the book's cover and then set it aside, turning my attention to the envelope, the front of which read "To Levi, From Hamia". I opened it and found a folded sheet of paper tucked inside. It was dated one day after I had spoken to Hamia Diab the week before.

November 26, 1997

We meet the angels, the messengers of divine help, on the frontiers of our own freedom and our own capacity. They touch us when we reach our natural limits, when we ourselves are at the end of our strength, or of our endurance, or of our understanding, or of our capacity to hope and to believe. The angel appears when we ourselves are reduced to the center of our deepest need.

—Thomas Merton

Dear Levi:

Thank you for being an angel and messenger to my son.

May Christ's Love Guide You,

Hamia Diab

P.S. I have included a copy of Brother Llewellyn's letter from this
past August. Since you asked about the nature of my response,
I thought this letter would provide context so you may better
understand that to which I was responding. Please understand that
the original is dear to me, so a copy will have to suffice.

I STOOD AND quietly shut the office door. Returning to the desk, I read
Hamia's letter again before setting it gently on the desk. Picking up the
book, I turned to the title page, which read "Sir Thomas Malory's History
of King Arthur and his Knights of the Round Table". The copyright
year was 1922. As I flipped through the foxed pages, the book naturally
opened to a piece of folded paper marking one of the illustrations. I set
the paper aside and studied the illustration. It depicted a white-bearded,
wizened old man carrying a baby away from what looked like a stone castle. A maiden in a red dress with a light blue cloak and white habit looked
lovingly at the child in the old man's arms as two stoic knights stood in
sober observance of the scene. Beneath the illustration was a description
that read "So the child was delivered unto Merlin, and so he bore it forth".
I set the book down, unfolded the piece of paper, and read.

August 17, 1997

My Dear Friend, Hamia:

Greetings in the spirit of our Lord, Jesus Christ! It is my hope that
Moussa has received the book I mailed to his apartment in New
Orleans. The tales of King Arthur have given me great joy ever
since my father made a gift of *The Boy's King Arthur* to me when
I was just a boy, myself. As you know, I have strived even in these
later years to retain a sense of the questing spirit that I had as
a young boy when I explored the woods, fields, rivers, and knobs
of my beloved Nelson County. Even as I near completion of my
sixth decade, I hold to the sense of wonder that infuses this life
with adventure and joy. God has blessed me, my friend, and it is
my hope that the quest I have prepared for Moussa will be both
enjoyable and enlightening as he discerns the path that God

wills him to walk. After all, the Christian life is a journey, so let us celebrate along the way!

Though it has been three years since your last visit, I hold you and your dear husband in daily prayer, seeking the intercession of St. Raphael the Archangel as Nassar continues to adjust to the reality of his health limitations. Please know that your letters are a great source of joy to me, though I do hope you and Nassar will be able to join us at Gethsemani during our 150th jubilee next summer.

May the peace and love of Christ be with you and your family, Hamia. Until we meet again, I anticipate with great enthusiasm the quest that awaits Moussa upon his arrival at Gethsemani. Be it known that a great treasure of immeasurable value awaits the one who is worthy!

In the Friendship of Christ's Love,

Brother Llewellyn

I PLACED THE letter on the desktop and put my head in my hands. For a long time, I contemplated all that had happened since the day I saw Moussa Diab holding his cryptic sign. I thought about Hamia's belief that my path and Moussa's were supposed to cross, and how she found meaning in the brief time that we shared together. And then I thought about my life and the choices I'd made, wondering if I had the depth to believe those choices had really led me to this moment. I picked up Hamia's letter, looking closely at the name of the man she quoted, Thomas Merton. Then I read one of his lines out loud.

"The angel appears when we ourselves are reduced to the center of our deepest need."

As I pondered those words, I considered for the first time that maybe it was Moussa Diab who had been the good Samaritan, the angel of God's Providence, and that the man in need of help had been none other than Levi Motley. I picked up the book, and again leafed through the pages. It didn't take long to discover another piece of paper tucked next to the illustration of an armored knight mounted on his steed at the edge of a vast ocean. The description beneath the illustration read "When Sir Percival came nigh to the brim, and saw the water so boisterous, he doubted to overpass it".

With a deep sigh, I picked up the piece of paper and saw it contained a message for...

Who? I thought. *Moussa? Me?*

I read the message, which turned out to be a clue.

✝✝✝

"The secret of the Holy Grail, the Cup of Christ, resides at the Abbey of Our Lady of Gethsemani.

To find the place where it hides, you must first follow the clues and then solve the mystery.

A questing man, stout of heart and clear of mind, will surely discover where the Grail stays.

Lift your eyes to Almighty God above, for He is the True North that will guide you on your way.

For it is true, my friend, the Secret of the Grail lives here.

Not discovering this Sacred Truth is now your only fear.

Begin from whence the wizard emerged gently bearing the child,

And find that place that stands in the land of Lancelot the Wild.

Therein find the hearth, and the brick that appears askew,

For upon its smooth face is written the second clue".

M.O.T.G.Q.

B.L.

CHAPTER
TWENTY-THREE

Looking at the objects laid out on the desk, I couldn't help but laugh in wonder at what I had gotten myself into. The book, the letter, the clue. Each represented an element of a spiritual quest that had been designed by a now deceased monk and intended for the now deceased hitchhiker I had picked up and taken to, of all places, Gethsemani.

"What the hell am I supposed to do with this?"

It was an honest question. I really didn't know what to do. I had reasoned that Moussa's death though tragic, was probably the result of him being in the wrong place at the wrong time in the wrong skin. And even if his killing hadn't been racially motivated, I fundamentally agreed with Jerry Edelen's point that a man can't go wandering into places where he's not invited. Sad as it was, that's what I thought probably happened.

Then there's Sandoval, I thought. *But how can I accept anything she said as pertinent to the truth when it was offered under the guise of deception?*

"On the other hand, why would she go to such lengths unless there's something to all of this? And there's the connection between Brother Lew and Conrad Westcott to consider."

I shook my head, befuddled. After struggling for some time with the question of my underlying motivation to pursue the matter of Moussa's death, I had finally admitted to myself that I was primarily driven by a sense of wanting to find out who Regina Sandoval was and what her beguiling presence in my life had been about. But what now? It was clear that Hamia Diab had a deep belief in both my encounter with her son and my pursuit of the truth regarding his death. After all, she had made me the guardian of a quest that was not mine to pursue.

"Or is it?"

I picked up the letter from Hamia and silently read another of Merton's lines.

"We meet the angels, the messengers of divine help, on the frontiers of our own freedom and our own capacity..."

"At the point of our deepest need," I said, finishing the thought.

Just then, there was a knock at the door followed by George poking his head around the corner.

"Speaking of angels."

"From your lips to God's ears." I shook my head and chuckled. "It's good to see you laughing, Motley. Very good, indeed. But you've been in here so long I thought I might have to bring in food and water."

"I'm good on that front, George. What I need is sage advice."

He made a move like he was going to flee down the hall. "That's a damn dangerous thing to ask of a man, Motley. It is, indeed. But I do recall a verse from the Good Book that says something about a father not givin' his son a stone when he asks for bread. Not to imply I'm your daddy, you see, but do you remember that one?"

"Been a while since I went to Sunday School."

"Yeah, I reckon that's true for me, too, but that one had some stayin' power."

He sat and regarded me with a serious look. I sighed and said, "I don't wanna go through the whole rigmarole right now. Let's just say I'm at an impasse."

"What's standing in your way?"

"A question of whether I'm getting too personally invested by taking on something that wasn't meant for me. Does that make sense?"

"Sure, it does. There's been plenty of times I've had to ask myself that same question. But you didn't ask for my experience, you asked for my advice. Problem is, I ain't no sage, so I need to ask a couple of questions to try and give you what you're looking for." He leaned forward in his chair. "First off, if this thing wasn't meant for you, then who was it meant for?"

"Moussa Diab."

"I had a feeling you might say that. What is it people normally say about such things? It's a damn shame or some variation on that theme?"

"That's what they normally say."

"Well, there ya go. It's a damn shame, just like people say. But if this thing was meant for him, then how is it it's landed on you?" I pointed to the book and the documents on the desk. "Try to be more specific son. I got eyes, but a little exposition is part of the writer's job after all."

"It's a book that belonged to him, and a letter that sheds light on what he was doing at the monastery. And there's also...a clue."

"Umm-hmm. And you came to be in possession of these, how?"

"His mother sent them to me."

"And why'd she do that?"

"She has it in mind that there was some reason why my path crossed her son's path, and well..." He waited. "I think she thinks I was part of his, I don't know...part of his quest." He kept waiting. "Hell, I don't know, George. I guess she thinks that I'm supposed to pick up the ball and run with it."

"And is that what Nathan Hadley was snoopin' around about?"

I shrugged and said, "I don't know what else."

He looked at me for a long moment. Then he slapped his hands on his thighs, stood, and walked toward the door.

"Hey. What about the sage advice?"

"Aw, get the hell outta here," he said with a frustrated wave.

"What do you mean?"

He turned to look at me and I was surprised to see contempt in his expression as he said, "What I mean is you're one of them sorts that likes to tie himself in knots just to have the challenge of getting out of it. You're like that, what's his name, that magician guy. Houdini. Yessir, that's the one. That Houdini guy. That's you, Motley. You wrap yourself up in chains and throw yourself in the river just to prove you can get out of it and swim to shore. Well, shit fire, son, I say to hell with the chains. Just jump in the damn river and have yourself a swim for cryin' out loud."

"That's your advice?" I stood and ran a hand through my hair as I paced the room. "Seems like you gave me a stone there, pops."

He pursed his lips and said, "Well perhaps that was a bit harsh."

"A bit?" He motioned for me to have a seat. "I don't wanna sit. I'd rather go find Nathan Hadley and beat the shit out of him."

"And I'd like to join in that worthy task. But then we'd both be in jail, and Cotter would have to bail our asses out." He walked over to me and put his hand on my shoulder. "If this work ain't meant for you, if it's not yours to pursue, then what's it doing sittin' there on your desk? I'll tell you what. That dead boy's mama gave you the opportunity to pick up where her son left off. Meaning she chose you to find what her son barely had a chance to get after."

I shook my head as I turned to look out the window. It seemed apropos that there was no view on this side of the building other than the brick wall of the neighboring building, which I found myself dumbly staring at.

"At some point in our lives, we all got to dive into the deep end, Levi. That's how a man finds out who he is. Life gives you enough of a burden. I can't see how them chains you like to wrap around you are gonna do anything other than make you sink."

I heard him, but did not turn to face him.

"You may not think that's any kinda sage advice, son. But it damn sure ain't no stone, neither."

He walked out, closing the door behind him.

CHAPTER
TWENTY-FOUR

FOR A FEW days after my conversation with George, I wrestled with his assessment of what was holding me back from acting on the quest that Hamia Diab had apparently placed in my care. When I first received and opened the package from Mrs. Diab, I was filled with what I thought must have been the sense of wonder that Brother Simon had described as being in short supply in the world today. But when reality set in and I was faced with the responsibility of doing something about that sense of wonder, I defaulted to my typical position of cynicism.

As I wrestled with what to do, I thought about wonder and cynicism, imagining those two feelings as poles on opposing ends of a worldview continuum. It occurred to me that despite all the wandering I had done, I had mostly been tethered to the latter pole, and I wondered if I could change that. It was with the question of change in mind that I entered the monastery and walked down the hall toward the retreat director's office.

Brother Simon didn't appear overly pleased to see me darkening his doorway. Being the honest man that he was, Denny had relayed the content of our conversation to him, and the wary monk seemed to think that I had cajoled the impressionable postmaster into talking about things that were better left alone. I assured him that was not the case, and that I had come to the monastery that day looking to speak to Brother Simon himself but instead found Denny sitting in his office. When I explained that it was Denny who had been eager to open up to me, the monk shook his head, lamenting the idle chatter of those who were better off biting their tongues.

"Let your yes be your yes, and your no be your no," he said. "Anything else is from the Evil One."

"That seems a bit harsh. I don't think Denny meant any harm, much less any evil."

"Of course not. I simply mean that a man is bound by his oath, and he must remember that oath in matters great and small." He looked at me sternly. "What oath binds you, young man?"

"I'm still trying to figure that out, brother. But I'm working on it."

He nodded and said, "That's a fair answer. But still, there must something driving you onward."

I considered that and said, "I suppose right now it's Moussa. I mean, I haven't made any oath or vow, but...well, I guess I'm at least trying to leave some good tracks in my search for the truth."

"So you are now of a mind that that there is a truth to be found?"

"I suppose I am. I don't know what it is, but there is some truth to know in all this."

His posture relaxed a bit, and he sighed. "Well, one often comes away with new information despite oneself when conversing with dear Denny. But if you came here today expecting that I have information not previously disclosed, then you are bound for a disappointment."

"I admit that I'm looking for some information, but it's not something you could have previously disclosed. You see, I need help deciphering something." He looked bemused, so I clarified my meaning. "I'm trying to find...a place."

I pulled out my notepad, which contained the notes I had scribbled down at the office. Despite my initial trepidation, I had delved into the King Arthur book, looking for anything that might be related to the clue that Brother Lew had left for Moussa. It was clear that the bit in the clue about the place from whence the wizard emerged with the child referenced the illustration depicting Merlin carrying the baby away as the maiden wept. I learned that the baby was the son of Uther Pendragon and was given up after Pendragon ordered the knights to deliver the child "to what poor man you meet at the postern gate of the castle". Based on the text and the picture, it was not difficult to surmise that Brother Lew's clue referenced a castle as the place from whence Merlin bore the baby away. But what was the likelihood that a castle existed somewhere on the grounds of a monastery in rural Kentucky?

Unless it's a reference to the monastery itself, I had thought.

But that didn't seem to jibe with the next part of the clue, which stated that the castle stood in the place of Lancelot the Wild. Finding the chapter on Lancelot, I discovered an illustration of the famed knight appearing, I was surprised to see, as a bedraggled man living "by fruit and such as he might get" as he ran wild in the woodlands. Based on this information, the only explanation I could come up with was that the clue referenced a castle in the woods.

Brother Simon gave me a quizzical look and said, "And what is this place you are looking for?"

"I don't know exactly, but I think it's here on the grounds of the monastery." I was a bit embarrassed to lay it out there, thinking I wouldn't blame him if he found this all wildly implausible. Still, I summoned my courage and took a leap of faith. "I don't know if this makes any sense, Brother Simon, but I think I'm looking for a castle in the woods."

To my surprise, he didn't find the idea to be crazy. Instead, he seemed to be considering the matter with some care. "There are various structures in the woods surrounding the abbey, and there are other properties adjacent to our own. But you must understand that the surrounding area encompasses thousands of acres. How do you know the place you seek is on monastic property?"

I hesitated to reveal the full extent of what I was pursuing, but he had been honest with me, so it seemed only fair that I reciprocate. "Brother, you've been generous with your time and open with the information you shared about Moussa and his stay here." He gave me an expectant if somewhat wary look. "Moussa's mother gave me the King Arthur book that Moussa brought to the monastery. There's a clue in the book that indicates Moussa was supposed to go to this castle or whatever, to find another clue. I don't know where it all leads, but I've decided to follow the path that Moussa was on."

"And you think this will reveal what exactly?"

"I don't know. Hamia Diab said this was all part of some kind of spiritual scavenger hunt that Brother Lew designed for her son."

He gave a wistful smile. "That sounds like Brother Llewellyn."

"So, you did know Brother Lew?"

"Know him? Of course. Brother Llewellyn came to the monastery in nineteen-sixty-two, and I arrived in sixty-five. That means I was a brother to the man for thirty-two years."

"Well, I don't mean to be, umm...rude or anything. But I've heard that you aren't exactly chummy with the other monks."

I thought that might offend him, but he gave a soft laugh. "Denny," he said, shaking his head. "Perhaps I am not, as you say, chummy, but I am sincere in the fraternal bond I share with other members of this community. Brother Llewellyn was a good man, and whether I engaged in small talk with him or not, I know my guests, and many of them looked forward to the adventures that Brother Lew devised for them. They would often show me some artistic component of the adventure that he created. These became cherished objects for many of our guests. So, while I may not have known his family background, I knew of his propensity toward these spiritual scavenger hunts, as you referred to them."

I raised my hands, surrendering to his guidance. "Well, here I am on one of those hunts. And believe me, this is not a place I ever expected to find myself."

"Is that so?" he said, giving me a narrow look. "Perhaps in the future you will become more open to the guidance of the Holy Ghost?"

I gave a nervous chuckle and said, "At this point, I'd have to say anything is possible."

He regarded me closely. "For those that are led by the Spirit of God are children of God." I gave him a blank stare. "From Paul's letter to the Romans."

I didn't know what to say to that, so I kept silent, waiting to see if he would help me.

"So, you're looking for a castle in the woods, is that it?"

"I think so."

"Hmm. Well, I hate to disappoint you, but while there are hermitages and other such buildings on our property, I am not aware of any castles. Why a castle, anyway?"

"The clue references an illustration in the book that shows a door to a stone structure, which I take to be a castle. I guess I'd call it a stone castle."

He looked pensive. "A stone castle?"

"That's what it looks like to me," I said with a shrug.

"Well, I don't know of any stone castles, but I do know of The Stone House."

"The Stone House?"

"Yes. It was an abandoned hermitage that was often used by teenagers for, umm...unsavory activities." He gave a disapproving shake of his head. "A local man who used to be a monk here received permission from the abbot to restore the place."

"You mean to make it livable?"

"No, not exactly livable. But he tuckpointed the structure and put a new roof on. He cleaned up the inside, repaired the windows, things like that. Essentially, he stabilized and waterproofed the structure, and it's now used by people who are out hiking as a place to rest or to get in out of the elements."

"Am I allowed to go there?"

"Of course," he said with uncharacteristic cheerfulness. "As I told you the first time we met, the monastery grounds are a place of welcome and peace to all who wish to pray and reflect."

"Okay, then how do I find it?"

Brother Simon proceeded to tell me to walk about a quarter of a mile down the highway until I saw a gate on the opposite side of the road. "Walk through the gate and follow the trail. You'll see a sign pointing toward The Stone House. Simply follow the sign."

Ten minutes later, the dirt was crunching under my boots as I trekked along the path. I had walked for about twenty minutes when I saw a post displaying two white signs with black lettering. One sign read "Cross Knob" with an arrow pointing west, and the other read "The Stone House" with an arrow pointing south. I headed south.

The path inclined for most of the remaining hike until I came around a bend and saw The Stone House. Approaching the small structure, I saw its walls were constructed of brown stones, and that it had a flat aluminum roof whose edges, though rusted, were intact. Two thick trunks supported the front part of the roof, which served as a pergola with an Adirondack chair sitting on the concrete porch beneath. I pulled a wooden wedge free from the front door and it swung open.

The fireplace was directly in front of me as I stepped inside and scanned the small room. There was no furniture except for a wooden lectern that stood at the opposite end of the room. I walked over to the lectern and saw a notebook and pen laying on its surface. Opening the notebook, I saw prayers and reflections of various kinds had been left from people who had visited from as nearby as Springfield and from as far away as Seattle. Several messages of gratitude had been written to Brother Kieran "For restoring this place of sanctuary and rest for the weary travelers of the monastery's vast trails, both worn and new".

I closed the notebook and walked over to the fireplace. On the mantle above were various objects, such as a pinecone, the glass figure of a white rose, a small cross made of two sticks held together by black masking tape, and a small prayer card. I read the prayer in a soft voice.

"I SAID A PRAYER FOR YOU TODAY
AND KNOW GOD MUST HAVE HEARD.
I FELT THE ANSWER IN MY HEART
ALTHOUGH HE SPOKE NO WORD.
I DIDN'T ASK FOR WEALTH OR FAME,
(I KNEW YOU WOULDN'T MIND).
I ASKED HIM TO SEND TREASURES
OF A FAR MORE LASTING KIND!
I ASKED THAT HE BE NEAR YOU
AT THE START OF EACH NEW DAY
TO GRANT YOU HEALTH AND BLESSINGS
AND FRIENDS TO SHARE YOUR WAY!
I ASKED FOR HAPPINESS FOR YOU
IN ALL THINGS GREAT AND SMALL.
BUT IT WAS FOR HIS LOVING CARE
I PRAYED FOR MOST OF ALL"

AS I FINISHED reading, I heard what I thought to be the sound of footsteps outside. Hurrying onto the porch, I scanned the area but didn't see anyone. I listened for a long moment, but the only sound was the gentle stirring of the leaves. I walked around to the back of the house and peered into the forest stretching into shadowy depths of trees and underbrush. Seeing nothing out of the ordinary, I returned to the front porch, looking up and down the path for signs of a hiker. Not seeing anyone, I pulled the collar of my coat tightly around my neck and walked back inside the house.

The fireplace was constructed of the same brown stones that comprised the walls of the house. I bent down and ran my hands along the walls of the fireplace but none of the stones felt loose. But as I felt along the back wall, my hand came to rest on something loose behind the firep- it. I pulled the piece out and set it on the ground in front of the fireplace. It was a smooth caramel-colored brick.

Again, I thought I heard footsteps on the path outside, so I darted out the doorway and ran up the path to see if someone had passed by. Not seeing anyone, I ran in the opposite direction but found no one. Suddenly, I was seized by the thought that someone might have lured me out of the house to abscond with the brick I left lying on the dusty floor. So, I sprinted back to the house where I found the square-shaped brick lying undisturbed where I had left it. For several minutes after, I stood at the window and looked out at the path leading to and beyond the house, but I neither heard nor saw any sign of human or animal.

Returning to the brick, I knelt and picked it up, turning it over in my hands. The clue was written in black on the brick's smooth surface. As with the first clue, there were three crosses sketched above the text and a Greek symbol underneath. In the right corner were the letters M.O.T.G.Q with B.L. written below. The clue read as follows...

"CONGRATULATIONS, GOOD AND BRAVE SOUL,
ARE MOST HEARTILY DUE,

FOR YOU HAVE PROVEN THAT YOUR MIND IS CLEAR
AND THAT YOUR HEART IS TRUE.

TURN NOW TO GOLGOTHA WHOSE FOUNDATION
CAN BE FOUND HERE.

AND THOUGH THE CROSS BE NOT SEEN,
ITS FOOT STILL DRAWS YOU NEAR.

IT IS THE PLACE HIGH UPON THE ROCKS,
WHERE CHRIST ENDURES IN PAIN,

THE SIN OF ALL HUMANITY,
AND THE WORLD IT SEEKS TO GAIN.

WITH SPADE IN HAND DIG BENEATH THE CROSS
INSCRIBED ON THE STONE,

AND THERE YOU WILL FIND THE GIFT I OFFER
AS AN INHERITANCE TO YOU, ALONE".

CHAPTER
TWENTY-FIVE

"Turn now to Golgotha whose foundation can be seen here," I said in a whisper.

The room was small and mostly empty, so there was nothing I hadn't already examined except for a gathering of stones that lay against the wall adjacent to the fireplace. I scooted over and looked at the stones. In the middle of the pile, I saw that the trunk of a small tree jutted a few inches from the rocks. The trunk had been cleanly cut, leaving a stump with a flat grainy surface into which three nails had been partially driven. Standing, I turned in a circle, looking to see if there was anything else in the room I had missed. Seeing nothing new, I turned my attention back to the stump. It was not difficult to imagine the full height of the trunk subdivided by a beam that would form a cross. With that image in mind, I took up a place behind the lectern and faced the wall against which the cross would have stood, its base buried in the pile of stones.

"What is this?" I said, bewildered. "Golgotha?"

Whatever the scene represented, I knew it would be best to capture images of the scene that I could examine and reflect upon later. I knelt to read the clue once more, writing down each line in my notepad before photographing the brick, the stone pile, and the tree stump. Next, I made sure to capture photographs of the stone structure both inside and out. Once finished, I stood for a moment looking up and down the path as the soft wind blew cool against my face. I took several more photographs of the surrounding area and then began the hike back to the monastery.

I was about half-a-mile down the path when I was seized by a sudden thought. I stopped, pulled out my notepad, and read the clue.

"And though The Cross be not seen, its foot still draws you near."

The foot of The Cross draws you near, I thought, and then read on.

"It is the place upon the rocks, where Christ endures in pain, the sin of all humanity, and the world it seeks to gain."

The place upon the rocks. The foot of The Cross.

I contemplated the meaning of the words for a moment and then smiled with the realization that I knew where the clue was leading me.

Doubling my pace, it took only fifteen minutes to make my way to the large cross that stood beside Monk's Road. It was anchored high atop a rock mound encircled by the barren limbs of wild shrubs. The rock mound itself sat atop a hill that was about fifty feet in elevation. Considering the height of the mound, I figured the cross stood roughly seventy-five feet above the highway like the steeple of nature's cathedral overlooking the surrounding landscape. I climbed the hill and made my way gingerly through the underbrush and onto the base of the rock mound. Circling the perimeter, I searched for some sign of a cross inscribed on a stone. The first time around, I didn't see anything. But about halfway around my second effort, I hit paydirt.

The stone was not part of the mound itself but lay underneath the row of dead shrubs. It was a semi-flat, oblong stone with a red cross painted on its surface. The elements had worn the image, and I wondered if the sign would be recognizable after another month of exposure. I pushed back the sticks of the barren shrubbery and tested the weight of the stone. It was heavy enough that it wasn't going anywhere unless someone intentionally moved it. I slid the rock to the side and felt the ground beneath. It occurred to me that the ground must have been warm and loose when Moussa had determined that a small shovel would do the trick on it. But in the months since, the packed ground had become cold and hard. I cursed at the realization that the small shovel was leaning against the wall in my office. To make matters worse, the creeping gloam of twilight seemed to be both rising from the ground and descending from the sky. Realizing that time was growing short, I jogged back to my truck, got in, and sped off toward New Haven.

Pat Edelen was standing behind the counter at Brothers Hardware Store. It had to be him, I reasoned, based on the near carbon copy resemblance the man held to Jerry Edelen. I hurried down the aisle that contained shovels and selected a longer and sturdier version than the one Moussa and I had both purchased during previous visits to the store. Then I grabbed a mattock that was small enough to be held in one hand, but heavy enough to do some damage. I took the items and set them on the counter, anxious to pay and get back to my task.

"Hey there, mister. What kind of project ya got goin'?"

"I'm on a grail quest," I said, flashing the man a wide grin.

Pat Edelen shot me back a dubious glance and then looked down at the shovel and mattock, shaking his head as he said, "I swear, it's gettin' to be I ought not even ask."

I paid for the items and dashed out the front door, calling out for him to "Tell Jerry not to let Tommy Johnson get his goat" as I went.

Back in the truck, I paused at the realization that I had come as far in this effort as Moussa ever had. With that thought in mind, I looked around, half expecting someone to be hiding in the shadows of a doorway or peeking out through curtains. But all I saw were people going about their business, as oblivious to me as they were to the ghost of the young pilgrim from whom I had inherited this quest.

I drove down Monk's Road and eased the truck off the highway, figuring any vehicle that passed by would be indifferent to my presence. That was taking a good deal for granted given how things had turned out for Moussa. But time was not a friend, so unless I wanted to come back another day, I had to act fast.

I scrambled up the hill, tools in hand, and went to work breaking up the ground with the mattock. After a couple of minutes, my right hand ached, so I switched to my off hand. Once I had loosened things up, I moved in with the spade. But the ground was harder than I thought, so I had to go another round with the mattock. Darkness was creeping over the cross, the mound, and the surrounding landscape. Realizing I had to go now or give up the fight for another day, I went hard at it with the shovel. After a few minutes of digging, the tip of the shovel scraped against an object. I cleared the perimeter with the spade, and then got down on my knees, clearing away dirt with my hands. The top of what appeared to be a box wrapped in plastic was barely visible in the failing light. I used the mattock to free the edges so I could pry the box out. The box came free, and I set it aside as I got to work backfilling the hole.

By the time I put the rock in place, twilight had turned to the early stage of nighttime, and I had to watch my step as I walked back down the hill to my truck. I threw the tools in the truck bed, placed the box on the seat beside me, and made my way back to Bardstown, the thrill of the hunt tickling my nerves the entire way.

My nerves were tickled in a different way as I drove toward *The Observer* offices with a police cruiser cozied up behind me. I circled the courthouse and pulled to the curb in front of *The Observer* building. The cruiser did not follow suit, instead pulling into a spot on the opposite side of the street. I got out of the truck and looked over to see Officer Nathan Hadley eyeballing me as I made my way inside the building, box in hand.

"Working late, boss?" I said, stopping at the open door of George's office.

"The grind ain't ground me down yet, Motley. No sir, indeed. What're you up to there?"

"Looks like I decided to dive into the deep end."

"Yessir, that's what I like to hear," he said, clapping his hands together. "Although I think the parade that kicks off the Christmas around town festivities begins in about twenty minutes. And unless my early senility is kickin' in, I do believe that is your assignment."

"Shit."

"Oh, come on now. Whatever tasty little tidbit you got there in that box won't grow stale while you tend to your professional responsibilities."

"Probably not," I said with a sigh. "But you know how it is when you're on a roll."

"A rolling stone gathers no moss, yessir that is the truth. But it's also true that a man sees a thing with fresh eyes in the light of day. Umm-hmm, he surely does."

I looked down at the box. The plastic was torn where the tip of the shovel had pierced it. I wanted to tear that hole open right then and there, but George was right. I had a job to do and for a guy in my position, a job was something I should be damn grateful to have.

"Is there someplace I can put this? This and the other things in my...I mean, umm, the spare office?"

"Oh, come on now, don't feel like ya gotta apologize for claiming that space as your own, Motley. You got squatter's rights as far as I'm concerned."

"Thanks, but I'd feel better if I could put these things someplace secure. I damn sure don't want to take them home since Hadley's outside sniffin' around, again."

"Got a safe right here in my office," he said, standing. "And I dare Officer Nathan or any other of God's creatures to try to get after anything I put inside of it."

I thanked him and walked briskly down the hallway to retrieve the book and documents that lay out on the desk in what was by proclamation of the boss man, my office. I placed everything in the safe and George sealed it up tight, daring even the Devil and his minions to try and get after the items as he did so.

CHAPTER
TWENTY-SIX

THE COURTHOUSE WAS lit up in a cascade of green, gold, and red as people gathered in anticipation of the annual lighting of the tree to mark the beginning of the Christmas Around Bardstown festivities. Parade floats lined up for the procession down the main thoroughfare as wisps of smoke curled up from cups of coffee, hot chocolate, and mulled wine. The Stephen Foster Music Club performed a rendition of "Gabriel's Message" as children waited in line to sit on Santa's lap. When the song ended, an announcer's voice came over the loudspeaker, encouraging the crowd to join him in counting down to the official start of the Christmas season. When the count hit zero, an explosion of light emanated forth as the first float rambled down the street to the cheers of the assembled crowd.

I walked up and down the street, capturing the celebratory scene with my camera. Occasionally, I stopped to chat with an onlooker about their hopes for the season, or to tease a child for being on Santa's naughty list. Shopkeepers regaled me with the gift items they had on display and the mayor crowed about the impact of Christmas tourism on local trade. I had just stepped out of a gift store on the west side of the street when I saw Olive McGill marching down the opposite sidewalk. My call to her was swallowed up by the noise of the crowd, so I darted after her, dodging in and out of revelers to catch up to her determined pace.

"Hey, Miss Olive. Wait up."

She turned as I caught up to her just in front of the Farmer's Bank and Trust building.

"Well, if it isn't my good buddy, Levi Motley. And him chasing after me like a happy-go-lucky teenage boy."

"How about a little recognition for the effort? I had to dodge two floats and play bumper cars with a crowd of eggnog-soused partiers just to catch up to you."

"I am rightly honored by your effort," she said with a slight bow. "However, I'm due to start a tour in five minutes, so you will need to walk and talk if you wish to confer with me." At that, she turned and proceeded down the sidewalk, and I strode after her, amazed that her short legs could propel her at such a speed.

"But the stable," I said as we passed the tour stand. "It's empty. So, where are you headed?"

"To the old opera house."

"There's an opera house in Bardstown?"

"I said the old opera house. You should listen more carefully."

"Okay. So why are you going to the old opera house?"

"Obviously, we have to avoid the main drag due to the parade, so the parking lot of said location is serving as our makeshift stable this evening."

"Makes sense," I said as we turned and hustled down Broadway.

She shot me a sideward glance. "And will you be joining a tour this evening?"

"Well, I think I've got what I need for my story. But where are you taking people if you have to avoid downtown?"

She abruptly stopped and her hands went straight to her hips. "Have you not yet learned that there is more to this gem of a town than Main Street? After all, Judge Harry McGill always did say that you have to get off the beaten path if you want to discover something new."

I got ready to reply, but she stomped down the sidewalk before I could utter a single word. "I happen to agree with Judge McGill," I said, following after her. "But I thought the main drag was Third Street, not Main Street."

She gave me a sour look and said, "You've got a lot to learn."

I shrugged and said, "No arguing that. So, what new destination are you taking me to this evening?"

"Well, depending on whether you have the five dollars required to join the group, you may or may not be on your way to Federal Hill."

"Federal who?" I said, prompting another abrupt stop.

"Hill, you nincompoop. Federal Hill." I looked at her with a blank stare. "Have you learned nothing during your time in this beautiful town?"

I began to venture an answer in my defense, but she again hurried away down the sidewalk.

"It is disappointing indeed to learn that you have lived these many weeks in our rose garden of a community and have not paid a visit to My Old Kentucky Home."

"Oh, that place. Yeah, sure. I've driven by there."

"Driven by?" she said, with a huff. "You are quite the insufferable bag of bones, Levi Motley."

We crossed the street and headed for the makeshift stable. "I don't see Roscoe or Moots."

"We are running two carriages this evening due to the volume," she said in explanation. "Thus, we are joined this evening by this delightful little mare, Starlight. And over there is Moots's cousin, Possum, who is not delightful, but who does know how to handle a horse and buggy." She stroked Starlight's white mane, and the horse pressed her snout against Olive's cheek. "Now if you are quite finished, then perhaps you will answer the question I put to you."

I reached for my wallet and pretended to search its depths before triumphantly displaying a bill for the fare. She gave me a wry look and prepared to climb up onto the carriage.

"Hey, before we go, let me ask you something. Why were you so interested in that label?" She looked confused, so I explained myself further. "That day at the Getz Museum. You said that bottle of Old Relic reminded you of something."

"Ah, and so it did," she said with a pensive look. "But I haven't had time to research the matter due to my preparations for the Christmas tour of homes."

I wanted to inquire further but before I could, Olive climbed onto the carriage and announced that the tour was set for departure to Federal Hill. I climbed aboard and passed over the bill with a toothy grin, taking my seat alongside the other passengers.

As we settled, Olive provided a quick survey of the history of the old opera house, explaining that it had once been called The Town House, "where the William Comedy Company performed once a year. For twenty-five cents, patrons were treated to a show called *Moonshiner's Daughter*, not to be confused with the movie about that little lady from Butcher Holler."

The guests smiled and nodded, and Olive gave me a disappointed look as she read the lack of recognition on my face.

"Now, let us proceed to Federal Hill where a candlelight tour awaits you, along with bourbon barrel cake and a glass of hot cider."

As Starlight pulled the group out onto Second Street, Olive encouraged her guests to visit the live nativity scene at Bardstown Baptist Church, saying they should head one block west on Broadway, and two blocks south on Third to locate this charming annual Bardstown tradition. The carriage meandered down Second Street and on past East Flaget and Raspberry Alley where, our guide pointed out, the Old Coopersmith House still stood over 200 years after its construction in 1790.

"And now we are approaching East Stephen Foster Avenue, which was once called Market Street. To our left, you will see a home that once served as a general store until fire damaged the structure in eighteen-fifty-six. Thereafter, it became the home of the late Mrs. Dixie Ward, who died in nineteen-sixty at the ripe old age of ninety-seven."

As we made our way down the street, Olive provided background information on the various homes, including the modest abode where Lieutenant General Hal Moore was raised with his three siblings. "This honored son of Bardstown earned the Distinguished Service Cross for valor when he courageously led his troops in the week-long Battle of Ia Drang during the Viet Nam War. He was known as Yellow Hair to his troops as a tongue-in-cheek homage to the legendary General George Custer, who commanded that very same Seventh Cavalry Regiment at..."

She paused, a bemused look creasing her face in a way that confused me given her normally confident bearing. But after a few seconds, her bemusement transformed into a look of enlightenment that caused her countenance to beam with pleasure. I had always marveled at Olive's ability to recall and articulate with great mastery the history of her hometown, but I couldn't fathom what new insight could have led her to stop in the middle of her oration. After a few more seconds of silence, she looked at me with a satisfied smile and gave me a single nod before picking up where she had left off.

"General George Custer, who commanded that very same Seventh

Cavalry Regiment at the Battle of the Little Bighorn just under a century before."

Olive was in her element, her face glowing in delight at the sight of a brick mansion off to our left. "Ladies and gentlemen, this lovely example of Georgian architecture was built in eighteen-twenty-three by Walter Beall, a wealthy merchant for whom one of our downtown streets is named. The home passed to local distiller Conrad Westcott and his wife Isabelle in nineteen-eighty-three." She paused and gave me a pointed look before she continued. "The foundation is of limestone and the bricks used in the eighteen-inch walls were burned right on the property and laid in Flemish bond. Just look at that magnificent doorway. Ladies, it's wide enough for a hoop skirt and then some."

The ladies in the group smiled as I gave Olive an almost pleading look. She frowned and shook her head, taking my meaning. "Mr. Possum, I think one of our guests would like to exit the tour to get a closer look at the Westcott residence." She shot me a stern look. "However, I am certain he will rejoin our tour at his earliest convenience."

The carriage came to a halt. I gave Olive a quick wink and leapt onto the grass as she shifted her focus to the nineteenth-century Greek revival mansion across the street, explaining that it had once been the home of one of the most celebrated legal minds in the history of Nelson County, "who also happened to be a great lover of thoroughbreds. Hence, he constructed a racetrack right on the grounds, though sadly, it no longer remains."

Turning, I walked up the sidewalk and through an ornamental gate supported by two stone pillars. In the front yard, a small crowd of people were gathered around a man who looked like a figure straight out of a Dickens novel. I joined the group as the man provided an overview of the history of the residence, including a biographical sketch of the current owners.

"The name Westcott may ring a political bell for some of you as the son of the esteemed owners of this estate, Rogers Westcott, is a Kentucky state representative who may well occupy the governor's mansion in the coming years."

The guide, who called himself Stephen, ushered the group inside where a woman, also garbed in Victorian era dress, was serving brownies with chocolate bourbon icing and cherries jubilee generously infused with the finest Old Royal bourbon. The house was spectacular. The guide explained that the fine crystal chandelier was a gift to the original owner from a prominent family in New Orleans. The light from the glass gleamed and reflected in the foil ornaments adorning a twelve-foot Christmas tree generously arrayed with strings of popcorn and cranberries and red paper streamers.

"Governor Charles Anderson Wickliffe himself made a gift of that exquisite eighteenth-century federal mirror you see on the opposite wall there, when Governor Wickliffe resided nearby at Wickland," the guide said. "Just look at how it fits perfectly with the Italian damask wallpaper pattern that stretches from the foyer all the way up the stairway, which, by the way, is made of ash and has a cherry railing." The guide went on to point out the candles on the table at the foot of the stairway. "If we were visiting a hundred years ago, these candles would have been put out to light the way to our sleeping quarters as we retired for the evening."

As the eloquent guide moved into the grand living room, he focused our attention on the fifteen-foot ceilings embellished with stately cornices and a Greek anthemion pattern stenciled in each corner of the room. At this point, I split off from the group and made my way down the hallway to what looked like the study.

As I entered, several people were milling about the room, and I joined them in perusing the pictures along the wall. I heard a woman comment on the French furniture, saying, "It gives the room an elegance befitting a bourbon industry elite."

"And look at those fluted window casings," her friend said. "The acorn design of the corner plumes is just stunning."

"Regal." The two women turned toward me with matching expressions of amused derision. "You say stunning, I say regal. You know, to-may-to, to-mah-to?"

The women rolled their eyes in unison as I chuckled inwardly and moved down the wall, stopping in front of a black and white picture of what I took to be Conrad Westcott. He was standing in the foreground of a large still with a rickhouse in the distance. He wore overalls and the sleeves of his shirt were rolled all the way up to his biceps. The image was of a cocky young man with eyes narrowed by the sunlight and lips curled upward at one end. He had the look of a man who not only knows his secrets but your secrets, too.

Moving on, I stood in front of the bookcases and examined the titles. On the shelf below the books was a framed picture, again in black and white, of a man in military-dress trench coat and cap. The man was holding a towheaded blonde boy in each arm.

"Sergeant Thomas C. Westcott," a voice from behind me said. I turned to see a man dressed in a turtleneck and tweed blazer. "And his two boys, James and Conrad. I'm the smaller one there in the crook of Daddy's right arm. The other boy is James, my dear brother who has done shuffled off to receive his heavenly reward."

He looked directly at me, and there was nothing for me to do but introduce myself. "Levi Motley," I said, extending my hand.

"Connie Westcott," he said, shaking my hand without warmth. "But then, I suspect you already knew that, now didn't you, big 'un?"

I turned back to the picture, ignoring his question. "Was he leaving for the war?"

He picked up the frame and looked at the photograph. "He was on leave, home for three weeks as I recall. I remember he said I'd growed like a damn weed since the day he left. Told me if I kept growing like that, I'd be a linebacker for the Cats by the time he came home for good."

"Is he still with you?"

"Well, now ain't that a polite way of asking a man if his daddy was a casualty of the Great War."

"I didn't mean to..."

"He made it back, all right," he said, cutting me off. "Only to buy the farm in a goddamn car accident. Can you imagine such a thing? Making it through a gauntlet of Nazis only to be done in by a drunk redneck?"

"I can imagine it." He gave me a doubtful look as he set the frame down on a desk. "My old man survived Nam. He died when I was nine."

"Car accident?"

I shook my head. "To tell you the truth, I'm not sure."

His eyes narrowed in either curiosity or suspicion, I couldn't tell which, but he let it go without further inquiry.

"So here we are," I said. "Two sons of veterans. One living in a Georgian mansion and the other renting a frame house month to month. Given that I'm the latter, maybe you could tell me the secret to becoming the former."

"Ain't got no secret. But I reckon I been at it a few decades longer than you, and a man does tend to accumulate according to the talent he applies over time. I hear you gotcha some talent, so I reckon it's just a matter of time."

He was a square-shouldered man who, despite the slight paunch that his cashmere turtleneck couldn't hide, did not look like one to back down from a fight. And though his hair was thinning with middle age, he still sported a slicked back, salt-and-pepper coif that gave him an air of respectability.

"I would say I hope you're right," I said, scanning the room. "But I've never really had any use for accumulation."

He grunted and said, "Well, a man does find his perspective changes. But don't get no twisted idea that all this is some sorta inheritance. By God, I earned what I have."

"Self-made man, huh?"

"From the dairy farm to the distillery, and don't you forget it."

Just then a man who had been circling us took advantage of an opening in the conversation and introduced himself. Westcott's demeanor changed in an instant as he glad-handed and worked the man with the practiced ease of a seasoned politician. I watched as he gripped the man's arm, listening intently to every word he said and occasionally offering a hearty laugh or a thoughtful nod. After a few minutes, he sent the man away with a bottle of Old Royal that he autographed right in front of him with a black marker. The man thanked him and beamed as if he'd just been given a baseball autographed by Mickey Mantle. Turning back to me, the beguiling ease of his friendly banter evaporated and was replaced with a demeanor that was not so much cold as it was businesslike.

"Any chance I can get one of those?"

He gave me a wry smile, walked over to his desk, opened the bottom drawer, and pulled out a fifth of the fine single barrel bourbon. He signed the label and presented it to me without ceremony.

"Appreciate it."

"Don't go thinking it comes without a string attached."

"Well, is it a gift or a bribe?"

"It's an exchange is what it is. The bottle for a straight answer to my question." He took a step toward me, attempting to back me into the corner of the room, but I held my ground. "Just what in the hell is it you're up to in my town, Levi Motley?"

I snorted a derisive laugh and said, "Your town, huh?" He glared at me and waited. "Which means what exactly? That I'm not welcome here?"

His face broke out in a wide grin and his voice dripped with good ol' boy charm. "Oh, come on now, big 'un. Nothing could be further from the truth. After all, we are a hospitable bunch around here. Just ask any ol' body and they'll tell ya. We are chock full of hospitality in this here town. And dang it if I'm not the most hospitable sumbitch of 'em all."

"Yeah, I've heard that about you," I said in a flat tone. "All evidence to the contrary, as far as I'm concerned."

"Now, that there's an interesting word. Evidence. To my simple, country boy way of thinking that word means 'proof of somethin'. So, tell me, Mr. Motley. That what you're up to? Tryin' to find some kind of proof?"

"I'm trying to find out what happened to Moussa Diab."

"Who?"

"Yeah, right. Play dumb all you want, Mr. Westcott, but that dog won't hunt. Isn't that what a grand old southern gent like yourself would say? Some dumbass phrase like that dog won't hunt? Am I using that phrase correctly, Connie?"

He glared at me as a woman appeared in the doorway, her eyes sharp as she probed the nature of our conversation from across the room. She floated over to us and placed a hand on Westcott's shoulder. "Come now, Connie. We have guests to entertain." The woman's dark eyes blazed and burrowed into mine as she spoke.

He smiled and said, "Mrs. Isabelle Westcott, please make the acquaintance of one Levi Motley." I nodded and offered a greeting, but she did not reply. "He's just about to leave, now ain't ya, big 'un?"

"Actually, I thought I might rejoin the tour, so I can learn more about you and the missus. Oh, and Rogers, too. You must be so proud."

He put on a wide smile and his affect was one of a southern predator charming his prey. "Oh, you better believe it. Got to stand by your family, 'cause you see, there ain't nothing more important than family. That's especially true this time a year, don't you think?"

I looked at him with a cautious expression and said, "Yeah, I guess so."

"Aw hell, you know so," he said with a wave. "Now you done told me you lost your daddy. But what about your mama? She still around?" I shook my head, and he put a comforting hand on my shoulder. "Well, now it's a special kind of pain to be without your mama and your daddy."

He picked up the frame and looked at it with a wistful gaze. "And I surely do miss my brother James. Hurts like the dickens that he's gone. Hurts all the more around the holidays. Just like you surely hurt for your mama and daddy."

He set the frame down.

"But say there, I hear you gotcha a brother that's still around. That so?" My stomach muscles tightened as I looked from Conrad to Isabelle Westcott, who had a slight smile forming at the edges of her red lips. "That's all right," he said with a wave. "You don't have to answer seein' as how I know it's true. Tell me something, you gonna be seeing that brother of yours during the holidays? You know, sittin' around the fire, drinking eggnog, and celebrating the coming of Our Savior?"

I opened my mouth to speak, but no words came out.

"Well, hell's bells, big 'un. You look like you just seen a coyote come out of the woods and snatch up your prized puppy." He gave me a look of faux sympathy. "I tell ya what, Motley. My son Rogers...you know the one you say we oughta be proud of? Well, you just don't know how right you are, 'cause you see he's on a train bound straight for glory. I tell ya it's the goddamn truth. Straight for glory and won't stop 'til he gets to Frankfort and who knows what lies beyond."

He stepped in close to me and adopted a conspiratorial tone as his wife regarded me with a bewitching gaze. "Now, seeing as how it's Christmas and all and you ain't got no mama or daddy around, I reckon my boy Rogers might be able to do you a good turn, Levi Motley. Yessir, I think he could do you a damn good turn. Wanna hear about it?" He continued before I could reply. "Here's the deal. You see, I believe my boy could throw some of his political weight around so you and that brother of yours get to share in the wonder of Christmas together like family ought to."

I felt the blood pulsing in my jugular as he spoke.

"Now, it's probably too late to get the job done for the upcoming celebration. But I have a vision of the two of you next Christmas just a ridin' on out to the cemetery to put poinsettias on your mama and daddy's grave just like I intend to do for my own. Because after all, Christmas is about family. And I tell ya it just breaks my damn heart to know you ain't experiencing the joy of the season with your brother." He leaned in, his face just inches from mine. "Now, what is it I hear your brother's name is? Could it be Declan?"

My jaw clenched and my grip on the bourbon bottle tightened as he whispered in my ear.

"What do you say there, big 'un? I do that good turn for you and that convict brother of yours, and you bring me that goddamn treasure you're after. Sound like a deal?"

For a moment, the rage building inside me was doused by a splash of confusion. He must have seen it in my eyes, because his lip curled derisively, and he shook his head.

"Don't play dumb with me, boy. This is my town, and I got a home-field advantage you just wouldn't believe."

Just then a woman came up to Isabelle, and the two burst into energetic conversation. Isabelle introduced her husband, who gave me a sinister look before he transformed into the warm gentleman host. I stood watching as he charmed his guest, the particulars of what I had learned in my investigation flashing through my mind.

What is he talking about? I thought, utterly perplexed by his offer. *What treasure?*

For a moment, I grasped at the notion that perhaps Moussa Diab had stumbled onto something apart from the spiritual quest that he had embarked upon. Did the monastery house some kind of treasure that Westcott thought Moussa had access to? I recalled Brother Lew's letter and his hope that Hamia and her husband would be able to visit the following year for the monastery's one-hundred-fiftieth celebration.

One-hundred-fifty years, I thought. *That's a long stretch for...how had Westcott put it? The accumulation that happens over time?*

"And just what have those monks accumulated over all that time?"

As if he had overheard me, Westcott turned and flashed that predatory look to let me know he'd get back to me once I had wilted like the cornered prey that I was. I picked up the black marker that lay on the desk and walked to the center of the room where Conrad and Isabelle could see me over the shoulder of their delighted guest. I took the marker and scratched out the autograph on the bottle. Then I opened the bottle, took a long draw, and tipped the edge so that a shot glass's worth of bourbon spilled out onto the Oriental rug. Westcott looked ready to explode as I raised the bottle in mock toast and walked away.

As I exited through the magnificent doorway that was wide enough for a hoop skirt, I felt a sense of confused dread at the realization that my brother was in danger, and the only way I could help him was to figure out just what in the hell Conrad Westcott had been talking about.

CHAPTER
TWENTY-SEVEN

THE NEXT MORNING, I grabbed a coffee at Café Mozart and headed to *The Observer*, where I found George already on his second cup.

"You ever let the other early birds get the worm, boss?"

"Got to get up mighty early if you wanna beat this old cuss to the punch. You betcha."

I chuckled and asked if I could retrieve the items we had placed in the safe the evening before. He was happy to oblige but made a point of telling me that pleased though he was to see me taking a swim, he'd be needing my article on the previous evening's festivities post haste. I told him I'd have it in by deadline, but he was a wise man who knew his business. Which is to say he knew if I got started down the rabbit hole of questing, then I wasn't likely to come up for air until I had the furry little critter in hand.

"You know what a paper's made up of, Motley?"

"I've heard this speech already," I said in vain.

"A paper's made up of pictures and words and..."

"Advertisements," I said, hijacking his punch line.

"That is the damn truth. Pictures, words, and advertisements. And seein' as how you haven't brought me a single bit of advertising dough, you best be singing for your supper by handing over a first-rate account of the downtown Christmas party or whatever they call it. Hell, I can't be expected to remember such things."

"Don't worry, boss," I said as I walked down the hall to my office.

"I'll bring you some pretty words and pictures wrapped up with a big ol' Bardstown Christmas bow on it. How's that sound?"

I knew George wouldn't let me slide until I had delivered the goods on the article, but I was itching to dive back into the chase. So, I laid the items from the safe out on my desk and cut the cellophane wrapping away from what appeared to be a tin container. I gripped the lid, preparing to pry it off, but just as my fingers applied pressure, George's watchful face appeared around the edge of the doorway.

"That there box part of the story you're due to deliver into my greedy little Grinch hands?"

I shook my head, sighing as I set the box down and reached for my camera case. Retrieving the film from the case, I gave George a long-suffering glare and walked toward the darkroom.

"Lots of pretty Christmas pictures coming right up, bossman."

For the next few hours, I turned my attention to the task of giving my editor what he wanted, namely words and pictures of the Christmas Around Bardstown festivities. It was nearing noon when I felt I had the story in good shape. Having personally delivered news that a draft of my article was ready for my editor's hawk eyes to review, I prepared to shift my attention back to that metal box. I was in virtually the same spot, ready to pry open the container, when Dominick popped his head around the corner of my office door.

"Motley. Let's grab lunch."

"Can't do it. I just wrapped up this article for Hawley, and I've gotta get back to another project I'm working on."

Dominick walked into my office and sat down. "We need to talk."

"Come on, Dom. I told you I can't. I've got work to do."

He leaned toward me, his elbows resting on his knees as he said, "Look, man, I'm hearing some concerning shit about you."

"What kinda shit?"

"The kind that might require your boy to step up and be my brother's keeper, that's what kind. Now get your ass up, and let's grab lunch."

I shook my head in frustration as I began to offer another protest, but a sudden rumble in my stomach betrayed the fact that I was quite hungry. I looked at the box on the desk and let out a defeated sigh. "You drive."

"Damn skippy. Let's go to Hawk's."

"Hell no," I said, shaking my head. "I remember what you said about that place."

"Oh, don't be such a wussy. They got more than balls on the menu."

With that encouraging review, I grabbed my coat, and we headed out. Colonel Hawk's Restaurant was housed in a small block building in a historically black neighborhood. When we arrived, we found the restaurant packed with lunchtime patrons. Dominick greeted some friends at one of the tables as I perused a framed article on the wall titled "You Don't Fool Me About Food". The article detailed the exciting life of the restaurant's founder, Louis "Hawk" Rogers, who had been named a Kentucky Colonel by Governor A. B. Happy Chandler in the 1930s and who had hobnobbed with luminaries from Hollywood to Washington, D.C.

In addition to the article, the wall featured a caricature of Lyndon Johnson, a framed Kentucky Colonel bowtie, a picture of a racehorse named Civil Rights, and an autographed photo of none other than Thomas Merton. A descendant of the founder who was working the lunch crowd told me Merton used to visit the restaurant often, so much so that Hawk named a private dining area "The Monk's Smoker".

"Uncle Hawk said Mr. Thomas was a good and gentle man," the woman said. "Just one of the plain old folks you'd expect to meet at the grocery or at a soda fountain."

My interest surrounding Merton, who I found to be a surprisingly well-known figure for a monk, continued to spike. We took a table and Dominick greeted our waiter, another of Hawk's descendants, with a glad handshake and a slap on the back.

"Charles in charge. How you been, brother?"

"Hard work and clean livin'," the man said.

Dominick looked at him with a dubious frown and said, "You need some new material, my man. I know for a fact that only half of that line is true."

"You trying to say I'm not a hard worker?"

We laughed, and the man asked to take my order.

"What's the special?"

"Lamb fries," he said.

Dominick choked back his laughter as I glared at him over the menu. "I'll have the soup of the day."

Dominick shook his head and said, "Gimme the country ham."

The man thanked us and moved on to the next table. When he was out of earshot, Dominick leaned halfway across the table and questioned me in a hoarse whisper. "Just what in the hell has your dumb ass gotten into, Motley?"

"I don't know. Hard work, clean livin'?"

He looked at me thoughtfully and said, "Well, I'll grant that you seem to have kept yourself busy lately."

"And on the right side of the bar."

"Yeah, that's Sam talking," he said with a dismissive wave.

"Even so."

"Well, you may be on the right side of the bar, but from what I hear, you're on the wrong side of the law."

"Bullshit. I haven't broken any laws."

"Since when do you have to break the law to be on the wrong side of it?"

"Okay, so how am I on the wrong side?"

"That's my question to you," he said, pointing at me. "Word is that you are not in the good graces of the powers that be."

"That be what?"

"That be able to break you down like a folding chair, that's what."

I slumped in my chair like a teenager being lectured by an overprotective father.

"Look, my friend, things work different in a small town. Everybody talks, everybody knows what everybody else is up to, and the power structure does not want to be fucked with."

"And where in this country can you find a power structure that does want to be fucked with, Dom? Tell me where I can find that utopia, and I'll be out the door before my soup gets here."

He rubbed his chin, considering my point. "Fair enough. But we ain't any other place but this one," he said, tapping a finger on the table. "And I know what happened to that kid shook people around here. People idealize this town, Motley. And a man getting killed under strange circumstances is bound to cause people to squirm, even if it did happen out in the county."

I looked around the restaurant at the all-black staff waiting on a crowd almost completely comprised of white diners.

"I know what you're thinking," he said. "But I'm not talking about racism. Hell, this place was and still is owned and operated by a black man. Ain't nobody here kowtowing to no white man. Besides, everybody loves Hawk's, black and white."

I spun my fork on the tabletop.

"Okay, let me spell it out for you. You know my man in the department? The one who didn't want to speak on the shovel?" I nodded. "Well, he didn't have any problem speaking on you." I stopped spinning the fork and looked up at him. "Oh, do I finally have your attention?"

Before I could answer, Charles brought our food.

"You did have it. Now you're gonna have to share it."

He gave me about thirty seconds of peace before he moved in on me again.

"So, here's the deal. I ran into Eddie, that's my man with the po-po. Before I could even ask him what's up, he gets all up in my grill asking what my boy at the newspaper is up to digging around in the Diab case."

His eyebrows arched into his forehead as he looked at me, anticipating a response.

"What?" I said with a shrug. "You know I'm looking into it, so why the surprised look?"

"It's not surprise, it's concern. My man says you're getting all kinds of attention from people who you'd rather not know your name. He tells me the chatter around the courthouse is that you even bucked the county attorney by refusing to let him see what was in a package that came to his office."

"It was addressed to his office but intended for me."

"From that boy's mama?"

"Yeah, that's right. I already told you I spoke to her. Hell, you're the one that got me her number. So, if I'm on the hot seat, how come you're not snuggled up right beside me?"

He sniffed and gave me an indignant look. "Oh, I'm right there beside you, no doubt. Because I put myself there."

I sighed and said, "Yeah, I know that. I'm just being a smartass."

"Look, I'm with you, and you know that," he said, waving away my comment. "But what is it I'm with you on? And why are people getting riled up about it?"

They were fair questions. I had filled Dominick in on much of what was happening, but I hadn't shared anything about the package that

Hamia had mailed to me and what it had led me to discover. So, I summarized the most recent events, including the arrival of the package containing Moussa's book and the letter from Brother Lew. He listened with careful concentration as I described my meeting with Jack Merrick, and how Nathan Hadley had stopped me on the sidewalk in front of *The Observer* office building. When I told him how George had verbally undressed Hadley, he shook his head in appreciation.

"My man, George. He don't let his people twist in the wind." He gave me a direct look. "What was in the package?"

"Umm, well, let's see. There was a book."

"What kind of book?"

"It was, umm...a book that belonged to Moussa."

He gestured for me to continue, but I was hesitant. Dominick dropped his fork and gave me a deadpan look. "Your dumb ass is going to tell me what's going on, even if I have to turn you upside down and shake it out of you."

"Yeah, yeah, all right. It's just that recent developments have been... unexpected. And I'm still processing it all." He looked at me, waiting in silence until I finally relented. "It was the book Moussa had with him when I picked him up. It's about the legend of King Arthur."

I paused, waiting for some incredulous laugh or roll of the eyes, but he only stared at me with a thoughtful expression.

"Evidently the book once belonged to Brother Lew. He mailed it to Moussa as part of the spiritual quest I told you about." He gave me a blank look. "Remember? I told you Brother Lew liked to create these adventures to make a person's spiritual journey more exciting and fun."

"Yeah, I remember. That's actually a pretty cool idea."

I nodded my agreement and said, "The book contained a letter from Brother Lew and a clue that Moussa was supposed to follow."

"You think he did?"

"I know he did. The first clue led to a place out in the woods near the monastery. It held the second clue, which led to a box buried at this place near Monk's Road. That's why Moussa bought the shovel."

"And you have that box?"

"Yep."

"Back at the office?" I nodded. "What's in it?"

"Don't know," I said with a shrug. "I was about to find out but ended up having lunch with you instead." Dominick rubbed his chin. "What're you thinking, Dom?"

He let out a slow breath. "I'm thinking whatever is in that box is what's got people all fired up."

I shook my head and said, "I don't know, man. I can't imagine whatever that kid was up to would have attracted the attention of Westcott or Merrick or Hadley or whoever else you say has an eye on this."

"Maybe it wasn't what Moussa was up to, but something Brother Lew was up to."

My face screwed up in a doubtful expression. "A monk? Really?"

He shrugged and said, "Who else then? Fact is, Moussa is dead and whatever he was doing has touched a nerve. Or at least you following up on it has. And then there's the matter of the invitation from Westcott to Moussa."

"And the matter of Westcott being a brother to Lew."

"Exactly," he said.

We ate for a moment, processing in silence.

"Westcott knows about Declan."

Dominick stopped eating. "Knows what?"

"Knows he's my brother. Knows he's in prison."

"How'd that come up?" I told Dominick about my visit to the Westcott residence. "So, he knew who you were?"

"Indeed, he did."

"And how did Declan's name come up?"

"It was some kind of bribe, I think. But he was coy about it, giving me his good ol' boy schtick. Basically, the message was that golden boy Rogers could get Declan out early."

"And what was on the other side of that generosity?"

"Generosity my ass. It wasn't exactly offered in the spirit of Christmas charity, if you know what I mean."

"The question remains. What's he after?"

I hesitated, shifting in uncertainty. "He said he wants me to bring him the treasure."

Dominick's face wrinkled in confusion. "Bring him the treasure? The hell's he talkin' about? I thought you said this was all about spiritual stuff."

"It is about spiritual stuff. I don't know what he meant."

Dominick rubbed the back of his bald head as he tried to make sense of what I had told him. "Let me get this straight, you started down this path out of spite for being duped by that fake reporter lady whose part in this, I will remind you, remains unknown. Now you got some bigwig bourbon executive with a powerful son looking into your life and wanting to engage in a quid pro quo with you. I mean, damn, Motley. Just what the hell is this about?"

I threw a wadded-up napkin on the table. "I don't know, Dom. I mean, you don't get tailed by the cops or pressured by the county attorney for pursuing spiritual truths."

"No, you don't. And you don't get offers to get your brother sprung from the pokey for no spiritual treasure, neither." He gave an exasperated sigh and said, "Look, I said this before, but maybe you should back away from this. I mean, you're telling me Conrad Westcott thinks you're after something he wants, and you don't even know what it is? Are you really going to wait and find out the hard way that a man like that gets what he wants?"

I felt my face getting red as my own frustration quickly rose to the point of anger. "Yeah, I am going to find out the hard way," I said in a sharp whisper. "Because all you're talk of small-town politics and some dickhead that thinks he can screw with people's lives for his own purposes doesn't sit right with me. And by the way, it shouldn't sit right with you either. Maybe you're getting a little too chummy with the power structure, as you like to call it."

Dominick glared at me as he responded through clenched teeth. "Yeah, well not everybody can just pick up and leave when shit gets tough. Some of us are committed to the long haul. You ever think of that?"

We glared at each other across the table. After a long moment, I blew out my cheeks and rubbed my temples, attempting to calm myself down. "Look, man, I'm sorry. I didn't mean that. And you're right, I run away when things are tough. Or at least I used to."

Dominick's features softened and he looked like he was about to speak.

"Don't say anything. I'm saying you're right. But what I need you to understand is that I feel different about this, you know? I don't where all this stuff is heading, but I think you'd have to agree that it's heading somewhere. I mean, why would these powerful people you're talking about get their panties in a wad if that wasn't the case?"

He nodded, but I could see the concern etched on his face. "I'm worried about you, that's all."

"I get that. But someone recently told me that a man's got to jump into the deep end to find out who he really is."

"Someone?" he said with a knowing smile. "That right there is vintage Hawley."

I smiled, too, and for a moment, we sat in silence, each of us lost in our own thoughts. Finally, Dominick spoke up, posing the obvious question. "Okay. I get that you're sticking with this, and I respect that. But what now, Levi?"

I chewed on my lip for a moment, considering the next move. "First, I go back to the office and open up that box."

He nodded in agreement. "Then what?"

I locked eyes with my old friend.

"Then I go see Declan."

CHAPTER
TWENTY-EIGHT

W E WRAPPED UP lunch at Hawk's and returned to *The Observer*. I was eager to investigate the contents of the box, and I had it in mind to tell Dominick that I needed to do so alone. Thankfully, the better angels of my nature prevailed upon me, and I realized it would be wrong to exclude him. After all, if not for Dominick's brotherly concern, I surely would have hit the road and missed out altogether on the unique adventure I found myself taking part in.

"I feel like a kid on Christmas morning," I said, staring at the box.

"Yeah, well I'm thinking that might not be such a good thing. Especially since I doubt young Motley typically found himself on the good list."

Lifting the lid, I saw a soft cloth lining had been placed inside the tin. The same lining had been used to wrap the two objects contained within.

"Guess somebody knew we were a package deal," I said, handing one of the objects to Dominick and unwrapping the other.

It was a book accompanied by a large envelope with the name "Moussa" scrawled across the front. I ran my hand across the name, reminding myself that this had all been intended for the spiritual discernment of the deceased young pilgrim. Remembering that gave me a sense of melancholic pride that his mother had chosen me as the successor to his quest. Dominick read the feeling written on my face and gave me a nod as he unwrapped the second object.

"What do you make of this?"

He held up a circular, wooden disk about ten inches in diameter and roughly an inch thick. The image of a tree was carved in intricate detail on its surface. Dominick flipped the piece over, revealing four holes that had been bored into the wood, each about a half inch deep. He handed it to me, and I ran my hands over the image of the tree, admiring the craftsmanship.

"Well?"

"No idea."

"Same here," he said as he picked up the book and read the title and description. "*The Seven Storey Mountain* by Thomas Merton. The autobiography of a young man who led a full and worldly life, and then at the age of twenty-six, entered a Trappist monastery."

He handed the book to me, and I turned it over to examine a photograph on the back cover depicting four monks toiling with pitchforks as they placed hay in a thresher. The picture was captioned "Trappists at work in the fields (Author on the left)". I opened the book and saw the inside cover contained blurbs from literary luminaries such as Evelyn Waugh, Graham Greene, and Monsignor Fulton J. Sheen, who likened the book to a twentieth-century version of *The Confessions of St. Augustine*.

"Hamia quoted Merton in the letter she sent me. You know anything about him?"

Dominick frowned and said, "I don't recall the good Reverend Elijah at St. John A.M.E. ever mentioning his name."

"Right," I said, setting the book aside. I picked up the envelope and cut it open. Inside was a letter, the paper fragile and yellowed from age. It was dated July 25, 1954, signed by Father William French, and presumably addressed to a young James Westcott.

Dear James,

Let me begin by wishing you a most happy fourteenth birthday! What a young man you have become. You have a spirit for adventure that you come by honestly as a bona fide replica of your father, may God rest his soul. Oh, the adventures he and I had growing up in a time before the world was set afire in the chaos of destruction and madness. Yet the pride I feel for my friend's courage in joining the fray has never lessened, though my own call has been to contend in spiritual rather than military warfare.

It is in the interest of encouraging you to listen to God's call in your own life that I offer you the gift of this extraordinary book. It is the story of man whose search for God enabled him to overcome the self-contradictions that plague all men who choose to follow the world rather than Our Heavenly Father above. I pray this book will inspire you to know the joy of God's purpose for your life, a purpose that will most certainly lead you to happiness in this life, and many years from now, a heavenly reward in the world to come.

But lest you think I have forgotten that you are, after all, a growing boy with the heart of a knight, let me wish you a joyful birthday despite the challenge of your circumstances. For Proverbs tell us a glad heart makes for a cheerful face! So, I say to you, enjoy your birthday and accept this gift as my wish for you to know the adventure of seeking God is the greatest that any man can embark upon.

May God bless you and guide you on your way!

Warmest Regards,
Father William French

I REREAD THE letter, handed it to Dominick, and said, "The challenge of your circumstances? I wonder what that means."

As he read the letter, I reached inside the envelope and found it also contained a folded piece of paper. The paper was large and thick like construction paper and subdivided into horizontal thirds, each containing drawings sketched in pencil. The drawing on the top third covered the entire width of the page. It depicted a cross in the foreground of a deep valley that stretched and then rose into a hill. A bright sun appeared near the apex of the sky exuding rays of sunlight that flooded down upon the scene. A small clock was sketched in the bottom left corner of the image, its arms indicating eleven o'clock.

"A book and some kind of wooden plaque," Dominick said, joining me in examining the page. "And drawings?"

"Clues."

"To what?"

"Places, I think. Here, look at this middle section. It's divided into two images. Looks like the first is a tree trunk with a hole in the middle. And the second is..."

Dominck picked up the wooden disk. "This." He held up the wooden piece, comparing it to the drawing. Both showed branches flowing up and outward and roots that mimicked the branches as they stretched toward the bottom of the disk. Both the carving and the drawing showed the tree encircled by an interwoven series of lines that tied into the limbs and the roots.

"I'm thinking this piece of wood is supposed to be placed in that hole on the tree."

"Yeah, I agree," I said. "Check out this picture below."

The bottom third of the page contained a sketch of three bodies in repose. The background had been darkened with pencil except for a perfect, white circle appearing above and to the right of the bodies. A clock was drawn in the bottom right corner, its arms, again, indicating eleven o'clock. Dominick pointed to the clock in the top picture, and then moved his finger down to the clock in the bottom image. "Both of them indicate eleven o'clock," he said. "But up here it looks like the sun's out, while the bottom one looks like the moon is out."

"Eleven o'clock in the morning, and eleven at night."

"Okay. So, are you supposed to put that wood circle in the tree in the morning or at night? And what happens when you do?"

I shook my head in uncertainty as I turned the piece of paper over. On the back were the familiar images of three crosses and a Greek symbol. Underneath the symbol were the initials "M.O.T.G.Q." with the initials "B.L." underneath.

Dominick blew out a weary breath and said, "And what's this supposed to mean?"

"The crosses and letters have been on each of the clues so far. The 'B.L.' must stand for Brother Llewellyn, but I'm not sure about the other letters. Maybe something 'Grail Quest'?"

I looked up from the drawing and locked eyes with my friend. Without saying a word, we shared an understanding that we were being drawn into something truly fascinating and I was happy we were experiencing the moment together. I gave him a knowing smile and turned my attention back to the piece of paper.

"That Greek symbol there, it's also been on the other clues though I'm not sure what it means."

Dominick's eyes narrowed as he studied the symbol. "It's Chi-Rho. The first two letters of Christos."

I shot him a look of surprised appreciation and said, "Check out the big brain on Dom."

He put on a faux look of arrogant intellectualism and said, "Yes, well, the classics lessons Mummy and Daddy indulged me with do come in handy from time to time."

I copied his haughty tone. "And do you happen to have any Grey Poupon?"

"But of course, my good man," he said, keeping up with the bit. "And here, you can spread it with this silver spoon I keep up my..." Dominick froze in the middle of his sentence, his eyes on the doorway.

"Miss Olive," I said, following his gaze. "How long have you been standing there?"

She regarded our antics with an amused look. "Oh, just long enough."

I grunted and Dominick cleared his throat.

"Mr. Dominick Cotter, I presume," she said, extending her hand. "You are a fine reporter, sir. I enjoy reading your work."

"Thank you, umm...Miss Olive. That's very kind of you to say." We looked at each other in awkward silence. "Well, I best be going. I've got a umm...a piece I'm working on for that...you know...yeah." Dominick gave Olive a curt bow and said, "Later, Levi," before he slithered out of the room.

"You look surprised to see me," she said. "But then you're usually the one dropping in on me unannounced, as opposed to the other way around."

I offered her a seat, but she declined.

"Thank you, but I won't be long. I had a civic engagement next door at the library and thought I'd stop by to say hello. The lady at the front desk said I should just go on back."

"Yeah, I bet she did," I said, dryly. "Hey, sorry for that little umm... well, you see we were working and we just kind of uhh..." Her eyebrows arched in anticipation. "Anyway. How can I help you?"

She gave me a cryptic smile and said, "I think I will have a seat after all."

I motioned for her to sit as I took my own seat.

"I see you're reading Thomas Merton," she said, glancing at the book on the desk.

"Well, not yet. I mean, I just got the book from uhh...it was a gift."

"His is a conversion story."

She shot me a knowing look. I didn't really know what to say, so I waited for her to explain the purpose of her visit. But she didn't appear to be in a hurry, as she rather unabashedly perused the items on my desk.

"It appears you are engaged in some interesting research. Perhaps even a mystery?"

Her eyes were glowing with interest as she looked down at the pieces lying on the desk. I didn't want to appear rude, but I had the sudden urge to gather up the pieces and shove them in a drawer. I was about to make a move to do that very thing when Olive turned her attention to me with a soft grunt, indicating she had concluded her unsolicited examination.

"Well then. It is not merely to say hello that I have stopped by to see you, Mr. Levi. In fact, I am here because I have solved a mystery of my own."

I nodded and then shifted uncomfortably as a strange sensation of paranoia worked its way through my body. Again, I felt the urge to collect the items and get them safely out of sight. But Olive appeared to have moved on from her interest in my work as she perked up and began recounting the reason for her surprise visit.

"The mystery of that label," she said with a satisfied nod. I looked at her with a perplexed expression. "The Old Relic label from the whiskey museum. You gave me a picture of it and asked me about it on the Christmas tour. You must have slept since then." She tapped me teasingly on the knee.

"Oh, right. What'd you find out?"

"Well, the lightbulb went off, as they say, while we were on the Christmas tour. I was talking about Hal Moore and the Seventh Cavalry and that sparked my recollection of an image similar to the one on the Old Relic label."

"Yeah, I remember. You paused there for a few seconds, and I thought maybe you forgot your lines."

Her face began to turn red, and she gave me a stern look as she said, "I most certainly did not forget. I'll have you know that I rehearse my parts diligently, going over every syllable until I have mastered each word."

I shook my head in amusement and said, "I'm just razzing you, Miss Olive."

She pursed her lips and said, "Well, perhaps I did lose my concentration for a second or two. Be that as it may, my elocution on Lieutenant General Moore made me think about the insignia of the Seventh Cavalry, which is a seven at the intersection of two crossed sabers."

She looked at me with an intense gaze and I nodded my assent, though I had no idea what the insignia of the Seventh Cavalry was before that moment, nor what it had to do with the label on a bourbon bottle.

"It was then that I had a revelation about the image on the Old Relic bottle. It occurred to me that the snake on the label bears a distinct similarity to the insignia of another military unit, although I couldn't recollect which one at that moment. So, the next morning, I consulted a military history book in my library and found the insignia I was searching for."

She offered a satisfied nod, as if she had just figured out how the magician pulled the rabbit out of the hat.

"Okay," I said in a hesitant tone. "So, what was it?"

"The insignia of the Eighty-Seventh Armored Field Artillery Battalion."

I nodded dumbly, still unsure to what end she was driving.

"The Eighty-Seventh Armored Field Artillery Battalion," she said, repeating herself in a triumphant tone. "Without question, that label is designed in the image of the insignia of the Eighty-Seventh. The color scheme is different, but you have the triangular shield in both, and in both you find the image of a snake with a single eye and a sharp tongue darting out of its mouth. When I put the photograph you gave me next to the image in my book, it was undeniable."

"Huh," I said, scratching my chin. "That's interesting." She appeared ready to boil over in her excitement to tell me the rest of the story, so I prompted her saying, "Dare I imagine that you've already looked into why that label was designed to resemble the Eighty-Seventh insignia?"

"Indeed, I have," she said, clapping her hands together.

"And?"

"Well, I went to the library to research the records of locals who have served in the armed forces. And wouldn't you know I discovered that one

Thomas Westcott did, in fact, serve in the Eighty-Seventh Armored Field Artillery Battalion during World War Two."

"And what? You think his son designed that label in honor of his father?"

"It would certainly be a fine way to honor a father's service, don't you think?"

"I suppose that would be one way to honor his father's service," I said, remembering the picture of Thomas Westcott in military dress that I saw in his son's study. "But why Old Relic? Was he saying that his dad was a relic of the war, a remnant of the past? And why retire the brand name and label in favor of Old Royal? I mean, if he wanted to honor his..."

I stopped, a sudden thought occurring to me. Reaching for the letter on the desk, I read aloud the lines that had captured my thought.

"Oh, the adventures he and I had growing up in a time before the world was set afire in the chaos of destruction and madness. Yet, the pride I feel for my friend's courage in joining the fray has never lessened, though my own call has been to contend in spiritual rather than military warfare."

I looked at Olive and saw her eyes were alight with interest. Again, she looked down at the pieces lying on the desk. Instinctively, I stood and put myself between her and the desk and for a quick second, her face flashed anger at my protective move. But the look quickly faded as her demeanor shifted back to the prim self-confidence to which I was accustomed.

"Well then," she said, rising from her chair. "If I can be of any assistance to you in helping to solve your mystery, you know where to find me."

"Of course," I said in a hesitant tone. "Look, thanks for stopping by and for sharing your...discovery."

She gave me a tight smile, turned on her heel, and walked out the door. When she was gone, I gathered up everything on the desk and took it to George's office. As always, he was happy to store it in his safe. I told him I would be out of the office for a couple of days, but that I'd be on the job, pursuing that white whale of a story that I'd promised to bring him.

"Well now, Motley, you know I ain't one to perch myself on a man's shoulder, but just for giggles, where ya off to?"

I tossed him a one-word answer as I turned to leave.

"Manchester."

CHAPTER
TWENTY-NINE

THE DANIEL BOONE National Forest is comprised of over 700,000 acres of rugged, mountainous terrain covering twenty-one counties in the Appalachian region of Kentucky. It was named for the legendary explorer who made an expedition into the Cumberland Gap in 1769 to prepare the wilderness for westward expansion. As I drove alongside the jagged limestone cliffs and river valleys that pervaded the forest, I thought about Olive and how she would be pleased to know I took it upon myself to learn this bit of the region's history.

My research into the area also uncovered that the original name of the town I would soon be driving through was Greenville. But as fate would have it, there was already a Kentucky town called Greenville, so the name was changed to Manchester. The way I saw it that was a good thing, as I didn't think Greenville Federal Correctional Institution had the same foreboding strength as the prison's actual moniker, which referenced the industrial English city of the same name.

Thinking about Olive took me back to the day I first heard her practiced soliloquy on the frontier crucible that she posited as the key to understanding the character and identity of the archetypal Kentuckian. I had been entranced by her speech and felt a sense of pride when she made it a point to say that I, too, was an inheritor of the great cultural traditions of the state that she so loved. But as I thought about that, I heard a voice in the back of my mind offering a dissenting view on the matter of my supposed cultural inheritance. The voice belonged to Grandma Lenny, and her take on the matter was simple and direct.

"Bullshit."

With that succinct message in mind, it occurred to me that Olive McGill and Lenora Motley, had they ever met, might not have liked each other very much. I thought that not because their ideas on culture and identity were dissimilar, but because Olive McGill spoke of identity as if it were a cloak that any man, woman, or child from Ashland to Paducah could simply drape over their shoulders to magically assume the natural birthright of the Kentuckian.

But Lenora Motley didn't have any cloak to offer her grandsons though like Olive, she knew her history. Her family history. Her neighborhood history. A neighborhood inhabited by people who were tough, proud, and eminently situated in that ever-burgeoning class of America known as the working poor. Not that we knew we were poor. After all, knowledge is a comparative exercise and we were blithely unaware that we occupied one end or another of the city, much less that there existed some magical land beyond our borders known as suburbia.

As boys, we learned about our family and neighborhood history from Grandma Lenny, who schooled us with the wistful pride of someone longing for the ever-elusive stability of better days. She talked about life in Portland during its heyday, recounting stories about characters imbued with grandiose powers of strength, humor, honor, and the spectacular ability to imbibe copious amounts of grain liquor. The favorite of these mythical characters was her father, after whom Declan was named. A second-wave Irish immigrant, Declan Farrell was, as grandma told it, a quixotic figure beloved as a wit, storyteller, and jokester who could capture and command an audience anywhere, anytime. But Declan Farrell was also a mercurial man with an unpredictable temperament, a dockworker who supplemented his meager income with burglary and theft. That is, when he wasn't bellied up to the bar along with the working-class immigrants of his ilk, men who were more at home on the stools of the wharf taverns than they were in the pews at St. Patrick's or Notre Dame du Port.

I found Grandma Lenny's stories to be both entertaining and educational. But Declan came away from the telling with a sense of regret and bitterness, as if the stories represented a lost inheritance. Still the tales captivated him, especially those of Great-Grandpa Farrell, and he honed his suave, devil-may-care attitude according to the often embellished and largely apocryphal character of his eponymous forebear. Those cool aspects he crafted in the likeness of Declan Farrell comingled with the hard aspects he forged in the image of our father, Raymond Motley. The resulting figure that my brother cut was that of a cunning old-world crook endowed with the muscle of a modern street fighting man. Where the cruelty came from was another matter, but it all coalesced in the stage character that Declan Motley played with Faustian aplomb.

Declan, I thought as I drove through the foothills of the Cumberland Mountains. *What the hell am I going to say to him?*

I thought about that question for several miles, rehearsing one opening line after another. But eventually I gave up, knowing my brother would smell weakness in any man who had to prepare a canned greeting. Instead, I spent the rest of the journey thinking about Olive McGill and Lenora Motley, two summmae cum laude historians from two different worlds though each had lived her life not more than an hour's drive from the other. As I thought about the two women, I thought maybe they would have liked each other, despite the fact that one had a judge for a father while the other had a thief.

Maybe not in spite of the fact, but because of it, I thought. *After all, didn't Oscar Wilde once say the only difference between saints and sinners is that every saint has a past while every sinner has a future?*

I looked out the window at the jagged limestone cliffs and river valleys flashing by and decided that, yes, Grandma Lenny and Olive McGill would have liked each other after all. I decided that was especially true given my certain belief that both Judge Harry McGill and Great-Grandpa Declan Farell had been all too familiar with that old "saints and sinners" quip and that each had coopted it on more than one occasion to suit his own purposes.

CHAPTER
THIRTY

T HE DOOR BEYOND the Plexiglass divide opened and my brother entered the room. The prison guard unshackled his hands and feet, and Declan sat and picked up the receiver. I followed suit, my throat feeling like a kinked hose as I fumbled for an opening.

"Hey, brother."

Declan's lips curled in mockery. "All those hours driving down here and that's the best you could come up with?"

"Ah, you know, umm…I had something better, but I scrapped it."

He gave me a contemptuous look to let me know my discomfort was exactly what he had been expecting.

"Forget it," I said, but I knew he wouldn't. We were mere seconds into our interaction and already he had managed to intimidate me.

What the hell? I thought.

"This guy needs a job, right? So, he takes one as a toothbrush salesman. His first week numbers are squat, nada, zilch. Didn't sell a one. So, he goes to his sales manager and asks him for some pointers and the manager says to him, 'The trick is you gotta make 'em feel like they don't have a choice but to buy a toothbrush.' So, the next week the guy's number one on the sales board and the manager pulls him aside and says, 'My man, how'd you go from zero to top of the board?' So, the guy tells him that he went to the airport and set up a table with a sign that said 'free chips and dip, take a bite.' So, all the people passing by stop and try it out. But every time a person took a bite, they'd look at the guy and say, 'This dip tastes like shit.' And every time the guy would look at 'em and say, 'It is shit. Wanna buy a toothbrush?'"

Declan shook his head in disappointment. "Chrissake, Levi, I sat right next to you when Tommy Arnold told that joke at Scotty's Place. And besides, you're supposed to use that retard voice. That's what makes the joke funny."

I dropped my eyes to avoid his disgusted glare.

"Three years and you show up with a joke I already heard? And told better by a fuckin' ingrate like Tommy Arnold at that."

"Yeah, well about that. Look, I'm sorry. I've just, you know...I've been..."

"Don't give me that sorry I've been too busy to come see you crap. I didn't ask you to come down here. Christ, I'd respect you more if you'd just tell the truth."

"Oh, and you've got a handle on that, do you? And what do you mean you'd respect me more? I didn't know you respected me at all."

"Well, it's goddamn difficult when you show up after three years with a lame joke and some horseshit about how bad you feel that you ain't been to see me before now."

"Okay, fine. I didn't want to come because I didn't want to see you in this shithole. Is that truth enough for you?"

"It's a damn sight better than the pity I saw on your face when I walked through the door."

"It wasn't pity. It was surprise."

He barked a shrill laugh. "'Surprise,' he says. Leave it to little brother to be surprised when he sees a prisoner in chains in, oh wait, where are we? A prison." He slouched in his chair and regarded me with a face knotted in disgust. "You were always soft, Levi. A mama's boy without a mother. That's why I had to..."

He stopped and leaned forward, his eyes locking on my free hand as it lay on the counter.

"Where is it?" I withdrew my hand from the counter. "You best be telling me it's getting dialed in and polished at Frederick and Sons on Market." I started to speak but my face went flush with shame. Declan regarded me with a look of utter disdain and said, "I knew I shouldn't have given it to you."

"It wasn't yours to give."

"Yeah, well it was a mistake to let you keep it. What a complete and total fuck up you are."

"Look where you're sitting, asshole." I slammed my fist into the Plexiglas. "You wanna compare notes about who the fuck up is?"

A guard stepped forward and barked at me to calm down or get tossed.

"Yeah, yeah. I hear you," I said, raising a quieting hand. "Sorry."

The guard eyeballed me as he stepped back to his post. I drew in a deep breath and exhaled slowly as a smile played at the edge of Declan's lips.

"Look, I didn't come here to fight with you."

The smile fluttered maliciously on his lips, and I had to remind myself that to Declan, my visit didn't represent a moment of fraternal bonding. His stock in trade was knowing a person's motivations, desires, and weaknesses, so he could exploit them to his advantage. He wasn't on the streets, so the play wasn't for money or power or turf. His play was for a few minutes of amusement at my expense. But I wasn't going to let him run me out of the place by shaming me. To even the score, I decided to hit the bastard where he lives.

"I was down on Griffiths Avenue a few weeks back. There must've been a half-dozen cruisers a couple of blocks down from pop's old place. Lights everywhere." The flutter of Declan's smile faded, and his eyes were suddenly laced with a sliver of jealousy. "Turns out J.C. Turner..."

"I heard all about it," he said, cutting me off. "Ol' boy finally manned up and took care of business with Randy Johns. 'Bout fuckin' time. Randy had been bangin' J.C.'s old lady for the better part of a year."

"Tammy?"

"Nah, he dumped that bitch and got with Jamie Durbin. You know, Marvin's sister."

"Yeah, I remember. She worked at the department store on Portland Avenue." I put a hand to my chest and made a lifting motion.

"Yeah, that's her. Big ol' titties," he said, grinning. "Guess Randy thought they was too big for one man to handle, the horny bastard. Bet he don't think that no more."

"How'd you hear about it?"

"Bobby's people. They visit every month and give him the rundown."

"Bobby Chestnut?"

"Nah, Bobby Shouse."

"Shouse is in here?"

He nodded. "Almost a year. Counterfeiting charge." He leaned forward, unable to conceal his curiosity. "So, why'd you go down to the neighborhood? I mean, shouldn't a college boy like you be hanging out in The Highlands with all the other frat boys?"

I hesitated, girding myself against his inevitable disbelief at my reason for visiting our old haunts. He stared at me, waiting. Finally, I said, "I was, umm...taking pictures."

"Pictures? What kind of pictures?"

"You know, umm...of the old man's house and, uhh...different spots around the neighborhood." He gave me an incredulous look, his mouth hanging half-open. "Yeah, I know. Not the brightest idea I've ever had." He got ready to lay me open, but I moved on with the story before he could get the words out. "I about got into it with a couple of guys, too. This tricked-out Explorer pulls up in the middle of the street and some wannabe tough guy asks me what the hell I was doing."

"Yeah, I would've had the same question."

I ignored him and continued. "So, I come right back at him and say, 'What the hell are you doin'?' Then he points to some dude in the passenger seat, all shadowy and discreet, and he tells me that guy owns the old man's house now."

Declan listened with his mouth still slightly agape. But I could also see that covetous glint in his eyes, letting me know he was desperate for information about the goings on in his stomping grounds.

"So, this driver, you know, he's like maybe twenty-one but fronting like he's O.G. or something. And, believe me, I know I'm not walking away from this unless I take this guy on. I mean, after all, I am standing on the sidewalk with a camera, looking like some kind of narc. So, I walk out into the street and tell him my old man grew up in the house I was photographing. 'Who's your old man?' the guy asks, and I say, 'Ray Motley.' 'Never heard of him,' he says."

Declan's face contorted in disbelief. "Bullshit he's never heard of Ray Motley."

"Yeah, well, he was a pretty young kid. But I could tell the other guy knew exactly who the old man was, and I got the sense he wanted to split."

Declan nodded and said, "Damn straight he did."

"So, I look at the kid and he's got his right hand on the wheel, but his left hand is down by the doorframe."

"A gunsel."

"Exactly," I said. "But I'm not backing down to this punk. Not for nothin'."

For several minutes, I proceeded to relate the events that followed. Declan leaned back in his chair, processing what I was saying so he could later find a way to use it for his own manipulative purposes. I told him the punk driver continued to claim he'd never heard of Ray Motley and that I told the kid maybe he'd heard of Rock Motley. But the kid shrugged with a smartass look on his face and asked again why I was taking pictures of the house. It wasn't difficult to put two and two together to see that the house was probably a front for a drug operation. Still, I stuck to my story that I was a photographer and that I had just come around to visit the neighborhood where I had grown up.

I further explained that the young punk challenged me to drop some names of people from the neighborhood that I knew, but before I could, a red Mustang pulled up next to the Explorer. A woman leaned out of the Mustang and asked the punk kid if he'd heard about J.C., to which he responded that he heard Randy told J.C., "It ain't his fault Jay can't make his old lady cum", and that Jay straight blasted him. Not wanting to hear any more specifics, I walked around the Explorer and stood on the sidewalk.

I went on with the story, telling Declan I must've stared at that tinted window for a full minute before the mystery man in the passenger seat rolled it down. I asked the guy if he owned the house behind me and he nodded. I told the guy I grew up a few blocks away on Bank Street, but that some of the guys I ran with lived down that way. I told him I knew Marty Cooper, Dickie Hatfield, and Freddy Sadlow, explaining that we used to call him Ringo because he played the drums. He stared at me, but I didn't look away. Finally, the red Mustang moved down the block and the driver returned to sizing me up. His left hand was still hanging out of view, and he had a cocky look on his face, like he knew what was coming and I didn't. The guy in the driver seat then asked why I was taking pictures.

"I still can't figure that part out myself," Declan said, interjecting.

I explained to Declan that I told the guy again that my old man was

Ray Motley and that he grew up in the house I was photographing. At that, the smartass punk broke in and again said he had never heard of him. But my gut continued to tell me that the man in the passenger seat had heard of the old man and if the driver had not, then that probably meant the punk kid hadn't grown up in Portland.

"Hell no, he didn't," Declan said.

Continuing my story, I described how I had pointed out a vacant shell of a building at the end of the block, stating that it used to be the Shamrock Inn. I told the guy my old man had a buddy named Dave McGinty who lived above the bar and that the two of them would run the streets while their pops would get their load on. After I said this, the driver called bullshit, claiming the place had most recently been a video store with tanning beds and a liquor store before that. The cocky prick went on to say with grim satisfaction there had never been a bar there and then he spat out the window. But the driver locked eyes with me and nodded with appreciation as he confirmed that I had spoken the truth. He looked at the kid and told him many years ago, the building had, in fact, been the Shamrock Inn, explaining that his own father had spent so much time there he probably grew roots into the floor.

Declan gave a slight smile that if I didn't know better, might have been a show of pride.

"So, then the driver says, 'Your brother Declan Motley?'"

Declan's smile became a sinister look of self-satisfaction.

"I said, 'That's right.' Then he says, 'Yeah, I think I remember you, but you ain't been around for a while.' I told him, 'That's right, I moved away.' So now the punk-ass driver acts like we're cool and all and he says, 'Damn, brother, you got some Portland blood in you.' I ignored him, and said to the other guy, 'Look, I get it. It was a stupid move to stand out here taking pictures. I'm just visiting old haunts, that's all.' So, the man in the passenger seat said, 'Nah, man, you're good,' and before I could say anything more, the window went up and they drove away."

Declan looked pleased but I could see there was a question burning in his dark eyes. After a moment he said, "How come I heard about J.C. and Randy, but didn't hear nothin' about you running up against Square Teddy?" I shrugged and gave him a confused look. "It had to be Teddy. Don't know who the youngster was, though." Declan lit a cigarette, took a drag, and flicked ashes onto the floor as he said, "But you didn't stick around to get no names, did you?"

Declan made a sucking sound as he pulled on the cigarette as I shifted uneasily in my seat.

"Yeah, you talked your way out of it didn't you, little brother? Didn't mind dropping the old man's name neither, did you?" He looked at me carefully, but I didn't speak. "All's I'm saying is that it's good to be able to stand behind a name. Ain't that right, Levi?"

I didn't answer, careful not to fall into whatever trap he was laying for me.

"Too bad that little brown boy that got cracked in the head with a shovel didn't have no names to throw out." I sat up straight as Declan gave me a toothless grin. "But he wouldn't have had any names to give, now would he?"

"What are you talking about? What boy?"

"Hmm. Let's see, what boy could I be talking about?" He looked up at the ceiling, feigning ignorance. "What boy, indeed."

I shook my head, not wanting to hear anymore. "You know what, screw it. I don't need to know what you're talking about."

"Oh, but I think you do need to know, little brother."

I stared at him, trying to remain calm despite the sharp uptick in my heart rate. Declan snuffed out his cigarette, pulled out another, and offered it to me in a mock gesture of charity. I glared at him as he shrugged and lit up.

"But if you don't want to know. Hey, I understand. I mean, it must have all been so traumatic for little Levi."

How the hell could he know about Moussa? I thought, my mind racing.

I put the phone down and glared at him, wondering how he was planning to twist me up with this information. I had come all this way with just a sliver of hope that I could procure some instinctive advice from my brother about how to get deeper inside my investigation. But I didn't think for a minute that he had any real information about the case. Yet there he was, dangling something he knew right in my face, knowing I would take the bait. I picked up the receiver and said, "How do you know about that?"

"About what?"

"Come on, Declan. This is important. You can mess with my head all you want, but I need to know what you know."

He put his hands up and shrugged in a gesture of pure ignorance.

"Fine. Then I won't tell you how your name got thrown out in the middle of all this."

"Oh, come on," he said with a mocking snort. "You know you can't bluff me."

But I could see that whether he believed me or not, I had his attention. More than that, his ego demanded he know everything I knew, so he could build up his street cred on the information. In truth, we were in the same position, each of us wanting to know what cards the other held. We both had motives that were purely selfish and that made our standoff the most honest moment in the whole shitty conversation.

"You first. After all, you brought it up, big brother."

His lip curled derisively, and he stared at me for a long moment, calculating his possible moves. In the end, he knew I had an option he didn't, the option to get up and walk out. If I did, then he would be left not knowing how his name was being tossed around in the street. We both knew he couldn't allow that.

"There's some boys in here from down that way, down near where you've been staying the last few months."

"How do you..."

"Doesn't matter," he said, waving a dismissive hand. "I know things. That's the way the street works. You know things, or you suffer at the hands of those who know more than you. Not that you'd know anything about it, college boy." I bit my lip and waited for him to continue. "Anyway. There are some boys in here from down that way. Marion County."

I felt my heart pick up a pace. "You talkin' about those Cornbread Mafia guys?" He gave a slight nod. "I heard they got busted with like fifty tons of pot."

"Oh, it was a lot more than that. And those cunt feds couldn't get one of them to turn. Not one rat among 'em. Now that, I respect."

"Yeah, I heard that. So, what do they have to do with anything?"

"Simple. They hear stuff about their 'hood the same way I hear stuff about mine. And if some redneck got into a pinch in their 'hood the way you got into one in mine..."

"Ours."

His lip curled in contempt as he continued his point. "...the way you got into one in mine, then it would probably take some fast talk like the kind you pulled off to get out of it."

"For Christ's sake, Declan, just say it. You're talking about Moussa Diab."

"Think about it," he said, eyeballing me with a narrow gaze. "You got cornered for doing something stupid but got out of it because you dropped a few names and places from around the neighborhood. That's why they let you walk. Because despite being a first-rate asshole that ain't got sense enough to know better than to snap photographs in broad daylight, and a block from a murder scene at that, you were from there and could prove it."

It was plain enough to see he was talking about Moussa and before I got myself neck-deep in the investigation, I had thought Moussa's death to have been easily explained as a racially motivated attack. So, to that end, Declan had a point. Moussa would've had an uphill battle either way, but if he'd been able to connect with his attacker, to call out some name or place familiar to him, then maybe he would've had a chance to get clear of the situation. Maybe.

But that's only true if the official story holds, I thought. *And I'm way beyond the official story.*

"So, tell me something, baby brother." He leaned in toward the dividing glass. "Why the hell are you asking questions about some sand nigger that got what he deserved for being someplace he didn't belong?"

I felt the blood rush to my temples as my grip tightened on the receiver. I glanced over at the guard and then back at my brother, seething with contempt for his cruelty. Declan gave me a wicked smile, but I was past being baited. I was ready to stand up to my brother whether it be now, or on the street once his release came through.

"What's the problem, baby brother?" He lifted a hand and flopped it down at the wrist. "You got some kind of queer thing going on?"

"Go to hell, Declan. And leave Moussa's name out of your bitch mouth."

This time it was his fist that flew into the Plexiglas. "Easy to say on the other side of the glass, you punk motherfucker."

The guard standing beside the door shouted an order. Declan smiled and nodded toward the guard and then turned back to me with an evil look on his face.

"What's up, Levi? You turn fag since the last time I saw you?" I took a deep breath and fought to remain calm. "Oh, I forgot what a soft-hearted, sweet boy you are. Well, don't worry your innocent little head. I won't say anymore bad words about your little brown boyfriend."

He puckered his lips together and made a kissing sound.

"I'll see you on this, Declan. The day you get released I'll be the first person you see, and you will pay for this."

He feigned a look of fear. "Oh, no, what am I gonna do? Little Levi's going to see me on this once I get out. Maybe I should ask the warden to extend my stay here in Shangri-La."

"Oh, I wouldn't worry about that. From what I hear, your stay is getting shorter not longer."

Upon hearing that, Declan ceased with the smartass antics and his eyes burned into mine in a way that made me thankful I was, as he had said, on the other side of the glass.

"And just what in the hell are you talking about, Levi?"

I stared at my brother in silence. After a long moment, his hand smacked hard against the divider. The guard took a step toward him, but Declan raised his hand in a gesture of peace and smiled at the guard. Turning back to me, he waited for a response with no intention of repeating the question.

"The man's name was Moussa. And I swear on the grave of our dead grandmother, Declan, you will remember that name if I have to spell it in blood across your face."

Declan waited as he regarded me with a vicious, unblinking glare.

"It looks like maybe this guy Moussa got wrapped up in something. I don't know exactly what or if he even knew about it, but for some reason there are powerful people who are pissed-off at me for asking questions. I assume you heard about those questions from those Cornbread boys?"

He continued to glare at me but didn't speak.

"One of these pissed-off people has a son in state politics. The guy's name is Conrad Westcott, and his son's name is Rogers. He cornered me the other night and said he knew I had a brother in prison and that his son could get my brother out on early release. He was a smartass about it, talking about how family should be together over the holidays and how he couldn't stand to see me and my brother apart. Said he could make it happen before next Christmas."

"But that's not possible, since I've got two and change left on my term." His voice was unnerving in its placid ferocity. "And there is no such thing as federal parole and there are no reduced years, except when some fucking rat gives information over to the feds." He leaned forward, his nose almost touching the Plexiglas. "And you see the thing is, little brother, I ain't no fucking rat. So why would my stay be any shorter than what the judge handed me?"

I licked my dry lips and tried to swallow. "I'll get a handle on this."

"A handle on what?"

"They think I'm onto something they want. I think Westcott was trying to bribe me, but I didn't let on that you wouldn't want to get out early."

"Oh, no, no. It's not that I don't want to get out early, it's that I cannot and will not get out early. Because if I were to get out early, then the whole goddamn city will think I'm a fucking rat. Do you understand that?"

"Yes, I get it."

"Then don't just get a handle on it," he said through clenched teeth. "Choke it to death."

"Okay, I hear you. But you want me squash this, then you gotta tell me what these Cornbread guys have heard."

He gave me a bemused look as if I hadn't heard a word he had said.

"Come on, Declan. That's not ratting. You want me to get this under control? Fine. Tell me what you've heard." He shook his head as if he couldn't believe the level of my stupidity. "You said it yourself. These guys hear things about where they're from, just like you do. And I know you, Declan. You play people to get information that you can turn to your gain. That's your game."

His eyes narrowed as he regarded me with a cold stare.

"Tell me what you've heard."

I waited, but he only leaned back in his chair and folded his arms across his chest.

"Fine. I'll go back to Westcott and tell him to greenlight your release. Then I won't have to spend any more holidays without my big brother. Hell, maybe this guy can find mom and we can all be together, like one big dysfunctional family."

We sat and looked at each other for several minutes. Finally, I shook my head in frustration and was on the verge of leaving when Declan broke his silence.

"I don't know much."

"What do you know?"

He leaned forward and pointed a finger at me. "What I know is that I've got a weak-ass brother who's jamming me up."

I placed the receiver on the hook, leaned back, and folded my own arms across my chest. Declan glared at me for a full minute. Finally, he jerked his head toward the receiver. I waited another ten seconds and then picked it up.

"Artemis Ray. Those boys are talking about some guy named Artemis Ray. He's supposed to be some kind of badass." He snorted in derision. "They're saying this guy Moussa wandered into an operation."

"What kind of operation?"

"Jesus, Levi, if you can't keep up, then drop out before it's too late."

"Okay, I understand," I said, raising a hand. "A pot operation."

"Yeah, a pot operation. Your boy got too close to something, but the guy that took the rap for killing him was just some redneck clown. None of it went down the way the guy sold it, but so what? They closed the case, and nobody was asking questions until some city boy started poking his city-boy nose into it. I almost fell over when I heard it was you. I didn't even know you were in Kentucky, but then how would I? Baby brother doesn't want to be traumatized by seeing big brother behind bars."

"Is that it?"

"That's what I know. Whatever kind of cover-up got arranged, it's this Artemis guy who's pulling the strings."

"Artemis Ray?"

He nodded and I wrote the name down. When I was finished, I looked up at my brother and stared in amazement at the slight wrinkle I observed in the carefully crafted mask that was Declan Motley. In truth, I couldn't believe what I was seeing because I couldn't remember ever having seen it before. Despite every instinct in my body telling me I had to be imagining things, I could have sworn my brother's face displayed a look of genuine concern.

"You should be careful, Levi. If what these boys say is true…"

I continued to stare in utter amazement as for one rare moment,

Declan let me know he was, after all, my big brother. He held my eyes for a few seconds, then he blinked, and whatever wrinkle of care I had seen smoothed over and vanished.

"What's this really about, Declan?"

"What it's always about," he said with a knowing shake of his head. "Money and power."

"Gotta have one to get the other."

"That's right," he said, slumping back in his chair. "And what better way to grab some major cash than to step into the void left by these Cornbread boys being locked up and doing twenty?"

My eyes narrowed as I considered his point.

"The pot game," he said, expressing the obvious. "These powerful people you're talking about. They took over the pot game."

I nodded my head in slow comprehension of his hypothesis.

"Use your freakin' head, Levi. Those boys had a multistate operation raking in tens of millions off the books. What, did half of America suddenly stop smoking weed when the Cornbread Mafia got locked up? Fuck no. It's probably the same bastards that put 'em in here that are making millions off what those guys built."

"Nature abhors a vacuum," I said almost to myself.

"Yeah, well so does the black market."

Declan sat up straight, leaned in, and locked eyes with me.

"Money and power, little brother. And in case it's not obvious by now, that ain't your game. So, you better watch your back."

CHAPTER
THIRTY-ONE

A FEW DAYS AFTER my visit to Manchester, I sat at a table in Café Mozart, sipping coffee and nibbling on a blueberry bagel. I had spent much of the trip from Manchester to Bardstown ruminating on Declan's theory that there was a connection between the power brokers I was making nervous and the marijuana business that had previously been dominated by the Cornbread Mafia. It made sense that someone stepped into the vacuum left by the incarceration of those Cornbread boys. Of course they did. My problem with the theory was making the connection to Moussa. I simply could not imagine any scenario in which Moussa Diab insinuated himself in the cultivation or sale of Kentucky Bluegrass, which as it turns out was a strain of marijuana made famous by one of the leaders of the Cornbread Mafia, a man named Johnny Boone who had been dubbed "The Godfather of Grass".

I had learned that bit of trivia after spending a few hours in *The Observer* archives, researching those folk heroes of the pot trade. Just as Dominick had told me, George Hawley published some excellent work on the group and the archives contained not only his articles, but some fantastic photos to boot. Through my research, I learned that "Cornbread Mafia" was the name given to the group by federal prosecutors after seventy members were arrested in 1989. The group's operation included twenty-nine farms across ten states in the southeast and Midwest. Federal agents estimated they seized nearly two hundred tons of marijuana at the time of the group's arrest. But just as I had heard from both Dominick and Declan, not a single one of those arrested made a deal for leniency.

I reviewed this information in my notebook, thinking the story would make for an incredible book someday. But for now, I had enough on my plate trying to figure out the facts of Moussa's death and the angle that Conrad Westcott was playing with his quid pro quo. I scribbled out my original take on the matter, applying Occam's razor to the case to try and bring order to my thoughts.

Conrad Westcott is a bourbon baron whose deceased brother, James, became a Trappist monk and adopted the name Brother Llewellyn. Brother Lew had been friends with Hamia Diab for many years. Hamia's son, Moussa, made a pilgrimage to Gethsemani where Brother Lew was known to create spiritual adventures for people visiting the monastery. He devised a quest for Moussa to help him figure out his path in life. But brother Lew died before Moussa arrived, and the letter from Hamia to Brother Lew stating that her son was looking forward to his time at Gethsemani fell into the hands of Brother Lew's sister-in-law, Isabelle Westcott. She called to let Brother Simon know that Moussa was invited to dinner at the Westcott's, but Moussa didn't accept the invitation. A couple of days later, Moussa wandered into a place where he shouldn't have been and got sideways with Dale Goodlett. Whatever the facts are regarding what actually transpired, the end result was Moussa's death. Not wanting his name attached to what looked to be a racially motivated killing, Conrad Westcott denied to Regina Sandoval that any invitation was ever sent to Moussa Diab. The case was settled with Dale Goodlett going to jail, and life goes on.

I studied the summation. It was neat, clean, and plausible. That was, until you applied other factors to the scenario. I wrote out those factors.

Number One: Regina Sandoval. What's her role? And why would she go to such lengths to deceive both me and, presumably, Conrad Westcott, if there wasn't more to this?

Number Two: The invisible presence of powerful people who I am told are upset by my questions about what happened to Moussa. Who are these people, and why do my questions make them nervous?

Number Three: Conrad Westcott. Speaking of powerful people who are upset, the guy tried to bribe me offering Declan's freedom in exchange for the treasure I'm supposedly pursuing. That makes no sense. What treasure?

Number Four: Artemis Ray. Who the hell is he? I don't know, but

Declan said the Cornbread boys in Manchester are saying that the situation with Moussa didn't go down the way the official story tells it. And they say that somebody named Artemis Ray is behind the cover-up of whatever really happened.

I stared at the four factors I had identified. Reading each one was like pulling the pin from a hand grenade and throwing it into the neat summation I had written out. Individually, each factor caused serious damage to the simple logic model that my summation represented. But together, they obliterated the notion that Moussa Diab's death was anything close to an open-and-shut case. I sighed, placed my pen on the notebook, and reached for my coffee. But before I could even lift the cup, I heard a voice that made my jaw go slack.

"Well, Mr. Motley, it looks like you might have a future as an investigator after all."

Looking up, I stared with strained comprehension at Regina Sandoval standing before me. I tried to speak, but words refused to form on my lips. Instead, I continued to stare at the woman in disbelief until the awkwardness of the moment prompted her to sit down.

"I hate to be presumptuous, but if you sit there with your jaw on the table much longer then people will start to wonder if you're having a stroke."

"I think I might be," I said, still processing the unreality of her presence.

"Well, I suppose that's understandable given the way we parted after our last meeting."

"You mean, after I confronted you about being a lying piece of shit. Let's not sugarcoat things just to be polite."

"Oh, don't worry, Mr. Motley. I haven't mistaken you for a man who hides his feelings in the interest of diplomacy."

"Then you've read me correctly. Given that fact, I suggest you get your ass away from me before I come across this table."

"You're not going to do that," she said, shaking her head.

"And why is that?"

"Because that's what your brother would do. And you're not the criminal in the family, now are you?"

I felt my face go flush as blood began to pulse in my temples. "You don't wanna be saying things like that to me."

"Why? Because you don't want to appear a foregone conclusion? Don't worry. You are anything but."

I glanced around the café and then back at the woman sitting across from me.

"Trying to see if I've got back up somewhere? Well, I don't. I'm here alone"

"Here for what? You can't possibly think that I'd..."

"I'm here for the same purpose I had when I first called you," she said, cutting me off.

"Which is?"

"Oh, don't be coy. I have the same purpose you have. I'm looking for something. The only difference between us is that you're still trying to figure out what it is."

"Lady, there's a lot more that separates us than that. So, I suggest you leave before you find out just how different we are."

She looked at me without expression for several seconds but made no move to get up. One of the owners of the café appeared, remembering us from our previous visit. As the owner spoke, I forced a smile and nodded as if everything was normal.

"May I get a cup of chai?"

I shot a disbelieving look at her, but my companion only smiled at the owner who said she'd bring the tea right away. The owner scooted away, and Sandoval looked at me with a carefree expression.

"Leave. Now."

She feigned a look of incredulity and said, "It would be an act of discourtesy to place an order and then depart before the order has arrived. And I have no intention of wasting that fine woman's time."

"Listen to me. You've got as long as it takes her to come back with that drink before this takes a nasty turn."

"Are you threatening violence, sir? In a public place?"

"I'm not playing with you, lady." My tone was low and ominous. "Start talking or leave."

She sniffed and gave me an indignant look. Regina Sandoval, or whatever her name was, clearly preferred to control the conversation. But my words, and more likely my demeanor, seemed to convince her that the timer on this particular conversation was running out. So, she gave up whatever rhetorical strategy she had planned and got to the point.

"I have a proposition for you."

"What could you possibly offer that I would want?"

"The truth, of course. Or is that something that no longer interests you?"

"I'm doing just fine on my own," I said.

"Yes, you are. But the trail you're following will only get you so far." It was clear from our earlier interaction that the woman had her ways of finding things out, so I didn't react to whatever it was she thought she knew about my investigation. "Play it cool all you want. But I know more than you might imagine. Especially after speaking to Hamia Diab."

I looked at her with disgust and said, "Do you have a soul?" She returned my look with a deadpan stare. "Posing as an Assistant U.S. Attorney? You're giving that woman false hope, making her believe there's justice to be had for her son. What the fuck is wrong with you?"

She looked at me narrowly and said, "Haven't you figured out what this is about?"

"Money and power. What else?"

"Oh, don't be naïve. That's only the force behind it. If you really want to know the truth about this, then you'll listen to what I have to say."

The owner of the café brought her tea. She thanked the woman and then turned back to me, tipping the delicate cup to her lips.

"Okay, Sandoval or whatever the hell your name is. Sure, I want the truth. So, tell me, are your eyes blue or green?" She shot me an icy glare. "I mean, come on, the most interesting thing about you is that you're a chameleon. So, which is it?"

"Do you want to hear what I have to say or not?"

"Blue or green? Tell me that first."

"They're blue."

"Well, that's a damn shame," I said, leaning in closer. "You see, I halfway wanted to fuck you when I thought they were green."

Her face went flush, and her lips started to tremble.

"Oh, I'm sorry. Did I offend your delicate sensibilities?"

She laid her hands flat on the table, attempting to steady herself. I gave an indifferent shrug and said, "What can I say? Green eyes really do it for me."

She put a hand to her chest as she attempted to get her breathing under control.

"We could've had a good time, you and me. But then again, maybe you're out of my league. I mean a classy broad like you, I'm sure you've got all kinds of studs lined up to…"

"Artemis Ray."

I stopped talking and stared at her.

"Oh, do I have your attention now, you juvenile asshole? Are you suddenly interested in what I have to say? You better be, because whether you know it or not, you're into it up to your eyeballs. But then again, maybe a gutter rat like you is too stupid to see he's about to get washed away by the oncoming storm."

She took in a breath and closed her eyes. Exhaling a slow breath, she opened her eyes and said, "Now, do you want to hear what I have to say or not?"

We glared at each other for the better part of minute. Finally, I gave a slight twitch of my head.

"We can help each other," she said.

"Why would I help you?"

"You don't know what you're looking for. I do, because I'm looking for it, too." I eyed her cautiously, waiting for her to continue. "I can tell you the what, who, and the why. Isn't that what you reporters are always looking for?"

"You forgot the where and how."

"I don't know the where and how. That's where you come in." I gave her a blank stare. "I know you have the book. And I know you've uncovered information that may have put you on the path to finding it."

"Finding what? All I'm after is the truth about what happened to Moussa."

"I can help you with that, Mr. Motley. I know about your quest."

"What are you talking about?" I shook my head in disbelief. "This so-called quest is nothing more than some spiritual choose-your-own-adventure game. The only reason I'm entertaining any of this is because of Hamia Diab, because she appreciated me being kind to her son. You're crazy if you think Moussa was tied up in some play for whatever the hell it is you're after."

"I don't think he was. I think what Brother Lew devised for Moussa is exactly what you've said it is. But Moussa was killed, and the reasons for his death make this spiritual adventure something far greater than what Brother Lew ever intended it to be."

"Okay, fine. So, what is it that according to you, we're both looking for?"

She shook her head and said, "It's not that easy."

I scoffed at that and said, "How am I supposed to believe you, much less help you, unless you tell me what you're talking about?"

"I give to you, and you give to me."

"Then, damnit, be out with it already," I said, my voice rising. "What the hell are we talking about?"

A few of the café patrons turned to me with looks of concern.

"Sorry," I said with an apologetic wave. "Work stuff."

Sandoval reached into her leather satchel, and I stiffened, remembering the last time she had made that move. She gave a slight shake of her head as she pulled out a piece of paper and slid it across the table. I picked it up and examined it. It was a photocopy of the front of an envelope. The return address was Hamia Diab's and the addressee was Brother Llewellyn in Trappist, Kentucky. I shook my head and said, "What is this?"

"It's a letter from Hamia Diab that fell into the hands of Isabelle Westcott."

"The letter that Denny gave her at Brother Lew's funeral?"

"So, you did learn something on your visit to the monastery." My face was a stone mask. "Anyway, yes. This is a copy of the envelope."

"Where's the letter?"

"I have a copy of that as well. But it doesn't contain anything you wouldn't already know after talking to Hamia."

"How do you know what I know?" She shot me a sardonic frown. "Right. You're amazing at your job. I almost forgot."

She gave me a look that said when you've got it, you've got it.

"Well, if the letter doesn't offer anything more, then why are you showing me the envelope?"

"Look at it more closely."

I studied the photocopy and saw that in the bottom left corner someone had written "See Rogers about activating A.R."

"Given the way you reacted earlier, I take it you've heard of Artemis Ray?"

I hesitated in answering, and she arched her eyebrows, giving me a look that anticipated fair play.

"Yeah, I've heard of him. Word is he had something to do with covering up what really happened to Moussa."

"What else have you heard?"

"That he's some kind of a badass. Somebody I best be watching out for."

"Whoever told you that was correct on both fronts. This is not a man to be taken lightly, Mr. Motley. And he is on to you. That I know for a fact."

"I haven't seen anybody following me. At least nobody other than Nathan Hadley."

"Don't worry about him," she said with a disdainful snort. "Westcott uses him to bully people into giving up local scoop. And you shouldn't expect to see Artemis Ray. That's not the way he works."

I looked down at the photocopy. "So, what? You're telling me this proves a connection between the Westcotts and Artemis Ray? Ergo, if Artemis Ray had something to do with Moussa's death, then that implicates the Westcotts?"

"Correct. I am telling you that."

I held up the copy and shook my head. "You're making quite a leap."

"Maybe. But the letter does prove that the Westcotts knew Moussa was going to be at Gethsemani. And the envelope indicates that they wanted Rogers to contact Artemis Ray, presumably about Moussa's visit."

I gave an incredulous laugh and said, "Yeah, assuming A.R. stands for Artemis Ray. But how do you know this wasn't just a note that someone scribbled on whatever piece of paper was handy at the time?"

"Too big of a coincidence. Especially given that you've heard the name Artemis Ray from someone independent of me. This envelope is corroboration of what that person told you."

"Fair point. But how'd you get a hold of this?"

"Well, I, umm..." She hesitated in a way that was totally out of character for her.

"What?" I said, pressing her.

An embarrassed look came over her face and she said, "I was the Westcott's maid for a day."

I didn't want to laugh, but she flashed me a knowing smile, so I did.

I'll give her this much, I thought. *The woman is resourceful.*

Her smile faded and she leaned across the table with a serious look. "Time to give, Mr. Motley. What have you found?"

I looked at the envelope and considered her conjecture that it was evidence of a connection between Moussa, the Westcotts, and Artemis Ray. She was right. It was independent verification of the name Declan had given me, but I maintained a healthy skepticism that it proved the Westcotts had something to do with Moussa's death. Still, I had to admit it was interesting. Thus, I decided to share the recent developments in my investigation. I told her about the book and the clues but stopped short of telling her what I had found at The Stone House and what I found in the metal box. She listened with an eager attentiveness, devouring me with her eyes as I spoke.

"You're not giving me the whole story," she said when I finished.

"And you haven't told me what it is you're looking for."

"What we're looking for, Mr. Motley."

"I've given equal to what I've received."

She sighed and said, "Then how do we advance the conversation?"

I eyed this woman sitting across from me with wary contempt, considering whether and to what extent I wanted to reengage with her duplicity. And I knew that's what I would be doing. She wouldn't be sitting in front of me if she didn't need me, but the same question that had existed during and after our first go around existed now, namely what was her primary motivation? I didn't know, but her offer to provide the what, who, and the why of Moussa's death was something I had to consider. What I really needed was time to think, so I decided to punt.

"I think we're good for now. Give me a day or two to follow up with my leads while you follow up with yours, and we'll see where we are." I wrote my number on the back of the photocopy and slid it across the table. "Call me at home the day after tomorrow and we'll see where things stand."

She gave me an amused look and said, "You have a home phone?"

I gave an indifferent shrug, not ready to get too chummy with someone I still believed to be a liar. She got up to leave, but I stopped her. "Let me ask you something before you go."

"Okay," she said in a wary voice.

"That story you told me. Did you really lose a brother to violence?"

She looked at me for a moment and then slung her satchel over her shoulder. "No," she said without apology. "But Regina Sandoval did."

I felt my face go flush with anger, but before I could say anything, she turned and walked out the door.

CHAPTER
THIRTY-TWO

The lamps ensconced on the library walls emanated a light that reflected off the pine-colored stacks, creating the effect of a room aglow. Outside, nearly three inches of snow had fallen, and although the clock on the wall read only six-thirty, darkness had fallen on the Abbey of Our Lady of Gethsemani. Still, the hour of Compline had to be completed before the monks' day of prayer and labor would end. Brother Simon had related this fact to me as he compelled me to attend one of the earlier canonical hours, Vespers. He had spotted me as I walked down the hallway on my way to the restroom.

"Still tilting at windmills, Mr. Motley?"

"No rest for the weary," I had said. "But I'm smart enough to know when to come in out of the cold."

"And I see you have done so just in time for prayers."

"Oh," I said, giving him a surprised look. "Have I?"

"Indeed, you have. And I dare say, you are overdue to join us for an hour of prayer."

"Overdue, you say?"

"Mmm-hmm," he said, eyeing me closely. "After all, you've paid enough visits to our humble community to know that prayer is the central component of our reason for being."

"Okay," I said, scratching the stubble on my chin. "Well, I'm headed to the restroom. But you know, I'll, umm...do my best to catch up with you."

I went into the restroom and did my business. When I came out, I found Brother Simon standing in the hallway with his arms crossed and a stern look on his face.

"I am more than happy to show you the way to the chapel, so you don't get lost, of course."

"Of course," I said with a nervous chuckle. "Lead on, Brother."

I followed him down a series of corridors that led to a vestibule outside the chapel where Brother Simon stopped and pointed toward a door. "The steps to the balcony are through that door. From there, you will have a better vantage point and the sublime experience of Gregorian chant rising up to meet you."

He shot me one last pointed look as he turned and made his way into the chapel. I felt like a teenager wanting to pick up a bulletin to prove to his parents that he'd been to church. But then I thought about the many ways Brother Simon had helped me, and it seemed like my attendance at evening prayer was a small sacrifice to make in gratitude for his assistance. Besides, I still had several hours to kill before the clock would strike eleven, so I ambled over to the steps and made my way to the balcony.

Taking my seat, I watched with interest as the monks readied themselves for prayer. They stood in stalls facing each other and on cue, turned toward the altar at the far end of the chapel. Each monk made the sign of the cross as a single note from an organ filled the silence and a cantor chanted, "O God, come to my assistance." In unison, the monks chanted the response, "Lord, make haste to help me." The monks then turned back toward each other, bowed, and chanted, "Glory to the Father, and to the Son, and to the Holy Spirit. As it was in the beginning, is now, and will be forever. Amen."

For the better part of the next hour, I sat mesmerized by the repetitive chanting of hymns, psalms, and gospel passages that Brother Simon later explained were part of the Divine Office of the Church. When Vespers ended, I felt a sense of peace and was glad that I had stayed for the hour of prayer when my instinct had been to bolt.

That experience had been earlier in the day. Now I sat in the library, tapping my pen on the open journal as I thought about the rest of the day's events.

Before I had left for Manchester, Dominick and I agreed that he would follow up on the letter we found in the metal container by seeking out Father William French. Neither of us had much hope we could locate the old priest, that is if he was still kicking, but we agreed it was worth the effort if for no other reason than to see if he could provide insight into the relationship between James and Conrad Westcott. Before I headed to the monastery that morning, Dominick had left a note, telling me that Father French was still extant, that he had spoken to the man, and that he needed to see me right away. But when I had gone looking for him, George told me Dominick had been called out to cover a police chase that had predictably ended in a fiery crash on Louisville Road. I left a note on Dominick's desk letting him know that I was headed out and wouldn't be able to catch up with him until the next day. Then I left for Gethsemani.

Throughout the drive, I thought about the drawings I had found in the metal box. The image of the three sleeping figures eluded my understanding. But I thought I knew what the image of the cross with the hills in the background referred to, and the clock in the corner of the picture clearly indicated eleven o'clock. That the sun in the picture was just shy of its apex indicated that the time referred to eleven in the morning. There wasn't any great mystery to the drawing of the tree with a hole in the trunk, as it seemed to me that somewhere a tree stood with a hole in its trunk proportional to the carved wooden disk. Based on my understanding of the clue, I planned to make my way to Cross Knob by ten-thirty, so I would have time to find the tree and place the disk in the hole on its trunk by eleven o'clock. Next, I would find Brother Simon and ask him about the drawing of the sleeping figures to see if he could help me understand what the image meant. After that, I figured it would be a long day since the clock relating to the image of the sleeping figures indicated eleven o'clock at night.

Putting pen to paper, I headed a page in my journal "The Quest Continues" and began to record my experiences, beginning with my arrival at the monastery when I had pulled my truck into the same spot where I always parked, put on my gloves, retrieved my backpack, and headed out.

I hiked across the frozen ground in the direction of Cross Knob, heading west across a path that inclined as it led into the woods. The way upward became more steep and less sure as I went. It wasn't impassable by any stretch, but it was not well-worn and lacked the aid of switchbacks. I traversed the final hundred meters of the path, which were rocky and steep, and came to a clearing on top of a knob. The scene was exactly as depicted in the drawing with a gray metal cross standing in the foreground of hills and valleys that stretched for miles beyond. I wish I could've stood there six weeks earlier when the foliage would have been on fire with the colors of autumn. Still, I took in the surrounding landscape with appreciation despite the muted effect caused by the onset of winter.

Setting my backpack on the ground, I scanned the area for a tree with a hollowed-out spot in its trunk. It didn't take long to find as it stood beside a trailhead at the edge of the woods. I examined the circular gap in the trunk, noticing four carefully carved knobs that I surmised would align perfectly with the four indentions on the back of the wooden disk. I retrieved the disk and ran my hand across the intricate image that was carved into its surface. Then lining up the holes with the knobs on the trunk, I pressed the wooden disk into place. It covered the hole in the trunk perfectly.

Having completed the task indicated by the drawing, I walked around the perimeter of the clearing. Scanning the area, my attention was drawn to a stone cairn that had been erected just beyond the clearing maybe thirty yards from the cross. Searching the ground for a stone to place on the mound for good luck, I found a smooth oval stone that was ivory with light brown lines running through it. I added it to the top layer of the cairn and then turned and took a few steps before I stopped and returned to the stone mound. Without knowing why, I took the stone off the cairn and placed it in my coat pocket. Then I walked back to the clearing where I sat for a while on a bench in front of the cross.

After fifteen minutes or so, I hiked back down to the monastery where I hoped to find Brother Simon. As I neared the monastery, a light snow began to fall, and for the first time since I'd arrived back in my home state, I found myself missing Colorado.

Back in the library, I set the pen down on the open journal and rubbed my eyes. Taking a sandwich and thermos from my backpack, I took a break to eat and then continued my account of events from earlier that day.

When I got back to the monastery, I found a note on Brother Simon's office door, stating that guests in need of help should call the phone number listed. I found that to be odd given Brother Simon's hands-on approach to caring for guests, but then remembered he said there wouldn't be many retreatants at the monastery during the winter months. I thought about buzzing the number on the note, but instead decided to take another crack at deciphering the cryptic image on my own.

So, I walked down the hallway looking for a spot to sit and ruminate on the clue and found the entrance to the library where I took a seat at the same study carrel where I am sitting now. I took out the drawing and focused on the bottom third of the page. It appeared to me that the artist intended the image to be of three people sleeping outside at night. Where, I couldn't tell. Studying the drawing more closely, there was a detail that captured my attention. It appeared that the three bodies were laying on a thick surface of some kind, like a rock or a foundation. At that, an idea occurred to me, so I gathered up my things and headed back out into the cold. The snow had picked up, forming a solid white coating on the grass. I walked along the outer wall of the enclosure and followed it as it turned parallel to the highway. I crossed the highway and stood at the head of the trail where I had stood the day I first spoke with Brother Simon. The sign next to the trail read "To the statues".

I started down the trail, which eventually became a snow-covered path leading to a set of wooden steps that traversed a rock wall. Clearing the steps, I continued down the path, which led over a plank bridge that spanned a running stream. All along the path beyond the stream stood crosses and plaques containing prayers and poems. There were also several statues of Mary, the most striking of which was a brown statue of The Blessed Mother holding Baby Jesus in the crook of one arm while her foot pressed down on the neck of a serpent whose mouth was open and ready to strike. Clearing the snow away, I saw there were colorful stones, rosaries, and pinecones that had been placed at her feet. Nearby was a statue of Joseph holding a carpenter's square. The statue was green and black with mossy decay, but in a strange way the decrepitude enhanced the intensity of the image. There were other statues depicting various images such as Jesus with the lost sheep draped over his shoulders and St. Francis with a bird perched on his arm.

As I continued up the path, I saw a clearing atop a small rise near the end of the path. Sitting within the clearing was a life-sized obsidian statue unlike any other along the path. I stopped in my tracks, certain that I had found the place that the clue referenced. Brushing the snow off the statue, I saw it depicted the three disciples who slept while Jesus, depicted by a statue several feet away, knelt on a rock as he looked to the sky with his hands covering his face. My breath appeared as a billow of smoke in the cold air as I looked from one statue to the other. The images conveyed a powerful contrast of agony and apathy that was moving in its effect. I reached for my camera and captured the images, knowing that whatever appeared on film would be woefully inadequate to the real thing.

When I was finished, I looked around, half expecting someone to walk up the path to greet me with congratulations for having deciphered the clue. But then I remembered that, if I understood the clue correctly, I had to come back at eleven o'clock at night to truly understand its meaning.

The library clock was nearing seven-thirty as I again laid my pen down on the journal.

More than three hours to go, I thought as I stretched and yawned.

To keep myself awake, I retrieved the second clue so I could look over it one more time to make sure I hadn't missed anything. As I examined the image, I heard footsteps out in the hallway. I got up to have a look, but no one was there. Returning to my carrell, I picked up my pen and recorded one last note in the journal.

Having found the statues, I decided to hike over to The Stone House. I entered the small abode where I knelt and reached for the caramel-colored brick in the fireplace, wanting to have another look at the clue. It was gone. I guess it doesn't really matter, though. It won't do much good to whomever took it because even if they decipher it, they won't find anything buried under that stone.

I tapped my pen on the journal and then took that thought to its logical conclusion.

Which means they'll have to find me if they want to know what was buried there.

A sly smile crossed my face as the image of Regina Sandoval, or whoever she was, came into my mind. At that moment, her sudden reemergence at the café made perfect sense.

CHAPTER
THIRTY-THREE

FOR THE NEXT half hour, I sat at the study carrell and reviewed each piece of documentation related to both my quest and my investigation, although the line between the two had essentially blurred to the point of erasure.

When I finished my task, I pulled out Brother Llewellyn's copy of *Seven Storey Mountain* and read about Thomas Merton's early life in France and New York, his years as an undergraduate at Cambridge, and his eventual conversion to Catholicism in 1939. I had just started reading the chapter describing the author's decision to join the Cistercian order when my eyelids began to feel like deflating balloons. Thinking a nap would do me well before I headed out into the snowy night, I lay down on a bench, closed my eyes, and started counting to forty. I didn't even make it to ten before I was out.

Sometime later, my body jerked upright and for a moment I didn't recognize my surroundings. Rubbing my eyes, I scanned the room as recognition gradually seeped into my brain. As I looked around at what I now knew to be the monastery library, my eyes came to rest on the wall clock, which to my dismay indicated the time was eleven-oh-seven.

Cursing, I leapt up and rushed to gather my belongings, stuffing the items roughly into my backpack. A moment later, I ran out of the library and down the hallway, pulling on my coat and fumbling with my gear as I went. I flung open the door and stepped outside, my foot sinking in a deep snow drift. Again, I cursed, realizing that I would lose precious minutes trudging through several inches of snow to get to the statues.

I made my way across the highway and onto the path that led to the statues. Arriving at the wooden steps, I attempted to scurry quickly up, but my foot slipped, bringing my knee down hard on the edge of the wooden board. I cursed for the third time, and then climbed on. Hobbling down the path, I arrived at the clearing where the garden statues stood in what I estimated to have been about fifteen minutes.

It should be around eleven-twenty-five, I thought.

Anxious but not frantic, I looked around the clearing with the familiar feeling that I didn't know exactly what I was looking for, but that I'd know it when I saw it. There was nothing. Not a movement or a sound other than my own heavy breathing. I walked further up the path and cleared away the snow from a cherubic statue that held a sign that read "Trail Ends Here". My heart fell as I stared at the sign, fearing it was a harbinger of my failure.

I returned down the path and stood next to the three disciples as they slumbered under a blanket of snow. Clearing off a section of the statue's foundation, I sat and placed my head in my hands as I joined the fallen men in their plight. With each minute that passed, I was both sure that I had failed in this phase of my quest, and unsure if I would have a chance to redeem myself.

I waited a few minutes longer, and then guessing the hour must be approaching midnight, I decided to make my way back to the monastery. I had just slung my backpack over my shoulders in dejected preparation for the trek back down the trail when I heard a voice behind me.

"Giving up so early?"

At the sound of the voice, I spun around and nearly fell as my boots lost their grip in the snow. Steadying myself against the statue of the sleeping disciples, I saw a man standing beside the statue of the agonized Jesus. Perhaps it was the effect of hope springing up inside me, but for a moment I was struck by the notion that the man was an angel. I laughed out loud and strangely, tears pricked my eyes. The man regarded me with a thoughtful expression as he waited for my answer to his question.

"Actually, I thought it was way late," I said, dabbing my eyes with the sleeve of my coat. "After all, I was supposed to be here at eleven and it has to be pushing midnight by now."

"It's close, but not yet the hour that Our Lord was betrayed and arrested," he said, motioning for me to sit. "So, there is still time to pray."

The man proceeded to kneel next to the statue of Jesus. He closed his eyes in prayer as I stood watching him with an overwhelming desire to talk to Brother Simon so I could tell him that I had discovered what it felt like to truly have a sense of wonder. After a moment, I shook myself out of my reverie, thinking it some kind of spiritual voyeurism to stare at a man while he knelt in prayer. Blowing out a soft breath, I rejoined the sleeping disciples, thinking myself better suited to the company of those flawed men.

For several minutes, I sat with my eyes cast downward, not wanting to be rude and not knowing what else to do. But after a while, I found myself thinking about the sleeping figures beside me, trying to remember all I could about the story of the Garden of Gethsemane. I knew the basics were plain enough even to a miscreant like me, so I ran through the story in my mind.

Jesus went to Gethsemane where he prayed for God to take...take what? I thought. *The cup. He prayed that God would take this cup from him, but then he ultimately left it up God. And these guys beside me, they went out with him but couldn't stay awake and that made Jesus angry. Can't say I blame Him. I mean, what kind of friends are they to sleep while he's trying to convince God to let him live? Anyway, I guess the bottom line is that his friends slept while Jesus figured out that he had to surrender to God even if it meant...*I shook my head at the thought. *Even if it meant his own death.*

The idea of a man giving himself over to the will of God with full knowledge of the awful fate in store for him was tough to reconcile. I closed my eyes and tried to crystallize it in my mind, the idea of surrendering to something greater than myself no matter the cost. I gripped my head, unable to grasp the enormity of the concept. But I kept searching myself, trying to understand how someone could make that kind of sacrifice. As I did so, my mind drifted through all the years I'd spent thinking I was on some great adventure because I was unencumbered, and that it was the lack of encumbrance that made me free. But that wasn't true. I was neither free nor unencumbered. I was uncommitted. And it was that lack of commitment, that lack of a will to sacrifice, that kept me alone. As I thought about this, I had the sense of grasping for some thread of truth that was just beyond my reach. It was like trying to get a grip on a ray of light, on something that could be perceived, but not held. It was something on the edge of my consciousness, something I knew without knowing how I knew it. It was there, just on the edge of my consciousness. I thought I could reach it if only...

"Did you say something?"

"I said it's time," he said, standing. "Follow me."

The man set off, his confident stride cutting through the snow as he walked down the path away from the statues. For a moment, I felt disoriented, like I had been shaken from a dream to which I longed to return. I started out after the man, but then stopped and looked back up the trail to where the statues stood in silent testimony to the events of a night that happened almost two-thousand years ago. For a moment, I felt compelled to stay in that place and continue my contemplation of the evasive truth that was just beyond my reach. But then I heard the snow crunching under the man's boots, and I turned to see him disappear around a bend in the trail. So, I again shook off my reverie and set off down the trail.

We hadn't gone far when the man split off from the trail and headed toward an open field that shimmered like a white lake under the moonlight. We crossed the field and entered a forest of gray trees and barren underbrush. To our left, the moonlight reflected off the surface of a lake and I found myself longing to see the water in summertime with the fish jumping and the turtles snapping and dragonflies buzzing above the water's surface. Eventually, we came to a gate that led into a yard outside a small house where smoke billowed from a stone chimney. We walked inside the house, kicked off our boots, and shed our coats. The house was small, and it reminded me of my own spartan abode, although this home radiated more of the presence of its inhabitant. The man poured two mugs of coffee, and we took chairs at the kitchen table.

"I'm Brother Peter."

"Levi Motley."

We shook hands and he regarded me with a curious gaze. "Given that Brother Lew has been dead for several months, you can imagine my surprise when I saw this during my afternoon walk." He motioned to the wooden disk that lay on the table.

I sipped my coffee and said, "If you think you're surprised, imagine how I feel drinking coffee with a monk at half-past midnight."

"You're on a quest. And a quest takes you to places you don't normally go to do things you don't normally do."

"If that's so, then this definitely qualifies. And while we're on the topic of questing, I wonder if I could ask what exactly it is I'm doing here?"

He cocked his head, and his brow furrowed. "Why ask me that question? Don't you know your own purpose, your own mind?"

"Well, I assume you're like the dungeon master or something, right?" He took a gulp of coffee and eyed me carefully. "I mean, isn't that what all this cloak-and-dagger stuff is for? So, you can let me in on your little secret handshake or whatever?"

He set his cup down and leaned toward me. The sleeves of his flannel shirt were rolled up, exposing forearms muscled like twisted cables. I guessed him to be in his sixties with features that bespoke a life of some hardship, although his eyes held a deep resolve that told me this was not a man prone to defeat.

"I'm going to tell you something and I want you to hear me. This is not a game. I suspect you wouldn't be here if you thought it was."

"No, I don't think this is a game." I let out a deep sigh. "I didn't mean to give that impression. I sometimes use sarcasm to hide my nerves, that's all."

He considered this and said, "The best thing to do when you feel your nerves on edge is to remind yourself of your objective and then imagine the worst-case scenario. When I do that, I find that my focus overcomes my fear and the voice in my head slows down and becomes reasonable rather than irrational."

"And what's the worst-case scenario? That you'll die?"

"No. That I'll let my men down and they'll die because of it."

"You talk like you were in the military."

"Twenty-two years."

"Seems like an odd training ground for the monastic life."

He grunted and took another gulp of coffee. "Did you serve?" I shook my head. "Then how would you know?"

"I guess I wouldn't. But it still seems like you took a hard left turn from a life of action to a life of..." I waved a hand over the space around us.

He grunted again, and said, "To pass through life without an opponent is to never know what you're capable of." I arched an eyebrow, waiting for him to explain his meaning. "Seneca."

"So, what? Your opponent was the Viet Cong and now it's the devil?"

"A man faces no greater opponent in life than himself." I frowned, not understanding where he was leading the conversation. "What I'm saying is that a man must contend in this life. Can you think of any adversary with whom to contend that's greater than yourself?"

I considered his point but was unsure how it related to whatever it was I was supposed to uncover or learn during this cryptic meeting.

"Why are you here if not to contend with some part of yourself that you need to overcome, to master?"

"Well, this isn't really my quest. So, I don't know what it is I'm supposed to overcome."

"If it's not your quest, then how'd you get here?"

He got up and refilled our mugs.

"I guess I inherited it." I thought about my answer for a moment and then nodded. "Yeah. That's it. It was given to me."

"Well, if it was given to you, then it stands to reason that it's your quest."

He handed me a fresh mug of coffee. "No, you don't understand," I said, taking the mug. "What I mean is that it wasn't intended for me."

"Okay, then who was it intended for?"

"Don't you know?" I said with an incredulous huff.

He sat and folded his hands. "What I know is that I saw the Celtic Tree of Life on the trunk of an ash tree on Cross Knob. And when I see that sign, I know to be at the statues at eleven o'clock."

"Why eleven o'clock?"

"It's symbolic of the holy hour that Christ spent praying in the Garden of Gethsemane."

"Okay, then why eleven in the morning? Is that a holy hour, too?"

"No, it isn't," he said. "But you're ignoring my question and wasting my time."

"Your time? Hey, I'm the one on the quest."

"I thought it wasn't your quest."

"Well, I'm the one who it fell to, and I'm the one sitting here. Right?"

"Yes. You're the one sitting here. So, tell me something. What is that brought you here?"

I leaned back in my chair and let out an impatient sigh. "It seems to me you would know something about Moussa."

He gave me a quizzical look and said, "Who is Moussa?"

"Oh, come on, man. You mean to tell me that you haven't heard what happened to…"

"Yes, that's what I mean to tell you," he said, cutting me off. "Why are you here?"

I stood and paced around the house, which was essentially one big room with a loft bedroom and a door that led to what I assumed was a bathroom.

"Why do you live like this?" I said, scanning the room. "I mean, why aren't you with the other monks?"

"Because I'm a hermit. I live alone and commune with God."

"What a contender you are," I said with a snort. "It sure takes a lot of guts to set up shop away from the world in a place where you don't even have to contend with everyday life."

"Everyday life happens here, too." He regarded me with a narrow gaze. "Have you ever spent time alone? Ever spent time in isolation with no one but yourself?"

"Yeah, in fact I have."

"Then you should know something of the guts it takes to live alone. And what would you know about contending with anything? You can't even tell me why you're here." His eyes were hard in that weather-beaten face. "Have you even thought about it? Even asked yourself the question?"

"Yes," I said in a defensive tone. "I've asked the question."

He spread his hands apart and said, "Then why are you here?"

"I'm just…I don't know…following the trail, I guess."

"What trail?"

"Obviously the one that led here."

"You're obfuscating."

I laughed and said, "Yeah, well, I'm known for my Mot-logic."

"Otherwise known as bullshit."

I tensed as I felt my face redden. He stood and placed his hands on the table, his look intense and demanding as he leaned toward me. "Why are you here?"

I shook my head, searching for an explanation that made sense of it all. "It was just…I don't know…random, you know? It's not like I planned it."

"Planned what?"

"To meet Moussa, I guess. That's what started it all. But I didn't ask for this. I didn't ask for what happened."

"Which was?"

I grunted in disbelief and said, "Get the hell outta here, acting like you don't know."

He burned me with his glare. "If I knew, I wouldn't ask. What happened?"

"Whatever, man," I said, shaking my head. "He died, okay? That's what happened."

"And what was he to you?"

"Nothing. He was nothing. That's the point. This is all bullshit. I shouldn't even be here."

"What was he to you?"

"Just some guy, all right? Just some random guy I saw hitchhiking. He was hitchhiking, so I gave him a ride. Big fuckin' deal. Like that's some kind of heroic act."

"Did he say it was heroic?"

"No."

"Then what?"

"I don't know what he said. Just...I don't know. He said I was..."

He stepped around the edge of the table, waiting for my answer.

"He said I was, just, you know...like, some kind of angel or something. An angel of God's providence." I barked a sharp laugh. "But it's all bull-shit. I mean, you can see that right? I'm not supposed to be here. He is. But he fucking died. Do you understand, now? Do you?"

"And how did you come to meet him?"

"I told you," I said, rubbed my temples trying to slow the adrenaline rushing into my brain. "I picked him up hitchhiking."

"And where were you coming from?"

"What? What the hell does that have to do with anything?"

He took a small step toward me. "Where were you coming from?"

"Bowling Green, man. I was coming from Bowling Green. What's that got to do with anything?"

"What were you doing there?"

I let out another sharp bark of laughter. "What I've always done. I was getting hammered with idiots like myself."

"Where were you before that?"

"What the hell, man? This is ridiculous." I walked to the door and picked up my coat. "You're seriously messed up, you know that? I mean, you must have some serious post-traumatic stress or something. I mean, to live out here alone and catch people up in some kind of weird web and ask all these dumbass questions."

"Where were you before you got to Bowling Green?"

I threw the coat on the ground and said, "As if it's any of your damn business, but okay, fine. I was in Colorado. Satisfied? I mean what are you plotting my movements on a map or something?"

He fixed me with an intense gaze. "Why did you come to Kentucky?"

"Because I'm from here, that's why."

"No, it isn't. Why did you leave Colorado?"

"I don't...I don't remember."

"Why?"

"I don't know. I just left."

"If you just left, then you do know."

"No. I mean, yes. Right." I pressed hard into my throbbing temples. "I just left. So, there you go. That's it."

He took another step toward me, looking at me with a face wrought with concern. "Why did you come home?"

"Just because," I said, throwing my hands up and taking an instinctive step backward as he moved toward me.

"Why did you leave Colorado, Levi? Why did you come home?"

Blood and adrenaline pounded in my head, and I longed to bolt out of the house and get away from this hermit with his incessant questioning.

"Why?"

"I don't...I just..."

"Why did you come home?"

My head swam and for the second time that night, tears pricked my eyes. I fought them back, not wanting to appear weak, but there was nothing I could do. I felt exposed as I looked about the room, but there was nowhere to retreat, no shelter to be found.

"Because I lost it," I said, my voice breaking.

Brother Peter put a hand on my shoulder. "What did you lose?"

I hesitated just a moment longer and then looked into the man's eyes. "His watch." The tears spilled onto my cheeks. "I lost my father's watch."

His weathered face showed deep compassion as he guided me to take a seat. "Tell me what happened."

My jaw quivered and every nerve ending in my body cried out for leaving. But I didn't leave. I stayed. And I did something that I hadn't done for a long time. I told the truth.

"I, umm...I really don't wanna get too deep into this," I said, biting my lip. "Let's just say I was someplace I shouldn't have been doing things I shouldn't have been doing."

I glanced over at the man, expecting to find judgement in his expression. But the deep lines in his face registered only care.

"I passed out and the next morning I came to with somebody shaking me by the shoulder. I was on the sidewalk and..." I gave a heavy, labored sigh as Brother Peter nodded encouragement. "I don't remember much. I know I blacked out at some point, but I don't know how I ended up on the sidewalk. But this lady was shaking me and telling me I needed to get up, that I couldn't stay there. It was early, still dark out. I tried to get up, but I could hardly move. So, she helped me get to a spot off some alley. She laid me down in high weeds. You know, like an overgrown yard. That was the best she could do, and I couldn't go any farther."

I wiped my cheeks and dabbed my eyes with the collar of my shirt.

"I was out again for a while, and when I woke up, the sun was blazing. I rolled over and tried to get up but ended up doubled over, vomiting. After a while, I was able to sit up and look around. I knew I needed to get out of there, but I felt sick every time I tried to get up. Finally, I stood and balanced myself against a building. That's when I reached down to my wrist...just an instinct, you know. It was gone. The money I had on me was gone, too, but I didn't really care about that. All I could think was that my father's watch was gone, and it was my fault."

I swallowed hard and looked at the man again expecting to see disappointment or pity written on his face. But he continued to regard me with a look that I could only describe as sincere empathy.

"So, there's your answer," I said, blowing out a deep sigh. "I left Colorado because I'm a fuck up who can't get his shit straight. And because of that, I lost the only thing I had left of my father. I left because that's what I do. I'm too much of a pussy to make a stand someplace, so I leave and pretend to start over someplace else. But I end up doing the same thing wherever I go."

For a long moment, the house was silent as each of us sat lost in our own thoughts.

"My given name is Albert," he said, breaking the silence. "When I entered the monastery, I chose Peter as my monastic name. Do you know why?" I gave a slight shake of my head. "Because I'm a knucklehead like he was. I'm hot-tempered and impulsive, prone to leap without looking, and given to weakness when my faith is tested. You seem like a man that can relate."

I gave a weak smile and said, "Obviously."

"But Peter was also ardent in his belief, a steadfast man who displayed great love for his friends, for Jesus. So much so that Christ gave Peter the keys to the Kingdom of Heaven." He gave a soft laugh. "It's amazing, if you think about it. He had to know the guy would screw things up, but he gave him the keys anyway."

He shook his head in wonder at the thought.

"Now, I'm just an old soldier, so who cares what I think? But I believe Jesus did that because he knew people are flawed, and a flawed person ends up either bitter and vicious or empathetic and compassionate. How a person ends up usually depends on how they're treated in moments of vulnerability, when a person is at their weakest. I think Jesus knew a man like Peter would remember his own humanity when ministering to others in their vulnerability, in their worst moments."

He gave me an earnest look and said, "I'm sorry about your father's watch, Levi. But you know what this means, don't you?"

My face wrinkled in puzzlement. "I'm not sure I follow."

"It means you know why you're here."

I wiped my face with the arm of my shirt and looked at the man, unsure of where he was going.

"You're here because even in the midst of your shame and anger and sadness, you showed kindness to a stranger. Even though you were, as you say, a fuck up who couldn't keep his shit straight, you found it in yourself to be charitable to someone who was vulnerable, someone who was in need. And for that charity, you've been granted something special. You've been granted the grace to confront your own failings, to contend with your own shame. You're like Peter, like me. You're like anyone who's lost something they can't get back, but in confronting the reason for the loss, they gain something greater in return."

"What? What do they gain?"

"They gain forgiveness. And once a man understands and accepts his own forgiveness, he can share that grace with others. That's a gift, Levi. And it's the first step to becoming the man your father wants you to be."

"How can you know that?" I said in a small voice, bewildered by his words. "How can you know what kind of man my father wants me to be?"

"Because you told me why you're here, that's how. And on that journey from there to here, you lost an heirloom, but you inherited a quest. Seems to me you traded one for the other. If that's so, then the question you have to ask yourself is...was it a good trade?"

I stared at the man, contemplating, as he had said the "journey from there to here". After a moment, I looked away and found myself staring off at nothing as I thought about his question. Was it possible? Of course, I could never replace that heirloom, but I got his point. Losing that watch was the impetus for my journey back to Kentucky, and what I had gained in making that journey? Could it be that having lost something I treasured, that I gained something greater in its place? Had I traded that terrible moment out west for...

Well, shit fire, son. Out west ain't a place.

Tears pricked my eyes, again, and I smiled, remembering that Brother Peter wasn't the first person to have asked me where I had come from before arriving in Bardstown. My smile turned into a soft laugh as I thought about George Hawley with his peccadillos, his quirks, and his profanity-laced style of conversing. I thought also about his stalwart defense of his people, about his work ethic, and how he'd go to the mat to protect his values, his integrity. And then I thought about what he said to me that morning when he sent me out to find him a good story.

It's the people that tell a story, Motley. Focus on the people, son, and you can't go wrong.

Focus on the people, I thought, and the images of all the people I had come to know, or know better, since I came home popped into the frame of my consciousness like a photo projector had been turned on in my brain.

Suddenly I saw Daphne Rose, standing beside me at the bar, telling me how she'd probably fall in love with me if only I'd stick around long enough to learn how to love her back. I saw Dominick, steadfast in his long-suffering loyalty as he told me he wished I could've met his Great-Grandma Beatrice, who after five minutes with me would have said,

"Thank the heavens that after God made that fool, he broke the damn mold."

Images played through my mind of Moots and Roscoe, Brother Simon and Denny, the Edelen brothers, and the Bosnian couple with their wonderful café and a sense of warm hospitality that had not been extinguished by the pain of losing their country. And though I had never met him, I pictured Brother Kieran, and the kindness he'd shown to weary travelers by giving them a place for respite in The Stone House. I pictured Sam standing on the right side of the bar at The Prep Room. Hell, I even saw the fleeting image of Vernon the gas station clerk, and the gray-bearded man, and Regina Sandoval.

Would I be here without her? I thought. *Probably not.*

And then there was Miss Olive, telling me she was going to put St. Jude on my case, and that I could expect him to be tapping me on the shoulder any day now. And there was Hamia Diab, thanking me for being an angel, a messenger to her son.

And then I saw Moussa. There he was, standing on the side of the road, trying to hitch a ride at the exact moment a hungover vagabond fleeing his latest personal tragedy came rolling by. Moussa, smiling as he looked at me and said, "I think the scales might be tilting in your favor, Levi Motley."

Unashamed, I let a tear run down my cheek as I thought about Ray Motley, Grandma Lenny, and Declan.

As I pictured each of these people, the voice of a man long dead came to me saying, "The angel appears when we ourselves are reduced to the center of our deepest need."

The images having run their course, I let out a breath that felt like air rushing from a tomb that had been opened after centuries of being sealed shut. Brother Peter looked at me, a piercing glint in his dark eyes. He had let me wander through my own consciousness, through my own memories and my own thoughts of the people who had come into my life in the days, weeks, and months since I'd lost my father's watch. I nodded slowly as I looked at the man, this hermit who anyone could see had his own regrets, his own pain, and yet through his compassion had shared with me the forgiveness he had found for himself, a forgiveness I was certain had been hard won.

"It was a good trade, Brother Peter. A good trade."

I stood, walked to the door, and pulled on my boots in preparation for the trek back to the monastery. Brother Peter watched me without comment, sipping his coffee and ruminating, I imagined, on his own life's quest and the many trades he had made. The door creaked open, and I was about to leave when I suddenly heard George Hawley's voice, repeating something he had said to me that morning when we first met.

"Bring me the story it still wants told, Levi Motley, and this old town will forever remember your name."

Shutting the door, I turned back to the hermit and said, "I think there's more to this quest, brother. Something more that I'm meant to find." He cocked his head and gave me a look of intense curiosity. "I need to know what really happened to Moussa Diab."

He began to slowly nod his head. "So, you want to know how well I knew Brother Llewellyn. Is that it?"

"No, Brother Peter. I want to know how well you knew James Westcott."

CHAPTER
THIRTY-FOUR

I HAD A GOOD dream going. Because of that, the ringing telephone did not register in my unconscious mind as such, but rather as a foghorn, bellowing caution to a ship captain unaware of how close he'd come to running his vessel against the craggy rocks at the foot of a cliff wall. But the ship captain ignored the foghorn, secure in the knowledge that he was, of course, merely a representation of the subconscious thoughts of the dreamer, and thus, the only consequence of running the ship upon the rocks would be that the dreamer would awaken with a faint memory of what subliminal danger feels like.

But in the midst of my dream, I became vaguely aware of sunlight beaming through the curtainless windows. And with the light came an emerging clarity and clarity being anathema to fog, the intrusive sound no longer registered in the dreamer's unconscious mind as a foghorn, but rather as a ringing telephone representative of the unassailable reality that comes when a person awakens from a dream with the faint memory of what subliminal danger feels like, and a strange desire to experience the real thing.

I slipped out of my sleeping bag and shuffled across the floor groggy, grumpy, and in need of caffeine.

Whose bright idea was it for me to get a phone? I thought.

I picked up the receiver and spoke my "hello" through a vast yawn. Naturally, the voice on the other end was that of the woman whose bright idea it was for me to get a phone.

"It's ten-forty-five, Mr. Motley. Been howling at the moon?"

"More like walking the path of angels."

"Hmm. That doesn't strike me as your usual late-night routine."

"Yeah, well, it was a late night to be sure. But routine? Not even close."

"How's that?"

"Well, if you must know, I spent the entire day and night at the monastery."

"And?"

I yawned again. "And that's why my voice sounds like slurry."

I heard a curious grunt on the other end of the line, but I didn't let her goad me into saying more. After several seconds of silence, I blew my nose loud enough to make a point.

"All right, Mr. Motley. I'm the one who called you after all. But I'll remind you that I am following your instructions."

"Well, I've slept since we last talked, so you're going to have to remind me of my instructions."

"The last time we spoke, you told me to call you the day after tomorrow. And just in case you don't have a calendar handy, please be informed that would be today."

I held the phone away from my ear as I rubbed my eyes into focus. I could hear her voice through the receiver as she said, "Mr. Motley? Are you there?"

"Yeah, I'm here. So, tell me, Sandoval, where are we on all this?"

"Well, that depends."

"On what?"

"On what you know and what you're willing to share," she said.

"Well then, right back at ya."

Several seconds passed with our collective breathing the only sound passing between us.

"I can fill in a lot of blanks for you," she said, entering the fray.

"Umm-hmm."

"That's it? That's all you're going to say?"

"No. But you'll have to forgive my cynicism since you are, Miss Sandoval, its primary source."

"So, I'm going to have give if I want to get. Is that it?"

"Isn't that what a quid pro quo is? You tell me, lady. It's been a while since I've brushed up on my Latin."

Again, there was silence, and I knew she was recalibrating her tactics.

"Fair enough. I have failed to retain your good graces, so I've got to improve my standing with you if we're going to resume our partnership."

"'Partnership' is an awfully strong word. If I were you, I'd settle for getting me back to the table."

"And I haven't given you enough yet to do so?"

"No," I said, dragging the phone line into the kitchen.

"Okay then. I've got a proposition for you. Do you want to hear it?"

"Hey, any day I get propositioned before my first cup of..." I stopped, sighing as I poured water into the coffee maker. "Yes, Sandoval." I pushed the brew button. "I want to hear your proposition."

"Glad to hear it. My proposition is this. A two for one deal. My two pieces of information for your one answer to a question."

"Sounds fair," I said with an ironic undertone of wariness.

"Good. Then here goes. I know what it is, Mr. Motley. I know the source of this whole bloody affair. That's the first piece of information. Ready for information item number two?"

"I'm ready. Although technically, you already told me you know what it is, so..."

"Be that as it may, here is item number two. I am this close to locating the other man."

"The other man?"

"The other man that was present when Moussa Diab was killed," she said, conveying a sense of drama through the phone line.

"Killed or murdered?"

"That remains to be seen."

"Either way, are you saying the other man was responsible for his death along with Dale Goodlett?"

"That also remains to be seen," she said. "Once I find him, then we'll both know. That is as long as your answer to my question is sufficient to the cause."

"Whose cause?"

"At this point, I think it's safe to say we have a shared cause, even if our motivations aren't the same."

I considered her argument as I poured a cup of coffee. "I'm not sure that's true."

"Oh, but I think it is. In fact, I think what you know will go hand in glove with what I know. And if we add to the mix what Mr. Cotter knows, well then..."

I was about to take a drink but stopped my cup in midair. Again, I heard her voice on the other end of the line asking if I was still there. Of course I was still there, but what I was wondering was where Dominick was, so to speak, and why Sandoval suddenly wanted to include him in our conversation.

"What's Dominick got to do with this?"

"A good deal, I suspect. Especially now that he's talked to Father William French." I took a long gulp of coffee. "Oops. Did I say that out loud? I guess I did. And would you look at that, I've given up three pieces of information instead of two. So how about it, partner? Are you ready to live up to your end of the bargain?"

I set my cup on the counter, watching the smoke swirl upward from the brim.

"Mr. Motley?"

I drew myself up and said, "Yeah, I'm here."

"And?"

"Shoot."

She hesitated for just a beat or two before she asked the $64,000 question.

"I know *what* it is. But my question is...do you know *where* it is?"

I took another drink of coffee before answering. "No. But I know how to find it." The moment stretched, and we both knew the implications of our exchange belied the silence on the telephone line. "Is that sufficient for the cause?"

"Meet me in an hour," she said.

"Where?"

"Some place we can talk openly without prying eyes or ears."

"Okay. How about we get lunch at The Prep Room?" She didn't answer right away. "I'm going to go out on a limb and assume you know where that is. Will your backup be joining us?"

Another long pause stretched before she answered. "I'll see you there at noon. Bring Dominick Cotter. If my hunch is correct, he has information we both need to hear."

"How do you know that? Sandoval? Sandoval?"

I hung up the phone, and for the better part of ten minutes, I stood in the kitchen drinking coffee and thinking about the information she had shared.

There was another man there, I thought. *And she's close to finding him.*

I had to admit that tidbit was worth the price of admission. But of course, that raised the question of how this second man was roaming the free world while Dale Goodlett sat idly in a jail cell. How could he have gotten away while Goodlett took a deal and confessed? And why didn't Goodlett put the other guy in to save himself some time or maybe even get out of it? I didn't know the answers to those questions, but if Sandoval was on the level, then there was a fair chance of finding the answers somewhere in the hunt.

And then there was Dominick. It occurred to me that whoever was on the trail of man number two had been tracking Dominick as well. How else could she know that Dom has spoken to Father French? That my friend was wrapped up in something that appeared to be growing in its sinister complexity didn't sit well with me. But I had to admit to my curiosity about what Dominick had learned in his conversation with the good priest. At least I hoped he was good. With that hope in mind, I called Dominick and asked him to meet me for lunch.

"Prep Room at noon. I'm buying."

"Damn skippy. See you there, Motley."

CHAPTER
THIRTY-FIVE

I ARRIVED AT THE Prep Room a few minutes before noon and sat at a corner table that allowed for a full view of the place. A waitress stopped by, and I told her the other two members of my group would arrive shortly. She shuffled off and I sat back and waited, the calm demeanor I hoped to convey belying the butterflies flitting about in my stomach. A few minutes later, my lunch companions arrived. Introductions were made, small talk ensued, and we placed our order before lapsing into a cautious silence. It was Dominick who broke the ice with a dose of humor.

"So, a black guy, a Latina, and a white dude walk into a bar in the bourbon capital of the world."

I fought back a smile as Sandoval furrowed her brow and said, "So, what's the punch line?"

He looked at her deadpan and said, "Bartender says, 'Two Black and Tans and a White Russian coming right up.'" I shook my head and laughed and even Sandoval managed to crack a sly smile. "Hey, somebody's gotta get this party started."

I told him that was one way to do it and brought us to the business at hand. "So should we call you Regina Sandoval or Cynthia Wilcox?" Before our female companion could answer, I made the decision for her. "I think we'll go with Sandoval as a devil you know kind of thing."

She looked at me coldly but did not object.

"Well, I know why I'm here, and I know why Dom's here. That leaves you, Sandoval."

"It's quite simple," she said with a small shrug. "I'm looking for something and I need your help to find it."

"And you're trying to find this something for you or for someone else?"

"Is that your way of asking if I'm the primary or a representative of the primary's interest?"

"Actually, that's not at all how I would've put it, but okay. Which one are you?"

"Why does it matter?"

"'Cause a man's gotta know who he's getting in bed with," Dominick said with a coy look. "In a manner of speaking, that is."

She returned his look with a coy look of her own.

"All double-entendres aside," I said, glazing Dominick with a disapproving stare. "It would be nice to know who we're working with and for."

Dominick gave a sheepish half-grin and said, "Right. That's what I meant."

"Who I'm working for is immaterial to the effort as far as you're concerned," she said, looking from one of us to the other. "If you want to move forward, then you'll be working with me. As to who you would be working for? You tell me. *The Observer*?"

Dominick and I shared a concerned glance. "Not good enough," I said.

"Why not?"

"Because an unknown party is a poisoned pill," Dominick said. "What happens when the man behind the curtain turns out to be the Wizard of Lee Harvey Oswald? We end up guilty by association, that's what."

Sandoval considered this as she calculated how much she wanted to reveal to us.

"Okay, yes. I'm working for someone. But I'm not going to tell you who that someone is. You must understand that I can't break confidence with my client."

"Meaning what?" Dominick said. "That you're a lawyer?"

She shook her head. "I'm an independent contractor with expertise in recovering things that are rare and valuable."

I felt my heart pick up a pace as Dominick continued his line of questioning. "And this client of yours...he wants this rare and valuable thing to do what? Sell it?"

"Why do you assume it's a he?"

"He, she, whoever. Just answer the question," he said. "Is your client looking to sell this thing?"

"Why is that pertinent?"

"Because your resistance to transparency makes this smell like a deal that's off the books," I said.

"Meaning?"

"Meaning it smells like black-market shit," I said. "Come on, Sandoval. You can't expect us to get deeper into this on a blind. You gotta be straight on this now, or we're out."

Again, she appeared to be running through her options. I thought she might walk, and I was okay if she did. After making good progress on my own, I wasn't about to let myself become a pawn in her game for a second time. But she didn't walk. Instead, she reached inside her bag and produced a cell phone. "Excuse me for a moment, gentlemen," she said and walked to the other side of the room.

While she was gone, the waitress brought our order. I picked at my food as Dominick dove into his with abandon. We didn't talk because we didn't need to. We were both thinking the same thing...namely, what was the story behind this woman who called herself Regina Sandoval?

"Okay," she said, reappearing at the table. "I'll give you enough to let you know how far in you'll be if you choose to work with me. I won't give you his name..." She shot a perturbed look at Dominick. "But I think you can deduce enough on your own to decide how you want to go."

Dominick and I looked at each other and we both nodded in agreement.

"You've got the basic picture so far," she said, taking her seat. "I'm an independent contractor with expertise in locating scarce objects of great value."

"You mean art?" Dominick said.

"Primarily, yes. Although I have on occasion appropriated my skills to recover objects of a more specific nature." She looked at us to see if we were still with her and then continued. "On this occasion, I'm looking for an object of extraordinary value that was taken quite a long time ago. Rumors have persisted about what happened to this object, but its location...actually, I should say the location of its peer objects, has only been uncovered in the last several years."

I noticed Dominick had stopped eating as he paid close attention to what Sandoval was saying. "Taken from where? And what do you mean by 'peer objects'?"

"I'll get into that in due course, Mr. Cotter. What you need to know is that I work for a man who wants me to obtain this object. He does not intend to sell it, since you asked, but rather use it for..." She paused as she, again, seemed to be considering how much to say.

"Collateral?" I said, guessing. "A display in a museum? What?"

She pursed her lips as if she didn't want to say more.

"You said you'd tell us enough to let us know how far we'd be in," Dominick said. "That's only fair."

Her look turned to one of concern as she regarded Dominick. "You're not in so far that you can't turn back, Mr. Cotter." Then she turned and looked at me. "But you, Mr. Motley." She exhaled a slow breath. "Well, as I said when we spoke before, you're already in up to your eyeballs."

Dominick gave me a curious look, and I felt my face going flush with a slow-building anger. "And just how in the hell am I up to my eyeballs in something I didn't even choose to be a part of?"

"What can I say?" She raised her hands in a helpless gesture. "You were the one who picked Moussa Diab up and delivered him to his fate."

"His fate?" I said, my anger building. "What the hell are you talking about?"

"I'm talking about the game we don't choose to play, but it's being played just the same."

My face contorted in confusion as I looked at Dominick, who wore a pensive expression. I ran a hand through my hair and took a deep breath, trying to regain some sense of balance in the conversation. As I tried to focus, my mind went back to my conversation with Declan, and it was there I found the balance I was searching for.

"It's all about power," I said. "That's the game you're talking about, right? Money and power..."

"And politics."

We both looked at Dominick, whose pensive expression had become one of calculating self-assuredness. "It's all three, isn't it, Miss Sandoval? Although really, it's all the same game when you get to the root of if."

I looked at Sandoval and her eyes dropped to the table.

"You gotta shoot us straight, lady," Dominick said. "If my boy is already in, then I'm putting myself in the mix with him. The least you can do is tell us what we're into."

"Oh, she'll tell us, Dom," I said with an ironic smile. "She'll tell us because she needs us more than she's letting on. She wouldn't be sitting here if that weren't true."

Sandoval raised her eyes and looked from one of us to the other. "It's not collateral. And it's certainly not for display in any museum." She hesitated, holding out just a moment longer before acquiescing to our pressure. "It's leverage. It's...a weapon."

"To be used on who?"

The question had barely escaped my mouth before I knew the answer.

"Ah, hell." I shook my head as it occurred to me that it wasn't Moussa, but the Westcotts who were the nexus of the whole affair. "Rogers Westcott. That's why you're snooping around Conrad and Isabelle. You're trying to find dirt to use against the golden boy, who everybody seems to think is headed for political glory."

Dominick's face screwed up in a worried expression. "You want us to go to work for a political enemy of the Westcotts?"

"As I said before, Mr. Cotter, you wouldn't be working for anyone other than yourselves or your employer. As far as I, we, are concerned, you would be partnering with me and me alone. I often utilize such partners in my work."

"You mean you often use such partners in your work," I said in disgust. "Call a spade a bloody spade already."

"Nonetheless," she said, straightening in her chair. "Under the terms I am proposing, you would be operating as willing partners in my effort to locate and recover this object. That's it."

"And how is this object going to be used as a political weapon against Rogers Westcott?"

Sandoval gave me a firm look and said, "My client's motivation and purpose are none of your concern."

"Okay, then what's our end?" Dominick said.

"Well, I assume if you're on the job for your paper, then you'll get quite the story out of this."

Dominick snorted in disbelief and said, "So we get a story, and you get this, how did you put it? 'This rare and valuable thing'? That's not much of a sales pitch."

"And how could we ever write about it anyway given your...affiliation?" I said. "Not to mention your unspoken endgame."

She looked from one of us to the other as she calculated her next move. "Okay, how's this? I can assure you that you will be properly compensated. Both of you. That is, if we find and recover the object."

"I don't want your money, Sandoval," I said, my face knotting in contempt. "You know why I'm doing this."

"Yes, I do," she said, leaning toward me. "And you will find what you're looking for if you cooperate with me. As I told you before, I'm quite certain I can fill in the blanks for you regarding the death of Moussa Diab." She leaned back in her chair and sighed. "Still, the compensatory offer is on the table. Whether you choose to avail yourself of it or not is up to you."

Dominick's face screwed up in confusion. "I still don't get why your client would go after something like this if he's not interested in profiting from it. That makes no sense."

"As far as my client is concerned, there is a profit margin associated with this endeavor that transcends capitalistic values."

I looked down at my half-eaten plate of food and pushed it away. "All part of the game, huh, Sandoval?"

She managed to put on an empathetic look, but I looked away in frustration.

"I know what Great-Grandma Beatrice would say about all this," Dominick said. We both looked at him as Dominick slowly shook his head and said, "'Pick up the hem of your dress and roll up your pant legs children, 'cause the shit's about to get deep.'"

CHAPTER
THIRTY-SIX

W E SAT IN silence as each of us pondered the gravity of our next move. After a few minutes, Sandoval threw a wadded-up napkin on the table and sighed in frustration. "Well, there you have it. I've said all I have to say. Either work with me or don't. It's up to you."

"Oh, I'm gonna work with you, Sandoval. I'm going to work with you, so Hamia Diab and her son get their due."

Dominick blew out a long, slow breath and nodded. "Yeah, I'm in. But right now, I think I'm too sober for this business." He stood and pointed to me, but I shook my head. "What about you, Sandoval? You down for a drink?"

She glanced at me and then back at Dominick. "Sure. Vodka Tonic."

"What about it, Levi? You already the odd white man out. You gonna be the only one not drinking too?"

I looked at him and again, shook my head. "I'm good."

He made his way to the bar, leaving me with my erstwhile adversary. At least that's what I hoped she was. I figured the next hour or so would tell the tale.

I folded my hands on the table and leaned toward her. "So, Miss Sandoval. What is it?" She shot me an annoyed look. "Well, isn't that the logical next question?"

"Maybe it is, but I seem to be the one doing all the talking here."

"Fair enough. Where do you want me to begin?"

"How about where we left off from before?"

I agreed, and without delay launched into the details of my

investigation, starting with my visit to Brothers Hardware and my confusion at seeing the diminutive shovel that Moussa had purchased at the
store. I followed that up with an account of my visit to the monastery
and my conversation with Brother Simon, sticking mainly to the broad
strokes.

Dominick returned with the drinks as I was sharing how I learned
about the dinner invitation the Westcotts had extended to Moussa. He
set the rocks glass down in front of Sandoval and placed pints of beer in
front of himself and me. My look of agitation was met with a shrug that
seemed to indicate I could take it or leave it.

"What did I miss?"

"Nothing you don't already know. Let me fast-forward and tell you
about my conversation with Denny."

With that, I related the account of how I learned about the letter that
fell into the hands of Isabelle Westcott, confirming the obvious point
that the Westcotts knew about Moussa's visit prior to his arrival at the
monastery.

"Now let me ask you a question, Sandoval. How'd you find out about
that letter?" She gave me a quizzical look. "Don't even try it. You must
have known about it. Otherwise, how did you know to go looking for it
at the Westcott residence?"

"Look," she said in an impatient tone. "You've been working your side
of the street, and I've been working mine. That we came up with the same
information is verification that we're both on the right track."

Dominick looked from one of us to the other and said, "Umm, can
someone tell me what it is we're talking about?"

"We're talking about the letter that Hamia sent to Brother Lew. The
one Denny told me about." I nodded toward our female companion.
"She's got a copy of the letter and the envelope it arrived in."

Dominick looked at Sandoval and said, "And how'd you manage
that?"

I stifled a look of amusement as Sandoval cleared her throat and said,
"I posed as a member of the Westcotts' cleaning crew."

At that, Dominick gave a deep laugh of appreciation. "Go on, girl.
Bloom where you're planted."

Sandoval gave him an embarrassed smile.

"Anyway," I said, refocusing the conversation. "The envelope had a note on it saying something about Rogers getting with A.R. We think A.R. is someone named Artemis Ray."

Dominick's laughter faded and his face grew serious. "You're shittin me."

I eyed him narrowly and said, "You've heard of this guy?"

He took a drink and set his pint glass down. "Hell yes, I've heard of him."

Sandoval's eyes were gleaming with intensity as she said, "What have you heard?"

Dominick's face was grave as he offered his response. "There's a whole mythology around that name. He's like the guy in that movie. You know, Motley, that one we liked about the guy who makes up the story in a police station."

"*The Usual Suspects.*"

"That's the one," Dominick said, snapping his fingers. "He's like the dude in that movie. Keyser Soze."

Sandoval shot us a puzzled look. "Keyser Soze?"

"Soze is a character in the movie," I said. "He's some kind of powerful shadow figure that pulls everybody's strings. All the other characters know of him, but nobody's ever seen the guy."

"Yeah, that's who this Artemis cat reminds me of," Dominick said. "Word is the guy's a bad dude, but nobody I know of has ever met the guy. I'm telling you, Levi, it's like that movie when they say I know a guy who knows a guy who knows a guy who did a job for Artemis Ray. See what I mean?"

Sandoval shot him a dubious look and said, "No, I don't see what you mean. Can you tell me anything specific about the man?"

"Yeah. I can tell you it's bad news that his name is wrapped up in this. Is that specific enough for you?" She slumped back in her chair and let out a frustrated sigh. "Sorry, but that's all I got," Dominick said. "But how do you know A.R. is Artemis Ray?"

I looked at Sandoval and then back at Dominick. "Well, like she said. She's working her side of the street, and I'm working mine."

"Oh, well, that really clears things up for me."

"Okay, okay. I hear you. I got the name from Declan, who got the name from those Cornbread Mafia boys he's with up in Manchester."

Dominick perked up at this and said, "Declan knows those dudes?"

"Getting to know people is what Declan does. And he's impressed as hell with those guys. And impressed with the empire they built."

"Right. And he wants to know how it all came crumbling down, so he can learn from their mistakes."

"If it came crumbling down."

"Good point," Dominick said. "Could be that it's still going."

"That's actually a theory I've been turning over in my mind. But right now, I'm not seeing the connection to what we're talking about."

Sandoval gave an exasperated sigh. "I'm sure this is all very fascinating. But can we focus on one criminal endeavor at a time?"

Dominick gave her a sidelong glance and said, "So you're saying this is a criminal endeavor?"

"Oh, grow up."

"Okay, okay," I said, hands raised. "Let's get back to it."

I watched Sandoval take the top third off her drink and I sensed the presence of this Artemis Ray character had her a bit spooked. I found that interesting since she had already indicated to me that she understood the guy was dangerous.

"What else can you tell me, Mr. Motley? What else have you learned?"

I finished up my part of the story by relating my experience during recent trips to the monastery. Though he knew part of the story already, Dominick looked genuinely fascinated by my account. For her part, Sandoval listened with the intense scrutiny of a human lie detector, though she, too, had already heard part of the story. I took them through each phase of the quest, describing how it unfolded and what it led to. I stopped short of a full description of my time with Brother Peter, but Sandoval didn't press me to provide more information. Instead, she seemed satisfied that the information I had provided aligned with whatever thesis she had devised in the course of her own investigation.

"So, Brother Llewellyn really was passing it on to Moussa," she said in a voice that was little more than a whisper. Suddenly she shot me an accusing look. "I didn't hear you say anything about how you figured out how to find it."

"Huh?" I said, feigning ignorance. "Didn't I?"

"Yeah, play it that way if you want," she said, glaring at me. "But you'd do well to remember the interest that I represent."

My face contorted in disdain. "And you'd do well to remember that

I'm working for Hamia and Moussa Diab. So, I don't give a damn about your so-called client or any upper hand he's looking to gain by finding this...whatever it is."

We glared at each other as Dominick cleared his throat, seeking to bring the temperature down a few degrees. "Excuse me," he said, knocking on the table. "Hello. Can we maybe, I don't know, raise our glasses and have a toast to our common purpose of finding the truth and maybe, just maybe, getting paid while we're at it?"

I picked up my untouched pint and knocked back half the brew. Sandoval withered me with a sour expression as she raised her glass without drinking.

"There now. That's better." Dominick gingerly sipped his own brew. "Now who's up? Miss Sandoval?"

She looked at Dominick and gave a soft grunt. "I believe we have yet to hear anything from you on this matter."

Dominick played up his newly acquired role as the keeper of the peace as he responded to her. "Yes, yes, well, that may be. But you see, Miss Sandoval, I'm at something of a disadvantage seeing as how I don't have the context that you and Mr. Motley possess regarding our..." He looked from me to Sandoval. "I think I am correct in saying 'our'?" I answered in the affirmative, but Sandoval only gave him a tiresome look. "Our investigation," he said, concluding his thought.

Sandoval pursed her lips tightly and she looked to be on the verge of losing what was left of her patience.

"I suppose what I'm saying is I don't know where to place my newly acquired puzzle pieces," Dominick said. "Perhaps you could show me a corner of the picture to help me get started?"

Sandoval raised her glass and, this time, took a drink as she measured her approach.

"Well, tell me this, Mr. Cotter. Do any of the puzzle pieces you so recently acquired, presumably through your conversation with Father William French, display the image, partial or whole, of a World War Two soldier?"

Dominick played it cool, but Sandoval's question clearly hit the mark she'd aimed for. "I believe I've got that piece somewhere in my collection. But how does it fit?"

Sandoval shook her head, her patience running out. "Don't be coy with me, sir. If your motivation lacks the altruism of your saintly friend here, meaning you want to get paid, then start talking."

Dominick shot me a glance, but I could only raise my hands and shrug. "That's why we're here. Time to lay all the pieces on the table."

"And here I thought we were playing poker," Dominick said.

"Yeah, well, you're the one that went and mixed metaphors," she said.

I concealed a smile as Dominick's usually confident bearing sagged a little.

Sandoval sighed in frustration. "For God's sake, it'll be opening day at Santa Anita by the time we get into this."

I shot her a curious look. "California track, huh?"

She huffed, ignoring my question as she turned to Dominick. "Father William French. How did you find him?"

At this, Dominick looked at me, appearing to have regained a bit of his usual swagger. "She don't know, does she?"

I looked at Sandoval and said, "Dom's something of a savant in the art of finding and cultivating sources."

"Great," she said in a flat tone. "Where did you find him?"

"He lives across the river on a little piece of land in Southern Indiana." Dominick pulled out his notebook. "He's been retired five years. I thought I surprised him, but he said he's been waiting for someone to come along ever since James died. Of course that's Brother Lew to us, but he's still James to Father French."

"Makes sense," I said. "He knew him since he was a kid."

"That's right, he did. You see, William French and Thomas Westcott were childhood friends. Grew up here in Nelson County on farms that butted up against each other. The way Father French tells it, they spent their days exploring, hiking, camping, canoeing. Of course, that's when they weren't working the farm."

Sandoval cocked her head and said, "This would have been in the late twenties, and early to mid-thirties?"

"Yeah, that's about right."

"A different time," I said, wistfully. "A different world."

Dominick looked at me and said, "That's just what the priest said. Made it sound like their childhood existence was a glorious adventure. And he said Thomas was a regular Don Quixote."

"What did he mean by that?"

"I took it to mean he was an adventurer. What else could it mean?"

I considered the question for a moment and then gave a slight nod. "That's probably it."

Sandoval shot me a probing look as Dominick continued. "Anyway, Father French always knew he wanted to be a priest, so he went off to seminary at sixteen while Westcott stayed on the farm and later married Ruth Goodwin, also from a farm family. She gave birth to James in nineteen-forty and to our boy, Conrad, just eleven months later."

"Irish twins," I said.

"Yeah, well the twins were still in diapers when daddy Westcott volunteered for the big war in forty-three."

Sandoval's face screwed up in a perplexed look. "Why? He would have been dispensed from the war given he was a married father of two children."

"The priest said he thinks Thomas saw the war as the great adventure of his life. Like it was his chance to escape the farm that had dominated his existence. It was his chance to be a warrior."

"To be a questing knight on a noble mission," I said. "Brother Lew must've gotten his romantic notions of adventure from his father."

Dominick flipped a page in his notebook and continued. "Well, while Sir Thomas was off fighting the good fight, William French was ordained a priest in nineteen-forty-four, three days before Normandy. He found out later that his friend had been part of the invasion. Obviously, Thomas survived it, although it was some time before Father French got word from Ruth that he was okay."

"Can you imagine?" Sandoval said, shaking her head in wonder. "Taking care of two children while your husband is thousands of miles away playing soldier."

"Oh, no, no. Our boy Thomas wasn't playing nothin'. He was awarded the Silver Star for bravery in combat. The man was the real McCoy."

"The real McCoy," I said reflectively. "And a proud member of the Eighty-Seventh."

"That's right," Dominick said, flipping through his notebook. "I looked it up when I got back. Here it is. He was part of the Eighty-Seventh Armored Field Artillery Battalion."

"It was in honor of his father," I said in a small voice.

Sandoval leaned toward me with a blazing intensity and said, "What was in honor of his father?"

I hesitated for a moment as she leveled me with a demanding glare. "The label on Conrad Westcott's first single barrel bourbon. It's a shield with a snake on it. The colors are different, but it's a close replica of the insignia of the Eighty-Seventh. Olive and I saw the label at the Getz Museum. She got curious and figured out what it was."

Dominick gave a soft laugh and said, "Of course she did."

Sandoval continued to burn me with her trademark intensity as she said, "What was the name of the bourbon?"

I cocked my head, wondering at her curiosity as I said, "Old Relic."

Upon hearing the name, her eyes widened, and she looked away, her mind connecting dots I couldn't begin to see. Suddenly, she turned to Dominick, and I noticed her breathing had picked up a pace as she leaned forward and said, "Did he send anything back to Father French?" Dominick eyed her with a wary look. "Did Thomas Westcott ever send Father French a package? Something he asked him to keep safe?"

Dominick shot me a concerned look as Sandoval grew anxious.

"What kind of package? What are you talking about?"

"Oh, don't be dense, Mr. Motley. What do you think I'm talking about? Isn't this what you meant when you said you know how to find it?" She turned her attention back to Dominick. "He did, didn't he? He sent him something. What was it?"

Dominick set his notebook on the table and folded his hands as Sandoval's anxiety grew to the level of frenetic excitement.

"Don't play games with me, Mr. Cotter. What did he send him?"

I tried to intervene. "Look, you're going to need to..."

"What? Calm down? Goddamnit, don't you see? Father French told Dominick he's been waiting for someone to show up ever since Brother Lew died. That means Father French has it. He's got the treasure."

The worry in Dominick's face mirrored my own. I took a deep breath and leveled Sandoval with a stern glare. "I think it's about time you tell us what this is about."

"Don't be a fool," she said, her hands clenching and unclenching on the table. "There's no time for this." She gave us both a pleading look. "You're going to be rich men. You just have to trust me."

"But we don't," I said, shaking my head. "We don't trust you."

"There's no time for this." She pounded a fist on the table. "Don't you see? Father French has the treasure. The person he's been waiting for was supposed to have been Moussa Diab."

A couple at a nearby table gave us a worried look and the waitress came to ask if everything was okay. "Everything's fine," I said, taking a drink of my beer. "In fact, how about you bring another round? It's on me." I gave a casual smile as the waitress walked away. Then I turned and cautioned Sandoval in a harsh whisper. "Keep it together. Remember what you said about prying eyes and ears?"

"We're wasting time," she said through clenched teeth. "Father French has the treasure. We need to go and get it."

I looked at Dominick, who had leaned back in his chair, his arms folded across his broad chest.

"We don't work for you, Sandoval," I said. "So, if you think you've got all the answers, then there's the door." Her chest heaved with the quickened rate of her breathing. "Or you can tell us what the hell this thing is, and we can figure it out together."

The waitress returned with a round of drinks. I smiled at her and told her to keep the tab running. Then I turned to my companions and said, "Now, let's everyone have another nice little toast like we're happy, companionable, day-drinking colleagues."

Dominick and I raised our glasses and imbibed. Sandoval glared at us for a moment before finally raising her own glass. She took a quick sip and set the glass noisily down on the table causing part of the drink to spill onto the tabletop.

"Not exactly what I had in mind," I said in a chilly tone. "Now, I think it's time you tell us what we're talking about here."

Sandoval craned her neck, scanning the handful of patrons scattered at tables throughout the room. She studied each person, none of whom seemed to care in the slightest about our conversation now that the show Sandoval put on had ended. Apparently satisfied that we were anonymous, she looked at me and offered one last appeal.

"Look, there really isn't time for this. Other people are looking for the same thing we are." She gave Dominick a pleading look. "Just tell me whether Father French got a package from Thomas Westcott. If he did, then we can go back there and get it, and you'll be a wealthy man."

Dominick's stony expression never cracked as he stared back at her, silent. She closed her eyes in resignation.

"At this point, you're the one wasting time, Sandoval."

She gave a low laugh, picked up her drink, and shot me a caustic smile. "You think you're such a crack sleuth, don't you, Motley?" She took a drink, this time in a calm manner. "But for all your street smarts and integrity, you're just sinking deeper into the pit, and you don't even see it."

I stared at her, waiting her out. Finally, she sagged back in her chair and relented.

"Lieutenant Douglas Stone. That name mean anything to either of you?"

I shook my head while Dominick sat still as a statue.

"Of course not," she said with a sigh. "Well, let me tell you about Lieutenant Stone since we've got nothing better to do than while the day away with stories. It should come as no surprise that Lieutenant Stone was a member of the Eighty-Seventh Armored Field Artillery Battalion during World War Two." She said the last three words with deliberate emphasis. "In April of nineteen-forty-five, Lieutenant Stone and evidently Thomas Westcott...who was what, Mr. Cotter? A Sergeant?" Dominick gave a nod. "Yes, well Lieutenant Stone, an art aficionado from Nebraska, and Sergeant Westcott, the questing adventurer from Kentucky, found themselves in a place called Quedlinburg, Germany. Ever heard of it?"

I shook my head again, as Dominick remained stock-still.

"I suspect neither Lieutenant Stone nor Sergeant Westcott had heard of it, either...at least, not before the war. Just as I suspect they had never heard of the church of St. Servatius and the trove of medieval treasures that had been housed there for more than one thousand years." Again, she emphasized the final three words. "Do you see where this is headed, gentlemen? Need I continue, or can you bring to bear your powers of deduction to figure out how the story proceeds from this juncture?"

I gave a slight nod for her to continue, which she did after an exaggerated sigh.

"In a stroke of what was either fantastic or awful luck, depending on your perspective, Lieutenant Stone discovered this medieval treasure trove in a cave where it had been placed, ironically, for safekeeping after the Allied Forces began bombing Germany. Whether Sergeant Westcott was or was not with Lieutenant Stone when he made this discovery is an open question. What is not in doubt, gentlemen, is that Lieutenant Stone proceeded to abscond with the treasures, shipping them back to his home in Nebraska where he is said to have openly displayed them until his death almost forty years later."

"I thought there was a big effort after the war to return stolen art to the rightful owners," I said, my face screwing up in puzzlement. "Seems like they would have found him out if he was so open about it."

"Indeed, there was, Mr. Motley. And the Army did investigate the matter in forty-nine. But soon after, the iron curtain of communism came crashing down and Quedlinburg became a part of East Germany. Needless to say, that rather complicated any further investigative efforts."

Dominick leaned in with thoughtful intensity as he listened.

"Many years later when Lieutenant Stone died, the treasures passed to his heirs who decided they would attempt to sell them off. That's when things began to get dicey. You see, one of the treasures, the so-called Samuhel Gospel, was sold in nineteen-ninety, bringing the mystery of the Quedlinburg treasures into the full light of the public sphere for the first time in decades."

Dominick nodded and said, "And then the Berlin Wall came down."

"Precisely," she said. "And East Germany was no more."

I eyed her narrowly as I said, "What was the Samuhel Gospel?"

Sandoval's face took on a dreamy appearance as she described the treasure. "A jewel-encrusted, illustrated masterpiece from the tenth century. The Stone heirs received three-million dollars for it, but its value today is far, far greater than that."

I swallowed hard and looked at Dominick, who was chewing on his lower lip. Turning back to Sandoval, I said, "What else did he have?"

"Let's see, there was an ivory and gold comb, ancient in design. There was a sixteenth-century manuscript called the Evangelistar, a gold and silver chest, a five-hundred-year-old heart-shaped box." She let out a long slow breath. "Among other items of stunning magnificence."

I exhaled a long slow breath of my own as Dominick said, "So, how'd you come to find out about this?"

"Easy. It was in the news. Once the Samuhel Gospel sold, media descended upon the little Nebraska town where Stone had lived. The German government sued to have the items returned and eventually they were. But not before the heirs received a settlement in exchange for the return of the treasures."

"They got paid?" Dominick said. "The government actually paid them to give the stuff back?"

"They did, indeed. You have to understand that the value of these objects from a cultural and historical standpoint is incalculable. Whatever they paid to get the treasures back was a pittance in comparison to the importance of having the treasures back in German hands."

"Okay, I'm confused," I said. "If the treasures were found and returned, then what are we doing here?"

"Simple. We're searching for the treasures that were not returned. You see, Mr. Motley, two of the pieces have never been found."

"Do you know what they are? The two items that weren't returned?"

"I do," she said with a seductive gleam in her eye. "One is a reliquary made of rock crystal and the other is an enameled reliquary cross. Both are centuries old, and both are priceless."

I rubbed my chin in curiosity as I said, "What's a reliquary?"

"A reliquary, Mr. Motley, is...well, I guess the simplest definition is that it holds a precious holy object. Medieval artisans created them as brilliant works of art."

I took a long swig of my beer as Sandoval turned her gaze to Dominick, who suddenly looked like he wanted to crawl under the table.

"Well, Mr. Cotter? Satisfied? May we now return to the question at hand?"

Dominick tapped his fingers nervously on the table. "And that question would be?"

"Oh yes, of course. Allow me to reset the conversation. The question, sir, is did the good Father French ever receive a package from his old pal Sergeant Thomas Westcott?"

Dominick stopped tapping and placed both palms on the table. "The answer to that question, Miss Sandoval, is yes. Father French did receive a package from Thomas Westcott."

"And was Father French privy to the contents of the package?"

"Yes and no. He told me the letter from Westcott indicated there were three items in the package. One was an ordination gift for Father French, and the other two were for Westcott's sons."

Sandoval snorted in disgust. "I suppose Ruth Westcott was undeserving since she wasn't a member of the boy's club."

"I thought the same thing," Dominick said, referencing his notes. "I mean, damn, that's cold-blooded to not bring your old lady something back. But it's in here somewhere." Dominick searched the pages of his notebook. "Here it is. Father French said the letter that came with the package explained that Ruth, who evidently was some kind of artist, had told her husband she only wanted photographs of the landscapes that he saw. It seems she wanted to recreate the images on her own."

My mind went to the drawings and the carved wooden disk that Brother Llewellyn had crafted.

"And you say there were three items?" Sandoval said, her brow creased with confusion. "But there are only two items missing from the Quedlinburg treasures. What was the third piece?"

Dominick shrugged and shook his head as Sandoval ruminated on the information.

"Three items," she said, pondering. "And one was an ordination gift for Father French."

"What are you thinking, Sandoval?"

She considered my question for a moment and said, "It could have been a chalice, I suppose."

"Why a chalice?"

"It's a common gift for a newly ordained priest. Plus, I've seen chalices mentioned quite a few times in Army records of missing artifacts. You know, from churches that were destroyed and looted."

"Army records?" Dominick said.

"Sure. The military has all kinds of open cases with claims about pieces that were taken during the war. Still, only Father French can tell us what the items actually were." She levelled Dominick with an intense gaze. "Did he provide that information to you, Mr. Cotter?"

Dominick shook his head and said, "He's an old dude, you know. It seemed to me he was having a hard time thinking back on it all. Like it was somehow painful."

Sandoval's eyes narrowed as she probed further. "But why would he tell you about the package and then not tell you what was in it?"

"Like I said, he's an old man," Dominick said with a shrug. "Eventually, he got tired and asked if I could come back another time."

"You still haven't answered my question."

Dominick looked her square in the eyes and said, "No, ma'am. He did not tell me what was in the package."

Sandoval held Dominick's gaze, and the two stared unblinking at one another for a long moment. Their standoff might have continued, as Sandoval had said, until opening day at Santa Anita since neither appeared willing to back down. But the cell phone that lay on the table next to Sandoval began to buzz, so she begrudgingly gave in. She picked up the phone and spoke a curt greeting as she stood and walked to the other side of the room to converse with the person on the other end of the call. I took advantage of her absence to get the scoop from Dominick.

"Why do you think the priest opened up to you, Dom?"

"Well, for one, I had the letter he sent to James Westcott. I thought he might keel over when I showed it to him."

"Yeah, but there must be more to it than that. Why would he open up and tell you his story the way he did?"

"Like I said before, he'd been an expecting someone to show up ever since Brother Lew died. It seemed like he wanted to get it off his chest, you know?"

"And you think he's shooting straight?"

"Why wouldn't he be? I mean, he's got nothin' to gain from this. All those people are gone, now. And don't get me wrong, he was a stout old man, but he's gotta know he's not far behind."

"What about Conrad? He's not gone."

Dominick scoffed at my question. "Yeah, but Father William wasn't a fan of Conrad's. He obviously cared about James, though. When I showed him the letter, he could barely hold back the tears. Hell, at that point, I didn't have to push at all. He'd have told me damn near anything I wanted to know."

"So, then he did tell you what was in the package?"

He shook his head. "Nah, he didn't tell me that."

He shrugged, reading the incredulity on my face.

"The priest would tell you damn near anything, but he didn't tell you that?"

He frowned and shook his head, and I stared at him in disbelief. Sandoval was right. Why would Father French be so open about the package and then not reveal its contents? That didn't make sense, especially given Dominick's description of the man as wanting to get things off his chest. I gave my friend a suspicious look. In response, he nodded toward Sandoval who was walking briskly back toward the table.

"We'll talk later," he said.

Sandoval's arrival precluded any further comment on the matter. "We've got to move."

"What is it?"

"That was my colleague." I stared at her, not comprehending her statement as my mind was off kilter with the thought that Dominick might be lying to me. "My backup. Remember? He's sitting on the location of the other man." She read the continued confusion in my blank stare. "The second man. The other guy who was there when Moussa was killed."

"Oh," I said, snapping out of my confused fog. "Of course. Where?"

"An abandoned house out in Washington County. He gave me directions to a place where we can meet up and strategize."

I looked at Dominick, but he shook his head. "I'll find you later."

I turned to Sandoval who said, "This is me living up to my part of the deal, Mr. Motley." She leveled me with a warning glare. "Be sure you're ready to live up to your end."

I shot Dominick another questioning look, but he was staring down at the table. With that, I stood and pulled on my coat.

"You just worry about yourself, Sandoval. When my time comes, I'll show you exactly how to find what you're looking for."

CHAPTER
THIRTY-SEVEN

THE HIGHWAY WAS covered by a layer of packed snow, making our drive a slow-going affair. Sandoval looked pensive as she stared at the road, and I sensed she was struggling with a fair amount of disappointment. Not that I begrudged her any feelings of discouragement. When Dominick announced that Father William French had long ago received a package from his friend Thomas Westcott, it made sense she thought the package contained the treasure she was looking for. This was especially true given that Father French stated he had been expecting someone to come knocking on his door ever since Brother Llewellyn died. In the final analysis, her target remained unchanged, as did my own. The difference was that Sandoval remained uncertain of how to locate her target, while mine was coming into crystalline focus as we turned off the highway and crept slowly along a narrow state road in rural Washington County.

"I see you've switched up your rental," I said. "Next time get something with four-wheel drive."

"I had no idea it snowed so much here."

"Not from around here, huh?" She didn't respond. "Well, just so you know, it doesn't usually snow like this. Especially this early. But hey, why shouldn't the weather be as crazy as the rest of this mess?"

We slipped into a prolonged silence, her pent-up frustration feeling like a third passenger sitting between us. I decided to try to distract her from her disappointment with shoptalk.

"So, tell me something. How'd you get put onto this, anyway?"

"I told you, I'm an independent contractor who..."

"Yeah, I get that. You find things. But why this? I mean, how did your client learn about these treasures in the first place?"

"I already told you. It was in the news. And the reports were clear that two of the Quedlinburg treasures were never found."

"That's it? All this based on a news article?"

She shot me an impatient glance. "Look, Mr. Motley, there are a million different ways these things come about. People like my client are privy to certain information that the public is not aware of. A guy owes them a favor, or he needs to get out of a jam, and suddenly he's got diarrhea of the mouth regarding all kinds of potential schemes. Make sense?"

"Sure. Especially when your client is a bigwig politician."

"I never said that."

"Yeah, but you said this treasure you're looking for is a political weapon that your client wants to use against Rogers Westcott."

Her voice was low and steady as she said, "No, I didn't." She shot me a menacing sidelong glare. "You did."

"Fair enough. But whoever your client is, he calls someone like yourself when he wants to find a rare item like this thing we're after, and you go to work. Is that it?"

"More or less."

"Okay. But how'd you figure out this was somehow related to Thomas Westcott? I mean, there were thousands of G.I.s roaming around Germany when the treasure was taken."

"Of course. But you should know by now that's not how you work a case. You start with the facts you can confirm and work outward in concentric circles, steadily gaining new information that either confirms or contradicts what you think you know."

"Meaning you looked at the other guys in Stone's unit."

"Precisely."

"And none of them were driving luxury vehicles to their second home in the Hamptons?"

"None of them had a son who was working as a barrel roller in a rickhouse before suddenly coughing up fifty grand to purchase and reopen a shuttered distillery. How's a twenty-something orphan without any prospects pull that off?"

I thought back to my conversation with Conrad Westcott and the comment he made about his father being killed by a drunk driver. "Both his parents died?" She nodded. "Well, there's his wife. What about her?"

"Don't think I haven't thought of that. I've got a dossier on the former Isabelle Tuttle, who was a debutante from a wealthy Lexington family."

"Well, there you go."

"Not hardly. Her family disowned her once she hooked up with a hot-blooded redneck without a pot to piss in. But the future Mrs. Westcott was once a free-spirited hippie-chick who was..."

"Only too happy to piss off her Puritanical parents," I said, finishing her thought.

Again, she nodded and said, "What you end up with is a Dickensian pauper, orphaned and working in a Frankfort distillery during the day and hanging out at the university bars at night."

"Trying to hook a nice college girl," I said.

"Which he accomplished."

"So, he got the girl and then sprung for a dilapidated distillery, which in time would make him a baron of the bourbon industry. Why isn't that a classic success story as opposed to evidence of a smoking gun?"

"In my work, one rarely finds a smoking gun," she said. "However, one does often find a trail of breadcrumbs to follow. What you need to understand is that I'm here, and I'm committing my client's resources to this search. Given those facts, it should be clear I'm not operating on conjecture."

"So, what else do you have?"

"A letter from Thomas Westcott for one thing," she said.

"To?"

"Another member of the Eighty-Seventh."

"And?"

"And let's just say Sergeant Westcott liked to spout off at the mouth."

"Like father, like son," I said. "But according to Father French, James was quite the opposite."

"Indeed. I've done my homework on Ruth Westcott too, and by all accounts, she was a humble artistic woman. She was good-humored like her husband, but prudent and not given to his thirst for adventure."

"Sounds like Brother Lew got his sense of adventure from his father, and his talent from his mother."

"We all take a bit from both sides, now don't we, Mr. Motley?"

I looked out the window at a creek running parallel to the road. The creek was swollen and running fast, its current aided by the recent snow.

"Why didn't you just approach Brother Lew?"

"Never got the chance. By the time I was put on the case and learned about Moussa, Brother Lew was dead."

"And that's when you learned about me?" She gave a single nod. "So, why is this second guy important? We've already determined Moussa didn't know anything about this mess. So, what's this guy going to tell us?"

"Maybe you've determined that," she said, giving me a sidelong glance.

I sighed and said, "Okay, but the question remains. What do you expect to learn from this guy?"

"One thing I've learned, Mr. Motley, is that people don't realize what they know is important until they tell it to someone who can see the bigger picture. There are details that in a vacuum seem unimportant, but when those details are fit into a broader frame, they illuminate aspects of the picture that were previously dull."

"And that's why you wanted to hear the entirety of my story?"

Again, she gave a single nod and slowed to a creeping pace as we approached a gravel parking lot next to an abandoned grain silo. A car flashed its lights twice, and we pulled beside it. The man inside the car gave me a hard look, but Sandoval assured him all was good. He spoke directly, telling us the person we were looking for was in an abandoned shack about three miles up the road.

"It fronts the highway, so we'll have to ditch the cars and approach on foot."

"Any cover?" I said.

"There's a gulley behind the house," he said, still eyeing me warily. "We can bound through the adjacent fields and come up behind the house through the gulley. That's the best approach."

"And then?"

"We waylay the bastard when he comes outside to take a piss."

"That simple, huh?"

"This ain't the movies, pal," he said. "No need to get overly complicated. When he grabs his johnson, we pounce on the guy."

"Is he carrying?"

He nodded. "A forty-five."

"Well, then I really do hope it's not like the movies, 'cause in the movies the guy being waylaid usually takes out his pistol and puts a hole in at least one of the guys doing the waylaying."

He gave me a dubious look. "If you're going to get out there and freeze up, tell me now."

"Not a chance, pal. Let's go."

I jumped in his vehicle, and we headed down the snowy road.

"What do I call you?"

"Joe."

"Joe? Are you serious?" He shot me a guarded expression. I shrugged and said, "Joe it is."

We hadn't gone far when he pulled the vehicle onto what appeared to be a spot for maintenance vehicles. Sandoval trailed behind us and did the same. Joe walked over to her vehicle and motioned for her to lower the window.

"When we've secured the target, I'll hit you on your cell phone. You drive up and park in front of the house. Back the car in the driveway and come through the front door and be quick about it. This place is pretty isolated, but you never know who's creeping around and these hillbillies are all armed to the teeth." He looked at me and then at Sandoval. "Whatever you want to ask this guy, do it quick. When the job's done, Elaine will bring us back to my car, and then the two of you go back the way you came."

"Elaine?"

Sandoval leveled her colleague with an incredulous glare, and he bit his lip as he lowered his eyes in shame.

"Don't worry, sweetheart," I said, flashing her a caustic smile. "You'll always be Sandoval to me."

She raised the window, and I didn't know if her look of disgust was meant for me or for Joe. I decided it was probably meant for both of us and with that question settled, I followed Joe as he jogged out into the field. If we'd been hunting, our prey would have heard us coming a mile away as the crusty snow crunched beneath our boots. Of course, in a way we were hunting, and I suspected that given our clandestine tactics, Joe must have had it in mind that our prey would be on guard.

"How do you know he'll come outside?"

"What's he going to do, piss on the floor?" he said. "Besides I've already scouted his movements."

We picked up our pace, trying to stay low as we made our way across the field. After a few hundred yards, we moved in a flanking motion that eventually took us across the gulley Joe had referenced. That took us into a wooded area that provided cover for the next hundred yards or so of the trek before we eventually turned our march back toward the road.

I could see the rear of the shack in the distance. Joe was right in saying that the gulley would provide cover for the immediate approach. What he didn't say was that we would have to sprint across an open field before we made it to the gulley. The snowy conditions would slow us down and leave us exposed longer than we would have liked, but there was no way around it. If our target saw us, I suspected his move would be to bolt out the front. I suddenly wished that Sandoval was positioned to alert us if that occurred, but there was no way to make that happen now. Besides, he'd probably bolt anyway if he saw her vehicle lurking anywhere nearby. We stopped at the edge of the trees and assessed the situation.

"You see that old shed behind the house?" I nodded. "Our best bet is a full sprint to the gulley. We stop once we get into the gulley and out of view so we can listen for any indication that he spotted us. If there's nothing, then we go up the far side of the gulley just behind that shed. Got it?"

"Got it."

"When he has to piss, he comes out the back and walks over to that wood pile to the left of the house. He carries the piece and sets in on that stump next to the pile and does his business."

"It looks like we'll have to cover, what, twenty yards?"

He nodded and said, "I'll go left and draw his attention. You go right and skirt the edge of the house. You can use the house for cover if he gets to his weapon before we get to him."

We looked at each other.

"Ready?"

I nodded and we sprinted across the field. The first shot came when we were about halfway to the gulley.

"Shit," I said.

"Keep going and stay low."

More shots popped off as we ran, and the snow crackled a few feet in front of me as a bullet penetrated the frozen crust. Joe dropped to one knee and let loose three shots of his own. That bought us enough time to breach the gulley before we encountered any response. I crouched down in the bowl of the gulley, looking up at the slope that would take us into the backyard of the house.

"We're fish in a barrel if he comes out," he said, breathing heavily. "As soon as I lay down cover, you get your ass up that side and get behind the shed."

Joe moved up the slope of the gulley far enough to get a partial look at the house and began to unload. As he did, I scrambled up the slope, slipping and grasping for something to hold onto as I clumsily made my way to the rim of the gulley. Joe stopped firing and did the same. The return fire came, and we kept our heads just beneath the crest of the slope. Joe looked at me and nodded as he let loose a flurry of shots. At that, I scurried over the edge and sprinted for the shed, collapsing behind it with my back against the rotten wood of the shed's outer wall. I watched as Joe came over the top and made his way toward me. As he did, a shot from the house put a hole in the left shoulder of his coat, stopping his progress. I rushed over to him, took the pistol, and fired at the house. I only got off two shots before the clip was empty, but it gave me enough time to grab my partner and help him over to the shed.

"Clip." He pulled out a fresh clip and I loaded it into the pistol. We sat listening, knowing he couldn't approach us without announcing himself in the snow. "How bad?" I said, as Joe grimaced and reached inside his coat.

He groaned as he pulled out a bloody hand. "It just grazed me, but Christ almighty that stings."

We stood behind the shed for several minutes, our breathing slowing to a more normal level as we listened for any sign of our enemy's approach. I was about to suggest a way forward when we heard three pops coming from the front of the house. I looked at Joe, whose eyes were wide as he processed what was happening. Then we heard a voice shouting demands.

"Sandoval."

"Who?"

"It...shit, I don't know," I said in frustration. "Elaine, or whatever her name is."

We looked at each other and then dashed through the backyard to the side of the house. We crept along the side and Joe peeked around the corner. He nodded to me and made an all-clear gesture. We made our way into the front yard where I was rather amazed to see Sandoval standing with pistol outstretched over the figure of a man lying face down in the snowy muck.

"I heard the gunfire, so I thought you might need some help."

Joe walked over to the figure on the ground and kicked him hard in the side. "That was an expensive coat you ruined, asshole." Joe stood the man upright, and I drove a fist into his gut. The man doubled over, and my partner delivered a boot to the man's head, sending him flailing back into the slosh.

"That's enough," Sandoval said. "Let's get him inside."

We hauled the man inside the house, and Joe shoved him into a chair.

"What the hell is this?" the man said.

Sandoval kept her weapon trained on the man as Joe reached inside his backpack and pulled out handcuffs and a length of rope. He took out a pocketknife and cut a section of the rope. "Bind his feet." I obliged as Joe handcuffed the man and then used the remainder of the rope to secure the man's torso to the chair. He then dragged the chair near a wall.

"Who the hell are you?" the man said.

Joe answered his question with an open-hand strike to the man's head. "We're asking the questions, Powell. Or should I call you Jay-Eddy?"

The man looked at us like a trapped animal. "I ain't done nothin'."

"Then you've got nothing to worry about," Sandoval said.

The man was breathing heavily as he looked from one of us to the other. "I told you, I ain't done nothin'."

"We heard you," Joe said. "Time to break in some new material."

I found my legs had gone a bit wobbly as I realized what was happening. An hour earlier, I'd been picking at a B.L.T. in The Prep Room. Now I stood before a handcuffed prisoner, drenched, muddy, and lucky not to have been shot by the man handcuffed and tied to the chair in front of me. To me, it felt surreal, but Sandoval seemed to be moving and thinking as if this was routine. She pulled a small notebook from her pocket and flipped it open.

"Jerome Edward Powell. That's your name, right?" The man's eyes were wide as he stared up at her. "As my colleague stated, Mr. Powell, we're here to ask you some questions. Answer those questions truthfully, and there's a chance you walk out of here on your own two feet. Fail to answer our questions to our satisfaction, and well..." She cocked her head toward Joe. "I mean, you did ruin his coat."

Joe made like he was going to strike the man, but Sandoval put up a hand. "My colleague is a temperamental man. You'd do well not to piss him off."

"Fuck him," the man said, his face contorting in derision.

Before Joe could act, I threw my fist into the man's sternum. The chair rocked back against the wall and the man wheezed and coughed, struggling to regain his breath.

"My other colleague appears to be a bit temperamental as well," she said, regarding me with a mixture of appreciation and surprise. "But then getting shot at will bring out the beast in a man, now won't it?"

The man took in deep breaths, attempting to regain his normal breathing rhythm. "That's it," Sandoval said. "That's good, Mr. Powell. Just breathe and relax." Slowly, the man's breathing returned to normal. "Now, ready for question number one?"

"I ain't saying nothin'. I ain't done nothin' and I ain't no rat."

Joe reached inside his backpack and retrieved some first aid materials to bandage his shoulder. As Joe saw to his wound, Sandoval looked at our prisoner and seemed to be deciding which tactic to employ.

"To hell with it," I said, an idea occurring to me. "Let's take him in and collect the bounty."

Sandoval looked at me, her eyes narrowing as she picked up on my train of thought. "Sure. We can do that." She turned to the man. "Five thousand seems like a lot for this squirt, but I guess he has his reasons for wanting to lay hands on him."

"Who goddamnit? Who wants to lay hands on me?"

"Artemis Ray," I said, ominously. "Who else?"

The man's eyes grew wide, and his breathing accelerated as he struggled against his bonds. When he saw the effort was futile, he gave up.

"That's who hired you for the job," Sandoval said. "Isn't that right, Mr. Powell?"

The man looked wildly around the room but didn't answer. Joe took a step toward him, fist cocked and ready. "Stop," the man said. "Just stop for a minute."

"Answer the question," I said, taking a step forward.

"Okay, okay," he said, as he tried to determine his best course of action. "Yeah, it was Artemis. He put us on it."

"On what?" I said.

"On that little 'Spic who was stayin' with them monks."

I grabbed the man by the shoulders and slammed the chair back against the wall. "Don't call him that, again. You hear me, you piece of shit?"

"Okay, okay. I don't know what he was. He just looked...different, that's all."

"His name was Moussa," I said, releasing the man. "Just call him that and leave out any colorful descriptors."

The man nodded and said, "Yeah, whatever. Artemis told us to follow him. Me and Dale."

"Dale Goodlett?" Sandoval said.

"Yeah, me and Goodlett."

"Why?" she said.

"Hell, I don't know. He don't tell us what for, just what to do."

"So, you've worked for Artemis Ray before?" she said.

"Well, not Artemis directly, but for some guy named Jimmy who works for him."

"And this Jimmy told you to follow Moussa?" I said.

"Yeah, but there wasn't much to it. He was inside that monastery most of the time. Except when he went walkin' in them woods."

"But then he went to the hardware store," I said. "You follow him there?"

"Hell, we give him a ride."

"You gave him a ride?"

"Well, shit yeah, we did. I mean why not? We went up and down the damn road just passin' him as he walked, keepin' an eye on him. We figured why not just give him a ride to wherever he was headin' to save time, his and ours."

"Did you talk to him?" Sandoval said.

"Nah, not really. I mean what do you say to a boy like that anyhow?" He shot me a worried look, but I stayed put. "We just drove him into town and dropped him off. He walked down the street and went into Brothers. Then he come out and walked down Center Street and kept going 'til he cut off into them fields that run along Newton Valley. When he done that, we knew he was screwed."

"What do you mean?" I said. "Why was he screwed?"

"I mean, I get what he was thinkin' trying to cut through them fields to get back to that monastery. But he was walkin' right through Spud Allen's property."

"Why was that a problem?" I said.

"'Cause Spud's got plants hid all over his land. He sees some fella walkin' along with a damn shovel in his hand, he's like to lose his mind and shoot the motherfucker."

"So that part of the story that Dale Goodlett told the cops was true?" Sandoval said. "He thought Moussa was out there attempting to narc or steal plants?"

"Nah, that shit weren't true. Like I said, what was true is that he was walkin' through Spud Allen's property and Spud would've lost his damn mind if he seen some 'Spic...'" I balled up a fist and leaned toward the man. "My bad. I mean, if Spud seen some guy walking across his property with a shovel, he'd a lost his shit."

"So, you and Goodlett were what, trying to help?" Sandoval said.

"As a matter of fact, we was. I mean, all we was supposed to do was follow the guy and tell Jimmy what he was up to. But if he'd ended up gettin' shot on Spud Allen's property that would've surely screwed up whatever it was Artemis was trying to do."

"What happened then?" I said. "How did Moussa's body end up down by the river?"

"You gonna let me go if tell ya?"

I looked at Sandoval, who gave a slight nod. "I can tell you that your odds will improve. Now how did Moussa's body end up down by the Rolling Fork?"

The man gave me a sullen look and remained silent. Joe kicked the chair, and it went over on its side, the man's shoulder thudding against the floor as it landed.

"This is not a negotiation," Joe said, heaving the chair back up to a sitting position. "Answer the damn question. Now."

The man glared at Joe for a moment but then continued his account of what happened. "We got outta' the truck and went after the guy once he cut onto Spud's property. He seen us comin' after him and recognized we was the ones who give him a ride earlier. That spooked him. Fair enough, I guess. I mean, if I'd seen two dumbass rednecks chasin' me through a field, I would've run, too."

Sandoval nodded, encouraging him to continue.

"So, then me and Dale heard some four wheelers, and we stopped runnin' after him. The fella stopped, too, so I guess he had at least some common sense. Anyhow, me and Dale said hell, we ain't gonna be found out on Spud Allen's property with some guy with a shovel. So, we took off back toward the road. That fella we was chasin' came to his senses and took off with us, but he tripped and fell as he ran. Them four wheelers was gettin' close, so me and Dale took cover while that boy was laid out flat as a pancake right out in the wide open. But he didn't move a hair, so them boys missed him and went on by. Hell, I don't know if they was checkin' on plants or was just out ridin', but when they was gone, me and Dale went over to the fella' and saw blood runnin' from his head. That's when we run back to the truck and went to find Jimmy."

"What's Jimmy's last name?" Sandoval said.

"Hell, if I know." Joe took a step toward him. "You can hit me all you want. I ain't got no idea about Jimmy's last name."

"So, you left him out there?" I said. "You left Moussa in that field?"

"What the hell else was we gonna do? If we'd a got caught out there by Spud's boys, we'd all of us have been screwed."

"So, you went to find Jimmy?" Sandoval said. The man nodded. "And he sent you back to get Moussa?"

"Hell yes, he did. We told him what happened, and Jimmy was more worried about Spud than that boy. I mean, if it turned out that the boy was dead, and somebody found him out on Spud's property, then there'd be all kinds of people runnin' for cover."

"Why's that?" she said.

"'Cause Spud's connected, that's why. He's got a big growin' operation. Jimmy said we let it be found out we was on Spud Allen's property, and it'd be our ass."

"Okay, go on," I said. "Then what?"

"Then we went back. And sure enough, that boy done expired from losing all that blood. So, we got the body and took it down by the fork and then them two boys canoeing came along and found it. But there wasn't no good explanation for why there was a dead body down by the river."

"And without an explanation," I said, picking up his logic, "someone was going to ask questions that Artemis Ray and the people he was working for in the weed business didn't want answered."

"Damn straight," he said, nodding. "And that meant one of us had to take the hit. But I done took my pinch three years ago, so it was Dale's turn. Jimmy told him what to say and he done it."

"And the shovel?" Sandoval said.

"Well, that boy's head was cut wide open from where he fell and hit the edge of a rock. He was carryin' this little toy spade, so it seemed like that was the way to go. That's why Dale told the story that way."

"But you planted a regular-sized shovel near the body?" I said.

"Well, wasn't nobody gonna believe Dale cracked him hard enough to kill him with no garden spade. So, yeah."

We were silent for a long moment, unsure of what else to say.

"We've been here for quite some time," Joe said. "If there's nothing else, then I think we better wrap things up."

"Are we taking him in?" I said, looking at Sandoval. "If he's telling the truth, then it was an accident."

Sandoval looked at Joe and said, "Do you believe him?"

Joe studied the man for a moment. "I doubt he has the wherewithal to come up with a story like that on the spot. So, yes, I believe him. But accident or not, he and Goodlett are guilty of a bevy of crimes. Obstruction, mutilation, tampering with evidence. There's plenty he could be charged with."

"If he ever made it to trial alive," I said. "Seems to me there's some powerful people with a stake in keeping this quiet."

Joe nodded his agreement.

Sandoval turned to the man and said, "Okay, Mr. Powell. It's best you forget all about this conversation. And keep in mind, I found you once, I can find you again."

The man's face was drawn and muddy, and the left side was puffy and red from the blows he had taken. "I just wanna get away from here. Far away, and I ain't never comin' back."

Fifteen minutes later, we dropped Joe at his car. Before he got out of Sandoval's rental, he gave me a knowing look and nodded. Then he got into his vehicle and drove away. We drove off in the opposite direction and it wasn't until we turned onto the highway that led back to Bardstown that either of us spoke.

"Do you believe him?"

"A guy like Joe knows how to spot a liar. I believe him."

"So, it was an accident," I said, shaking my head. "It was nothing more than a stupid, tragic accident." I put my face in my hands and rubbed my eyes.

"What about Westcott? What about his role in this?"

"He had the kid followed," I said with a shrug. "Big deal."

"Are you listening to yourself?" She snorted in disbelief. "Westcott was having Moussa followed for a reason. You're going to gloss over that?"

"I'm not glossing over it," I said, turning to look at her. "And by the way, what exactly was that reason?" She looked confused. "I mean, the letter from Hamia to Brother Lew. She told me it was just pleasantries. So, what made Westcott wanna have the boy followed in the first place?"

Sandoval shrugged and said, "She mentioned this 'treasure of great value' that Brother Lew had referenced in his own letter to her. Something Moussa was meant to find."

"Yeah, but that was about spirituality, about Moussa figuring out his path in life."

"According to you," she said, giving me a sidelong look.

As we drove along in silence, I tried to process all that Jay-Eddy Powell had revealed to us. Finally, I interrupted the quiet with my summary of what I thought had ultimately happened. "The way I see it, if Moussa hadn't wandered off the road into that field, then he would have made his way back to the monastery, completed his quest, and gotten on with his life."

Sandoval shook her head as she stared at the highway. "I can't believe what I'm hearing."

"Look, I agree that Westcott thought Moussa was going to lead him to this treasure you're both after," I said, testily. "But that was never going to happen."

"How do you know?"

"Trust me. I know."

"Trust me?" Her face screwed up in derision. "Like I'm supposed to trust this nonsense that you didn't already know what it is we're looking for before I told you?"

I turned away from her and looked out the window.

"But it doesn't matter anymore," she said, shaking her head. "I only have one question left for you. Where is it?"

"I never said I know where it is," I said, still staring out the window. "I said I know how to find it."

"Then it's time you tell me how to find it," she said in a voice laced with venom. "And for your sake, Levi Motley, you better not have lied."

"That's your territory," I said, turning toward her with a contemptuous look. "I didn't lie, but that doesn't mean you're going to like what I have to say."

Sandoval's expression turned anxious.

"Just head back to Bardstown," I said, again turning to stare out the window. "You'll see."

CHAPTER
THIRTY-EIGHT

T HE BOTTLES BEHIND the bar were lined up like a choir on the verge
of singing the first note of a Christmas carol.

Or a requiem, I thought.

I searched the bottles for a unique brand and saw a label that read
"Slippery Pig" with the tagline "Be fat and happy". I hailed the bartender.
"Can I have a look at that bottle? The one with a pig on it?"

She handed it to me and said, "That'll put hair on your chest."

"Never had much trouble with that," I said, studying the bottle. It was
a twelve-year old, 110-proof straight Kentucky bourbon whiskey with
a picture of a pig dashing through a hole in a fence. "Gimme' a double.
Neat."

She gave a nod and looked down at the journal lying on the bar in
front of me. "Well, damn if it don't warm the cockles of my barren heart
to see a man ready to dive into deep thought with a fine bourbon in his
hand."

I gave her a wan smile as she set the drink in front of me and moved
down the bar to the next customer who ordered a light beer.

"That ain't gettin' it done," she said, winking at me as she popped the
top on the bottle.

"Not for me it won't," I said, dryly. "Not tonight."

The previous couple of days had left me with a surreal mixture of emo-
tions and thoughts that needed to be sorted out and placed in some kind
of rational order. The best way to do that, I decided, was to think and
write amidst the low hum of human energy in an old tavern in an old

town with a fine old bourbon in hand. Resolved that I was in the right atmosphere for the task at hand, I tipped my glass allowing just a taste to cross the threshold of my lips before it eased across my tongue and down my throat, giving me a Kentucky hug that warmed the cockles of my own barren heart.

I set the glass down, blew out a slow breath, and opened the journal. Staring at the blank page, I thought about Moussa and his innocuous but tragic decision to cut across that property with no more intent than to shave some time off his trek back to the monastery. It occurred to me that my thinking on the matter had come full circle, and I found myself balanced right back on the edge of Occam's razor. Turns out that strictly speaking, the simplest explanation had been the correct one. Moussa had been in the wrong place at the wrong time, though the color of his skin did not seem to signify in the manner that I originally thought it must have. I didn't know what to do with that conclusion, but its stark simplicity made me sad as I realized I had been hoping for a more sophisticated explanation. Somewhere along the way, I began to operate from the false premise that complexity yields meaning, as if his death would have been imbued with a greater sense of profundity were it the product of some nefarious machinations.

On the other hand, I thought, *it kind of was.*

I picked up my pen and let it meander across the page in loops and swirls until it reached the edge on the other side. Then I drew a straight line under the topsy-turvy image. The image that lay on the page was instructive in both its randomness and simplicity. The meandering line represented the uneven topography of everything that had brought me to that moment, and the straight line represented the same thing. I wrote "The Search for Answers" between the two images and then retraced the convoluted path of the first line, darkening its topsy-turvy way. At the bottom of the page, I wrote Moussa's name and the words "It was an accident". Then I stared at the page, attempting to sear the images and words into my consciousness.

I took another drink and thought about what I had learned about Moussa's death. While I agreed with Sandoval's tacit assertion that Conrad Westcott's plan to follow Moussa bespoke of, at the very least, an arrogant manipulation that deserved a reckoning, I stuck to the basic conclusion that his death was in fact an accident. What was not an accident was everything that followed, including the incarceration of a man who had taken the fall for no better reason than Jerome Edward Powell had already taken his pinch.

But for what? I thought. *Or better yet, for who?*

I thought back to Dominick's words the day he told me things work different in a small town and that the power structure does not want to be fucked with. As if on cue, my thoughts were interrupted by my friend's beefy paw slapping me on the back.

"Lighten up, Lee-Mo."

"What do you mean?" I said, closing the journal.

"I mean I could see the wheels turning in that rust bucket from the other side of the room. What are you doing writing in a bar?"

"Actually, I didn't write more than ten words."

"Hey, ten words is enough as long as they're in the right order," he said, taking a seat. "What are we drinking?"

"Slippery Pig. I'm told it'll put hair on your chest."

He raised an eyebrow and hailed the bartender. "What's up, Jessica? Girl, you know what I like."

"Irish Car Bomb?"

"Damn, Jay. You tryin' to send me home early?"

"I didn't think that was possible," she said.

"Well, it's getting more and more possible every day. So, my old ass will take the Irish and you can keep the car bomb."

She gave me another wink as she reached for a pint glass. Dominick slipped onto a barstool and regarded me with a sidelong look. "It's feeling damn heavy in here, brother. You got the look of a man with guilt pressing down on him."

"It's not guilt, it's...to tell you the truth, I don't know what it is."

"Well, whatever it is, I'm guessing it's tied up in whatever you and that Sandoval woman went off chasing after?"

"Yeah. It is," I said, turning to face him. "And strangely enough, you haven't been around lately for me to tell you about it."

He sighed and stared down at the bar, perking up momentarily as the bartender returned with his pint. He took a drink and then turned to me with an abashed look.

"The priest told you what was in that package, didn't he?" He nodded. "Why, Dom? Why hide that from me?"

He pursed his lips as he considered how to answer. "I got caught up. I thought maybe Sandoval was right. I thought Father French had that treasure."

"And you thought you could get it from him?"

Again, he considered how to answer. "I lost my head there for a minute. What can I say?"

"Did you go back to talk to the priest?"

"Yesterday," he said, and then shook his head. "He doesn't have it."

I hesitated before asking the question I knew was on both our minds. "What would you have done if he did?"

"I'm glad I didn't have to find out." He took a drink of his beer and then locked eyes with me. "I'm really sorry, Levi."

I looked at the man, my friend, who had been there for me a thousand times before and then some. I put a hand on his shoulder and squeezed. "You're a good man, Dom. I'm proud to call you brother."

He managed a small half smile, and I moved on in the way guys do when it's time to shut up and let something go. "So, what about it? Learn anything new?"

"It was mostly going over ground we covered the first time. But just like before, he was happy to get the past out in the open. I mean, it felt like I was on the other side of the confessional." I laughed and sipped my drink. "Not that I know how you Catholics roll with all that. But hey, whatever it takes to get through the narrow gate, you know what I'm sayin'?"

I laughed some more as he turned and gave me a serious look.

"I get the feeling that maybe this thing is starting to wrap up for you."

"Well, I know what happened to Moussa. So, yeah. I guess a big part of it is wrapping up." I sighed and looked down at the journal on the bar. "Now, I just have to figure out what it all means."

Dominick considered that for a moment and said, "Tell me about it. I can fill you in on my part with Father French and then maybe we can put the pieces together and make sense of it all."

I agreed with that approach and launched into my account of approaching, subduing, and questioning Jerome Edward Powell. As always, Dominick listened with keen attention, but that attention morphed into concern when I described the barrage of gunfire Joe and I endured during our approach to the abandoned shack where Powell was hiding out. Like me, he found Sandoval's proficiency with a firearm, as well as her comfort level in questioning a de facto prisoner, to be something of a welcome surprise.

"Guess she was a good person to have watching your back. Although it makes me wanna rethink my strategy of stonewalling her on that package." Dominick craned his neck and scanned the bar patrons as if suddenly nervous. "She ain't hanging out around here somewhere waiting for me, is she?"

I gave him a look of certainty and said, "It'll be a minute before Regina Sandoval shows her face in this town again."

Dominick gave me a curious look. "Why is that?"

"Let's just say I held up my end of the bargain."

"Meaning she knows how to find this treasure she's after?"

"She knows," I said with a nod. "But trust me, she's gotten as close as she's going to get to it. At least for the foreseeable future."

His eyes narrowed a bit, and I had the sense that he was skeptical of my response. In that moment, I felt we were back in that space of mistrust, as if he was still trying to plot a way to get to his own desired end. Given that impression, I wasn't about to tell him more until I learned what he had to say about his chat with Father French. Dominick relaxed in his chair with a despondent look on his face. I knew that he knew that despite my understanding, his duplicity meant the matter was firmly in the position of once again being my investigation, my quest. Seeing he understood this, I gave him a hard look and asked the obvious question.

"Did Thomas Westcott send Father French those two reliquaries?"

He hesitated for a moment and then sighed. "Yeah. The two reliquaries were in the package. So, I guess Sandoval's instincts or research or tip or whatever it was that led her to the Westcotts was correct."

"And the third piece?"

Dominick turned to me with an open expression. "Honestly, Levi, I don't know. The old man just said one of the pieces was an ordination gift from Thomas Westcott. Maybe Regina was right. Maybe it was a chalice or some sacred object."

"You mean like a reliquary?"

He shook his head and said, "Man, I don't know. What do you give a guy when he becomes a priest?"

"Good question. Why didn't Father French just tell you what Thomas gave him?"

Dominick pondered that for a moment as he thought back to what Father French had shared with him. "You know the two Westcott boys were orphaned, right?"

I stiffened a bit and took a gulp of my drink before answering. "I knew from Conrad that his father was killed in a car crash. Sandoval filled me in that the mother also died in the crash."

"As the priest tells it, Ruth Goodwin's family wanted the Westcott farm, but didn't want nothing to do with those boys."

"Assholes," I said in disgust.

"Yeah. Anyway, the Goodwins got the farmhouse at auction, but not before Father French got in there and secured the two pieces Thomas had saved for his boys."

"Father French having given the pieces back to Thomas when he returned from the war."

"Exactly," he said. "And since William French practically grew up in that old farmhouse, he knew every nook and cranny where Thomas might have stashed those treasures. He found them easily enough and honored his friend's wishes once the boys came of age. James was the oldest, so he got out of the orphanage first. Father French told me he gave both treasures to James."

"How does he know James gave the other piece to Conrad?" Dominick stared at me with a stolid expression. "Yeah, I get it. Even Father French can do the math that Conrad sold that treasure to start his business. Sandoval said as much herself."

"You think that's what this is all about? That whoever Sandoval is working for wants to find the other reliquary to tie the Westcott empire to a piece of war loot?"

I considered the question for a moment and said, "Given the plain facts of Moussa's death, I don't see it connected to the weed business in the way I thought it might have been. I mean, it's clear from what Jay-Eddy Powell said that there are powerful interests wrapped up in that world..."

"No doubt," he said, interjecting.

"But this package seems to be pointing us in another direction. Did the priest say anything more about it?"

"Yes and no."

"Meaning?"

He thought for a moment and said, "Meaning he didn't want to get into that gift he received. But he did say...how'd he put it? Damn, I don't have my notes."

Dominick was a professional who always strived to get things right. So, for a moment, he was silent as he thought back to his conversation with Father French, trying to recall exactly what the priest had told him. Finally, he slowly nodded, remembering the details of what he had been told.

"The piece Father French was given was stolen. That part's easy enough to remember. What I'm trying to recall is how he put it." I looked at him with a quizzical expression. "He was all secretive about it. He said it was a big deal, some kind of theft that happened here in Bardstown. Something at the church."

"St. Joe's?"

"Yeah. It was kinda crazy. He said it involved the F.B.I."

"Huh?"

"Yeah, I know," he said. "I'm not totally sure what he was talking about. I just know he said when the piece he had been given was stolen, Thomas Westcott became nervous thinking they'd come after him...'they' being the feds. But Father French assured Thomas that he never reported the piece as missing for that very reason. He didn't wanna jam up his friend by making him explain where he got it."

"Because it was taken as a spoil of war. And like Sandoval said, the Army was investigating that stuff, so they could return stolen pieces to their rightful owners."

Dominick nodded and said, "That's right. But whatever it was, Father French didn't wanna talk anymore about it. He just said that for a while Thomas wanted to return the pieces because he was so freaked out about the theft at the church. On top of that, Father French said Thomas had begun to regret taking those pieces. Evidently, it was weighing on his mind, and he wanted to find a way to give the treasures back."

"Let me guess. He and Ruth were killed in that car accident before he got the chance." Dominick nodded "And that left Father French with no option other than to give the two pieces to James like his friend had originally intended."

"Exactly right," he said. "Plus, you gotta think about the years that passed before those boys got out of the orphanage. If nobody came around asking questions, why not go ahead with the original plan?"

I nodded in silent agreement.

"So where do we go from here, Levi?"

"Hell, I don't know," I said, letting a deep sigh. "Like you said, things are wrapping up." He turned to me with a surprised look. "Hey, it's not my job to expose Conrad Westcott's dirty laundry to the world. Who would care anyway?"

Dominic gave a snort of incredulity. "After all this? You're just going to let it go?" I shrugged and lit a cigarette. "What about Moussa?"

I took a drag off the cigarette and looked down at my journal. "It was an accident, Dom. If he hadn't cut through that field..."

"But he did. He did cut through that field, and those two jackasses followed him." I stared straight ahead, ignoring his gaze. "Think about it. If those two guys hadn't taken off running, then maybe Moussa wouldn't have tried to run."

"Yeah, well, if he hadn't run then..."

"Maybe they wouldn't have even seen him," he said, cutting me off. "And then maybe he could've made it back to the monastery unharmed."

I turned to Dominick and said, "Or maybe they would have seen Moussa Diab standing in their pot field with a shovel in his hand. A guy like that tends to stand out under those circumstances in case you didn't know."

"You think I don't know that?" His voice rose in anger. "And what the fuck would you know about it?"

"Right. I'm sorry." I raised my hands in a sign of truce. "I didn't mean to imply that I know what it's like."

Dominick's face was hard as he stared at me. "No, brother," he said in a sardonic tone. "You don't."

We sat for a few minutes in silence. Finally, I said, "I'm sorry, Dom." He gave a curt nod in response. "You know, Declan told me money and power ain't my game."

"Yeah, well don't forget to add racial sensitivity to that list," he said, withering me with an angry look. I did the only thing I could. I kept my mouth shut and gave a stupid nod. Thankfully, Dominick moved on. Sort of. "But to hear Sandoval tell it, it don't matter if it's your game or not. Doesn't matter if it's mine either, for that matter. The game's being played whether we like it or not. She was right about that."

Again, I looked down at my journal. "Yeah, well I've played my part in this game. I kept up my end of the deal with Sandoval, and I know what happened to Moussa." I turned to Dominick and said, "I'm out."

He shook his head in the way I had seen him do a thousand times before when he was disappointed in me. I looked away and was about to hail the bartender for another drink when I heard a woman's voice behind me.

"Well, if it isn't dickhead Motley."

I turned and saw the disapproving glare of Katie Jo Culver, one of Daphne's friends.

"Why you put all that shit all over your face, Culver? Daddy not give you enough attention when you were little?"

Her face contorted in disdain. "Screw you, Motley."

"Hmm. Clever retort."

Dominick stood and said, "I think I hear somebody calling my name."

He walked away, leaving me alone in Katie Jo's unwelcome presence. I hailed the bartender and ordered my drink, trying to ignore the woman. But she remained standing beside my barstool, looking at me with the satisfied smile of someone who knows something that she wants you to know but who won't tell you until and unless you ask for it first. I groaned, knowing I was taking the bait.

"What?"

She gave a coy shrug, but when I responded with a disinterested shrug of my own and turned away, she couldn't stand to keep her juicy little tidbit of gossip bottled up.

"I know something you don't know, Motley."

"Oh, I am quite certain you know all kinds of things I don't know, Culver. Like how to..."

"Daphne's with Lance," she said, unable to contain her glee.

"It's a free country," I said, trying to appear nonchalant though my gut had involuntarily tightened.

Katie Jo was only too happy to continue providing unsolicited details. "He came down to The Prep Room and sat in my section and I overheard him say that you was out with some cheap hussy." My eyes narrowed as I took in what she was saying. "That's right. He said it loud enough so that me, Daphne, and the whole bar could hear it. Said you was out with some skank and that he seen the two of you makin' out."

"Well, as you can see, that's not true. Unless he considers Dom a skank." She looked confused. "Oh yeah. Me and Dom were over in the corner earlier going at it. But hey, everybody in town knows Dom's one prime piece of meat. Not an ounce of skank in him."

"You're so full of shit. You think you can say whatever you want 'cause you're cute and all, but really you're just..."

"Bye, Katie Jo," I said, but she didn't go away. Instead, her face transformed into a mask of fretful worry. I sighed in frustration and said, "For fuck's sake, what?"

She looked at me with tears glistening in her eyes. "She left with him, Levi. She left with him to go find you."

"Okay, well I'm right here. So, they won't have to go far."

"But they're not coming here. They're headed out to Raywick."

I threw back my drink. "Can I get another?" I said, motioning to the bartender. I turned around in my seat to face the suddenly emotionally distraught Katie Jo Culver. "Why would they be headed out there when I'm sitting right here?"

"Because Lance was talking loud on purpose, that's why. He got Daphne's attention saying you was out with somebody at Bickett's and that you and her was making out. He got her all worked up and upset."

I turned away and shook my head, refusing to take her seriously. But she still wouldn't leave, so I turned to look at her again and saw her face did seem to register genuine emotion. Against my better judgement, I nodded for her to continue.

"Look, I ain't no fan of yours. But she thinks you hung the moon even though you're bound to break her heart and leave her."

"Stay on point, Culver. Are you saying he got her upset on purpose by telling her I'm out with someone?"

"That's what it looked like to me. And she left with him."

"To go find me?"

"Well, that's what he said, but I don't believe it. I mean, after all, here you sit. So why in the hell is he trying to get her out to Raywick?" She wiped tears from her eyes. "You know he lives out there, right?"

I shook my head and said, "I don't know where that asshole lives."

"Well, now you do. And I think he's trying to get her out and away from her friends to do something to her."

I felt a rush of adrenaline surge through me. I tried to temper it, reasoning that Lance Coleridge wasn't worth my time, but I couldn't shake the idea that Katie Jo might be right. Coleridge was a low life who would stoop to any means to get what was likely the best thing that ever happened to him back in his life. But would he hurt her?

"You got to help her, Levi. You owe her that much."

I downed the shot that had been delivered to me and threw some bills on the bar. "Look, don't worry about it. It's probably nothing, but I'll find her and see what's going on."

"Find her," she said with a pleading look. "Find her, Levi."

"Calm down. Like I said, it's probably nothing."

I picked up my journal and headed for the door. As I went, it occurred to me that I might need Dominick to come along. I turned to search the room and saw him smiling and conversing with a pretty woman on the other side of the bar. I started to call out for him but stopped, suddenly unsure of whether I did, in fact, want him to come along. I didn't know if that was because of the tense nature of our conversation, or because I thought there might actually be something to what Katie Jo had told me.

Which, ironically, would be the best reason for him to come along.

I put that notion aside and was headed for the door when I spotted Katie Jo with another woman, laughing and pointing to where I had been sitting at the bar. For a moment, I paused. The way she was talking in such a lighthearted manner struck me as odd, and in that moment, I thought her whole act had to be a ruse. On the other hand, I knew her to be a vapid creature that I thought would be hard pressed to come up with a scheme like the one she had described. So, I stood for a moment and watched her, unsure of what to do. But soon my thoughts shifted to the image of Daphne with that shitkicker Coleridge, and I decided that at the very least it might be fun to have another shot at that prick.

With that thought firmly in mind, I left. Alone.

CHAPTER
THIRTY-NINE

THE NEXT MORNING, I leaned against the kitchen counter with a cup of coffee, thinking about the dream I'd been having before the morning sunlight began roasting me in my sleeping bag. In the dream I was maybe eleven or twelve and standing near the dugout of a baseball field with my bat and glove, watching the game. A boy looked at me through the chain-linked fence and said, "You're up," and the next thing I knew, I was digging into the batter's box as the pitcher stepped onto the mound and readied his delivery. As I dug my right foot into the dirt and lifted the bat into position, I looked directly at the pitcher, confident I could handle anything he had in his arsenal.

As the pitcher made his windup, I heard a voice from behind the backstop say, "Keep your eye on the ball, son." As I turned to look, the pitch thwacked into the catcher's mitt and the umpire called out, "Strike one." To my surprise, no one was there. Turning back to the pitcher, I repeated my routine and as the pitcher entered his windup the same voice came from behind the backstop saying, "Keep your eye on the ball." I turned to look but again, there was no one there. The umpire threw up his arm as he emphatically called another strike. Repeating the routine for the third time, I heard the voice call out with the same message as the pitcher let loose with a blazing fastball. But this time I did not turn around. This time, I took a stride toward the pitch, picking up the rotating seams on the baseball with perfect clarity. As the ball neared the strike zone, I felt the bat swinging in a plane perfectly in line with the flight of the pitch. The bat *pinged* as it made solid contact, and I watched as the baseball flew high over the second baseman and headed into right field. I sprinted down the first base line and had just made the turn for second when I woke up.

I drank my coffee and thought about the vivid nature of the dream, convinced the scene was a part of my own past. I was about to record the dream in my journal when a knock at the front door brought me back to reality. I assumed it was Dominick and walked to the door prepared to apologize yet again for my insensitive remark the night before. But when I opened the door, I found Daphne Rose standing on the front stoop.

"Hey. I'm surprised to see you."

"I just came by to say I'm sorry," she said, her eyes glistening as she spoke.

I reached out and embraced her, holding on for a long moment before I invited her inside. She came in, and I offered coffee, which she declined. "I won't be here long."

"What's the hurry? Got a hot breakfast date?"

She sniffled as the glistening in her eyes spilled over and tears streamed down her cheeks. Again, I put my arms around her and assured her everything would be fine.

"I'm so sorry for the way I spoke to you."

"It's okay, Daphne. Really, I understand. I haven't exactly been an easy person to be around lately."

I looked around the room, knowing I didn't have any Kleenex or a handkerchief to offer her and feeling chagrined at my lack of hospitable preparedness. She wiped her face with the sleeve of her coat, and I managed to provide a paper towel for her to blow her nose.

The previous evening, I had set out in pursuit of Lance Coleridge on the premise that had conveniently been fed to me that he intended to take advantage of Daphne in some way. In truth, I had seen through Katie Jo's act, but my desire to exact some level of harm onto Lance Coleridge overwhelmed the rational instinct that none of what I'd been told was true. Thus, I had admittedly left the tavern with the goal of wrecking Coleridge's night firmly in mind. Instead, I walked to The Prep Room where Sam told me that Daphne said she was going to The Old Stone Pub after finishing her shift early.

As it turned out, Sam was correct. I found Daphne with two of her girlfriends at the pub. She was already imbibing the third of whatever fruity drink the bartender had concocted for her, which was unusual be-havior for the normally temperate Miss Rose. I sat down at the table and attempted a reasonable discussion, but it didn't take long for the conver-sation to go off the rails.

"Yeah, he said all that," she had said. "So what? Lance has a big mouth and a little dick. Not a good combination in my experience."

"So, he left alone?"

"If that's your way of asking if he left with me, then you must be dumb-er than he is. I mean, look around, Motley. You see the bastard anywhere?"

"But did he try to get you to leave with him?"

"What if he did? What do you care who I see? I doubt you'd lose a minute of sleep if I were to leave with some guy from right here in this bar. Which, by the way, I intend to do."

"I didn't come here to fight with you, Daphne. I was worried by what Katie Jo told me. That's all."

"Oh bullshit, you were worried," she said in a heated tone. "You don't care about me. Admit it, you wanted it to be true just so you'd have an excuse to kick Lance's ass."

The conversation did not improve one iota from that point onward. In fact, it quickly devolved into Daphne getting up from the table to flirt with some guy who had been eyeballing her from across the room. Her girlfriends took a few potshots of their own as I made my way to the door, but I never turned around to give them the satisfaction of knowing they had gotten to me.

But that was last night. This morning, Daphne was standing before me as she blew her nose and looked up at me with pitiful eyes that plead-ed for me to say something comforting. And I did. I comforted her and assured her and told her the truth, which was that I had not treated her fairly and that she deserved better.

"What's that mean?" she said, warily. "You don't want to see me anymore?"

"Actually, no. It means you deserve better from me. And I've, umm... well, I've been thinking a lot about my life lately...about how I live and what I've done and what I want to do different."

She swallowed hard and looked at me with eyes that were hopeful I might be letting her inside if only a little.

"I'm not saying I'm suddenly some changed man who's seen the light,

Daph." I hesitated for a moment, chewing my lower lip as I thought about what I wanted to say. "Let's just say I think I can be a better man. I don't know exactly what that means, but I've had some interesting experiences lately that have led me to wonder if I might, umm...well, you know, if I could maybe..."

The phone rang.

"Saved by the bell," I said in a relieved tone.

"And not a second too soon," she said in a husky voice. "I believe you were about to ask me to dance, Levi Motley."

I laughed nervously as I picked up the phone. The voice on the other end indicated the call was from Manchester Federal Correctional Institution. The voice then asked if I would accept a collect call from Bobby Shouse.

"Of course I will."

I heard a click and then the heavy voice of Bobby who wasted no time delivering the news. "They fucked him up, Levi," he said in an urgent tone. "Word got out and they fucked him up. Bad."

I fumbled for words as I tried to comprehend what he was saying. Lacking the patience necessary for me to formulate a coherent thought, Bobby kept repeating himself until I was finally able to spit out a question. "Slow down, Bobby. What are you saying to me?"

"I'm sayin' they put him in the infirmary. Declan's in a coma."

I tried to speak, but no words formed as a wave of thoughts flooded my mind. My vision seemed to narrow and go black, and I felt like I was about to pass out. I heard Bobby on the other end of the line, but his voice sounded like it was a thousand miles away. Gradually, I gained control of my senses, and Bobby's voice came closer as I gained some degree of clarity.

"You hear me, kid? Levi? Levi? Do you hear what I'm saying to you?"

"I don't...understand. What do you mean 'word got out'?"

"They're saying Declan's getting out early. That he ratted somebody out and got time shaved off his sentence. Why would he do that, Levi? Huh? Why would he do that?"

My head was swimming as I attempted to make sense of what I was hearing.

"Declan told me you got yourself in a pinch. Is that it? You get him to bail you out of a jam you little punk sonofabitch?"

"What? No," I said, incredulous to the idea. "Hell no. You know better."

"Do I? Do I know better?"

"Hell yes, you do. Look, this is somebody trying to mess with him, with me, to try and get something they're after. That's all it is. But it's not true. Declan's not giving up shit to anybody to get time off his term. You know he wouldn't do that, Bobby." There was silence on the other end of the line. "Listen to me. Declan's not talking to any goddamn feds."

Daphne looked at me with shocked concern on her face as Bobby's voice came through the line with menacing ferocity. I'd known the guy my whole life, and he was like a second older brother to me. But he was cut from the same cloth as Declan, and he wasn't about to let his friend go down for some bullshit that he thought I had convinced Declan to get me out of.

"You listen to what I'm saying, Levi. My friend is laid up in a coma, and you best believe that the guys who did it ain't never gonna piss straight again. But this is your brother. He's all you got. So, whatever you gotta do to straighten this thing out...fucking do it."

I heard him breathing across the line. "How bad, Bobby?"

"Bad enough. And bad enough will get worse if you don't handle your business."

"I understand. I'll take..."

"Do it," he said, cutting me off. "Now."

The line went quiet and a voice on the other end said, "The inmate has now hung up. The call is now complete."

CHAPTER
FORTY

THE ONLY SOUND was that of my own breathing as I sat watching George Hawley read the story I had spent the last two days drafting. I could see he was halfway through the piece, but he had yet to remark or ask a single question, leaving me time to ruminate on all that had occurred since I received that phone call from Bobby Shouse.

A few hours after the call, I had cleared security protocols at the prison and received admittance into the infirmary. As I stood beside Declan's gurney, the doctor explained that it had been the blows to the head that had put him in a coma. I asked what the prognosis looked like, but the doctor predictably dodged the question by offering a pat answer that might have been "We'll have to see where things are in another twenty-four hours," but I couldn't be sure as I was only half-listening. I didn't spend much time in the infirmary, just long enough to sear the battered image of my brother into my consciousness. But like Bobby had said, bad enough was bound to get worse, so I had to act quickly to protect Declan. Acting quickly meant a brief but pointed conversation with Bobby Shouse.

Bobby entered through the same door Declan had walked through during my previous visit. As he sat and picked up the receiver, I could see his face bore multiple bruises and cuts. I didn't need to ask where he got them, and I did not engage in small talk, opting instead to use a neighborhood vernacular that Bobby would understand to convey the message that I needed a piece. Not that I had any intention of pursuing violent means in the protection of my brother, but it was clear to me that Katie

Jo Culver's attempt to deliver me into the hands of Lance Coleridge was part of a larger scheme that I imagined to be the design of Artemis Ray. Given the timing, it had to be. They way I figured it, my brother's beat-down was the Plan B that got launched after Artemis Ray and his proxies failed to get their hands on me. Either way, I had been grossly off base in thinking that my part in the amorphous game being played had run its course. That meant my ass was still in play, and I wasn't about to find myself hemmed in without a Plan B of my own. To that end, Bobby had told me to go see Phil O'Connell at Wright's Grocery on Lytle Street and give him Shousey's best regards. I did what Bobby told me and left the establishment loaded for bear.

My next task was two-fold. I needed to apologize to Dominick and enlist his help with a hunch I wanted to play. He graciously accepted my apology, reminding me that we had been friends for more than ten years, meaning this wasn't the first time I had made a dumbass remark. He also told me how worried he was about Declan. I told him that went without saying, and we moved on to what I was going to do about it.

"First, I'm going to write up everything I know and can verify," I had said. "Then I'm going to let George tell me whether or not it can be published."

"You gonna include the stuff about Jay-Eddy Powell?"

"How can I? It's not like I recorded in my notes that we stalked and captured the guy and then compelled him through force to give up what he knew."

Dominick had nodded his agreement with that assessment but reminded me that the information I had gotten during that conversation was a valuable chip to play. "I assume you wanna tie Conrad Westcott to Moussa's death somehow. How can you do that without Powell?"

"I couldn't do that even with Powell," I said, shaking my head. "The only name he gave up was Artemis Ray and that was only through some go-between named Jimmy." Dominick regarded me silently with a face etched with worry. "But I get your point. I'll write it all up and see what George has to say about it."

Dominick nodded and said, "I think that's a good idea. And then you've also got the envelope that…"

He didn't finish his thought. We looked each other, both of us knowing that Sandoval had shown us nothing more than a copy of the envelope.

On top of that, there was no way to confirm who scribbled that note on it, much less prove that A. R. referred to Artemis Ray.

"So, what else do you have on Westcott?"

"I've got Father French's account to you. That is, assuming you identified yourself as a reporter?"

"No doubt. You know I play it according to Hoyle when I interview somebody. But where does that leave you?"

I sighed, knowing it didn't get me anywhere definitive. "Well, taking what I have and adding it to the other source material on the Quedlinburg theft, I can at least waft suspicion in the direction of the Westcotts."

His dubious countenance reflected my own sense of foreboding that this was not enough to shake the will of a man like Conrad Westcott. But I speculated that given Rogers Westcott's political ambitions, maybe it would be enough to cow the great bourbon baron into a stalemate if he thought the inference of impropriety would sully his son's political prospects.

"There is one other potential play here. And I'm wondering if you could help me see if it has any legs."

"You know I got you, Lee-Mo. What do you need, brother?"

I slid a piece of paper in front of him. "Can you help me with that?"

His brow furrowed as he examined the contents of the page. "That third piece that was in the package. What are you thinking?"

I shrugged and said, "It's probably a long shot, but I'm wondering why Father French didn't want to get into what happened with the piece that was stolen."

"You thinking because he didn't report it that maybe there was something suspicious about it?"

"There's no doubt it's suspicious. The only question is whether it casts Westcott in a negative light." Dominick nodded and went back to studying what I had written on the piece of paper. "I was thinking maybe you could contact that friend you have. The one that got Hamia Diab's phone number?"

He rubbed his chin as he thought about my question. "Yeah, that was a phone number. This is a, umm...heavier lift."

I waited as he thought through what I was proposing. Finally, he nodded and assured me he'd look into it and let me know what he found. That had been three days ago.

In the interim, Declan had come out of his coma but predictably wouldn't say a word about who had assaulted him. I had spoken to Bobby a couple of times and though he couldn't say anything self-incriminating over the phone, he assured me he had things buttoned down on his end, and that Declan was safe in the infirmary. So, while Dominick was off doing his thing, and Bobby was handling business of his own, I waited patiently for the honorable George Hawley to finish reading my article, so I'd know which way the editorial wind was blowing.

"Well, now," he said, laying the article on his desk. "By God, you have done what you wondered whether you were capable of on that first morning we met." George read the quizzical expression on my face. "Shit fire, Motley, it's us who are qualified for social security that ain't supposed to be able to remember things. You told me you wondered if you'd be able to surprise me. Remember?"

I gave a soft laugh and said, "Yeah, I did say that. I also told you I'd bring you a good one."

He picked the article up and studied it for another minute before laying it back down on the desk. "It's a good one all right. And unlike anything I've read before. But I wonder, are you thinking this is something that'll make Connie Westcott blink?"

"That depends. Are you gonna publish it?"

George leaned back in his chair and took in a deep breath. "You know I'll always shoot ya straight, ain't that right, Levi?"

"Of course."

He looked at me with a narrow, pensive expression. "Well, here's the deal. This here article ain't enough to accomplish what you want to do. So, even if I was to give it some space, it'd need a thorough goin' over before it'd go to print. And the thing is I don't think that matches up with your timeline. Not that I'm prying into your business or nothin'. I just hear things, if you know what I mean."

"Yeah, I know what you mean. And don't sweat it. You know I trust you."

My gaze dropped to the floor.

"What is it, son?"

I looked up and locked eyes with the man.

"I'm up against it, George. There's no denying my brother's an evil bastard, but he's all I've got."

He didn't respond, but his look conveyed that not only did he understand me, but that he, too, had been there before.

"I don't know if this enough for me to accomplish what I need to do, but what you need to know is that I've got no choice. I have to protect my brother, and confronting Westcott is the only way to do that. And I've got one more card I hope to play on top of this one."

"And you're expecting ol' buddy Cotter to deal it to you, is that it?"

I nodded as he considered which direction to steer me.

"Well, then here's my position on the matter, as they say. You take this here article with my blessing and make your play. And go ahead and keep the stuff about Powell. We can talk later about whether it'll pass legal muster. Then if Dominick's information improves your stock...well, just maybe you'll get that old blowhard to slow his roll."

I held back a smile as I said, "Slow his roll?"

"Damnit, boy, don't go critiquing my slang now. That's just something I overheard some hip youngster say, and I been tryin' to work into a conversation for damn near a week."

George leaned in and tapped his finger on the desk as he regarded me with an intense gaze.

"Now you listen close, Levi Motley. When all this is over, you and me are gonna sit down and recraft this here piece into the story that really needs to be told."

"And what would that be?"

"Your journey, son." George regarded me with a knowing look. "And how it's changed you."

I swallowed hard and was about to break Artie Goben's rule of not spoiling a good moment with my stupid words when Dominick showed up and saved me from myself. He appeared out of breath, but the look on his face was one of triumph. George read that look and waved us off, saying it was best that a couple of knuckleheads like us conspire somewhere out of his evidently expansive earshot.

We retreated to my office, where I anxiously inquired as to Dominick's findings. In response to my query, he slapped a large envelope down on my desk. I opened it and examined its contents. After reviewing the documents inside, I looked at my friend with a mingled expression of awe and disbelief.

"How'd you convince your guy to do it?"

"I didn't. He stone-cold turned me down when I told him what I needed."

My face contorted in confusion. "Then how'd you get this?" He sat looking at me in silence, a smile playing at the edge of his lips. I looked again at the document in the file and then back at my friend. "No way. You went to Washington?"

His smile widened into a satisfied grin. "Come on now. You know a magician don't reveal his secrets."

"But how? A freedom-of-information-act filing would have taken...I don't know. A long damn time."

"You disappoint me, my friend. You put the D.C. in D.C., and brother, ain't no tellin' what your boy can accomplish."

I wrapped the big man in a bear hug, joyfully laughing to the point that I thought I might cry. Then I released him and picked up the file, placing it in my satchel.

"When are you going to see Westcott?"

"Tomorrow night," I said. "He's throwing a big Christmas shindig at his residence."

His face wrinkled in worry as he said, "You sure that's the best time to confront the man?"

"There is no best time. But I'm hoping I can use the party to throw him off his game. You know, lots of people around and all that."

Dominick nodded and regarded me with a grave expression. "And you think you've got the goods to do that?"

"Almost," I said, pulling on my coat. "I just have to make one more trip out to the monastery."

"What for?"

I threw the satchel over my shoulder. "To say a prayer in the Garden of Gethsemane," I said, gripping my friend on the shoulder. "And to find Brother Peter."

CHAPTER
FORTY-ONE

THE SOIREE WAS in full effect as I approached the Westcott residence with the confident stride of an invited guest. The warm smile on the face of the woman at the front door fell into a cautious frown, indicating she thought I'd mistakenly come to the front door when I clearly belonged at the service entrance. I really couldn't blame her, though, as I was decked out in my usual finery of grunge fare, which hardly fit the couture of the black-tie jetsetters who were inside sipping champagne and eating caviar on toast.

"Excuse me," she said in a haughty tone, "but I think you've come to the wrong address."

"Is this the Westcott place?"

"Why, yes. Yes, it is. But this is a Christmas gathering for..."

"Then I'm at the right address. You see, me and Connie, we're what you might call colleagues."

Her wide-eyed caution morphed into a look of outright disbelief.

"Yeah, you're right. Maybe 'colleagues' is too strong a word. How about collaborators? Yeah. Collaborators sounds closer to the mark. So, go on inside and tell Connie it's Levi Motley here to respond to his offer to collaborate with me on my, umm...family issues."

The woman stared wordlessly at me.

"Go ahead," I said, nodding toward the door. "He should be expecting me. And I tell ya something lady, if he's not, then shame on him for thinking so little of Rock Motley's son."

"Who?"

"Just tell him."

She shook her head in wary confusion as she turned and walked inside. I lit a cigarette and took a long drag, exhaling a large billow of smoke into the cold night air. When the woman returned, I almost laughed as she told me to walk around the side of the house to the service entrance. I crushed the cigarette out on the stone porch and told her I'd be waiting for Connie in the study. "No need for an escort, miss," I said, barging past the woman and into the house. "I know the way."

I heard her pleading with me to stop as I walked through the foyer past the bemused guests, their gowns and jewelry sparkling in the light of the fine crystal chandelier. My boots squeaked and left little puddles of water on the marble floor as I made my way to the study, plucking a glass of champagne off a server's tray along the way. Party guests murmured in condescending amusement as I slipped off my satchel and leaned against the stately mahogany desk, waiting for the man of the house to arrive. It didn't take long for Conrad Westcott to appear along with a white-haired man with a flowing mustache and the palest blue eyes I'd ever seen.

"What do ya say there, big 'un?" Westcott said with his thick guvnor's accent. "It's good to see ya and all, but I have to tell you this is kind of a private affair. Invited guests only. No offense."

I took a sip of champagne and then spit the liquid back into the glass. "Damn, Connie," I said with a look of disgust. "You serving these invited guests piss water?"

He chuckled and gave me a good-natured smile. "Well, if it's bourbon you're looking for, young man, then you have come to the right place. You just say the word and I'll be only too happy to send you on your way with a signed bottle of Kentucky's finest."

"Sounds like a deal. You can inscribe it to Declan Motley with best wishes for a full recovery."

He didn't break character, continuing to play the jocular host that the guests gathering around surely wanted to see. "Well, now, I don't rightly know who that is. And generally speaking, I do like to be of an acquaintance with them that gets my name on a bottle. After all, puttin' the name of Connie Westcott on a bottle of Old Royal makes it an instant collector's item."

"You don't know who Declan Motley is?"

"No, I don't expect I do," he said glancing around at his guests with a befuddled expression. "Is he here somewhere? Iffin' so, then hell's bells, maybe we ought to look for him." He poked one of the guests in the gut and said, "That you, Devin Mobley?" This brought a wave of laughter from the assembled audience.

"His name is Declan Motley," I said, heat radiating through my body. "But don't worry about the bottle. It'd probably be wasted on him since contraband is frowned upon in the Manchester Federal Correctional Institution. Especially in the infirmary."

"Well, there you go, then. Although it would make for one hell of a fine Christmas gift, there will be no signed bottle for Devin Mobley. With that settled, I'll show you to the door."

"It's Declan Motley," I said in a menacing voice. "You'd do well to re-member that, Conrad Westcott. After all, you'll want to know the name of the man that cuts your heart out."

Westcott's jovial face sagged, and there was an audible gasp from the gallery. Westcott stepped toward me, bristling with anger. "Now that's where you're wrong, 'cause I don't expect he'll get that chance if I..."

"That's enough, Connie," the white-haired man said, stepping for-ward. "Not another word."

Another man approached and stood next to Westcott, his features indicating that he must be Rogers. Then a fourth man who was obvious-ly muscle, took up a spot to my right as onlookers gawked at the scene. Conrad Westcott gave me a pleasant look as he composed himself and reclaimed the mask of the unflappable southern gentleman.

"Mr. Adams, if you would escort this man out of the residence," the white-haired man said. "And please do so with all the prejudice warrant-ed by his unwelcome and offensive presence."

I reached for my satchel as the muscle took a step toward me. He tensed and put a hand inside his coat, so I raised my hands and moved with deliberate caution as I retrieved a file folder from the bag. I held the folder up and then placed it on the desktop. The muscle looked at the white-haired man who put up a hand as he walked over to the desk and picked up the file. He read the document inside with intense concen-tration. When he was finished, he shot Westcott a concerned look and walked over to hand him the document. Westcott scanned the page with a slight fissure running through his normally implacable poker face. But as he finished reading, Westcott regained his smooth comportment and turned to the murmuring crowd behind him.

"Folks, this here is just a small matter of a disgruntled employee. If you'll excuse me for a few minutes, then I'll clear this up right directly. In the meantime, you folks get back to your revelry, and I'll be along shortly to offer a Christmas toast that'll make your old grizzled grandpappy shed a tear."

He closed the French doors that led into the study and pulled a set of lush curtains across them. Then he turned toward me with a look of pure malevolence and said, "What kind of game you think you're playing here, boy? You best start talkin' sense or you and that piece a shit convict brother of yours are in for a world of pain."

"Connie," the white-haired man said urgently. "Not another word."

"Oh, bullshit. This asshole walks in here like he owns the place, and you want me to stand here and take it? I ain't standing for it, Sid."

I looked at the white-haired man and said, "So, I guess that would make you Sidney Marksbury?" The man gave me a flat stare and offered no reply. "And you," I said to the muscle, "You're Mr. Adams, strong arm extraordinaire." Then I turned to the polished debonair man, who looked to be in his late thirties. "And you'd be Rogers Westcott, the man who put Artemis Ray and his flunkies on the trail of Moussa Diab."

The younger man shot a glance at his father, who gave an almost imperceptible shake of his head.

"Well, since we're getting acquainted and all, you're looking at Levi Motley. And my brother, who Mr. Westcott so derisively referred to as 'a piece of shit convict', is Declan Motley. And what was that you were about to say about my brother, Mr. Westcott? Were you gonna say that you'll cut my brother's heart out before he can get to you?" I pointed to the document in Westcott's hand. "Best think twice, because if you go after my brother again...well, whoever it was that said there's a reason you don't pick a fight with a man who buys ink by the barrel was spot on."

The door to the study opened and Isabelle Westcott stepped inside. She shot me a contemptuous look before making her way over to her son. Isabelle whispered something to Rogers, who shifted his weight nervously before offering a whispered response.

"Been talking to Artemis Ray, Mrs. Westcott?"

"Don't say a word, Rogers," Marksbury said. "You neither, Belle."

I looked around the room as the five of them stared at me with looks of open malice.

"You know something, Mr. Marksbury, somebody I know once predicted that I might someday find myself rubbing elbows and having a drink with the local bourbon glitterati. To tell you the truth, I thought she was off her rocker when she said it. But wouldn't you know it, here I am at a party with the great Conrad Westcott and nobody's drinking."

Westcott laughed with the jovial air of a man with nothing to fear. "Well, what can I say there, big 'un, but when you're right, you're right." He walked over to a wet bar in a corner of the study. "I mean, after all, there ain't no reason for such dour faces when we should be celebrating the coming birth of Our Lord and Savior."

He poured neat slugs of bourbon into five crystal tumblers and passed them around. "Sorry, Mr. Adams, none for you. But the rest of ya? Well, here's to the health and happiness of you and yours."

I set the drink on the desktop next to the flute of champagne as the group drank.

"What's the matter there, fella?" Westcott said. "Hell, it was your idea to have us a drink, and it was a damn fine one in my book."

I glared at him and said, "Let's just say I'm having a hard time drinking to the health and happiness of my loved ones right now."

He polished off his drink, set the glass on the bar, and eyeballed me with a mischievous look. "Well, let me tell ya something I've learned that'll maybe help give you some perspective on the current state of you and your loved ones."

Marksbury stepped forward to object, but Westcott waved him off.

"Ya see, I ain't no kinda wise man, Mr. Motley. I'm not no philosopher nor a deep thinker. I'm just a simple distiller of fine bourbon and to me that is God's own profession. But you know something I've learned?" He cocked his head, waiting for me to answer. "That's all right, I'll tell ya anyway. In all my years on this here earth, I have learned that people tend to get all balled up and twisted in consternation when bad things happen to good people. You ever notice that, big 'un?"

I stood in silence and scanned the faces of the people in the room. Each one of them sported a look of mild amusement, like they'd seen this act play out before.

"Well, it's just something I've come to know through observation, that's all I'm sayin'. I mean, you hear it all the time. Something bad happens to a fella everybody likes, and sure enough you'll hear somebody say gosh darn it, why's bad things always gotta happen to good people?"

Westcott looked around the room with his arms outstretched like a lawyer making his case to the jury.

"Well, now I ain't claimin' I discovered plutonium or nothing. I mean it's just the plain ol' truth is all. People feel all kinds of rotten when bad things happen to good people. That's just one regular old thing I've learned in this life." He walked toward me, stopping a few feet in front of me. "But you know what else I've learned, son?"

"I'm not your son. My father was..."

"I'll tell ya what else I've learned," he said, cutting me off. "And that is while people get all bent out of shape when bad things happen to good people, nobody gives a good goddamn when some sonofabitch gets his due. And there ain't no worse sonsofbitches in decent society than piece of shit convict criminals."

My chest heaved as I stared at the man, and my fists were balled up and ready for battle. But I saw the muscle move forward in my periphery, so I held my ground. Westcott threw his hands up as he stepped back, still the picture of a country lawyer arguing his case.

"Now, I hear you telling me that your brother, umm...what was that name? Dylan?"

"His name is..."

"I hear tell that your brother Dylan is in prison. Hell, I'm sorry to hear it. And if I'm catching your drift, it sounds like something awful bad has befallen that convict brother of yours. Now, I don't know shit from Shinola about what's befell ol' Dylan, but I do reckon that little truth I've been expounding upon does apply to the circumstances at hand. Meaning don't nobody give a rat's patootie about what's happened to your brother down at whatever prison his hind end is rottin' away in." He stepped toward me and pointed a finger at my face as he offered his summation. "And ain't nobody gonna care if it happens again, 'cause to God-fearin' people, bad things happening to bad people looks an awful lot like justice."

He picked up the bourbon that I had set on the desk and threw it back in a quick snort. I could feel my hot breath flowing in and out my nostrils as I struggled against every instinct in my body to pummel this arrogant man into a mass of bloody flesh.

"And you know what justice looks like, is that it?"

He gave a casual shrug. "Know it when I see it."

"Then why don't you tell me what justice for Moussa Diab should look like."

"Moo, who?" He shot a look of confusion at the others in the room. "Oh, wait. You mean that poor fella who got killed a few months back? Yeah, I read about him in that news-rag you write for. And since you asked, I do believe justice has already been served on that front. In fact, ol' Sid here saw to it that the perpetrator fessed up to what he done to that poor boy."

"And the man responsible sits in jail as we speak," Marksbury said. "That is the very definition of justice."

"Not according to Jay-Eddy Powell."

They looked at me with flat stares, but the air in the room felt suddenly charged. I shot a look at Rogers, who appeared a shade paler than he had before.

"Well, ain't you one to throw out names like you was stuffin' stockings with candy canes," Westcott said. "You got a bag full of 'em hiding there under your coat?"

"Jay-Eddy Powell. It looks to me like your son knows who I'm talking about."

Westcott shook his head and continued to look around the room like a befuddled old man who can't find the glasses perched on his forehead.

"Play dumb all you want, Westcott, but I've talked to the man, and his story doesn't line up with the justice Mr. Marksbury claims he has defined."

Marksbury tried for an impassive look, but I could see the worry in his eyes as he said, "Stories, Connie. A made-up fantasy is all."

I took my coat and toboggan off and threw them on a couch.

"Oh, you planning on stayin' awhile?" Westcott said. "You shouldn't be. In fact, security boy, why don't you..."

"I don't want to be here any longer than I have to be," I said, interjecting. "I'm staying just long enough to tell you a story. Then I'm getting the hell out of here, and I'm taking a Christmas gift with me."

Westcott tried to maintain his supercilious tone, but his voice was tinged with concern. "Still wantin' me to sign that bottle to your brother Devin, are ya?"

"My brother's name is Declan Motley. And the gift you're going to give me is the assurance that he'll be left alone to do his time. All of it. That's all I want from you."

For the first time, Rogers spoke, scoffing at me as he said, "Or what?"

"I already told you what," I said, maliciously. "You leave him alone, or he'll cut your heart out."

Rogers attempted a laugh, but it came out more like a shriek. Sidney Marksbury withered him with a glare, and Rogers adopted a sullen look as he shut his mouth. Westcott, his false joviality now vanished, walked over to the wet bar. "And just for the sake of conversation, Mr. Motley," he said, pouring another drink. "Let's assume I know anything about what you're talkin' about."

"Which he does not," Marksbury said.

"But if I did," Westcott continued, turning toward me with the drink in his hand. "What makes you think I'm inclined to give a sanctimonious punk like you so much as a crust of bread swept off my well-laden table?"

"Like I said, Mr. Westcott, I'm here to tell you a story. The story of what happened to Moussa Diab."

"That case has already been adjudicated," Marksbury said. "You're wasting our time."

I ignored him, training my gaze directly on Westcott. "I think it's a story you'll want to hear. After all, he was a good person and something bad happened to him."

Isabelle Westcott sighed in exasperation and said, "For God's sake, Connie, there are guests waiting for us. Important guests. We do not have time to waste on some vagabond who wandered in off the street."

"'Vagabond' is a good word, Mrs. Westcott," I said. "It's sure as hell apropos for a no-account drifter like me. So, if what I have to say is too much of an imposition on your time, then so be it. Go back to your eggnog and insider trading, and you can read the story in *The Observer* along with everyone else."

Marksbury cleared his throat. "Mr. Motley," he said, in a patronizing tone. "I'm sure *The Observer* has adequate legal services at its disposal, and George Hawley is certainly a man who knows his business. Still, you would be well served to inquire as to the boundaries of what you can and cannot put into print."

"I know I can write about my own firsthand experience, Mr. Marksbury. And my firsthand experience includes a conversation with Jerome Edward Powell, who told me three things. One, how he got put on to follow Moussa Diab. Two, how that young man died. And three, how Dale Goodlett came to take the rap for it."

"And this Jerome Edward Powell," Marksbury said with practiced patience. "Did he make any specific reference to the Westcotts?"

Sidney Marksbury moved about the room, taking the place of Conrad Westcott as the attorney on stage, only with Marksbury it wasn't an act.

"No, I reckon he did not mention the Westcotts, because why would he?" He motioned around the room. "You see anybody here that looks like this so-called Jay-Eddy character? Or at least what I imagine he looks like?" I stared at him without answering. "No, I didn't think so. And the reason for that is Mr. and Mrs. Westcott don't consort with riffraff."

"Like you," Rogers said, regarding me with a scornful glare.

"And if I may ask a further question, Mr. Motley? How did you come to locate this Jerome Edward Powell to question him in the first place? And where is he now?" Again, I didn't answer. "And did you identify yourself as a reporter for *The Observer* when you spoke to Mr. Powell?" Marksbury said, continuing his cross examination. "No answer, sir?"

"I can write what I experienced firsthand with Jay-Eddy Powell. And that'll be enough to put the county attorney on his trail."

"Well, by all means do so," Marksbury said in a theatrical voice. "After all, justice must be served though the heavens may fall." He looked at me through shrewd, narrow eyes. "And I'm sure Jack Merrick will be chomping at the bit to chase down some ragamuffin so he can re-prosecute a case that's already settled. That's some strange logic you're employing, sir."

As I looked around at each person in the room, my gaze came to linger on the face of Conrad Westcott. He tried for a look of sleepy boredom, but as I stared at him, I could have sworn I detected a slight glimmer of light in his eyes, daring me to state the business he knew I had come there for.

"Moussa Diab," I said as Westcott tried for a look of utter indifference. "He was just a young guy trying to figure out what God wanted him to do with his life. He never got to find out because his search got cut short.

And why, Mr. Westcott? Why, Mr. Marksbury? To protect the power and wealth of people like you, that's why."

Westcott's impassivity vanished and his face went flush with anger. "Oh, to hell with this nonsense. I didn't have nothing to do with..."

"Father William French."

Westcott stopped and stared at me.

"I've talked to Father French. Well, not me. My friend Dominick spoke to him. And in case you're wondering, Mr. Marksbury, Dom's an experienced reporter who knows how to dot his i's and cross his t's. Dom approached Father French and interestingly enough, the old priest said he had been expecting someone to come looking for him ever since your brother died, Mr. Westcott."

The skin under Marksbury's eyes sagged a little and Westcott chewed on his lower lip. Isabelle looked like she wanted to go to her husband, but she remained standing next to Rogers.

"That's right. Father French had been waiting for somebody to reach out to him ever since James died. And talk about stories, Mr. Marksbury. Father French sure told one to Dominick. Wanna hear it, Mr. Westcott?"

The menacing threat in Westcott's eyes was not lost on me, but I summoned my courage and continued with what I had come there to say.

"I'm sure you already know it, but I'll tell you anyway. It was a story about a package that was sent during the Great War from Thomas Westcott to his childhood friend, William French. Apparently, Sergeant Westcott didn't want any suspicious eyes on this package, so he addressed it to a Catholic priest, which was a pretty good strategy. I mean, who's gonna question a package sent to a priest, right? Turns out the reason Sergeant Westcott wanted to keep the package a secret is because it contained three rare pieces of...I think 'treasure' is the right word. Yeah. The package contained three pieces of treasure, two of them stolen from a cave in Quedlinburg, Germany."

My gaze oscillated between Westcott and Marksbury and I could see their faces registered a slight confusion.

"Now, you've both read the summary of the story I've written, and you can say whatever you want, Mr. Marksbury, about what my paper can and can't print. But you're not George Hawley, and George Hawley told me he'll stand behind that story. All of it. So, my article plus the pieces about Quedlinburg that have already been published will be enough to put Army investigators on your trail, Mr. Westcott. And don't tell me Jack Merrick won't pursue the truth about Moussa's death once that happens. He's an elected official. He won't have any choice."

Westcott's jaw clenched and unclenched as he glared at me, but he remained silent. I decided to hit him where he lives.

"You sold your piece of that treasure didn't you, Mr. Westcott? You sold that heirloom your father left you and named your first bourbon in honor of your old man." The man looked like he wanted to tear my throat from my neck. "Old Relic in honor of that old relic he gave you. Right, Mr. Westcott?" Wescott's face was slowly turning the color of red wine. "Not that I blame you. What else could you do? You were a young man with a wife and a son. You had ambition and needed a way to get started. So, you sold that treasure to buy an abandoned distillery and look where you are now."

"All of the paperwork for the purchase of the Old Stump distillery is in order," Marksbury said. "That purchase was completely above board."

"Oh, I'm sure all the paperwork is in place, Mr. Marksbury. And to tell you the truth, I really don't care how Conrad Westcott built his empire. But I do care about Moussa Diab, and I think Mr. Westcott got it in his head that maybe his brother intended to pass his piece of that treasure on to Moussa. And I think that's why Mr. Westcott had Artemis Ray put his people on Moussa's trail, so they could find the treasure first and deliver it into the hands of its 'proper heir'. Problem is, the plan went sideways, and Moussa Diab died. Is there anything you want to say about that, Mr. Westcott?"

"Don't say a word, Connie," Marksbury said, as Westcott's bottled-up rage caused his face to turn puce.

"Does that mean your client has no comment, Mr. Marksbury? I mean, the story is already written and filed away in a safe in George Hawley's office. You sure you don't want your client to have a chance to go on the record before it goes to publication?"

Marksbury remained silent. I shook my head in bewilderment as I turned to Westcott and said, "Did you really think your brother would give that treasure to a kid barely out of college? A kid who was only trying to figure out what to do with his life?"

Westcott took a deep breath and exhaled slowly. As he did so, the discoloration in his face faded and his contemptuous glare transformed into a mask of dismissive arrogance. He made his way over to the wet bar and poured another drink.

"You don't walk into my house and lecture me about my family history." He threw back the drink and poured another. "You hear me, street urchin? I don't give a damn what Father French told you or that colored boy you run with. You don't give me what for about my family or my business."

I felt the heat radiating throughout my body as he turned to face me with a look that said he had nothing to fear from a no-account street urchin like me.

"But I tell ya what, big 'un. Let's say, just for shits and giggles, that this fantasy you've concocted is true. You ain't gonna print a goddamn word of it."

"Because if you do, we will own your ass," Marksbury said. "You, George Hawley, and the whole damn *Observer* operation."

"No, you won't," I said, not backing down. "Father French is on the record, and the rest I experienced firsthand. I know my business, Mr. Marksbury, and so does George Hawley. You're not going to bully me. The story is going to print."

The two men looked at me, unfazed. I took a deep breath to calm myself and decided to shift tactics, hoping to win some kind of middle ground through negotiation.

"Tell you what. I'll take out the parts about Jay-Eddy and what really happened to Moussa since Connie is too big a coward to answer my questions. It doesn't matter, anyway. The facts are what they are. The reader can fill in the holes and that'll be enough to sully the image of the big man and his self-made bourbon empire." I turned and leveled Rogers with an icy glare. "And his son's political ambitions."

Westcott and Marksbury exchanged looks and I saw they, too, were shifting tactics.

"Let's say I really am looking for this treasure that you think my brother had," Westcott said, swirling his drink in the crystal tumbler. "Theoretically speaking..."

"And off the record," Marksbury said.

"Of course, off the record," Westcott said. "Theoretically, if I were to find this treasure, then I could return it along with restitution for the piece that according to you, I sold in order to buy the Old Stump property and start my distillery. If I were to do that, I don't think the government would fault me one bit. And John Q. Public? Hell, to the average fella, I was just a young man, an orphan. For me to have sold such a thing as you've described to get started in life...well, I think every man in this county would say he'd have done the same damn thing. So, you can take your parts about this and that and shove 'em where the sun don't shine, 'cause ain't nobody gonna believe some redneck jackwagon and ain't nobody gonna care that a good ol' boy from Nelson County who didn't have two nickels to rub together sold some trinket to chase the American Dream."

His point was well made, especially given Sandoval's information that the Stone heirs had received a sizable amount of money to return the Quedlinburg treasures to Germany. If Westcott returned his brother's piece and paid the German government for his own, he'd be exceeding the standard set by the heirs of Douglas Stone. On top of that, I suspected Westcott would put sufficient spin on his story to make him appear like a figure straight out of a Horatio Alger novel.

Westcott walked up to me and set his drink on the corner of the desk. "So, theoretically speaking and off the record...if I find the item, I'll return it, pay my debt, and get on with my life." He raised his palms. "No harm, no foul."

We stared at each other for a moment. Westcott's mouth curled in a condescending smile as he said, "Mr. Adams, I do believe we have returned to that point in the conversation where you were about to show Mr. Motley to the exit with all the prejudice that was previously requested." Adams took a step forward, but Westcott put up a hand. "But before you go, big 'un. Let's talk about that Christmas gift you said you was leavin' with. Remember that?"

"I do. And I am leaving with that gift."

He clapped his hands together and said, "Where are your manners, son? Ain't you gonna offer a gift of your own? I mean, that'd be the right thing to do in the spirit of Christmas and all."

"What are you saying, Westcott?"

"I'm saying that if someone were to, theoretically speaking, help me rectify this situation in the manner I have described, well I might consider a...what do you call it? A gift exchange?"

"Meaning what?"

"Meaning good things can start happening to bad people. Hell, I'm a Christian. I believe in reconciliation, second chances, forgiving my enemy seventy times seven times and all that. I might even go so far as to say that a low-down dirtbag convict can be rehabilitated to the status of an upright citizen deserving of all the fruits that our great commonwealth has to offer."

He locked eyes with me and said, "Those that do for me are well rewarded."

"And those who don't?"

He put his face just inches from mine, and I could smell the liquor on his breath as he whispered, "Ask your brother."

Blood rushed into my temples, and I felt disoriented as my head swam. I tried to think of something more to say, but what was left? He already had the whole story, and it hadn't fazed him. I felt panicked, knowing brute action was a one-way ticket to my own demise. But I had to do something. I felt my chin quivering as I fought to hold it together, not wanting to show weakness, but feeling utterly helpless in the effort to protect my brother. My breathing was unsteady as I struggled to find clarity, to see a way forward. Finally, I took a deep breath and said in a small voice, "I know how to find it."

Westcott smiled like a man who had cornered his prey.

"But I'll only tell him."

Westcott's smile faded a little as he saw I was pointing to Rogers. Wescott looked at Sidney Marksbury who gave a cautious nod of assent. He turned back to me, shaking his head with amused tolerance as he said, "Belle tells me we got party guests that need tendin' to, so go on ahead and play your last card for whatever it's worth. Go on. Tell my boy there how we can find it, and let's wrap this thing up with a big ol' Christmas bow on top."

I walked over to Rogers and leaned in close. It only took a matter of seconds to tell him what I knew. When I finished, he appeared unable to move or speak as he processed the implications of what I had revealed.

"What is it, son?"

Rogers walked over and spoke into his father's ear. As he did, Westcott's face contorted in a look of disbelief. "But that's more than twenty years from now. And how can we be sure we'd be the ones to get at it first?"

I watched closely as Westcott quickly moved from processing the information to plotting his end game. "I'll talk to the pastor," he said, lost in his own thoughts. "I'll give a million dollars to the church. This thing's worth fifty times that, so it'd be worth every penny. That's the only way I can control the situation, the only way I can get to it before..."

Westcott looked at me, realizing he had been vocalizing his thoughts. Slowly, his expression became one of self-satisfied confidence, and I knew in that moment that Conrad Westcott had no intention of ever returning or making restitution for the treasures that he and his brother had been given. For my part, the fifty-million-dollar valuation Westcott put on the missing piece gave new meaning to Sandoval's description of the item as rare and valuable. I did a quick calculation of the value that a man like Westcott would place on my life, as well as the lives of Declan and Moussa, and came up with a combined total of less than zero. Knowing that, the appeal I made to the better part of the man's nature sounded vacuous even to me.

"You know everything I know, Mr. Westcott. You know how to find it. There's no more reason to go after my brother. Just leave him alone and let him do his time. Please."

Westcott and Rogers looked at me with nearly identical sneers, like there had never been a question in their minds that they would obtain the information they had been seeking. Now it was just a matter of sport, and neither Declan nor I were anything more than playthings for their amusement. Father and son moved to the bar and poured drinks for everyone, even shoving a drink into Mr. Adams's hands.

"Well, big 'un," Westcott said, handing me a drink. "I can't believe I'm saying this, but I'm damn glad you dropped by. This is gonna be a fine Christmas, indeed. Drink up, everybody."

"Tell me Declan is safe," I said, setting the drink on the desktop. "That's the only reason I came here. Give me that, and I'm gone. You'll figure out the moves to get what you want, and you'll never hear from me again, including my article. That's a good trade."

Westcott put on that befuddled expression he had worn the first time I mentioned Declan's attack. "Well, I don't rightly know what you're talking about there, fella. Like I told you before, I have no knowledge of any wrongdoing that's happened to your brother."

He threw back what must have been his sixth or seventh drink and regarded me with cold detachment.

"But like I said, Mr. Motley, I thank you for stopping by. I'll have Mr. Adams help you find your way to the service exit. Do wish that brother of yours a merry Christmas, now won't ya? I'll have my boy see to it that he gets that early release."

Rogers levelled me with a mocking glare and said, "Sure thing daddy. I'll get the word out right away that Mr. Motley's brother is cooperating with the, umm...proper authorities."

Blood and adrenaline rushed into my head and my temples began to pound as I looked around the room at the faces of the people staring at me, each bearing an expression of outright condescension bordering on pity. I shook my head, knowing that any appeal to fairness or justice would be offered in vain as the only thing these people cared about was the perpetuation of their own self-interested power. Since I didn't have anything to offer in furtherance of that end, I knew the only play I had left was a threat to tear it all down. Resolved to that course of action, I reached inside my satchel and pulled out the envelope that Dominick had given me.

"Mr. Westcott," I said, holding up the envelope. "Don't you want to hear how the story ends?"

"Oh, I do believe we've already come to the end of this story, Mr. Motley."

"No, we haven't. Because even if you find it, the second Quedlinburg treasure is still out there."

"But you see, here's the thing, big 'un..." Westcott regarded me with cocky amusement. "It ain't."

Marksbury cleared his throat, attempting to intervene.

"Oh, forget about it, Sid. All I got to do is say off the record, ain't that right, Mr. Motley? Well here goes. Strictly off the record, just so you hear me loud and clear...that piece I sold? Well, let me tell ya somethin'...I bought it back."

My heart pounded in my chest as I processed the implications of what he had just said.

"You heard me right, fella. I've got Daddy's gift to me, and soon I'm gonna have the piece he gave James, too. And I know people, son. People that can help me dispose of them two pieces without anybody knowing where or how or to who or for how much." He approached me with an unsteady gait, and I could, again, smell the liquor on his breath. "And that right there is the end of your little, umm...story."

I felt the edges of my lips curl into the kind of devilish smile I had seen on Declan's face a thousand times. "But that's where you're wrong, Connie," I said with a slow shake of my head. "You see, that piece you sold wasn't part of the Quedlinburg treasures."

Westcott let out a disbelieving snort as I opened the envelope and placed the contents on the desktop.

"That piece you sold was one your father plundered as the Eighty-Seventh made its way through a town in Belgium called Verviers. Thomas Westcott took that piece from a family that lived there. It was a family that prospered in textiles, if memory serves me correctly."

The room was silent and now it was my turn to take the floor to offer a final summation to the bloody sordid mess that had ensnared my life and ended Moussa's.

"It's true, Mr. Westcott," I said, feeling confident that my role was morphing from prey to predator. "Your old man took that piece from a Jewish couple named Joseph and Emily Kleban. It was a comb wasn't it, Connie? Or should I say, 'isn't it', since it's evidently back in your umm... personal possession."

The flesh around Westcott's bleary eyes sagged, and I could see he knew where the story was headed.

"That piece your father gave you was a pearl-handled comb set with diamonds and emeralds. You thought it was part of the Quedlinburg trove because there was an ivory and gold comb listed among the St. Servatius treasures." I picked the papers up off the desk. "But being the arrogant prick that you are, you didn't do your homework. My buddy Dominick on the other hand?" Westcott swayed a bit, unsteady on his feet. "Oh, you remember Dominick, don't ya, Connie? Well, I tell ya my brother Dominick is some kind of savant. I mean, he can find damn near anything or anyone. And unlike you, Dom did do his homework. This is what he discovered."

I held up the documents for everyone in the room to see.

"That piece you sold belonged to a Jewish couple that was executed at Treblinka. And these documents are part of an active case with the cultural affairs division of the military. You see, Connie, Joseph and Emily

Kleban had a daughter. Her name is Anna." I dropped the papers on the desk. "And Anna wants her family heirloom back."

"You're full of shit," Westcott said in a slightly slurred voice.

"Nah, I'm not full of shit. And now that I know where that family heirloom is? Well, let's just say there's a whole new set of players ready to enter this game."

Sidney Marksbury walked over to the desk and examined the paperwork as I pulled on my coat.

"There were two reliquaries stolen from the Quedlinburg treasure trove, Mr. Marksbury. But Westcott's old man didn't give him a reliquary. I mean, why would he? It was James who was the spiritually minded one, and it was Father French who from an early age cultivated James's call to the religious life. So, Thomas Westcott gave Father French one of the two reliquaries as an ordination gift, and he told his friend he intended to give the other reliquary to James."

I turned toward Westcott who was bleary-eyed as he swallowed hard and leaned against the desk to steady himself.

"You didn't know Father French received one of those reliquaries because it was stolen. But Father French never reported it stolen, because he didn't want his friend to have to explain how he came to be in possession of such a thing."

Westcott shot an anxious look at Sidney Marksbury.

"You know, it could be that Father French's piece is still out there. Hell, maybe it's sitting on some grandma's coffee table in some small town just like this one. And the reliquary that your brother was given? Well, Connie, now you know how to find it. But if you do anything to try to influence the priest at St. Joseph's to give you that clue? Well, let's just say I left an open page at the end of my story. You take one step toward that missing piece, and I'll write a new ending."

"You're full of shit," Westcott said, repeating the only comeback he seemed able to muster.

"A pearl-handled comb set with diamonds and emeralds," I said, looking at Marksbury. "Am I full of shit, Sidney?"

Marksbury's face was pale as he looked up from the paperwork. "But how do we know that...that this is real?"

I reached into my satchel and produced another document that I laid in front of Marksbury. "This is a sworn affidavit attesting to the veracity of that file. It's signed by Captain Albert Korsak, United States Army."

Marksbury reviewed the document and then looked at Westcott, crestfallen.

"You can try to find Captain Korsak if you'd like," I said, pulling on my toboggan. "But I tell ya, it's a hell of a task to track the man down."

I walked directly up to Westcott and locked eyes with the man.

"My brother's name is Declan Motley. His release date is March fifth, two thousand. You and your son and Artemis Ray and whoever else was involved in his attack will correct the record on my brother being a snitch. Believe me when I say he can take care of himself. But if things do go bad for him while he's inside or if you get him early release, then the last thing you'll have to worry about is my story."

"Meaning what?" Rogers said.

"I think you know what it means," I said, never taking my eyes off Westcott. "Leave my brother alone to do his time. Beyond that, I want nothing from any of you."

"How do we know you won't publish your story?" Marksbury said.

I turned to look at Marksbury. "I'm a man of my word, Sidney. Are you?"

Isabelle Westcott gave me a desperate look and said, "But how are we supposed to return that heirloom to the rightful owner without people knowing?"

"Not my problem. But I imagine that's what Thomas Westcott would want his son to do." I slung the satchel over my shoulder. "And to be my brother's keeper is what Ray Motley would want his son to do."

I turned back to Westcott. "So, Conrad. It looks like we both get the chance to be the men our fathers want us to be."

With that, I gave him a nod, turned, and walked out of the house the same way I had entered.

Through the front door.

CHAPTER
FORTY-TWO

I SAT IN THE Prep Room nursing a pint while Sam busied himself cleaning and stocking up after the busy weekend.

"Working on a work night?"

"Yeah, they called and asked if I could fill in and I said why not? Monday nights are slow, so I can grade papers while I'm on the clock."

"You like teaching, Sam?"

"It's like anything else. It's got its high and low points. But overall, yeah. The kids are great...well, mostly. But even the knuckleheads are good in their core and those are the kids that when you reach them, it really makes everything worthwhile."

I nodded and said, "Yeah, I can see that."

"You thinking about a career change?"

"Hey, you never know. Do kids care about literature these days?"

He leaned against the edge of the bar and regarded me with a thoughtful gaze. "Kids are smart, Levi, and for the most part they aren't jaded. So, when we try to bullshit them, it pisses them off and they tune out."

"Unlike adults who walk around in a perpetual state of being tuned out because they assume bullshit is just a part of life?"

"That's right," he said. "Kids want us to be honest, and they hold us accountable when we try to slip one by them. Ultimately, I think kids care about teachers who care enough not to lie to them or treat them like they're too young to comprehend the truth. So, to answer your question...sure, there are kids who care about literature. As long as it's taught by a teacher who cares about the kids."

That's why I liked talking to Sam. He made solid points that made me think. The point he made on this occasion made me wonder why we stop caring about the lies that life feeds us. Shouldn't we always care about that?

"You know I read somewhere this used to be a school," I said, looking around the bar with its arched passages and cozy alcoves.

"Don't I know it. At least once a week I get an alum in here who wants to tell me all about his days at St. Joe Prep. Know what their yearbook was called?" I cocked my head in curiosity. "A-Z-U-W-U-R."

"As you were," I said with a wistful smile.

"The alumni like to say they're undefeated since sixty-eight since that's the year the Xaverian brothers who ran the place shut it down."

I laughed softly and said, "Well, we all have to hold on to something."

Sam smiled as he moved down the bar to take care of a couple that had just come in. In his absence, I sat thinking about young people, about students. It occurred to me that I was in that stage of life when school felt both relatable and nostalgic at the same time.

What had I wanted to be when I was in school?

The question didn't require much thought. Truth is, I didn't have a plan for a specific career path when I went off to college. It was the experience that I had been after. So, I wandered through those years looking for one adventure after another, and that's pretty much what I had been doing ever since. I told myself this was the kind of life I wanted, a life not bound to anyone or anything that kept me in one place. But I knew deep down my penchant for moving on was just a way to keep myself alone. But lately, things seemed to be changing, and I often found myself in deep contemplation about what to do next. That's all Moussa had wanted. Just to figure out what to do next.

Moussa.

I sipped my beer, thinking about our random encounter and the impact of that encounter on both our lives. It occurred to me that I was caught in the contradictory web of wishing none of this had ever happened while being grateful that it did happen. And that left me with a feeling I could not remember ever having experienced before. It was a mixture of sadness and gratitude that I surmised must be the prevailing emotion of anyone who endeavors to be a part of something greater than themselves. The sadness comes from finding out that nothing turns out exactly as you had hoped it would be, and the gratitude comes from knowing it was worth the ride all the same.

"Here's to you, Moussa," I said, raising my glass. "I'm glad I turned around."

I took a drink of my beer and stood to leave.

"Take it easy, Sam."

"Where are you off to, Levi?"

The question stopped me in my tracks, and I suddenly had the overwhelming urge to get in my truck and drive away. To move on. To start over. To be in motion. To find a town that didn't know my name. Maybe I could meet someone and start over in a place like that. Maybe I would even stay.

"Where are you off to, Levi?"

"I'm not going far," I said. "I just need to finish what I started."

CHAPTER
FORTY-THREE

IT HAD BEEN exactly three months since Moussa Diab died. Three days before his death, I had arrived in Bardstown to spend time with a friend who had reached out just when I needed him most. On my way to meet that friend, I had stopped to admire the impressive façade of the Basilica of St. Joseph Proto-Cathedral. Now I sat on its porch, looking out at the sun sliding behind the knobs far off to the west as I thought about all that had occurred from that day to this one.

"Judge Harry McGill always did say a contemplative mind is the sign of a peaceful spirit."

I looked down and saw Olive McGill standing on the sidewalk below the porch steps.

"Or I could be avoiding the priest's invitation to go inside and pray. It's the second time he's asked, but I don't know if he remembered me from the first time."

"Well, you do tend to leave an impression on people, Levi Motley. So, I suspect he did."

I cocked my head and looked at her. "Is that a good or a bad thing?"

"Which do you intend for it to be?"

I thought about her question for a moment before answering. "I'm not sure I intend much of anything," I said with a slight shake of my head. "And I think that might be my problem."

Olive gave me a sad smile and walked up the steps to sit beside me. For a few minutes, neither of us spoke as we stared at the remarkable display of red and gold spreading across the horizon.

"May I ask you something, Miss Olive?"

"You may, indeed."

"Did you always refer to your father as Judge Harry McGill?"

After a long moment of silence, I gave her a sideward glance and saw she was struggling with some emotion or memory.

"I called him Daddy."

She retrieved a handkerchief from her handbag and gently wiped her eyes.

"Did he really say all those things, all those wise phrases?"

She smiled and a soft sound came from her mouth that was both a laugh and a sob. "Oh, he said them all right. Even if most of what he said wasn't exactly original."

"And you remember all that he said?"

"I do. And not just his words, but his mannerisms, too. Like the way he would tousle my hair and flick the tip of my nose with his finger." She looked at me and dabbed her eyes with the handkerchief. "I don't why, but somehow I knew even as a young girl that by remembering his words and how he said them, I could keep talking to him after he was gone."

I gave her a soft smile and then turned back to look at the horizon.

"My dad used to say it's a great life if you don't weaken."

Olive continued to dab her eyes as she looked at me with a curious gaze. "Do you know what that means?"

I hesitated for a moment before answering. "I think so," I said, turning to look at her.

Olive gave a soft smile of her own and nodded, encouraging me to continue.

"I think it means we all lose something of ourselves that we can't get back." I paused and looked up at the soft blue sky as it began to fade to black. "Sometimes that's because life takes it away from us. And that's going to happen. There's no way around it. But other times, it seems like we give pieces away and it's not until much later that we try to understand what it was all for, why we did that. Either way, it hurts to lose a piece of who we are, and it's that pain that makes us feel weak."

I looked at Olive. Her eyes were filled with tears, but she again nodded for me to continue.

"I guess what I'm beginning to see is that to not weaken doesn't mean to forget what you've lost or to resist the pain it caused. To not weaken is to show resolve, to trade that loss and make a sacrifice out of the pain to become someone better than you were before."

Olive sniffed as she wiped her eyes and said, "Do you think your father knew that?"

"I never really got a chance to know my father, Miss Olive," I said with a sad smile. "But from what I do know, I don't think he was afraid of pain. But I do think maybe he was afraid to appear weak."

Instinctively, I rubbed my wrist and wondered what time it was, though I knew the hour was later than it seemed.

"I think maybe he was like me," I said, still rubbing my naked wrist. "I think he was trying to figure things out, you know? But my fear is that by the time he did, he had lost too much of himself, and he didn't know how to get it back."

Olive looked at me with a quizzical expression. "What, Levi? Get what back?"

Her question evoked something inside me for which I had no name. I suddenly felt like I had traveled to the center of my being, to a place where I had always thought I existed, alone. But as I looked over at this diminutive woman who was my friend, I realized in that solitary place that there were footprints all around me, and I had a strong desire to know the people who had left them.

"That thing we're all searching for and trying to hold onto at the same time...hope. He couldn't get back his hope."

We sat on the steps of the cathedral for a long time, both of us lost in our thoughts. After a while, vehicles began pulling into the parking lot between the church and the school. We watched as children burst forth from the vehicles and ran in unabated excitement to meet their friends. The adults called out for the kids to be careful as they emerged carrying hanging bags, instrument cases, and Christmas decorations. We watched as the adults gathered their children close, holding their hands as they led the children inside the school building.

Olive smiled and said, "It's the school Christmas pageant. That's where I was headed when I saw you."

"You have kids in the play?"

She stood and straightened her back. "Good heavens, no," she said, flattening the front of her coat and pants. "I'm assisting with the production if you must know."

"Sorry, I..."

"You what? Assumed? Have we not trodden this ground before, young man?"

"Yeah, I guess we have." She walked down the steps. "So how are you helping out?"

She stood at the foot of the steps with her fists on her hips, looking up at me. "I'm a woman of vast abilities, Levi Motley."

"You mean your gift of gab?"

"I prefer the term rhetorical talent," she said, and then turned and walked briskly away. "After all, Judge Harry McGill always did say that..."

But I couldn't hear the rest of what she said.

I smiled as I watched her hug a young girl who enthusiastically screeched, "Miss Olive," as she ran up to greet her. Olive hugged the mother, too, and the three of them disappeared inside the school building along with the growing throng of Christmas pageant attendees.

I stood and made my way through the door and inside the cathedral. For some time, I walked along the periphery, perusing the paintings and statuary, the Stations of the Cross, and the stained-glass windows. It was beautiful.

When I arrived at the southwest corner of the church, I stopped at the place where I had brought Regina Sandoval after our meeting with Jay-Eddy Powell, when she rightly pointed out that it was time for me to hold up my end of our bargain.

"What is this?" she had said that day, giving me a confused look.

"There used to be a Marian grotto underneath," I said, pointing to a flat stone on the floor. "Makes sense that Brother Lew would choose a spot like this, don't you think?"

Sandoval's eyes narrowed and she bent down to get a closer look. The flat gray stone was inscribed with black letters and numbers and Jerusalem crosses were carved into each of the four corners of the stone. She read the inscription aloud and the last of her words was barely more than a whisper.

"April eighth, nineteen-sixty-nine. Time capsule commemorating the one-hundred-fiftieth anniversary of the completion of St. Joseph Proto-Cathedral, eighteen-nineteen to nineteen-sixty-nine. To be opened... April eighth, two-thousand-nineteen."

Sandoval looked up at me with a stupefied look on her face. She tried to speak, but her mouth seemed incapable of forming words. After a moment of struggle, she found her voice and slowly articulated her question.

"Are you telling me it's in a grotto underneath this floor?"

"If by 'it', you mean the final clue that leads to what you're looking for, then yes. It's underneath this floor in a time capsule..."

"That won't be opened for another twenty-two years," she said in a small voice.

"More like twenty-one-and-a-half, but close enough."

Sandoval stuck out a hand to steady herself against the wall. "What's the clue?"

"I don't know. I only know it's in that time capsule."

She put a hand to her forehead and leaned back against the wall. "My employer is going to lose his mind over this." The pace of her breathing picked up, as her incredulity burgeoned into anger. "I will have your ass for this, Levi Motley," she said, pointing at me. "Do you hear me? I will fry your ass you lying sack of..."

"Careful," I said, nodding toward the soaring image of Jesus on The Cross that hung above the high altar.

"My employer will..."

"Will do nothing, Miss Rivera."

She took an involuntary step back and stared at me.

"Miss Elaine Rivera, to be more precise." She continued to stare at me, dumbfounded. "Don't blame Joe," I said, shaking my head. "He only confirmed what I already knew."

"But how... how did you...?"

"How did I figure out who you are? Simple. I had Dom look into your rental vehicle. You know, the one you tried to cover with a fake tag? All he could get was a name, but I was able to narrow down the pool of candidates, which you helped me with, by the way, when you made that quip about opening day at Santa Anita the first day we met." She gave me a puzzled look. "I grew up in Louisville, Sandoval. I never miss a reference to horseracing. So, I asked Dom to dig around for any Elaine Riveras in California. Turns out, there's quite a few of them, including one who lives in Carlsbad, a nice suburb of San Diego. I guess this gig pays well, huh?"

Her eyes darted around the nave of the church, as she struggled to comprehend what was happening.

"You know, since I've gotten into this investigation stuff, I've learned that anonymity is a damned important part of our trade, Sandoval. So, what you're going to do is tell your employer that you ran into a brick wall...or a stone floor, for that matter. I don't care what you tell him. But if I have any problem from you or some mysterious third party who appears on my doorstep, then I'll know who to come looking for. Better yet, I'll tell the feds that if they want a line on some missing art treasures, then they should look up Elaine Rivera in Carlsbad. I know you're good at your job, but even the best can't cover all their tracks, now can they?"

She sat down on a nearby pew and put her head in her hands.

"Just ask the heirs of Douglas Stone and Thomas Westcott. Sooner or later, somebody comes around asking questions you don't want to answer. So, you keep my name out of your mouth, Sandoval, and I'll keep Elaine Rivera out of mine."

For a moment, I saw the familiar sight of Regina Sandoval running through her tactical options. But there were no negotiations, powerplays, or attempts at leverage to be had. All that was left was her own burning curiosity. That at least, I could understand.

"Is it a picture?" She gave me a pleading look. "A letter? A key? Or a map?"

I shook my head and said, "I honestly don't know."

"But how did you find out about it?"

"A hermit."

"A what?"

"Brother Peter. He's a hermit I met on my quest. He was friends with Brother Lew. I think it was as simple a matter as Brother Lew wanting to tell somebody his story. So, he told his friend, Brother Peter."

"And you met this Brother Peter when?" She eyed me suspiciously. "Before we made our deal?"

"I told you from the jump that I don't know where it is, but I know how to find it."

She leveled me with an icy glare and said, "And here I thought manipulation was your brother's modus operandi."

I took a deep breath and let that pass. "I'm not trying to manipulate you, Sandoval. I'm on a different mission than you, that's all."

She let out a bark of harsh laughter that echoed throughout the cathedral. "'A different mission', he says. Well, tell me something, smart guy. What's to keep me from going on a mission to find this...this hermit?"

"The same thing that kept me from finding him. But if you can figure out what that means for you, then Godspeed."

Sandoval sat for a long moment, cradling her head in her hands. Finally, she gave me a look of defeated resignation as she stood and prepared to leave. But she didn't leave. Instead, she turned to look at me and for one final moment, I got to see that keen glint of intensity shining in her eyes.

"Brother Llewellyn was already in the monastery in sixty-nine."

"That's right. He joined the Trappists in sixty-two."

"Then how did he manage to get...whatever it is, into that time capsule in April of sixty-nine?"

"His nephew."

Her eyes narrowed as she considered this. Then her eyes slowly widened with enlightenment and her face broke into an ironic smile.

"Rogers?"

"Rogers," I said, shooting her an ironic half-smile of my own. "He was a second grader at the school in sixty-nine. Brother Lew and Conrad were still close back then, so he joined his brother's family to celebrate Easter that year, just a few days before they sealed the capsule. That's when Brother Lew gave the clue to his nephew and told him to give it to the principal the next day at school. He told Rogers it was important that it be added to the items that were going into the time capsule. It went in, and three days later the capsule was sealed in the grotto."

"Was it a package? Could it be that the treasure is in the capsule?" Sandoval gave an exasperated sigh to my indifferent shrug. "After all this, don't you want to know? Don't you want to find it?"

I looked down at the stone and then back at the woman who, to a significant degree, had been responsible for getting me into all this in the first place.

"You and I have always been searching for different things, Sandoval."

Her face wrinkled in a bemused expression. "What is it you've been searching for?"

In that moment, a sense of peace came over me, and I felt like a child with my whole life laid out before me.

"A story, Regina. I've been searching for a story."

I was surprised to see her countenance soften in an expression of empathy.

"For a long time, I thought it was the story of a man running from his past. But now I see it's the story of a man with the strength to trade his past for something better."

CHAPTER
FORTY-FOUR

T HOSE WERE THE last words I spoke to the woman I had known as Regina Sandoval. As it turned out, she didn't have anything more to say when I told her what I had been searching for. Maybe somewhere deep inside, she instinctively understood Artie Goben's rule about not ruining a good moment with your stupid words. On the other hand, I don't imagine that was such a good moment for her, since I had admittedly been underhanded in the way I played her for the information we got from Jay-Eddy Powell. On the other, other hand, wasn't it Sandoval who started this whole bloody mess by telling me all she wanted was to know what really happened to Moussa Diab? It was. And maybe that was the reason she was able to empathize with me in the end.

Either way, I had found what I was looking for, and it was on me to make sure that Moussa's mother knew the truth of what really happened to her son. With that daunting task in mind, I looked down at the gray stone that marked the location of a time capsule that held one whale of a secret inside. As I stared at the stone, I wondered what else was collecting dust inside that box. Letters? Photos? Heirlooms?

A watch?

"Yeah. A watch."

A watch that stopped the minute it was placed inside that box, just a few months before a man would walk on the moon and a little music festival would be held in upstate New York. A watch representing a moment in time that would never be repeated, the definition of unique.

Yes, I decided that inside that box there must be a watch, and I wondered if the owner would show up to collect it on the day the time capsule was to be unsealed. Would the owner still be alive? Maybe. But if not, I decided one of the owner's children or grandchildren would be on hand to collect their family heirloom. And I imagined that upon collecting that precious item, the new owner would take it straight to the jeweler to get the watch in proper working order and to get it polished to a high shine. Then that child or grandchild would wear the watch until someday far in the future when they would put it in a tin can or in a jewelry box on the dresser. And then someday far beyond that one, that person would die, and the watch would fall out of memory until a random descendant unwittingly stumbled upon the watch while perusing the discarded remains of all the stuff that didn't end up in the will. I pictured that descendant lifting the watch from the bottom of an old box in the attic, lovingly dusting away the cobwebs from that lost family heirloom to bear witness to just a smidgen of the old watch's former glory.

But that distant person would never know that what they held in their hand once lay in a time capsule, sealed up next to a clue leading to a hidden treasure that once led a no-account drifter on a quest that would transform his life. By then, that old drifter would long ago have died, decayed, decomposed, fossilized, and dissolved into the sediment of bygone consciousness. But I'd like to think that before the end rushed up to meet him, he would have gone through that great adventure in life we call change, and that he would have become the man his father never got the chance to teach him to be.

"Until then," I said to no one, "it's a great life if you don't weaken."

I pulled the collar of my coat up and shoved my hands in my pockets to fish out a pair of gloves. As I did, I felt something hard and round in my right pocket. I pulled the object out and saw it was the stone I had picked up that day on Cross Knob. I looked at it as it lay in the palm of my hand. The stone was smooth and nondescript, but that didn't bother me. It felt good in my hand and that was good enough for me. I raised the stone to my lips, kissed it, and then placed it on the flat gray marker.

Before leaving the cathedral, I dipped my fingers in the Holy Water and crossed myself the same way I had done as a child when I went to Mass at Notre Dame du Port with Declan and Grandma Lenny. Then I made my way over to the school, thinking I might stand in the back and watch the Christmas pageant for a little while. As I walked across the parking lot, I thought about the joy pouring out of those children as they rushed to see their friends and the thought occurred to me that one of the teachers might ask which child I was there to see. Knowing I wouldn't have a suitable answer to that question, I reckoned I'd have to drop Olive's name to make sure I didn't get the boot. I smiled, imagining Olive's consternation at being called away from whatever task she was performing to vouch for some raggedy-ass vagabond who claimed Olive McGill as his friend.

As I opened the door to the school, my smile grew so wide it burst into a laugh at the thought of the lecture Miss Olive would surely give me the next time I went to see her, as she stroked Roscoe's mane and henpecked ol' Moots in preparation for another stroll through The Great Meadows, her beloved Kentucky.

THE END

Thank you for reading *The Great Meadows*! Independent authors rely upon reviews to improve their craft and attract new readers. Thus, I would be grateful if you would use the QR code below to leave a review. Thank you!

Use the QR code below to join my email list for articles, updates, and offers! And just for signing up, you will receive a complimentary copy of my short story, *Blood on the Bottle*. This story depicts a most intriguing alternate version of the first meeting between Levi Motley and Regina Sandoval. Again, thank you for reading *The Great Meadows*!